T0357492

By Gia de Cadenet

Getting His Game Back
Not the Plan
Give Me a Shot

GIVE ME A SHOT

GIVE ME
A SHOT

A Novel

GIA DE CADENET

DELL

New York

Dell
An imprint of Random House
A division of Penguin Random House LLC
1745 Broadway, New York, NY 10019
randomhousebooks.com
randomhousebookclub.com
penguinrandomhouse.com

A Dell Trade Paperback Original

ISBN 978-0-593-72276-3
Ebook ISBN 978-0-593-72277-0

Printed in the United States of America on acid-free paper

1st Printing

BOOK TEAM: Production editor: Jennifer Rodriguez • Managing
editor: Saige Francis • Production manager: Meghan O'Leary •
Copy editor: Crystal Velasquez • Proofreaders: Vicki Fischer,
Liz Carbonell, Deborah Bader

The authorized representative in the EU for product safety and
compliance is Penguin Random House Ireland, Morrison Chambers,
32 Nassau Street, Dublin D02 YH68, Ireland.
https://eu-contact.penguin.ie

Dear reader, this book is dedicated to you.
You, with all your flaws, with all your fears,
with all your doubts about yourself.
Maybe you wear a mask so the outside world can't see
all the things that are "wrong" with you.
Maybe you cover up by pushing the world away.
But the You deep down, the core of who you are, is okay.
I hope that one day you can fully see that.

GIVE ME A SHOT

CHAPTER ONE

Mo

"Who. The Hell. Are You?"

Mo did not raise his head. He took a slow breath in, noticing a few missed suds still glistening on his just-rinsed hands dripping over the sink. He willed his heart to slow after the shock of the unexpected voice behind him. He should have been alone in the empty workshop that shared a wall with his own.

"I asked you a question."

The woman's voice was cold, steely. No sign that she'd been hit by a wave of adrenaline like the one that was still coursing through his own body.

"I'm Mo," he said, his voice scratchier than he'd intended.

"How did you get in?" she asked.

While still hard, her voice had lost a bit of its edge, so he took the risk of lifting his head slowly.

"I have a key," he said. Between the harshness of the florescent bulb high on the wall and the large chunk missing from the mirror above the sink, he couldn't catch a glimpse of her without making a sudden movement. Which he was sure wasn't wise.

"Why?" she asked.

It occurred to him that it might be marginally safer for both of them if she could look him in the eye. He turned slowly, keeping his hands in view. Another blast of adrenaline cut his breath as he came face-to-face with a loaded crossbow, its arrow pointed squarely between his eyes.

Months earlier, at his auto shop, Mo had interrupted one of his newer mechanics watching a video on the shop floor with one of the delivery men. They had been far too excited to show it to him, and Mo was subjected to the sight of a deer being taken down by a crossbow. The deer's pain and terror had weakened his bones and forced Mo to look away. Now, at the business end of a bow that looked exactly like the weapon from the video, he was fully aware of the damage they could do. His Adam's apple was as heavy as a billiard ball when he tried to swallow.

"Is that . . . a crossbow?" he asked, slowly raising his hands.

She lifted her chin, but the crossbow didn't waver.

"Yes," she said.

"A . . . a real one?" he asked.

"Yes."

The silence was sharp and heavy. The absence of any other sound amplified the thudding of his too-fast beating heart. It clipped at the bottom of his throat. He wanted to shake the adrenaline burn out of his raised hands, but he didn't dare move them.

"So?" she asked.

Her voice widened his vision beyond the crossbow, and it was only then that he began to see the person holding it. She was about five foot six. Her jeans were covered in dust, as was her black shirt. Her hair was dark and long, pulled into a ponytail that fell over her shoulder, more like a cheerleader's than a potential murderer's. Her skin was pale, but he didn't know if that was from fear, or if it was her normal complexion. The depth of her narrowed eyes reminded him of the charcoal dust he'd been washing off his hands. At some point, she'd turned on the hallway light behind her.

"Listen," he said. "I'm just here to wash my hands."

"After you finished chopping people up?"

Chopping people up?

Confused, he glanced down at himself. Nothing out of the ordinary about his work pants. Yeah, his well-used leather apron was dingy, but it wasn't bloody. Was she freaked out about the respirator he'd pushed onto his forehead?

"I'm a blacksmith," he said, looking back at her. "I was working next door. But my sink doesn't work. So Arnie, you know, the landlord? He lets me use this one." Damn, he was having to talk a lot. Far more than he ever did with a complete stranger. But he pushed on through the tightness in his throat because he didn't want to die. "You can come take a look if you don't believe me."

"And go to a secondary location so you can murder me? No thanks," she said.

Right. But you're the one with a murder weapon.

"It's late," he said.

"No shit."

"I mean, why are you here so late at night?" he asked.

"I don't see how that's any of your business."

"Okay."

She still hadn't lowered the crossbow. And her arms weren't even shaking. She squinted at him.

"Why are *you* here so late? If you're really just working? Can't you blacksmith during the day? If you aren't up to something shady?"

Something shady? Sharp sparkles flashed across the back of his scalp. This woman just appears with a weapon in one of his few safe spaces, and he's the one who's up to something shady?

"'Scuse me?" he asked.

"Yeah," she said. "Most people do their jobs during the day. Why are you here so late at night?"

"Not that it's any of your business," Mo growled, his annoyance diminishing his fear. "But I'm a mechanic. Run my auto shop during the day."

She stared at him. The crossbow was still pointed at his face. He wished he was wearing his welding helmet so that his face was protected, but then he'd probably look even more threatening. Besides, even if he'd had a helmet on, she could still shoot him in the chest.

"And?" she asked.

"And?" he asked back.

"You weren't going to say anything else?"

"Uh . . . no. I told you. I came to wash my hands. You drew attention to yourself."

Her dark eyes went wide, and the crossbow wavered then fixed on him again.

"Excuse me?" she asked. "You trespassed in my—"

"No one's been here for nearly a year. Arnie said he's been trying to get in touch with you for months. He was going to have to do something with all your—"

"Not mine—" Her arms went slack, and the arrow pointed at the ground. The woman seemed to deflate completely. Mo was happy to see that he was no longer perceived as a threat, but the transition was far too brutal. A completely different person was standing in front of him all of a sudden. Both of her shoulders were slumped, and she turned slightly away from him, her face a little toward the wall.

"Arnie doesn't have to worry about all the stuff. I'm loading up what I can tonight." She looked back at Mo, assessing him differently this time. "Sounds like you all are friends. Let him know my parents got *all* of his messages. He'll be paid for the back rent. My sister didn't exactly have an estate, but our parents did have a life insurance policy on her. Arnie'll get his precious money," she spat. She turned her back on Mo and walked away down the hall.

At home, Mo opened the door of the microwave with one second left on the timer. The beep on this one set his teeth on edge. He'd been vacillating between buying a new one and just putting up with the sound even though it stressed him out right before eating. Getting a new one would be wasteful, and that bothered him, but so did the fact that he had to stand next to the machine to make sure the sound didn't set him off. He sighed. He was able to acclimate himself to some sounds, but not others. And the ones he couldn't handle forced him to take burdensome extra steps, to spend his limited energy on them. Like so many other types of stimuli.

Minimizing or Managing Strong Sensory and Emotional Stimuli: The Full and Complete Story of My Life.

Taking out his leftover soup, he stirred it carefully, resetting the timer to zero. He was trying not to think about the woman again. The corrosive fear that had bathed his muscles had abated enough for him to eat. At the table, where he'd arranged his placemat, napkin, and sparkling water, he stirred his soup again, telling himself to stop thinking about her. She'd threatened him with a crossbow for chrissakes. But then, in a few short words, she'd told him part of why she had: grief. Her sister had died, and the woman had been there, clearing out the space, dealing with her sister's things on her own.

Presumably, she'd been holding back her feelings. Mo hadn't seen any signs that the woman had been crying. But she'd been alone there in the night. Maybe in a place with which she's unfamiliar. She heard noises, someone coming in. And she grabbed a weapon to protect herself.

But why a crossbow? Was it her sister's?

After running a hand down his beard, he leaned over and started eating his soup, going over the encounter in his mind. It was interesting that she didn't hide. Mo didn't know she was there until she was right on top of him. She didn't wait for danger to find her; she went out and faced it.

He thought of Maddie. God, she'd be like that when she got older. She was already headstrong enough. He had trouble trying to balance teaching her to maintain her courageous streak when she should, but also to be cautious for her own safety. He picked up his phone and opened his messaging app to return to their earlier conversation, taking another spoonful with his left hand.

Diana:

Hi again Daddy (it's Maddie)

It always made him chuckle when she texted that. Like his ex-wife would write "Hi Daddy." But that was Maddie, always making sure he knew it was her talking. Which Mo appreciated. He knew Maddie didn't realize it, but he kind of felt like he was intruding on Diana's privacy, with Madison having to use her phone to talk to him. Madison had recently turned twelve. Maybe it was time to revisit the discussion about getting her her own phone.

Mo:

Hi Sugar Plum. Getting ready for bed?

Diana:

Yep. Just wanted to say good night.

Good night. Sleep tight.

Don't let the bed bugs bite.

Love you.

Love you, too.

He checked the time. They'd finished texting hours earlier, before he'd had his life threatened. She'd be well into dreamland by now. And Diana herself hadn't contacted him, so no sign of nightmares, either. He finished his soup and cleaned up. He could hear that the TV was on in the other half of his duplex. Mrs. Sargysan sometimes fell asleep before turning it off. He carefully made the rounds of each plant in the living room, adding a little water where needed. He checked the soil on his orchids, even though he'd done it the day before and knew it was too soon for water. Lights off downstairs. He went to Madison's room and flicked on the light. Everything was as it should be. Her desk was tidy. At her bed, he smoothed her yellow-patterned bedspread and fluffed her pink pillows. He went over to the peace lily on her dresser and ran his fingers over the leaves to remove any dust. Standing in the doorway again before turning out the light, he surveyed the room and smiled. The riot of color in her room matched the joyful, silly riot of energy that was his daughter. She'd wanted to liven up his bedroom with bright colors once but had quickly understood that Daddy needed a visually quiet space. His was perfect for him and hers was perfect for her. She knew he checked on her after she'd gone to sleep during her weeks at his house. She said it made her sleep better knowing that he did. What she didn't know was that he couldn't relax without his little routine of making sure that everything was right in her environment even if she wasn't in it. Especially on a night like this when he'd been flooded by his own painful emotions and those of someone else.

It was a little past eleven by the time he finished his shower. The very hot water and vigorous massage cycle usually helped clear out any negative energy from the day, but tonight it wasn't enough. He wasn't thinking about the woman in specifics anymore. He was just weighed down. While he was washing his hair, he'd made the mistake of putting himself in her shoes, imagining what it might be like to lose one of his brothers. And to have to touch, to pack away their personal things alone. At night. The pain that the woman might have been feeling flashed through his body, and it almost knocked him to the ground. No wonder her reaction to his presence had been so strong.

What if her sister had also been alone? Had been attacked somehow?

If she had, the woman's choice to confront him with a weapon in hand made sense.

He needed to get to bed. Get some sleep and let his mind reset. When he picked up too much from people, sleep was a good way to let go of emotions that weren't his own. Crawling under the covers, he ran a hand over his beard and groaned.

Emotions from people I care about, fine. But why do I have to absorb strangers' emotions, too?

CHAPTER TWO

Jess

Returning to her dining room table, refreshed mug of tea warming her hands, Jess stopped short.

"Steinem," she said. "The whole and entire point of getting you that toy laptop was so that you could mirror me and stop—" She put her mug on the table and cupped his sleek black-and-white bottom. "Stop parking yourself on mine every time I step away." She nudged, and after a bit of resistance, the cat yawned and stood. Jess tapped the toy sitting in front of the chair beside hers. "That's yours," she said. "This is mine."

Steinem shot a glance at the toy, a glance at Jess, then stalked to the other end of the table and sat, his back to her. Jess rolled her eyes.

"Okay, fine," she grumbled, picking up her mug. She glanced at the corner of the screen. Still another ten minutes before her video call with her close friends Alice and Stephanie. She straightened the papers on her desk with one hand as she sipped. The first day of school was the following week. Her first day as Dr. Anderson, University of Michigan professor, the career she'd been dreaming of and striving toward since middle school. Along with her excitement about work, she also counted herself lucky to have found a place to shoot. Her competition days were over, but she still loved archery and needed it to be a part of her life.

She hadn't been thrilled about the way she learned about the Michigan Folk School. Her car was the only one in the relatively empty teacher's parking lot with a flyer tucked under her wind-shield wiper. Jess had approached her car carefully, checking underneath it and in the backseat before getting inside. But once she'd read the flyer the anxious prickles that had shot over her skin faded, and curiosity bloomed.

She'd found a couple of indoor archery clubs that would have saved her the thirty-minute drive from Warrendale to Ann Arbor, but the ambiance of the Folk School, and the few people she'd already met there, made the commute more than worth it.

"Guess I'm doing all right, huh, Sty Sty?" she asked the cat, still giving her his back. "Back to the States. Truly started my career, my grown-up life." A shower of sadness passed through her, and she readjusted in her seat to get rid of it. Something was missing from that picture. Her sister should have been there to share in this new stage with Jess, but she wasn't. If Jess wanted a good start, she would need to keep doing what she had been—ignoring her grief, stuffing it away in the deepest corners of her mind. Allowing it the tiniest foothold would open the door for it to overtake her.

I already cried, I already grieved. Time to focus on the next thing.

According to the psychologist she'd seen briefly before she moved back, she was doing well. He'd shared that it was normal to just react to life after a cataclysmic event like losing a sibling, and that Jess would continue to do well if she lived one day at a time, focused on one step at a time. The fact that she'd started to regain interest in archery was a big deal. It meant that she was rebuilding her agency in life—beyond her career.

The video call ringtone went off from her laptop, bringing her back to the present.

"Buenas tardes!" Alice announced as she appeared on the screen.

The sight and sound of her friend brought a wave of excitement for an instant, but it quickly died down. Alice's skin was bright pink.

"Buenas . . . tardes?" Jess said, confused.

"Your pronunciation's getting better," Alice said, half-smiling.

"Though I probably can't talk. I still have a looong way to go before I communicate well. At least people are kind and patient about me trying."

"That's good," Jess said. "What is up with—"

"I'm late, I'm late, I'm late for a very important date," Stephanie said, interrupting Jess as she joined the call.

"The surprise would have been if you were on time," Jess said, smirking as she sipped a bit more tea.

With Jess in Michigan, Alice at an NGO in Mexico City, and Stephanie teaching at a university in Sao Paulo, they'd been staying in touch through video calls in addition to their group chat. They'd become close friends while finishing their doctorates in gender studies at the University of Sussex near Brighton in the UK. Finding a good time to talk with their newly differing time zones was taking a bit of an adjustment, but they were adamant about making it work.

Stephanie stuck out her pierced tongue.

"I am nothing if not consistent," she said. She got closer to the camera, raising an eyebrow as she angled her head to one side and ruffled her bright purple pixie cut. "Apart from the story behind this impressive sunburn you're rocking, Alice, what did I miss?"

"Ha," Alice said. "While Goth-girl skin wasn't an issue in Sussex, I need to get better about sunscreen now that I'm closer to the equator."

"Yikes," Stephanie said.

Alice nodded.

"Jess," Alice said. "The big day is coming up. I'm sure you're already prepared for work, but how about socially? Any exciting encounters in real life?"

Jess snorted. "As a matter of fact, I have had one . . . *adrenaline-filled* encounter."

"Excellent," Alice said. "Do tell."

"'Adrenaline-filled'?" Stephanie asked, squinting. "We're listening."

Jess quickly recapped her run-in with the weirdo dressed like a serial killer while she'd been emptying out Cassie's storage space. She couldn't remember if he'd mentioned his name, but it wasn't like it mattered.

"So you threatened an innocent stranger with physical violence," Alice said.

"Consistent for you," Stephanie added.

"Hey!" Jess said. "I'd like to see how you'd respond when an ax murderer cosplaying as a blacksmith shows up. And there's no way to know if he'd planned on remaining an 'innocent stranger.'"

"I wouldn't have announced my presence," Alice said, her shiny, posh British accent making the chiding worse. "He didn't even know you were there. You approached him."

Jess rolled her eyes.

"I wasn't going to let him get the upper hand."

"Of course not," Stephanie said.

"Anyway, it worked out fine," Jess said. "He went away and left me alone. I got everything out of the space, so we won't cross paths again."

"I suppose that's true," Alice said, chewing her lip a little. "You could cross paths with other people, maybe. Like your parents?"

Jess frowned.

"There's no need," she said. "I'm here, they're in Rockford. Everyone is just fine exactly where they are."

"I see," said Alice.

"I get it," Stephanie said. "But seeing them might actually be useful. It's only been a few months since . . . Cassie, and grieving together might—"

"Can we talk about something else, please?" Jess snapped, cutting her off. She had zero desire to see her parents. An awkward pause almost gave Jess time to start feeling bad about being rude. But Alice saved her by pasting on a bright smile.

"Sure we can," she said. "Steph, do you have your class schedule yet?"

Stephanie barked a laugh.

"I'm not getting the best vibe from the administration. It's getting . . ."

"Curiouser and curiouser?" Alice asked.

"I'm afraid they may all be mad here," Stephanie said.

Jess and Alice grimaced.

"Well, we can keep our fingers crossed," Alice said. "At least Steph's picked up tennis again, and I've got my second book club meeting next week. All work and no play makes Jack a dull boy, Jess."

"Right," Jess said. "I didn't tell you that I've found a place to shoot."

She minimized the window and pulled up a browser. After copying the link to the Michigan Folk School, she pasted it into the chat.

"This looks good," said Alice.

"Is it far from where you live?" Stephanie asked.

"Not too far," Jess said. "And actually, there's an open house there this afternoon."

"You are going, right?" Stephanie asked.

Jess raised an eyebrow.

"Why do you say it like that?"

"Well, you know how you get," Stephanie said, shrugging.

"What's that supposed—"

"Huh," Alice said, cutting Jess off. "Funny coincidence."

"What?" Jess asked.

"They have a blacksmithing program. Looks like it's following you around," Alice said.

Jess took another look at the site. She'd only focused on archery before.

"Oh, you're right," she said, scrolling through. There were a couple of photos of people taking classes. None of the people in them could have been the guy she ran into; they were too short or too slim.

"The guy isn't on here. Plus, he was working in the city," she said.

"Be funny if you ran into him again, though," Stephanie said.

"Yeah. Hilarious," Jess said, deadpan.

"Well, maybe awkward," Alice said. "Since you did threaten to kill him."

"Jess doesn't get awkward," Stephanie said. "She gets, like, closed-off ice queen."

"That's true," Alice said. "All sealed up, keeps everything inside."

"You know," Stephanie said, "it's a wonder she ever let us in enough to become friends."

"It is," Alice said, ignoring Jess gawking at the screen. "Probably because we're so awesome. Did take a bit of work to get her to actually share an emotion. Like genuinely smile at—"

"Ladies! I am right here," Jess said.

"What? We still love you," Stephanie said. "Your hermit crab nature is part of your charm."

Jess squinted at the screen.

"And look, Steinem loves you," Stephanie said.

Steinem had stepped into view, hopping onto Jess's thigh and rubbing his face on her jaw. She ran a hand down his back.

"I don't have to take this slander, do I?" she asked him.

Her friends laughed.

"I'm sure it will be fine," Alice said. "This is probably a great opportunity. It'll be good to join a new community. Make some new face-to-face friends."

"Just don't draw down on them," Stephanie said, winking.

Jess pulled into the parking lot of the Folk School. She couldn't get to the spot she'd taken the previous weeks; the lot was fuller than she'd ever seen it.

"Okaaay," she said to herself, turning down a different aisle. She thought to park a little bit away from other cars, hoping that she'd still be able to see under hers as she approached it when she decided to go home. *But what if it's dark by that time?*

She glanced up. No streetlights in the parking area. She sighed. *Just park, Jess. The "perfectly safe" space doesn't exist.*

She took a deep breath as she got out of the car, squaring her shoulders and walking toward the barn, its open doors decorated with balloons and streamers. Stephanie and Alice weren't wrong. Jess felt more balanced with her emotions nicely contained. Under her control. Left to her own devices, she could isolate herself in study, or work, or archery. It just happened that way. In England, she'd had her friends to pull her out into the wider world. Before that it was Cassie. Jess needed to clear her throat and rub her suddenly aching knuckles. She took another deep breath. Time for her to be present so she could meet new people.

"Hello! Welcome to the Michigan Folk School," said a perky female voice to Jess's left as soon as she crossed the threshold of the barn. The tiny woman behind a table covered in brochures and photos looked much older than her voice sounded. Jess tried to return her smile, but she was temporarily distracted by bright yellow shoots coming from behind the woman's head. There were small feathers dancing at the ends of the yellow strands.

"I'm Lana," the woman said, reaching for Jess's hand. "The millinery instructor."

"Millinery . . . ," Jess said, returning her handshake. "That's hat making, right?"

The woman beamed, her feathers vibrating.

"Exactly," she said. "Have you ever tried? We have an introductory class if you'd like to come try out the School."

"Jess is a bit past the point of *trying* the School," a familiar voice said from behind her. She turned with a smile on her face. Ned, the salt-and-pepper-haired archery instructor that she'd gotten to know during her visits, joined them at the table.

"How's it going, Ned?" Jess asked.

"Can't complain," he said, the wrinkles around his eyes deepening with his smile. "Lana, Jess is new to the area, but she's come shooting a lot these past few weeks." He leaned toward Lana, and she followed suit. "Internationally recognized archer," he said. "Probably gonna replace me." He winked.

"Ned," Jess said, "I couldn't do that. I'm just here to relax." She looked at Lana. "It's nice to meet you. Could I get some of those brochures about the other classes?"

"Nice to meet you, too," Lana said, pressing some materials into her hands. "Glad to have you among us."

Ned guided Jess around the barn, from one small group to another, introducing her to other teachers and longtime students. Everyone was warm and welcoming. The apprehension that had tightened her shoulders was gone, and she was enjoying herself.

They'd just finished chatting with a couple interested in longbow archery when Ned glanced over her shoulder. He nodded at someone, giving them a wry smile.

"Jess," he said to her, his gaze still over her shoulder, "I'd like to introduce you to someone. He's a little . . . well, don't hold on too tight to your first impression."

Confused, Jess turned to follow his gaze as a man appeared from behind her, reaching to shake Ned's outstretched hand. The air in the barn plummeted fifty degrees. The harsh clutching shock around Jess's heart should have been strong enough to teleport her halfway around the planet.

The Ax Murderer was shaking Ned's hand. Jess gulped, her adrenaline flaming through her.

"Mo," Ned said. "This is Jess." He gestured toward her. "She's an archer. She recently moved to Detroit and has been doing a little shooting on the range while she decides if she'd like to sign up for some classes. Jess, this is Mo. Our lead blacksmith instructor."

While she still had to tip up her chin to meet his gaze, as she had in Cassie's storage unit, physically he didn't strike the same fear in her in the plain light of day. The feeling saturating her muscles would be better described as . . . mortification. She gulped again, trying to dislodge the boulder that had formed in her throat.

His dark eyes went wide momentarily, and his lips pressed into a seam, almost making them disappear behind his full mustache and beard. She caught his brief grunt before he offered her a handshake.

"Hullo," he said.

"Hi," she said, shaking his hand and hoping the deep breath she'd taken would calm the tremble in her fingers.

"Even though Mo isn't our most loquacious team member, he's been the head of the blacksmithing program for years," Ned said, drawing Jess's attention back to him. "We're quite lucky; he's the highest-ranked blacksmith in the region." Jess was surprised by the brief hint of pink that flashed across the bare part of Mo's cheeks. He glanced down, like a shy kid, then cleared his throat and crossed his arms before he looked up at Ned and gave him a terse nod.

"Oh" was all that Jess could manage to say.

Who knew that an ax murderer could seem . . . bashful?

CHAPTER THREE

Mo

A t least she doesn't have that crossbow.

Mo was stuck. Seeing this woman again, this Jess, in another one of his very few safe places had caused a spark of anger to bloom from his solar plexus. It had been quickly doused by the memory that she hadn't reacted to him as an individual, but to her fear from being surprised by a stranger while she was in a vulnerable state. Between the reminder of what he'd guessed she'd felt that night and the shock he could feel emanating from her right then, he was worried that he might throw up.

He swallowed a mouthful of his sparkling water to calm his stomach. As he swallowed, he was surprised to catch a whiff of vanilla in the air. They were far from the refreshments; even with his pronounced sense of smell, he shouldn't have been able to pick up on the baked goods at that distance. He took another quick sip. The can was running low. He'd been nursing it as an excuse to avoid small talk since he'd arrived. Participating in the annual open house was one of his least favorite parts of teaching at the Folk School. It had always been torturous for Mo—the ambient noise frying his ears and brain, the mixing energies of other people flooding through his body, having to produce his own energy to answer questions and be pleasant. He'd have to spend a lot of time with his plants, or mercilessly lift some weights, or take a burning shower once he got home.

Jess opened her mouth slightly, glancing between him and Ned. It seemed like she was thinking of saying something, maybe even apologizing, but that would mean sharing how they'd crossed paths. Ned's attention was temporarily drawn away, and Mo narrowed his eyes and shook his head the tiniest bit at Jess. *No. You don't have to.*

Jess's eyebrows bent toward each other. Mo slow blinked while shaking his head again.

"Everybody, everyone!"

Wendy, the president of the Folk School, was standing on a chair at the front of the room. The conversations died down as everyone turned to her.

"I have an exciting announcement to make," she said. "We've been fortunate that our community outreach has brought in new interest and new students over the years. The leadership board and I have decided to expand our efforts and are pleased to announce that this year the Michigan Folk School is putting on its first Renaissance Faire! We're looking forward to showcasing the skills we develop here and making an even bigger name for ourselves in the state and the Great Lakes region. We're still in the early stages, but our goal is to make it a school-wide event—including everyone from our newest members to our old-timers." She winked at Ned. He frowned back.

Gasps went up from the crowd. The room filled with a positive buzz, but something was off. Mo had known Wendy for years, and while she'd enunciated to make her voice carry, it had been tight, the pitch had been too sharp. Mo made eye contact with Ned.

"Sound right to you?" Ned asked, raising an eyebrow.

"No," Mo said. "Something's up."

"I had the impression that this was just a teaching association," Jess said to Ned. "Keeping traditional skills alive."

"In the ten years I've been here, that's exactly what it's been," Ned said.

Mo noticed that Wendy had stepped down from her chair and was having a whispered conversation with Lana. Either he was reading too much into the creases in her forehead and the set of her jaw, or she was downright worried. Ned was looking at her, too.

"You know . . ." He turned to Jess. "You don't mind if I leave you with Mo, do you? I'd like to have a quick word with Wendy."

Mo caught Jess swallowing just before she cleared her throat.

"Of course not," she said. She glanced up at Mo and gave him a polite nod without eye contact. "We can get acquainted."

"Great," Ned said. "Mo, would you . . . at least try? Let's not scare her off after her first few weeks here."

Mo rolled his eyes. But then again, he'd already scared Jess once. He wouldn't clam up. He nodded once, and Ned was gone.

"I . . . guess you really are a blacksmith," Jess said, drawing his attention.

"Yep."

"I owe you—"

"Nope," Mo said. Jess had surprised him by speaking so quickly once Ned was out of earshot. Based on her expression, he'd surprised her, too. She tilted her head to one side, assessing him.

"What do you mean, 'nope'?" she asked. He shrugged.

"Don't owe me anything," he said.

"But I could have . . . seriously injured you," she said.

He rocked his can of sparkling water back and forth a little, to see how much was left. She'd better understand why he wasn't upset if he spelled it out for her. But he couldn't do that. He was too raw from being in the room for hours. If he talked about what he imagined she'd felt, it might be too painful for him to handle. And he didn't want to bring it up in case it caused her discomfort in such a public place. He knocked back the rest of his water.

"You didn't," he said.

"But . . ." She glanced to the side, her eyebrows drawn together. Maybe the plain facts would help her see it from his perspective.

"Woman. Alone. Night. Intruder," he said. He started to go for more water but remembered there wasn't any left. "Gonna get another," he said, raising the can as he turned and walked to the end of the refreshment table.

"Uh . . . okay," she said to his back.

As he was reaching for a fresh can, he realized that he hadn't kept his word to Ned to keep Jess company. He started psyching himself up to go back when a hand clapped onto his shoulder.

"Mo, just the man I was looking for."

For whatever reason, jumping from shock or growling low due to frustration was never enough for some people to understand how very much Mo hated being touched unexpectedly. Even when he'd pushed through the discomfort of being vulnerable and had outright said he didn't like it, some people still plowed through his boundaries. Until there was some way for him to blast the liquid fire that spilled across his skin, along with the sharp seizing of his heart, back onto the offender, Mo didn't know if he'd ever get the message across.

Scowling, Mo turned to face Doug, the Folk School's Community Relations Person/Resident Pain-in-the-Ass/Serial Touch Offender. Doug jumped back, laughing awkwardly.

"The touching," Mo muttered, scowl firmly in place as he crossed his arms and stood at his full height.

"Oh, yes, sorry," Doug said, shoulders falling a bit as he tilted his head to make eye contact with Mo.

"Been over this."

"Yes, yes, you're right. Again, sorry. I'm just so excited about this Ren Faire project! Wendy asked me to come find you."

Mo raised an eyebrow.

"She wants to talk to some of the teachers in the break room."

Glaring at Doug one more time, Mo stepped around him to go find Wendy.

Walking down the quiet hallway and distancing himself from the loud activity of the barn gave Mo a delicious chance to breathe. He knew he had a bad habit of not breathing fully in agitating situations and that he should remind himself to take deep breaths, to give his central nervous system the opportunity to regulate itself, but he always forgot. It was only once he found himself in the quiet that he was able to relax and let the air wash away the sharp sparkles tensing his muscles. The calm let him feel safe and like himself again. Crossing the threshold into the break room, Mo felt his calm shatter as he heard Ned's question.

"How much financial trouble are we talking?" he asked. He was leaning against the counter beside the sink and looking at Wendy, who'd taken the seat at the head of the table. Lana and Eric, the millinery and textiles teachers, sat on one side of her, Alex and Maryline, the woodworking and food-smithing teachers, on the other. A young man Mo didn't recognize was leaning against the pop machine with his hands jammed into his front pockets.

Wendy took a deep breath, sliding her hands down the arms of her chair.

"All the trouble," she said. "Our long-term benefactor died, and his son thinks their charitable contributions should go elsewhere. If this Faire doesn't work, we are S-O-L. We're going to have to close shop."

Mo hated roller coasters. The feeling of his stomach dropping during the falls shot an electric charge all through him that took a very long time to clear. The sensation that reverberated through him at Wendy's words was the same, but worse. There was a drop, then a blast, followed by a choking sensation so strong he couldn't swallow.

"So this Faire isn't just a good time, then?" Maryline asked.

"Nope," Wendy said, leaning forward and resting her palms on the table. "That's why we need all hands on deck. I need each of you to help us plan and to participate in the Faire itself because you all have skills that should bring in the crowds." She paused, glancing down at her fingers as she tapped them on the table. "Some of you more so than others." She glanced at Ned and then at Mo.

Drop. Blast. Choke.

———

Late that evening, luxuriating in the quiet, safe calm that was his home, Mo shifted the small golden pothos back into place on his bookshelf beside the philodendron he'd just repotted. The staticky energy that remained in his body from the open house was now low enough that a regular shower should be sufficient to clear it. He felt that he might be pushing it a little by not repotting the pothos as well, but he didn't have enough time to do it and clean things up before his brother, Khalil, called him in twenty minutes. He'd just finished rinsing the back deck and was washing his hands when his phone rang. He glanced at the time and rolled his eyes.

Early. Typical Khalil.

Mo finished cleaning up and went into the living room with his phone to call back.

"You said six," he grumbled when Khalil answered.

Khalil groaned.

"I said around six," Khalil said.

"It's still not six now."

"It's around six," Khalil said.

"It's a quarter to six."

Khalil sighed, then chuckled.

"You're lucky I love you so much, man," he said.

Mo grunted.

"Anyway. I must have made a mistake when I wrote down the day I'm supposed to take Maddie to the orthodontist. I have Thursday, but doesn't she have coding after school?"

"She does, but that's the only day we could get for that appointment," Mo said as he uncrossed the arm not holding the phone and pushed himself up more comfortably on the couch.

"Oh. She's gonna miss it? Poor kid," Khalil said.

"Yeah."

"Also, don't say no—"

"No."

"Seriously?"

"If you know I'm gonna say no, why are you asking?" Mo asked.

"Because this is something nice for other people and, more important, for *you*. And as much as I know that lots of strangers and attention and noise are not the thing for Mr. Highly Sensitive Person, I wouldn't ask unless the benefit outweighed the over-stimulation."

Mo's skin crinkled. Khalil very rarely invited him to *do things* that he knew Mo wouldn't like. As much as he got on Mo's nerves, he was a good brother and had researched Highly Sensitive People when Mo had told him about it. He'd even suggested Mo try therapy to help him more comfortably live as a neurodiverse person in a neurotypical world. Mo didn't feel comfortable with the idea of therapy. He'd learned to manage himself. Khalil had respected that choice. If he was even bringing up an event, Mo knew he'd seriously thought about it.

"Fine. What is it?" Mo grumbled.

"Since they couldn't do anything before the end of last season, the parents of the youth basketball team are planning a thank-you banquet for last year's sponsors. It'll just be a little dinner and dance party for the kids on a Saturday evening, and of course you can bring Mads, too," Khalil said in a rush.

Mo's skin started itching and his throat got tight. Anticipatory sensory overload was unfortunately a thing. And it did not help that he was still battling the residual overload from the open house.

"We didn't really sponsor that much," he said. "And they already said thanks."

Khalil scoffed. "I saw the check, man," he said. "I'd want to publicly say thank you for that, too."

Mo rolled his eyes. It wasn't that serious, and he hadn't sent a check anyway. His shop had transferred the money, but that seemed beside the point. Donation amounts should be private. He opened his mouth to say so, but Khalil spoke first.

"Don't forget I'm on the league board," he said.

"So you should have put a stop to this nonsense."

"Come on, it's not nonsense. They really want to show their appreciation, and think of how much fun the kids will have—

a party. Kids love parties, even though Curmudgeon Brother never did."

Mo scowled and crossed his arm over himself again.

"What do I have to do?" he grumbled.

Khalil chuckled.

"Just show up, make a little small talk—"

Mo didn't restrain his loud groan.

"I know, I know. Just a little small talk, have dinner, and receive your award. Then come hang out with me while Mads tears up the dance floor with the other kids."

"There's an award? Like a little plaque or something? Please don't tell me I have to go up on a stage."

"Well . . ."

Mo tried to ignore the knot forming in his stomach. He leaned forward and rested his elbow on the coffee table, plopping his forehead into his flattened palm.

"Look," Khalil said. "I'll see what I can do about the awards. But this is a good thing, I promise. It's fostering a sense of community. And as much as you hate being the center of attention, I know community is important to you."

Mo groaned again.

"Come on, say you'll do it," Khalil said. "For the kids. For the parents. For Mads to go to a party on a Saturday night?"

Mo rolled his eyes. "Fine," he said.

"Great," Khalil said, with his ever-excited-about-everything tone. "Thanks so much, man. I'll get Maddie to the orthodontist on Thursday and let you know asap about the banquet."

"Mmkay," Mo said, forehead still on his hand.

"Knew I could count on you. Talk soon," Khalil said and hung up the phone.

Mo slid his onto the table and sat up slowly.

A sense of community. Khalil wasn't wrong. Community was important to him. Just . . . not being in the middle of it. Being the center of attention went completely against the calm, quiet life he needed to maintain. He rubbed his eyes and ran a hand down his beard. *The parents will be happy, the kids will be happy. Maddie will have fun.* That was also important. *Guess Khalil is right; he can count on me.* Mo stood. Heading for the fridge, he remembered who else said they hoped to count on him. Wendy and the others needed him to accept that blacksmithing would be a key draw for the Renaissance Faire. And apparently, they expected him to take a visible role in it.

Why can't I just help prepare? We've got several students who could be the face.

He groaned, opening the fridge door. An event like a banquet was always difficult and draining. He'd have to spend the following day on the couch recuperating from "people-ing" with near-strangers for several hours. This Faire business would be worse.

Aren't those things several days at a time? Complete disruption, rather than calm and stable—the way I need things to be.

But Mo loved the School too much not to be actively involved in trying to save it. Even if it killed him to try. He sighed.

The School could count on him, too.

CHAPTER FOUR

Jess

Returning to her office from lunch with the dean, Jess felt her phone begin buzzing away in her pocket. She slid it onto her desk, but she didn't recognize the number and let the call go to voicemail as she shook the mouse to wake up her computer. When the notification popped up, she listened to the message on speaker.

"Hi? Jess? This is Wendy Davis, the president of the Folk School. We met briefly on Saturday. We're having an organizational meeting about the Renaissance Faire this evening and after speaking with Ned, I was hoping that you could join us. I'm swamped today so you can just text me to confirm if you can make it tonight at seven. At the School. Thanks."

Ned must have told her about Jess's research background. She'd already shared with him that she taught Greek through Renaissance Women's History. It would be logical for Wendy to think that Jess could contribute to the accuracy of the event. She mindlessly clicked on a new email in her inbox. Historical accuracy wasn't the most important thing at a Renaissance Faire, though. She'd learned that lesson with Cassie.

Clearing her throat, Jess reached for her mug while opening the attached pdf in the email. Then she glanced into the mug because it didn't feel right.

Of course, I need to make the tea before I can drink it.

She got up from her desk and went over to the electric kettle she'd placed with a few boxes of tea on top of a low bookshelf. Electric kettles had become an indispensable part of her life in England, and now she was taking comfort in having one in her new life that was coming together differently than planned.

"A market, a feast day, festive, joyous," Cassie had once said years ago, looking up from the etymological definition of "faire." *"Not a history lesson with an exam at the end, Ms. Professor."*

And so Jess had relinquished a bit of her need for historical accuracy in all things and gone along with her whimsy-loving sister to the Bristol Renaissance Faire at least two weekends of each summer that she'd been an undergrad. It hadn't really been a surprise that Cassie came to love Renaissance Faires. She'd always been the "fairy tale" sister, Jess the "feet squarely on the ground" one.

The gurgling kettle caught her attention. Once she had a new cup of tea steeping, Jess returned to her desk, taking a deep breath and releasing it slowly, trying to expel the new ache in her lower back along with the air. Even though the connection to Cassie might make it strange, she could do a bit of consulting for the Folk School if that would help. She could probably just go to this organizational meeting, give her two cents, and then get out of the way. She picked up her phone and opened her texting app.

Jess:

> Hi Wendy. Happy to help. See you at seven—Jess

While she couldn't yet say that the Folk School felt like a place that was *hers,* pulling into the much emptier parking area felt right. Certainly much better than it had when she'd arrived for the open house. After finding a safer-feeling spot beside a silver truck, she walked inside briskly. She'd gotten a bit held up at work and again at home and was a few minutes late. Following voices down a side hallway, she knocked on the slightly ajar door of a classroom and pushed it open.

"Jess, wonderful, so glad you're here," Wendy said from the head of an oval-shaped table.

"Sorry I'm late," Jess said.

Wendy waved a hand in the air and shook her head.

"Please, have a seat," she said, gesturing to the only open spot. Directly across from Mo, the Ax Murderer. Jess sat after a quick gulp, returning the nods of everyone else at the table. Where the others seemed engaged—leaning forward, forearms resting on the table, or flashing bright smiles and open expressions—the vibe she got from Mo was . . . threatened hedgehog? His back was pressed firmly against his chair, arms crossed tightly, his bearded chin tucked down into his chest. He glanced up at her out of the corner of his eye and his lips pulled lightly to the side as he nodded at her.

Was that a smile?

She gave him a brief smile back. He returned his attention to Wendy, and his face shifted back into its previous expression. Jess realized it was not anger, as she'd initially read, but wariness. Getting settled into her seat, she took another look around at the others. Ned was notably absent.

"Yes," Wendy said. "While I tried to present this as a fun way to make our name known in the community, during the planning process we need to keep the stakes in mind. If we don't replace the funding we've lost, the School is going to close, plain and simple."

The clutching sensation she'd felt when Ned introduced her to Mo snapped itself around Jess's heart again. She'd need to do a whole lot more research in order to be up to the task of consulting if the School was at risk. It was one thing for her to potentially lose a place that she'd just begun to enjoy. But based on the gasps and fearful expressions, the School meant much more to the people around this table. She didn't feel equipped to manage the pressure of potentially letting them down.

"Let's not be all doom and gloom," said a man with an open laptop in front of him in the seat beside Wendy. His face was familiar, a little snarky and self-satisfied-looking. She remembered that Ned had steered her away from him the other day. "This is going to be a blast," he said. "We can create a magical world and draw people in. We have all sorts of skills to dazzle them. I'm sure they'll be happy to empty their pockets."

"Thank you for that contribution, Doug," Wendy said. "But I don't think it's wise to come at this from the perspective of getting people to *empty their pockets*. That sounds . . ."

"Predatory," Lana said from the chair beside Jess.

"Exactly," Wendy said. "You are correct about our skills, however. That's why I want this team to work together closely to bring this to fruition." She took a brief moment to make eye contact with everyone. "So that we know who's doing what, Doug will deal with logistics and organization. And because I'll also be very busy seeking out alternative sources of funding, he will lead the team."

Doug sat up straighter, like he was barely containing a preen, then his grin slipped at the sound of smothered groans and sighs coming from around the table. Everyone was shifting in their seats or covering their mouths to suppress coughs. Mo was the only one who stayed perfectly still, his eyes narrowed at Doug.

"The board and I thought it best for Doug to take the lead as he does not have a specific skill to offer at the Faire. Your plates will likely be overloaded with preparing your contributions and maintaining our class schedules," Wendy said, looking around the table again. "Doug has assured us that he will . . . keep his enthusiasm in check. Right, Doug?" She made eye contact with him.

"Of course, of course," he said. "This will be a team effort, for the future of the School." Jess couldn't help but notice that he seemed to be bouncing in his seat a little, his fingers flat against the table in front of his laptop.

"Good," Wendy said. "Lana will manage textiles and headwear to sell. Mo will of course manage blacksmithing, which is quite the draw at Ren Faires according to Theo." She gestured to a relaxed young man seated at the end of the table. He stood out in more ways than one—his light brown hair was shaved around the sides and back, long on the top and flipped to one side, the ends falling just below his ear. He was younger than anyone else in the room by far, closer in age to the freshman students Jess would meet the following week.

"Theo's only been with us a year," Wendy said. "But he's worked on Ren Faire circuits, so he'll be our realism consultant, in addition to impressing our guests with his sword-fighting and knife-throwing skills."

Jess's mind shuttered to a halt at "realism consultant." If this Theo guy was there for realism, what could she contribute?

"Jess," Wendy said, drawing her attention. "I can't tell you, *we* can't tell you, how much we appreciate your participation. Like Mo, your skills will be a *very* big draw for us."

My skills?

Everyone was looking at her expectantly, pleasant closed-lipped smiles on their faces. Except for Mo. His arms were still crossed, his chin still tucked. But his expression was less wary and more resigned.

"I . . . I'm not sure I understand," Jess said, returning her attention to Wendy. "How would my skills be a big draw if Theo will already be consulting? I can provide historical accuracy due to my research, but if he already has Faire experience, I'm not sure what I can add."

"Oh, don't be so humble, J. C. Anderson," Doug said, waggling his finger at her.

The breath flew out of Jess's body. Doug was smirking at her. She narrowed her eyes back.

"How do you know my competition name?" she asked.

"A little bird told me," he said, looking even more satisfied with himself. Other than raising an eyebrow, Jess remained perfectly still.

"Okay, fine," he said. "Ned mentioned that you were a competitive archer when I asked about you. I like to learn about new students." He grinned.

The brief flash of irritation at losing some degree of anonymity waned but didn't go away. She hadn't told Ned not to mention her competitive experience, but she knew she'd never told him what name she competed under.

Wendy was looking back and forth between them.

"You didn't ask her directly?" Wendy asked.

"Google is more efficient. Even though it took a little digging since she didn't put that name on her information card."

He turned the laptop around so that it faced the table. A photo of Jess taken during the World 3D Archery Championships filled the screen.

The hairs on Jess's arms went on end. Warmth flooded her neck and into her cheeks as she took a breath to tell this guy off.

"Again, Doug?" Mo growled low before she could speak. Doug jumped.

"Yes, again?!" Wendy snapped, turning on him. "My office when we finish here; do you understand?"

Looking chastised, Doug nodded and turned the laptop to face himself again.

"Jess," Wendy said. "I'm very sorry. I understood that Ned *told* Doug that you were a competitive archer. That's why I thought you could help us with the Faire. An archery show starring someone of your caliber could draw huge crowds. From well beyond Detroit."

Jess's stomach dropped through the floor. She gulped and glanced around the table again. Everyone was looking at her. Except for Mo. Arms still folded tightly, eyebrows furrowed, his gaze darted from person to person, before falling to the table a few inches in front of him. He shook his head almost as imperceptibly as he had when they'd been introduced. After a quick sigh, he looked up at her. His eyes seemed almost apologetic.

"A show?" she asked. She remembered watching the shows a bit when she'd gone with Cassie, but they'd been about entertainment mostly, not skill. Archery was a sport for her, not . . . an act?

Doug scooted to the edge of his seat and leaned toward Jess a little. Her irritation with him was still high enough that she needed to stifle a lip curl.

"Here's the thing," he said. "We don't want people to just come visit and look around. Archery and blacksmithing are dazzling. Therefore, you two will be the public faces of the Faire."

Jess looked at Mo just as he snapped a glare at Doug.

"Me?" he grunted sharply. Jess admired his commitment to keeping his arms crossed. It seemed to be his default position. But now his intimidating biceps were flexing. He cocked his head to one side as he narrowed his eyes.

Doug flashed him an anxious grin before returning his attention to Jess. He took a breath to speak, but Mo cut him off.

"Wendy?" he grunted again. "*Public face?*" He continued glaring at Doug until Wendy looked up from the notepad she had in front of her.

"We don't have to decide who exactly is the face of the Faire today. Or even next week," she said.

"Rick exists," Mo said.

"He does," Wendy said. "And he's a great blacksmithing teacher. But the two people with the most accolades would draw in more fairgoers and even potential students."

Remaining still in his seat, Mo slid his gaze to Jess. She barely concealed her shock at finding an anxious teenager hiding in his eyes. The thought to ask if he was okay bubbled up but before she could, his gaze shifted away, and his face slid back into a mask screaming "back off." Just before she looked around the table, she caught Mo dragging a hand down his beard. The others were very occupied by their phones, or their own notepads, or they seemed to be counting the ceiling tiles. She took a deep breath and shook out her buzzing fingertips.

Thirty minutes later, the small group filed out of the School and toward their parked cars. The core Ren Faire planning team had been set—Jess, Mo, Lana, Doug, and Theo—and had exchanged numbers so that they could schedule another meeting once they'd spoken to other students and teachers in fields related to their own. Jess fumbled in her bag, not really focused on where she was going as she approached the parking area.

"Jess," a gruff voice said from behind her. Mo jogged to catch up. "You dropped this," he said. He held out a keyring just as she hooked her finger into her own inside her bag.

"That's not—" She lifted hers out, but her office keys weren't there. "Right," she said, looking at it. "That ring keeps popping off." She reached out, and he put the keyring in her hand. "Thanks."

"Sure," he said. He shoved his hands in his pockets and took a few steps to the side but continued walking in the same direction as she was. She realized that the truck she'd parked next to must be his. It was strange for him to walk a little away from it.

"Are you . . . did you purposefully give me space just then?" she asked, looking at him. He shrugged.

"I make people uncomfortable sometimes," he said.

She hesitated to make the joke but decided to risk it.

"Especially in dimly lit hallways."

He looked confused a moment, then his eyebrows went up, and he let out a quick exhale. Almost like a laugh.

"Learned my lesson with you," he said as they reached their cars.

"Wonder if my crossbow would work on Doug," she said. "A lesson on not prying into people's lives."

Mo's face darkened.

"He'd deserve it," he said.

"You know, I really like the School so far, and I don't want to be rude," she said. "But that was kind of an ambush."

Mo nodded slowly, shoving his hands deeper into his pockets.

"Sorry about that," he said.

"You don't have anything to be sorry for," she said. "It looked like you got ambushed, too."

He nodded again.

"I guess it's kind of a compliment," she said. "If they think we're that good."

"Suppose." His eyebrows furrowed, and his jaw moved like he was stretching it as he glanced back at the School.

"And for a good cause," she said.

He sighed.

"For the best cause," he said, looking back at her.

Jess wasn't sure what else to say. She'd never have imagined that she'd want to continue a conversation with someone who had scared the life out of her in the middle of the night. But Mo was surprising. This huge, imposing guy—aware of the negative effect that could have on others and willing to take the initiative to mitigate it—who seemed to be hiding an anxious kid inside. She wondered what other contradictions he was hiding. She didn't want to be weird, though. She sighed loudly.

"Have a good evening, Mo," she said. "I'll see you around. Or at the next meeting."

"Good evening, Jess," he said. He walked around to the driver's side of his truck, got in, and pulled away.

CHAPTER FIVE

Mo

"Okay, sugar plum, serpentine belt," Mo called out to Madison as he straightened up from the open hood of the lifted car he was working on. The shop was closed on Sundays, but he'd decided that it was important for Madison to have some good automotive skills, so he'd taken to bringing her into the shop with him from time to time on their weekends together. That particular Sunday was doing double-duty for him; the basketball league's thank-you banquet had been the previous night, and Mo was in desperate need of some quiet, reflective time to evacuate the remaining tension from the hours of being in an enclosed space with loud music, excited kids, and painful small talk. While he was appreciative of what the parents had wished to express, the hand-drawn cards from the players touched him much more than anything else. That, and seeing Maddie have a good time dancing with the players and their siblings.

Refreshed from the previous evening after sleeping in quite late, Maddie hopped off the stool on the other side of the bay where she'd been doing her homework and started over to him, then stopped.

"Gloves?" she asked.

"Yep."

She bounced over to the workbench and grabbed a pair of purple nitrile gloves from the box he'd purchased specifically for her.

"Okay, Daddy, serpentine belt. Let's get crackin'," she said, snapping the second glove at her wrist and smiling at him.

He chuckled.

"First, let's set the stage," he said. "The belt's job is to transfer energy from the engine's crankshaft to other components that need energy to function. If the belt breaks while driving, it's not a crisis situation, but it can become very dangerous. The goal is to change the belt before it breaks. They're usually good for a minimum of fifty thousand miles."

"Fifty thousand miles. Got it," she said, standing beside him, close enough to look at the engine but still keep her pink-and-purple outfit clean.

"If it needs to be changed before that, you might hear a squeaking noise while you're driving. If it has cracks, or tears, you definitely need to change it."

"Squeaks, cracks, tears. Got it."

He grinned.

"So let's dive in. Can you find the belt?" he asked.

She leaned forward a little more, resting her hands on the frame as he was. She tilted her head to one side, leaned a little closer, then leaned back again. He noticed that her bottom lip was a little tucked in on one side, a focusing habit she'd had since she'd started reading. A wisp of dark hair from her slipping ponytail fell across her forehead and she pushed it out of the way with the back of her gloved hand.

"Is that it, Daddy?" she asked, pointing.

He followed her gesture and smiled.

"Great eye, sugar plum. Now, it won't look exactly the same on each engine, but the path is similar. You see how it goes over a couple of different pulleys? We have to look from underneath to see everything."

She nodded.

He drew her attention to a diagram on the inside of the hood.

"Here's the path the belt takes. Keep this in mind as we work to remove it and as we get the new one on."

She frowned, looked at the engine, then back at the diagram.

"What's wrong?" he asked.

"Um, okay, but . . . Can I take a picture instead?"

Why hadn't I ever thought of that?

"Uh . . . of course." He fished his phone out of the pocket of his work pants. She leaned in, slipping her glove off to take a few shots and zoom in and out on one. She nodded her approval.

"Okay, let's get underneath," she said, smiling.

They grabbed creepers and slid under the car together, Mo picking up a slim light and switching it on. Before he pointed out the pulleys that the belt wove over, Madison had taken two more photos and slid back out from under the car to judge them in the sunlight coming through the open garage door.

"Looks good," she said, sliding back underneath and handing him the phone.

Dropping the phone on his chest, he began to explain the process. As always, Madison was attentive and anticipated the right questions to ask. When it was time to loosen the tensioner, Mo got it started but let her do the rest. She wound the belt off with ease, and as they slid out from under the car, she took a closer look at it.

"I need to line up the grooves on the new belt with the grooves on the pulleys, don't I?" she asked.

Mo smiled. Observant twelve-year-old.

"Yep. It's easy to do. The challenge is getting the new one into position from the top and the bottom."

He walked her through verifying that the new belt and old belt were the same size, pointed out the signs of wear on the old one, and handed her his phone. She glanced between it and the pulleys a few times then rested it on the frame so that she had both hands free to thread the belt in place. She was focused, and Mo watched, letting her approach the task the way she saw fit. She'd taken quickly to all the projects they'd worked on together so far—changing the oil, the spark plugs, and the battery. Changing a tire had required extra help from him, but he was confident that she'd be able to do it on her own when she was older and stronger. That one was particularly important to him. He wanted to be sure she could handle that even if it was cold or dark or raining. He hoped she'd never find herself in a position to have to depend on someone else to do it for her. She was already pretty fearless, but he wanted to add a layer of confidence from extra skill.

"Okay. I think the top is good," Madison said.

He took a look.

"Nice job. Down we go."

Madison grabbed the phone from the frame, and he held the light. He started to help her tug at the belt, but she wanted to do it, so he only watched. Once everything was in place and she'd tightened the tensioner, he gave it one last tug. He handed her the phone so she could verify with the photo she'd taken. Suddenly it rang.

"Here, Daddy," she said, handing it to him.

"Jess" was lit up at the top of the screen. Shocked, Mo barely noticed Maddie sliding out from under the car.

"Hello?" he asked, answering as he followed her.

"Hi, Mo? It's Jess, um, from the Folk School."

He caught a whisper of timidity in her voice. She hadn't sounded like that in front of the School the other day.

"Yeah," he said. "Hi, Jess."

Maddie had just finished standing and was pulling off her gloves. *"Who's Jess?"* she mouthed, a grin pulling at her lips. A hot blast went through Mo's chest, and he couldn't breathe. He didn't know why Jess would be calling him, and the look on Madison's face was messing with his head. She looked like—

"I'm calling about the meeting this week," Jess said, drawing his attention back to the call.

"Oh, right," he said. Teaching Maddie was important for her development, but it also gave him the chance to forget about any outside stressors. Although it was Sunday and the organizational committee's meeting wasn't until the end of the week, he'd already had to start his mental pep talks about feeling trapped in the room and preparing an overstimulating event. He'd been out to the School and taught classes over the past couple of weeks with zero problems. It had even been nice to see Jess at a distance when he'd been there. But the meeting would force him to face *This Thing* and the threat to one of his safe spaces.

"Actually," Jess said, helpfully interrupting the anxiety cycle set to begin, "I'm surprised to be calling you. Probably as much as I imagine you're surprised to get a call from me."

"Uh, yeah." She had a point.

"From what I understand, you aren't a fan of texting. Since you hadn't replied in the group chat, I was nominated to call and check that you're coming to the meeting," she said.

Mo smothered a small chuckle. She was absolutely right about him and texting. Maddie was the only person he ever texted with voluntarily. He'd seen the progress of the discussion in the chat. There hadn't been anything for him to add, so he hadn't thought to say anything. And he certainly wasn't going to spontaneously participate. Jess's word choice had caught his attention, though.

"Nominated?" he asked.

"Well, they nominated, I volunteered, potato-potahto," Jess said.

In Mo's opinion there was quite the gulf between those two options, so he wasn't sure what to say. A weak "um" was all he could get out. Looking down, he kicked at the tag that had been on the serpentine belt with the inside of his shoe. Maddie strolling by caught his attention in the corner of his peripheral vision. She was smirking a little. He raised an eyebrow, and she dropped the smirk, walking toward his office and out of the garage.

"I . . ." Jess said. She paused and then sighed. "I don't know about the dynamics at the Folk School, but it seems like everyone . . . gives you a wide berth. Which I don't get. Yes, you can be intimidating at first glance. But it seems like . . . well, like you can also be empathetic."

Mo's face flashed hot. *Nobody* caught on to his empathy without knowing him for a long time. They just took his exterior at face value, not understanding that it was there to keep all his stupid empathy inside. The empathy that wouldn't let him *not* feel what other people were feeling and get submerged by it if he let them get too close. He crossed his free arm around himself and squeezed. Then he caught Maddie peeking at him from the open shop door. He tilted his head and raised his eyebrow again. She disappeared.

"Um, yeah . . . I . . ." He wanted to say something. To thank Jess for seeing that, for using the word "empathetic" with him, about him. But he felt kind of exposed, and that feeling always made him retreat into himself to get away from the sticky prickliness blooming over his muscles. He hugged his arm even tighter around himself for courage.

"It's . . . uh . . . Thanks for noticing," he croaked out before his throat closed up. He immediately wanted to kick himself. He should have been able to say more, but he just couldn't. Plus, his face was on fire, and it was keeping him from thinking straight.

"Sure," Jess said. There was a little pause and Mo figured that maybe she didn't know what else to say. He wanted to push the conversation along—which surprised him—but he didn't know how. She cleared her throat, and he figured she was about to say goodbye.

"Actually," she said, "I noticed something else, too."

"Yes?"

"You don't seem to want to do this Faire. At least, you didn't during the meeting. But when we were outside, you said that doing it would be for the best reason."

She was right. He was impressed that she remembered what he'd said.

"Uh, yeah," he said.

"Is that because you kind of like to keep to yourself? That won't really be possible if they want to draw a lot of the attention to our skills in particular."

Mo didn't know what to do. This woman not only *saw* him; it sounded like she *got* him.

"That's exactly it," he said, mind still reeling a little.

Jess sighed again. Long and heavy.

"I don't really want to do it, either," she said. "Not because I don't think the School should be saved," she added quickly. "If I can help, I'll do it. It's just that Ren Faires . . . they bring up some personal stuff."

"Oh."

Mo had an inkling that the "personal stuff" might be related to her sister, but he didn't want to pry. He hated when people did it to him. He wanted to be supportive, but short of saying that she really didn't have to participate, he wasn't sure how.

"You know," she said, "maybe we could help each other. Be a personal sounding board if we need to gripe about it. Or have each other's backs if the rest of the committee tries to put too much on the two of us?"

She was open to talking to him? Letting him vent? His smile bloomed on its own. That was the exact moment Maddie chose to pop her head out of his office. Her eyes went wide, and she giggled. He scowled and she disappeared again.

"That would be great, Jess," he said. "Thanks. A lot."

"Thank you, Mo," she said. "Feels better not to be alone on this."

"Yeah."

"I'll let you go," she said. "Been talking your ear off."

He wanted to say that she hadn't at all. Which was weird because he only ever had phone calls this long with family. However, Maddie had been getting a little too curious and he would be relieved to remove the source of her curiosity.

"Um, okay," he said. "Thanks for calling."

"Have a good day, Mo. See you Friday."

"You too. And see you then."

After ending the call, he looked at the phone, holding it in both hands. He took a deep breath, trying to clear out the lingering shock from Jess seeing what most other people missed. His worry for the Folk School and how he could possibly deal with the Faire was present, but it had taken a backseat to the amazement of being seen. Jess's fortitude had been on full display the night they'd crossed paths, as had her desire to make things right at the open house. What he hadn't anticipated was her ability to be observant. Especially about someone like him. He wanted to do something nice for her, too. The question was, what? Then he remembered that she'd said her keychain was always—

"Dad-dy? Who's Jess?" Maddie sing-songed less than a foot away from him.

He nearly jumped out of his skin. She'd appeared in front of him without making a sound. She'd done that less and less with time, but still managed to now and then.

"Someone from the Folk School. We're working on a project to get funding for it," he said.

Madison tilted her head to the side and squinted.

"You smiled with her, but you don't talk to her like you talk to me," she said.

Mo was confused.

"Why would I?" he asked. "I don't know her very well."

"You should talk to more people like you talk to me. It would help you make friends."

Mo frowned. Making friends was an annoying, recurring conversation with everyone related to him. Just how carefully had she been listening in, anyway? He leaned forward and kissed her on the forehead.

"I'm fine, sugar plum. But thank you for being concerned about me."

"No, wait," Madison said. "You talk to Mrs. Sargysan the way you talk to me. She's your friend."

Even though they spoke multiple times a week, Mo doubted that his next-door neighbor would consider him a friend.

"You're right, I do talk to her. But I don't know that she's my friend."

Madison shook her head as she stuffed her pink MP3 player into her pocket. It was what they'd settled on so she could listen to music before she got a cell phone. She shoved the cord down too, and her headphones slipped from around her neck. Mo caught them and handed them to her.

"She's your friend, Daddy. Trust me."

"I trust you, Mads," he said, sliding an arm around her shoulders. "Let's finish up and get out of here."

"Can we get some fruit for Mrs. Sargysan on the way?"

"We can do that," he said.

Mo tapped on his horn as Madison disappeared into Diana's house. He put the truck in gear and pulled away from the curb. He was always a bit sad when Maddie left, even though he knew they would talk that night, at least by text.

After pulling into the driveway of his house, he took his sunglasses off then slid his mesh grocery bag across the seat and brought it with him as he stepped out of the truck. He never wanted to seem disrespectful to Mrs. Sargysan, and he probably wouldn't get a headache from the little sun he'd pick up while they were talking. Maddie had chosen so much fruit, she'd had difficulty carrying the bag out of the store. Mrs. Sargysan was sitting on her porch, reading, and she waved at him.

"Where's my little kuzu?" she called out.

Mo smiled.

"Your little lamb is back with her mom. Just dropped her off," he said, climbing her steps. "But she sent something for you." He carefully placed the bag on the metal patio table beside her chair. The oranges and grapefruits pulled in multiple directions, so he decided not to let go.

"Ah! Always thinking of her bonus grandma. Such a sweetheart," she said.

"Shall I take them inside?" he asked.

Mrs. Sargysan's eyes went wide.

"All of that?" she asked.

"All of that," Mo said, nodding.

"Goodness, I'm spoiled," she said. "I hope she chose something for herself."

"Yes, but I had to be a bit firm. Natural sweets are healthier than man-made."

Mrs. Sargysan nodded.

"Good dad. I'll make her a fruit salad when she comes back. No way I'll be able to eat all of that by myself. Let's go get everything put away." She began to rise, but Mo shook his head.

"I'll handle it; you rest here."

Mrs. Sargysan rolled her eyes.

"Enough resting. I'll rest myself to death, and then there'll be even more resting. Out of my way, young man."

She got up and went into the house first. Following her into the kitchen, Mo noticed that it was a little warm.

"Is your A/C working right?" he asked as he put the bag down on the table.

Mrs. Sargysan harrumphed.

"I don't know. I set the thermostat like normal, but it doesn't feel like it should in here," she said.

"Do you want me to take a look?"

She patted him on the arm.

"Don't worry about it, I already have a man coming tomorrow," she said.

"Want me to hang around, make sure he doesn't try any funny stuff?" he asked, waggling his eyebrows.

"Ha! That'll be the day," she said. "I think it'll be all right."

"If you get too warm, you know you can come over."

"Thanks, Mo, but I'm fine. You go relax. I'm gonna watch my shows and go to bed."

"Okay. If you need anything, bang on the wall."

She saluted him.

"Will do."

CHAPTER SIX

Jess

Wednesday afternoon, the simultaneous video call ringtone coming from her phone and laptop jolted Jess upright from her knees and she slammed her elbow into the edge of the shower door. Confused, she quickly dropped the scrub brush, got her hands out of her gloves, and hurried to her dining table. Steinem dropped down from his perch on the bathroom counter where he'd been supervising her cleaning and followed.

"Hey," she said when Alice appeared on the screen. "Is everything okay?"

"Everything's fine. I think you sent me the wrong file yesterday, though. The doc is only like two pages long."

Jess blinked. Alice had agreed to look over a paper Jess was going to submit for a conference at the end of the month. Her latest draft was much longer than two pages.

"Lemme check," Jess said, opening her sent emails. Alice was right, the attachment name was incorrect.

"Yeah, sorry, brain fart," Jess said. She found the correct file and sent it. "I didn't mean for you to start on it right now. I know you have a lot on your plate."

Alice waved Jess's words away.

"I wanted to dive in. As crazy as it probably sounds, I'm starting to miss reading academic research." Jess's jaw dropped and Alice laughed. "I know, I know. When I had to, I couldn't wait to stop. Now that I don't have to . . ." She shrugged. Jess let her laughter die down with her friend's. Alice's face suddenly shifted to concern. "Are you all right?" she asked.

"Yeah, why?"

"You keep rubbing your elbow."

Jess stopped rubbing. She hadn't realized that she was doing it.

"Oh yeah," she said. "I banged it right before I answered."

"Oh," Alice said. But she squinted her eyes a little and looked off to the side. "You know, you kept rubbing one of your shoulders the other day."

"I did?" Jess asked.

"Yeah. I'd meant to say something about it but got sidetracked. Are you sure you're doing okay?"

Jess had been dealing with some achiness in her joints for a while—pretty much since she'd moved to Detroit. She might have jumped back into archery a little too quickly. She had had to put it aside during her final semester, and then after Cassie . . . Her forearms started aching a little. She cleared her throat.

"Just archer aches and pains," Jess said.

"Oh, okay. Since I have you, catch me up. Do you feel better about being on that committee at the Folk School?"

Too frustrated after the ambush meeting to wait for their next scheduled call, Jess had emailed Alice and Stephanie to vent. Both agreed that the way she'd been recruited was problematic, but that it would be a good way to really get to know the people there. Alice, with her irritatingly good memory, had brought up a framed photo of Cassie dressed for a Faire that Jess kept in her bedroom in Sussex. Jess had significantly downplayed how much Cassie had enjoyed them. It would probably be best if she kept that information as sealed away as possible. Returning pain in Jess's elbow drew her attention away from old memories.

"Yeah," Jess said, rubbing again. "Mo and I talked about it. He's uncomfortable with it, too. We said we'd participate, but we'll have each other's backs so neither of us feels railroaded again."

Alice didn't say anything. Her eyes had gone wide at the mention of Mo, but she'd remained quiet. Then she leaned forward, posed her elbow on the table, and rested her chin in her palm. She smiled.

"You and Mo *talked*?" she asked. "Mo the *Ax Murderer*?"

Jess was enraged that technology had not sufficiently advanced for her to reach through the screen and rub the smirk off Alice's face.

"And?" she snapped. "*Yes, Alice,* I spoke to Mo. I spoke to an empathetic human being who seemed massively uncomfortable at the meeting, like I was, and we agreed to help each other through this."

Alice was dead silent, but she'd shot up in her seat and covered her mouth with both hands. She began to giggle.

"What now?" Jess asked, narrowing her eyes.

"How do you know he's empathetic?" Alice asked.

"It's . . . a vibe," Jess said. Clearly, she'd provided too much detail and needed to change course. Alice squinted at her.

"He did forgive you for trying to kill him, so there's that," Alice said. "And now he wants to *help* you—"

Jess glared at the word "help."

"You know, maybe it's time to put your whole 'Atalanta, epic female archer ever eschewing men' thing to the side," Alice said. "But . . . maybe not. If this Mo is willing to run with you—"

"Life does not reflect Greek myth. Even if it did, Mo is no Hippomenes," Jess snapped. She crossed her arms and sat back in her chair. "More . . . Hephaestus." She shrugged. "Physically intimidating, muscular, blacksmith . . ."

"Even *better*," Alice said, smiling broadly. "I like what I'm hearing. A little romance is just the thing for the new life you're building."

Romance?

"I would like to invite you to shut up now," Jess said.

Grocery list freshly typed into her phone, Jess checked that it was safe and headed to her car after locking her door. Even though she'd taken the time to finish cleaning her bathroom and make a thorough list after her call with Alice, she was still shaking her head. It was rare for Alice to push her about dating. What was even more rare was that Jess kept finding her thoughts returning to a man someone had nudged her toward.

So what? He seems like a nice human. That doesn't mean I have to throw myself at him.

She got in and locked the door.

Pretty sure I've never met a guy who looks like that and is empathetic.

She put on her seatbelt and dropped her keys into their spot.

And who's willing to help me with something difficult, even though I haven't told him why it is.

She pressed the ignition. Nothing happened. She looked down, watching the button move as she pressed it again. She glanced at her keys. They were with her; it wasn't like they weren't close enough. She pressed the ignition again. Still nothing. She sighed.

Looks like I might have to call and ask him to help me with something else.

The tow truck pulling Jess's car parked in the lot of Mo's shop an hour later. Jess shouldered her bag and climbed down along with the driver. Mo had sent the truck when she'd called and explained her problem. Without her asking, he'd stressed that the driver was trustworthy and safe, so she'd felt better about getting into a vehicle with a strange man.

"I'm not sure how this works," she said to the driver once she joined him beside the controls to lower her car. "Do I pay you now? Or will you send me a bill?"

The older man shook his head, the ends of his gray beard grazing the potbelly straining against his overalls.

"Don't worry about it now, ma'am," he said. "I'll settle it with Mo."

"Oh, okay," she said. "Well, thank you again for arriving so quickly."

He shrugged as he walked around Jess's car in the spot he'd chosen, seeming to check that everything was as he wanted it.

"Like I said on the way, Mo's good people, raised right. He's not a talker, so when he does, says something's important? Means it is. Gonna take care of that right away. You have a good one, young lady."

He climbed back in his truck and waved at her as he pulled away.

Jess stood in front of her car for a moment and watched the tow truck roll down the street.

Very forgiving. Empathetic. Respected by his elders. Made sure to let me know that I'd be safe with the tow truck driver. Maybe Alice could have a tiny point?

Jess turned toward the shop and caught sight of Mo walking around a raised white sedan in one of the open garages. He was looking up at it, rubbing his hands on a cloth mottled with dark stains. There was a younger man in similarly stained coveralls following him closely, talking to him, but from where she was, it looked like Mo was only nodding or giving one-word replies.

"Doesn't talk much." I mean . . . in a way that's kind of refreshing. Guess he chooses his words carefully?

By the time she'd woven through the cars exiting the lot and made her way to the small reception area, Mo was well out of sight.

"May I help you?" an older Black woman asked, looking over a pair of glasses, once it was Jess's turn at the counter.

"Yes, hi," said Jess. "I'm here about. . . ." She got a little annoyed with herself. She wanted to be precise in naming the problem with her car, but she didn't know what it was. "My car wouldn't start a little while ago, and Mo sent a tow truck. We just arrived, and it's in the lot. He said he would look at it."

"Oh, you must be Jess. Mo said a friend's car was coming in. Grab a seat, and I'll let him—"

"Beverly, I finished the Caddy. Mo's gonna be busy all day, so—" a different young man in stained coveralls had cut the woman off, approaching her from the side. She'd silenced him with one look.

"David. Did you interrupt me while I was talking?" she asked.

"Yes, ma'am," David said, dropping his gaze.

"Have we discussed this?"

"Sorry, ma'am," David said, his cheeks reddening.

He took a step back and tucked his hands behind him. Beverly looked at Jess with her lips pressed together.

"Just grab a seat, hon. I'll have David let Mo know you're here."

"Thanks," Jess said, turning and following her instructions.

There were several open seats, but they were all next to men. Jess didn't want to make a thing of it and took a step toward the vacant one next to a nicely dressed gentleman who looked to be in his seventies. A different man got up, freeing a seat next to an earnest-looking woman with a Tupperware-style container on her lap. Jess took that seat.

As she sat down, the woman smiled at her, then returned her expectant gaze to the open door leading to the garage. Her body language was much different from everyone else's. She was sitting at the edge of her seat, back straight, her leg tapping and shaking the container a little. Maybe she was running late and needed her car. But she didn't seem annoyed. Jess shrugged it off, got settled into her seat and started to reach for her phone as Mo stepped through the door. Catching her eye, he nodded, then saw the woman next to her. The color drained out of his face.

"Mo!"

The woman leapt out of her chair, knocking it against the wall and made a beeline for him.

"Mo, I had to come by and say thank you!" she said, throwing an arm around his neck and hugging him. Mo looked like he was terrified. Jess had no idea it was possible to return a hug so awkwardly.

"Uh . . . was nothing," he said.

"Nothing? No, no, it wasn't nothing, not at all," the woman said, letting go of him and wiping away tears that had started running down her cheeks. Jess glanced around. The entire reception area was watching. Mo's eyes darted around, too, and he turned bright red.

"Um . . . glad to help," he said, looking horribly embarrassed. He slowly ran a hand down his beard.

"My lawyer said finding the tracker was so important." She wiped at her tears again. "You were so smart to have known what it was."

"I just . . . uh . . . knew it didn't belong there," Mo said, looking at the ground.

"Here," she said, thrusting the Tupperware at him. "I wanted to thank you but I'm kind of low on cash right now. I hope you like chocolate chip."

Mo took it and nodded.

"My favorite."

The woman sighed.

"Oh good. I was worried. Okay. I won't bother you anymore. The container's disposable, I don't need it back."

Mo's relief was palpable. She hugged him again, and he looked like he was going to throw up.

"Thank you, Mo," she said, putting a hand on his cheek.

His smile was close-lipped, and it looked like it pained him.

"Welcome."

She patted him on the upper arm and walked through the door to the parking lot wiping her cheeks. When Jess looked back at where they had been standing, she saw that Mo had disappeared.

He found a tracker in that woman's car.

Jess folded her arms across her cramping stomach. A lump began to form in her throat, the room spinning, her nose burning. She wasn't going to start crying in this room full of people. There was no reason to cry. She had already cried over Cassie. But the "what if" question wouldn't stay stuffed down.

What if someone had found . . . What if I had been here and protected my little sister like I was supposed to?

A single tear escaped, and she wiped it away instantly. Mo knew enough to help the woman, but he didn't go rushing in and try to be the hero. The ache in Jess's stomach became almost unbearable. If she squeezed any tighter, she'd cut herself in two. David came out of the garage, munching on a cookie. He had two on a clean paper towel and offered them to Beverly, who didn't look up from what she was typing.

"Why are you eating Mo's cookies?" Beverly asked.

"He said we could have 'em," David said around a mouthful.

"Oh, that's right. He's not a fan of chocolate," she said, accepting them.

Jess took a deep breath. Then another. Her nose stopped burning, the room came into sharper focus. Mo had lied to that woman, but it was a kind lie. So she could feel that she'd done something to thank him. Beverly pointed at Jess with the end of a pen, and David gestured at her to follow him.

Through the door leading into the garage, he paused, looking around.

"Can you wait here a second?" he asked. "Maybe he went back into the office."

Jess nodded. The smell of oil and gas displaced the last of her overwhelming emotions, and the chorus of drills and shiny bright car bodies brought her back to herself. It seemed like there were men all over the place, going back and forth, deeply engaged in their work. Jess was fighting the instinct to sink into herself, to make herself less visible in a room full of men, until she caught the black ponytail restrained by a bright red elastic on a shorter mechanic who walked past. Another quick look around and Jess saw a second female mechanic and another person who didn't seem to fit the macho mold of most of the other employees. They'd slid out from under a car and stood up. Even with the coveralls, there was something different about them. It wasn't so much the short blue hair, or the small, thin stature. It was something in the way they moved. Jess couldn't read their gender.

This is his shop; he must have final say on employees. Has he tried to recruit a gender-diverse staff?

"Um, hello," Mo grumbled as he walked over. His voice was barely audible over the background noise of the shop.

"Hi," she said, surprised out of her thoughts. "Thanks again for agreeing to take a look at my car."

He shrugged. Then he turned a little and tipped his head toward the open garage doors. Jess guided him out to her car in the lot. She wanted to say something about the woman with the cookies. Ask him how he knew what to do, or even thank him again on her behalf. But with the way he had responded in the reception area, she decided not to bring it up. At her car, she handed him the keys. He unlocked the door and popped the hood.

He leaned over the engine with his hands on the frame. She followed suit.

"Won't start, right?" he asked.

"Exactly."

"Had it a while?" he asked, glancing at her.

Jess shook her head.

"It's used," she said. "I bought it a month ago from a dealership in Illinois. I'm not into cars, really. Just a means of transportation."

He nodded, gaze roving over the engine.

"They check it out first? Certify it?"

"Yeah," Jess said.

Mo nodded again. He crossed his arms as he stood back up and ran a hand down his beard. Jess stood straight as well.

"You buy it on your own? No one went with you?" he asked.

"Yeah."

He ran a hand down his beard again, brows furrowed. Jess sighed.

"I should have taken a man with me, huh?" she asked.

Mo shrugged one shoulder.

"Or your crossbow," he said.

Jess laughed and to her surprise, Mo smiled at her. A full smile. Probably the first display of happiness she'd ever seen from him. It even reached his eyes. She was so surprised that she stopped laughing. His smile disappeared and he looked down to kick at nothing with his toe.

"Got a couple of ideas," he said, leaning over the engine again. "May take some time, though."

Surprising her again, he looked bashful, almost sorry. If he was sensitive to other people's emotions, she was worried about how his own were treating him. To go from deeply embarrassed to laughing to maybe sorry so quickly was quite the ride.

"I'm not . . . I'm not in a rush," she said.

Rumpling his brow, he looked at the engine again.

"You need it for tomorrow," he said.

Right. She'd forgotten about the committee meeting. She had class, too, but he couldn't know her schedule.

"Please," she said, waving a hand. "Don't worry about my schedule. I'll Uber around if necessary."

Mo wasn't looking at her. He was chewing his lip, his gaze intent on the engine block. His eyebrows tight together, fingers crimping on the frame of the car, he looked like he was trying to make a decision, and it was costing him. She began to feel really bad about bothering him, but she was also wary about just taking a guess and choosing a random shop.

"I can pick you up," Mo mumbled with his eyes closed. Jess had barely heard him.

"I'm sorry?" she asked, leaning in. He let out a puff of air.

"I can pick you up," he said. "Give you a ride to the meeting. If you want." He slowly turned to look at her, and Jess's heart started hammering in her chest.

Don't you dare! Don't you dare get all weak at the knees and googly-eyed at some adorably sexy— Stop it!

She cleared her throat and straightened her spine. Which was a bad idea because it made the woozy feeling she was getting from looking in his dark eyes lined with lush eyelashes even worse. She clutched the D-ring on the strap of her purse to ground herself.

"I—" She stopped to get her voice back to the correct pitch. "I would really appreciate that, Mo. Thank you," she said.

She saw a little pink in the skin above his beard as he looked back at the engine.

"Okay, good, you're welcome," he said.

"You know," she said, speaking before she could stop herself, "there's nothing wrong with accepting credit for having a positive impact on someone's life. Nothing to be embarrassed about."

He was looking at her car again, but he turned bright red, and his eyes got big.

"I wasn't going to say anything, but I hope you weren't uncomfortable because of what you did," she said in a rush. Her knuckles were aching again. She probably should have loosened her grip on her purse, but she was too nervous. He shook his head but still didn't look at her.

"Just . . . a lot of people," he said, scratching at his beard.

"Okay," she said. She left it at that because she'd said too much already.

He cleared his throat and tipped his head back toward the shop. At the desk, Beverly had her sign an estimate that made her eyes swim a little. Then Jess sat down to order an Uber. It arrived much more quickly than she expected, and as she was walking through the parking lot to meet it, she saw Mo leaning over the engine again, shaking his head. As she got into the car, she remembered what David had said, that Mo was going to be busy all day. She hoped he wasn't starting on her car right away.

Nah, he's got so many employees. I'm sure someone else can handle it.

CHAPTER SEVEN

Mo

Rachid, the second Sarda son, was visiting their parents for a week, so Mo drove out the next day. He took his time so he could think without thinking, without forcing it. Allow his eyes to half-focus and go to his parents' house on autopilot, enjoying the quiet hum of the wheels on the highway, the low growl of the engine. Normally, he would have benefited from the drive. It would have helped him to get away from the discomfort of that embarrassing moment in his shop. But the anxiety about driving Jess to the meeting the next day had anchored tension in his body.

Sheer madness.

He didn't know what had come over him, what he'd been thinking when he offered to bring her into yet another one of his safe spaces. Particularly one that he adored for its quiet.

Well, she needs a ride. She doesn't need to waste money on Ubers when we're both going to the same place.

But it would be an hour. An hour total, there and back, and they would have to talk. Even if they turned on the radio, there would still be the pressure to talk. Mo swallowed hard, trying to push down the lump that had formed in his throat. She might be understanding about it, if he got all twisted up and couldn't talk. She'd already shown him enough understanding, demonstrated that she could see what made him different from other people, for him to make her the gift he planned on giving her the next day.

Fingers crossed, she'll be understanding enough to not find my surprise gift weird.

Taking the exit for Grosse Pointe Farms, he followed his habitual detour to the florist to pick up a bouquet like he always did for his mom. As always, the garage door was open when he pulled into the driveway.

"Mo! There you are," his mom said when he walked into the kitchen from the garage. "My firstborn never fails to brighten my day." She went up on tiptoe to kiss his cheek as she accepted the flowers.

"Hi, Mom," he said. "What's all this?" he asked, gesturing to the kitchen island covered in stapled printouts.

"Your dad and I are trying to decide where to go on vacation," she said, returning to him after putting the flowers in a vase.

Mo looked closer and saw that each small set was a destination with accommodation and itinerary options.

"Mom, you've planned multiple vacations down to the last detail but haven't actually booked anything?"

"Not yet," she said, looking at the options, tapping her chin.

"Um, you couldn't have done this in multiple tabs on a browser?"

She looked up at him.

"Mo," she said flatly. "Staring at a screen all day is one of the occupational hazards of forensic accounting. Sometimes I need paper."

He nodded. Made sense.

She returned to her study of the printouts.

"Rachid and Khalil are in the study. ESPN highlights or some such."

"Okay," he said. He kissed her on the head and went down the hall.

As usual, Mo heard Khalil before he saw him. If it had been anyone else, that character trait would have gotten on Mo's last nerve. But with Khalil, it just made Mo roll his eyes.

"There's the man of the hour!" Khalil announced as soon as Mo walked into the room. Mo didn't understand. His face must have shown it.

"Only kidding, man. Come on, sit down." Khalil patted the couch beside him.

"Hey," Rachid said, in his much more appreciably quiet tone from the matching burgundy club chair to the left. Mo nodded back. The leather of the couch creaked as he sat. The sound was welcoming, familiar, but of course Khalil couldn't let Mo fully enjoy it.

"What's good with you?" he asked. "How's the little lady?"

Mo smiled, about to answer, but paused. Did Khalil do that on purpose? He always ribbed Mo for being prickly, a grouch, for not wanting to talk. But Madison always put him in a good mood, and it was easy to talk about her. Could Khalil tell that Mo had been a little annoyed when he sat down and was trying to push him into a better place? Or maybe it was just uncle stuff.

"She's good," Mo said. "She's on her way back to Diana's from a Girl Scout campout, but next weekend she wants to have some friends over for a slumber party."

"Oooh . . ." Khalil said.

"Yeah," said Mo.

"Any way to convince her to do it at Diana's?" Rachid asked. Mo shook his head.

"She's out of town. I think I'm going to have to bite the bullet and say yes. I mean, I don't want to say no. And the two girls she wants to invite over are sweet kids. I know they'll be well-behaved. It's just . . ."

"Mo and his space," Khalil said.

"Mo and his quiet," Rachid said.

Mo frowned. He'd already felt guilty enough when Madison had asked, and he hadn't immediately said yes. He wanted to. But other people. Especially children, with all their energy, in his space? Overnight? His skin started crawling, and his heart started racing just thinking about it. He needed to change the subject.

"Rachid," he said. "What's new? Mom said you're here for a conference?"

"Yes," he said, straightening in the club chair somewhat dwarfing him. "Most of it will be about pediatric cardiomyopathy. And there will also be talks about the latest research into techniques for Tetralogy of Fallot and the developments in atrial switch operations for d-TGA. I'm really looking forward to those."

Mo had no idea what the hell had just come out of Rachid's mouth. He glanced at Khalil, but he looked like he didn't know, either.

"You're doing it again," Khalil said to Rachid.

"What?" asked Rachid.

"Your thing," said Mo.

Rachid sighed.

"Sorry. Um. Kid heart stuff. I . . . I don't want it to sound boring." He slumped back into the chair.

"Nah, man, it doesn't sound boring. Just confusing," said Khalil. He turned to Mo. "Bro, you gotta let him tell you about the kid's life he saved last week!"

Mo raised his eyebrows.

"You saved a kid's life last week?" he asked.

Rachid waved a hand in the air, as if it were no big deal.

"My team and I worked to help a patient together," he said. "That's all. We did our jobs."

" 'My team and I' . . . 'We did our jobs,' " Khalil imitated him. "Dude, do not play it down; you saved a child's life. Tell Mo what happened."

Rachid leaned forward again and explained. As far as Mo could understand, he—or he and his team—had come up with a new process for a particular type of surgery for kids. Mo might have understood more if Khalil had been able to keep himself from interrupting every other sentence with a "wow," "that's so cool," "man, that shit is amazing," again and again. It wasn't that Khalil was wrong. It was just that he was, as always, incapable of being quiet.

"So, if I understand correctly," Mo said, "in this instance, the child wouldn't have made it without this process?"

"No, probably not," Rachid said, shaking his head.

Mo looked at Khalil.

"So he saved the kid's life, right?" Khalil asked Mo.

"Sounds like it to me," Mo said.

Rachid shrugged.

"It was a group effort."

"Rachid," Mo said, scooting forward. "There's nothing wrong with accepting credit for helping people. Jess told me that, and she's right. I know it's hard to feel seen, but this is one instance where it's important to accept the credit."

Both Rachid and Khalil looked at him sharply. He thought it was because he'd said a lot.

"Jess?" Rachid asked.

"Who is *Jess*?" Khalil asked.

Mo's face got hot. His ears were on fire, his heart felt like it was going to shoot out of his chest.

"Uh . . . a person . . ." he stammered. He scratched the side of his beard, then smoothed the hair into place.

Khalil's face bent into a wicked grin.

"A *female* person," he said.

Mo slipped back, wanting the couch to swallow him up.

Rachid cleared his throat and tapped his glasses higher on his nose. Mo caught the grin he tried to stifle.

"I appreciate what you said," Rachid began. "I will take that under advisement. But . . . um . . . I am curious. About Jess? She sounds wise."

Mo ran a hand through his hair. He wanted to curl into a ball. This was ridiculous. Now, to make his comment make sense, he was going to have to tell them not only about Jess, but also explain about Petra and finding the tracker. He most certainly couldn't tell them that Jess was going to be in his car for an hour the next day. It was all way too much.

"I thought we were talking about you," he said to Rachid.

Khalil shook his head.

"Nice try, bro," he said to Mo. "Tell us about Jess."

Mo flushed hot again and growled under his breath.

"No," he said.

"Don't make me bring out the big guns," Khalil said, smiling.

"Huh?" Mo asked.

"MA!" Khalil called out at the top of his lungs. "Mo's talking about a girl!"

Slack-jawed, Mo couldn't even collect his thoughts before their mom called back.

"What?"

"Mo's talking about a girl, come quick!" Khalil answered, laughing.

Mo was dead. No. He wasn't dead. He was going to kill Khalil, then he could die himself. Their mom was in the room with them in half the time it should have taken to get down the hall.

"Mo?" she asked him. "You've met someone?"

He glared at his brothers. Clearing his throat, he tightened his crossed arms.

"I spoke to another human being. She made a good point. I shared it."

The three of them looked at one another. Maybe if he kept his mouth shut, all the excitement would die out.

Their mom raised an eyebrow.

"There's more to the story than that, Mo," she said.

"There always is," Khalil said, grinning again.

Mo grunted.

"Um . . ." Rachid said. "If you think Jess is worth listening to, that says a lot about her as a person. You don't let anyone in enough to give you advice."

"You are *very* careful about who you listen to, Mo," their mom said.

Mo let his head slump back against the couch, closing his eyes.

"You know," Khalil said, "if you refuse to tell us anything, it's only going to feed our imaginations. . . ."

Mo opened one eye to glare at Khalil's grinning face. Unfortunately, he wasn't wrong. And if Mo didn't want Mr. Family Gossip Column to get too overexcited, he should set the record straight in advance. He rolled his eyes and lifted his head.

"She was in the shop. Overheard me talking to someone who wanted to thank me. Saw I was uncomfortable. Said it's okay to accept credit. Satisfied?" He glared at Khalil again.

"I got, I got it, man," Khalil said with his hands raised.

"That's . . . unusual," Rachid said. "For another customer to just walk up to you and give advice after eavesdropping."

"Not just a customer," Mo said, having relaxed a bit once Khalil backed off. Rachid raised an eyebrow and looked at their mom. Mo glanced up and saw that her eyebrow was raised as well.

"She's not *just* a customer, but she was in your shop? Close enough to *you* to overhear your conversation?" she asked. Her cheeks hollowed a little, like she was biting the insides. Khalil was looking at the TV, but Mo knew he wasn't grinning like that because of what was on the screen.

Mo sighed, scratching at his beard. Only, *only* because they were his family and he knew they meant well and he loved them, and in a weird perverse way he felt at peace and somewhat recharged after he spent time with them instead of totally spent like with the rest of the world, did he not explode. He sighed again.

"She just started coming to the Folk School," he said.

"Is she a blacksmith?" Khalil asked.

"No. Archer. We're on the Ren Faire committee together," Mo said.

Khalil and his mom reeled like bowling pins and Mo realized his new mistake with a wave of itchy skin.

"You're doing a Ren Faire?" Khalil asked, eyes wide.

"What's a Ren Faire?" At least Rachid sounded like his usual inquisitive self, no shock that made Mo feel unbalanced. He sighed and tugged a little at his beard.

"Folk School needs funds," he muttered. "Think we can make it if we have a Ren Faire."

Khalil tittered.

"Are you gonna dress up?"

Mo shoved himself off the couch and onto his feet.

"Mo!" his mom said, reaching for him. "Khalil, you're not helping." She scowled at him.

"Mo, come on, man, I'm sorry," Khalil said, reaching out a hand.

Mo grumbled, shaking his head, and made his way to the kitchen. He needed some water. He heard the swish of his mom's caftan as she followed him, but she didn't say anything as he went into the kitchen, found a can of sparkling water in the fridge, and closed the door behind him. She waited until he'd had a sip before she came up next to him and rested a hand on his upper arm.

"Do you want to talk about this Jess?" she asked.

He wasn't sure what to say about Jess. He couldn't tell his mom about the way they'd met; it wouldn't exactly paint Jess in the best light from his mom's perspective. He could say that she was willing to do something for a group of people she didn't know very well. That showed she had good character. Coupled with how attractive she was—

Attractive?

His cheeks flushed hot. He took a quick sip of water before clearing his throat.

"Not much to say," he said. "Working with her on the Ren Faire project."

"Okay," his mom said, her eyes twinkling. She patted his arm and returned to her printouts on the kitchen island.

A few hours later Mo left his parents' house, a large container of Bahgrir for him and gazelle horns for Maddie in his hand. His mother always sent him home with their favorite desserts. He paused before opening the door of his truck. The truck that Jess would be getting into in less than twenty-four hours' time. He'd forgotten while inside, but now looking at it, the prickly anxiety of driving with Jess to the meeting formed a lump in his throat. This anxiety was deeper than the constant, low-level buzz of it that he lived with every moment he wasn't in one of his safe spaces.

Maybe it's so strong because I've just stepped out of one of my safe spaces.

He got into the truck, settling the container carefully in the passenger seat so it wouldn't slide around on the drive home, and tried to parse why he felt so . . . scared about the drive with Jess the next day.

It's not like she's going to attack you.

He knew it wasn't physical safety that was bothering him. It was emotional. Jess had *seen* him. And she hadn't judged. That should have made him want to be around her, not run away. Maybe that's why he'd been honored when she'd reached out to him for help about her car. That's why he'd been stomach-wrenchingly nervous as they'd talked beside it, her hypnotizing brown eyes too intense to look into. Why, even when they hadn't spoken, he'd been happy to see her occasionally at the School, her beautiful sable hair gilded by the sunlight when she was on the archery range. He turned on the engine.

In spite of feeling the need to make her a gift, Mo hadn't fully acknowledged that he was attracted to Jess until that afternoon. Some deeper part of himself must have realized it and made him open his mouth and put him in a situation where he couldn't run away. He sighed, scratching at his beard.

I swear, I am my own worst enemy.

That was the deeper anxiety. She made him feel seen and appreciated for who he truly was. She'd given him the opportunity to help her in a concrete way with his skills. Like many men, for Mo that was all it took. Her beauty was just the icing on the emotionally overwhelming cake. He sighed.

I have a huge crush on Jess.

CHAPTER EIGHT

Jess

Sitting on the couch in her apartment, bag already on her shoulder, keys in her hand, Jess wondered what was wrong with her. Mo had called to say he was on his way—she raised her wrist to check her watch—seventeen minutes earlier, and she'd immediately gotten ready to leave. Once she was, she'd just sat down and folded her hands in her lap. No finding any last-minute detail to take care of, no taking out her phone to pass the time; she just sat. In part, it had been a good reflex. She hadn't noticed that her lower back was a little bit achy until she was seated and still. Her current inertia was surprising, though.

Just want to be ready when he gets here. Don't want to keep him waiting.

Mo had seemed very uncomfortable when he'd offered her a ride. At first, she'd thought it was because he's a reserved person and it was awkward for him to offer. But that morning, she'd begun to worry that he somehow felt obligated. She couldn't guess why that might be, though. Meowing slowly and low, Steinem drew her attention to where he was sitting on the floor watching her, just out of reach.

"I'm okay," Jess said.

Steinem narrowed his eyes and sniffed at her. He meowed again.

"I am," Jess answered. "You don't have to believe me."

Steinem turned his ear to the right, his head following. Jess caught the sound of a car pulling up to the front of her house.

She hopped to her feet, peeked through the blinds, and saw Mo's truck at the curb.

"Later, Sty Sty," she tossed over her shoulder.

Her heart was pounding as she took the steps too quickly. She reassured herself that she just didn't want to make Mo wait, it wasn't like she had a reason to be nervous or excited about seeing him. He was just a nice friend giving her a ride—

Holy. Shit.

Mo was stepping out of his truck, time slowing down. His hand on the truck's door, his muscled forearm revealed by the rolled-up sleeve of his dress shirt. His jeans were dark and not tight, but not so loose that Jess couldn't pick up on the fact that his thighs were impressive, too. His face seemed relaxed—as far as she could tell behind the reflective sunglasses and dark beard.

Has he always been this hot? How did I—

Her mind shut off when he looked up at her and gave her a cute half-smile.

"Hi," he said.

Damn you, Alice.

"Hi," Jess said back, willing her voice to sound normal.

"Lemme get your door," Mo said, walking around to the passenger side and opening it for her.

"Thank—" A long, brightly beaded necklace clattered to the pavement, cutting her off. Mo chuckled.

"Sorry," he said, bending to pick it up and shaking his head a little. "That's Maddie's." Jess caught a little smile on his face, a balance between endearment and exasperation. She got in and he closed the door behind her. The bright, loud beads were in stark contrast to the vibe she'd gotten from him. Her curiosity was high as he rounded the truck.

"My daughter," he said once he joined her inside.

"Oh," Jess said, glancing at his ring finger before she'd thought to check.

"She's twelve. Definitely a pre-teen, but the little girl is still there," he said as he settled into his seat.

"Oh," Jess said.

"I miss her when she goes to her mom's, but sometimes her forgetfulness leaves me nice surprises." The bemusement on his face was clear as he wiped the necklace with a tissue and gently nestled it into the center console. Watching him treat his daughter's forgotten belonging like a fragile treasure made some things click for Jess—his care to make sure he wasn't crowding her in the Folk School parking lot; his focus on making sure she knew she would be safe with the tow truck driver—Mo was a Girl Dad. The best, big mushy kind. The kind her own father had never been in spite of having only daughters. Jess cleared her throat to remove the forming lump.

"Are you two close?" she asked.

Mo shrugged.

"Like to think so. Was worried the divorce would change things. Worked hard so it wouldn't," he said. He gave her another half-smile.

"Ah. That's great," Jess said. She needed to change the subject. The positivity he was radiating was so enticing that she wanted to crawl inside his chest to know how it felt. Positive feelings that strong had been great in the past. But now that Cassie was gone, feelings like that . . .

"You look nice," she said quickly. His cheeks reddened as he tucked his chin.

"Thanks," he said softly, putting on his seatbelt. "Had a business owner's meeting. With the city. No time to change."

"Oh."

What? Were you hoping he dressed up for you? Get serious, Jess.

Facing forward, Mo scratched at his beard and ran a hand down it. She'd noticed him do that during the meeting and at his shop. It didn't seem like he was trying to groom it, but she was coming up empty on what else he might be doing. He sighed.

"So, um . . . I'm . . ." He trailed off as he gripped the steering wheel.

Jess's stomach began to turn as her gaze danced over the dashboard. It seemed like she'd put a lot of pressure on him by accepting a ride. He was so tense, she thought to tell him that she was perfectly fine getting an Uber, or she could call in to the meeting on Zoom or some other app. Then she heard him take a deep breath and suddenly he was talking again.

"I'm . . . kind of odd, right?" he said. "The thing is, I'm not angry all the time, I just pick up on a lot from other people, and you figured that out, which *never happens*. So, again, thank you for that; it means a lot." He paused and took a quick breath. "Because I pick up the emotions of other people, it's difficult when they're in my space and when we have to talk because I'm bad at small talk. So if I'm weird there and back, it isn't you. I'm not angry or anything. And I'm happy to give you a ride. Even . . . even if I seem weird."

Jess blinked. For a moment, it was the only thing she could do. Her lungs had frozen; her mind put into a sort of standby mode at the deep, rumbly purr of his extended speaking voice. Up until then, she'd only heard curt, short phrases or grunts and had no idea he could sound like that. She knew he was uncertain, knew that she needed to say something to address the vulnerability he'd just displayed, but she was struggling to get back into her *mind* and out of her tingling *body*. Angry that she failed to maintain control of her reaction to him, she forced a light cough. She thought she caught him gulp and glanced at him. He'd sort of crunched into himself while speaking, his considerable height reduced in his seat.

"I don't think you're weird," she said.

"Heh. You haven't known me long enough."

Jess didn't care for that. The dislike pushed her more fully into herself.

"I *know* you're not weird," she said. "You're a kind person who wants to help others. Even if it makes you uncomfortable. You've proven that to me, to that woman at your shop, and you're proving it by doing this Ren Faire. I appreciate you telling me not to take it personally if you're quiet on the ride, but I'm not going to sit here and listen to some crap about you being weird."

Then she was certain she heard him gulp. Slowly, he turned to face her.

"You don't think I'm weird?" he asked, incredulity etched around his eyes.

"Would you feel better if I did?" she asked. The laugh that shot out of him, and the smile that spread across his face, warmed her to her toes.

Fine, Alice. Maybe you can kind of be right.

He started the car, and they set off. Jess was happy to sit in silence the whole way there if it would help him be more relaxed. However, she also wanted to be sure she could support him during the meeting.

"Mo, just so I understand how to help, the 'picking up from other people' and being uncomfortable when they're in your space—is that what makes participating in a Ren Faire challenging for you?"

He nodded.

"It's the energy of a lot of people, their emotions. I can feel it in my body, and it drains me. Having to use a lot of my own energy to stay steady, and even more to *perform*? Plus all the noise and changes to my schedule." He shrugged. "I can understand that an event like this is very exciting and a lot of fun for other people. For me, it's the opposite. I know I'm going to need days to recover afterward."

"Hmm . . . thanks for explaining," she said.

"Thanks for trying to understand. What about you?"

Of course he would ask about her. She hadn't anticipated the logical next step in their conversation. And she didn't particularly want to touch on it. Giving voice to her *why* might bring up too much. However, Mo had been vulnerable; it would be wrong for her to refuse to do the same.

"My sister," she said. "She adored Ren Faires. I even let her drag me along a few times. It was never my thing. I'm a stickler for historical accuracy, and it was sorely lacking in the Faires I attended."

"I get it," Mo said. "Cosplay blacksmiths are a danger to themselves and others. They like the look, but they aren't respecting the craft. Just playing around."

Jess nodded.

"About your sister . . ." He paused, sighed. "That makes *a lot* of sense."

"What do you mean?"

"That participating in this Faire would be difficult. Having that connection, Faires being linked to her—I'm sure everyone would understand if you don't want to do it. If it's just too much. And if they don't want to understand, I will make sure that they do."

There was something in his enunciation, in the way he slowed down and dropped the tone of his already deep voice as he finished his statement . . . a wave of heat cascaded up her body and cut off her ability to breathe again. The skin-tingling thrill of letting herself be attracted to Mo was alluring. But she had to fight it. Being attracted to Mo, to anyone, wasn't what she wanted or needed. Keeping her composure, her control, was always the best, safest option.

"That's kind of you, Mo," she said. "But I'm sure it will be okay." She gave him a friendly smile when he glanced at her then turned her attention out the window, letting the silence settle between them.

Thirty minutes later, Mo pulled into a space in front of the School. He took a deep breath and let it out slowly.

"Here we go," Jess said, reaching for her door handle.

"Wait. Almost forgot," Mo said, opening the center console and handing her a small, brown paper pouch. "Here," he said, handing it to her.

Confused, Jess opened the pouch and tipped the contents into her palm. A small, wrought piece of dark metal fell into her hand. It was a particularly serpentine S, the curlicued ends looped around small keyrings. She'd never seen anything like it.

"What's this?" she asked.

He shrugged.

"You said your keys kept popping apart. The two rings. It seemed like you chose to keep them separate. So I put one ring on each end of this keychain. That way the two groups of keys don't mingle while staying linked together."

Jess's heart dropped and then took off.

"You *made* this?" she asked softly. "For me?"

His cheeks reddened.

"Yeah." He shrugged. "I wanted to say thanks. Um, for seeing me, seeing the empathy and that I'm not mean." His cheeks reddened, and he looked away, out the windshield. "Wanted to give you something useful. It's okay if you don't like it."

Jess snapped her hand closed, squeezing until the key ring bit into her palm.

"No," she said. "I do. I like it . . ." She softened her grip and looked at it again. "I like it very, very much. Thank you."

Jess hadn't realized that she'd walked into the organizational meeting on a cloud. She and Mo had joined Lana, Theo, and Doug inside. Jess had greeted the others, taking a seat beside Mo, and accepted a stapled packet that Doug distributed with *Project: Renaissance Faire* on the cover. As Doug began, Jess followed along on autopilot, the keychain in her hand drawing her attention a few times. She glanced down at it, still surprised that Mo had actually *made* it for her. She didn't know if anyone had ever handcrafted something for her—especially to meet a need they'd noticed but that she hadn't articulated.

". . . covers the structure," said Doug, drawing Jess out of her haze and back into the room. "Let's look at some examples of Faire hierarchy and costumes on the next page." He turned his page and the others followed suit. Jess tucked the keychain into her purse then did the same.

"One thing," Theo said, a long, thin finger raised. "It's garb."

"I'm sorry?" Doug asked him, eyes narrowed.

"We don't wear costumes. We wear garb," Theo answered, smiling.

Jess barely heard them. The clothes were like a punch to her solar plexus. As her gaze bounced around the page from one woman to another, each one's face morphed into Cassie's. The room began to dim and there was no air. Something bumped against her leg, knocking her knees together. She looked up at Mo beside her. He didn't say anything, but she understood that he was concerned, that by bumping his knee against her, he was silently asking if she was all right. She shook her head a little without meaning to. Mo cleared his throat.

"Garb later," he announced to the table. The others flinched at the command in his voice. He turned the page of his packet. Jess, Lana, and Theo did as well. Doug did not.

"Why? I thought it would be fun to start with costumes—er garb. Especially for you girls. You get to play dress-up!" He grinned at Jess and Lana. The comment and stupid look on his face slammed Jess back into herself, and she took a breath to snap at him, but Mo spoke first.

"No," he said to Doug, much more loudly and deeply than anything else he'd said before.

"What?" Doug asked, cowering in his seat a little.

"Sexist," Mo said. Jess was kind of glad he was looking at Doug because she wouldn't have wanted that facial expression aimed at her. Not from such a big guy. She swallowed.

"Yes, Doug," she said, looking at him. "That was a sexist thing to say."

Lana was practically hiding her face in the printout.

Doug sighed.

"Fine," he said. "Let's, um . . . let's talk tasks." He took a deep breath and straightened in his chair. Jess squinted, wondering what was coming. He flipped forward a couple of pages in the packet and held it up, pointing to a photo that took up the top half of the page. The others found the correct page. "These are examples of hand-forged goods sold at Faires. Sold for a lot of money." He pointed to two photos at the bottom of the page. "These are photos of some similar goods that Mo has made. Tell us yours aren't better, Mo."

Mo's cheeks briefly flashed pink. But as he pulled his chin closer to his chest, scrutinizing the relevant page in his packet, Jess could tell that they were getting redder.

"Mo, he's right," Lana said. "Yours are much better. We could sell yours and make a good bit of money off them." She looked up at him, smiling.

Jess wasn't sure, but she thought she saw his chest rising and falling faster. She could almost taste his distress. She scanned the page.

"Are you all sure the ones at the top weren't made in a factory?" she asked Doug quickly. "There are so many." She turned to Lana. "This seems like an awful lot of intricate work. Mo isn't a machine."

He looked up from the packet at her. There was a panicked little boy in his eyes and a flash of appreciation.

"Let's ask our resident expert." Doug sighed. He looked at Theo. "Do you know if Faire-goers like things like this?" Theo was looking at the photos as well. He whistled low.

"You crafted these yourself?" he asked, looking at Mo. "We could make bank."

"See?" said Doug. "Handmade. Artisanal. Higher price point."

Mo slumped back in his seat.

"And of course, people would be amazed watching you make them. So you have to fit the theme, in cos—garb," Doug said. Mo had gone pale.

"Um, people watching, Doug?" Jess asked. "Did you consider asking Mo if he wanted to produce and perform for people at the same time?"

"Once the board found out about the possibility, they were all for it," Doug said, suddenly intent on his laptop.

"And I bet we can guess who suggested it to them," Jess said.

Doug shrugged.

"They're also looking forward to your shows," he said, still not making eye contact.

"*Shows?*" Mo and Jess asked in unison. She was surprised and . . . felt somehow lifted that his reaction had been the same as her own. They made brief eye contact, Mo's gaze softening as he gave her a tiny nod. It sharpened as he looked back at Doug and crossed his arms. Mo seemed to have returned to hedgehog mode, but this time looked ready to attack.

"Ren Faires often have archery shows," Doug said, continuing not to look at Jess. "Isn't that right, Theo?"

Theo looked up from his packet, an eyebrow raised.

"I mean, yeah," he said. "But aren't we in the planning stage, here? You're talking like Jess having shows has already been decided." He glanced at her, looking unsure. Doug still didn't look up from his screen.

"Doug," Mo growled. Doug jumped.

"I mean, we are here to agree . . . on the details," he said softly. *Ah. Ambushed again.*

It was easy to have a quiet ride back to her house. Jess felt so defeated that it would have been difficult to talk. A small wave of relief washed over her as they turned down her street. She'd be inside soon and could take a long bath to soothe her head-to-toe aching muscles. The pain had flared in the middle of the meeting and still hadn't abated. It seemed that Mo had needed to process on the drive back as well. Several times, she'd heard him taking slow deep breaths, his lips firmly sealed together.

"I'm very sorry," he said after he opened her door at the curb. He shoved his hands in his pockets as he walked her to her front door. "I didn't do enough to keep them from piling more stress on you."

It had been decided that in addition to manning the archery stand and teaching guests to shoot, Jess would headline a fully choreographed show that would take place a minimum of three times per day, each day of the Faire. She had relented because of the extremely solid argument that doing so could bring in guests beyond Faire fans—people interested in archery who might become long-term paying students. Something else strange had happened. Cassie's face had appeared in her mind's eye, almost like she was nudging Jess to do it. Like giving her all to this Faire would make her sister happy. And since Jess had failed to make Cassie happy before the end . . . She cleared her throat.

"If you owe me an apology," she said, "I owe you one. I

couldn't get them to see past their own excitement to how difficult this is going to be for you." They walked side by side up the steps of her porch.

He shrugged, hands in his front pockets.

"I'll be okay," he said. "Just put my head down and be mean, grumpy me." His lips bent up on one side, but no hint of a smile reached his eyes. The sad, defeated look there broke her already battered heart. Before she could think, she cradled his cheek with her palm. The shock that blasted out of his perfectly still body nearly bowled her over.

"You are *not* mean," she said, stepping closer to him and grazing his cheekbone with her thumb. "You are not grumpy, or weird. You . . ." She fished in her purse with her free hand as she let the other drop to his chest, finding his gift and holding it up for him to see. "You're a forgiving person who pays close enough attention to others to *hand make* them something that they *need*. Please don't say negative things like that about yourself anymore."

At some point, they'd gotten even closer. Jess didn't know if she'd moved, or if he had. The urge to kiss him was there. An urge she hadn't fully registered during the evening, in spite of the bursts of attraction she'd felt but kept stuffing down. That urge that hadn't manifested itself until it became an imperative. But she just couldn't bring herself to move closer. She felt him take a slow, deep breath, which drew her attention to his slightly parted lips. She moistened hers and looked into his widened eyes.

"I—"

Mo darted forward and kissed her, cutting her off. Surprised, she smiled against his lips and immediately started kissing him back. His lips were warm and soft, his beard and mustache tickling her skin. The tingles coursing through her waned and surged again, her previous nervousness melding into arousal. She was aware of his hands coming out of his pockets, gently cupping the backs of her arms as he pulled her close. A moan slipped out of her, and she kissed him back harder, opening her mouth. He followed the invitation and did the same. She allowed herself to spread her fingers, to enjoy the hard warmth of his chest against her hand. A low, grumbly sound escaped him, shocking her enough to pull back and break the kiss with a smile.

"Wow," she sighed. "Thank you for that."

He cocked his head to the side.

"Why would you thank me?" he asked, voice soft and grumbly.

"I don't think that was very easy for you," she said, letting her hand fall to her purse.

His cheeks reddened as he glanced down, a shy smile escaping him.

"How do you *get* me?" he asked, looking up at her. "Almost no one does."

She didn't understand. He didn't seem like that much of a puzzle. She shrugged.

"I dunno," she said.

"I'm glad you do," he said.

She smiled. He returned it as they enjoyed a little more silence together.

"I think we'll be okay," she said finally, maintaining eye contact but getting her key into her lock.

He took a small step back, nodding, returning his hands to his pockets.

"We will."

"We can do this. Together," she said.

He chuckled, his cheeks turning a bright shade of pink as he glanced at the ground again.

"Good night, Mo."

"Good night."

CHAPTER NINE

Mo

Mo took a closer look at the bar stock he'd been working. The piece that would become the blade of the blacksmith's knife was warped. It looked like a novice had made it. If he had to chuck this one and start from scratch, it would be the second piece of stock he'd wasted that evening.

Maybe I need a break.

He set the stock aside and left his hammer on the anvil. His palms were sticky and uncomfortable, so he wiped them down the sides of his jeans before opening the mini fridge he kept in the corner of his workshop. He grabbed a can of sparkling water and drank for a long time, long enough to finish more than half of it. He'd intended to clear his mind by working on a project that evening, but it kept shifting to another subject: his kiss with Jess.

That memory kept pushing out all his other thoughts. It bounced him around between disbelief, happiness, and guilt. The happiness part nearly overwhelmed him at times. He usually hid from too much happiness unless it was related to Maddie, trying to tamp it down so it didn't create expectations or become so strong that his hands shook or his heart beat too fast. The disbelief made him wonder if he'd dreamed the whole thing. He had a lot of trouble with the guilt. Because he didn't understand where it was coming from.

It's okay to like someone, to be attracted to them. To kiss them.

He tossed the empty can in the recycling bin. He started to return to his project but gave himself another moment to lean against the old tool chest he'd placed against the wall. Even with its wear and tear, it was still sturdy enough to support him. He crossed his arms, closed his eyes, and sighed, letting his head fall back.

He hadn't been attracted to anyone in years. It was normal to feel out of sorts. Mo knew that he felt out of sorts more than other people; that was what had essentially led to his divorce. Diana had tried to be supportive of the way that he managed his sensitivity, but his need to withdraw from the world led to her feeling smothered when she tried to live the same way. After that, he'd slipped easily into withdrawing from women, though it hadn't been an active choice. It made sense that he would feel anxious or off-kilter when intrigued by someone for the first time in years.

Shouldn't feel like I'm in middle school again, though.

He felt like he was going insane. The period of time between his full realization of his crush on Jess and his choice to act on it by kissing her had been so short. Minuscule. For him, at least in the past, he would have ruminated on a crush for weeks at a minimum. He'd talk himself out of the possibility that it could be requited, shutting down completely in the presence of the woman because his shyness and anxiety were short-circuiting his brain and making his body jittery. There was something about Jess that pushed him through all those crippling overwhelming feelings and made him act without ruminating. Was it her inquisitiveness? Her determination? Her dark, piercing gaze and rich flowing hair, or that comforting vanilla fragrance he'd noticed recently but hadn't connected to Jess until she was sitting in his truck?

At least she didn't seem to notice me sniffing the air like a maniac so I could feast on it.

It had likely been a combination of all those traits that made him take a chance without worrying as much as he had in the past. Maybe he shouldn't compare the present and the past, even if doing so might help him feel steadier about the present. He pushed off the chest and returned to his task. Sliding a third bar stock off the bottom shelf, he placed it in the forge to start warming up.

Novelty shouldn't provoke guilt. If anything, it should pique curiosity. But maybe it would be wiser not to follow that particular feeling. It loaded him up with too much shaky energy. He pulled the glowing bar stock out of the flames and returned to his anvil. Hammer raised, he put his thoughts aside and started over. Things were going well until his mind replayed Jess's reaction to the kiss. Her soft moan and her hand on his chest. He brought his hammer down too hard on a part of the stock he'd unintentionally pushed past the edge of the anvil. The piece bent, giving what should have become the blade a bend of about eighty degrees. He stopped, stood up straight, and examined it.

I need help.

But from who? He hadn't thought this much about a woman—noticing the way she moved, the fact that she stood up for him with others and even stood up to him when she said she wouldn't listen to him calling himself weird—since the earliest days with Diana. Now here he was, so distracted that he couldn't do a simple task that he'd done countless times. He put the stock and his hammer down on the anvil and flicked off the forge blower. After rubbing both hands on his jeans again, he pulled out his phone. This was about a woman, about relationships, so Khalil came to mind first. But Khalil was too excitable, like a puppy. There was Rachid, more analytical. But Rachid had always been in a committed relationship to his studies, then his career. Karim was shy, like Mo was, but he was doing well with Isadora. Maybe he would be a better choice. Amir was too young, still learning himself. Mo groaned. He was making things too complicated.

He checked the time. If he hurried . . .

The chime rang out as Mo walked through the door at the Original Fade barbershop. Darius, Khalil's business partner, was brushing off his chair.

"Mo!" he said when he looked up. "It's good to see you." He reached out, and Mo shook his hand.

"Good to see you, too, Darius," he said. He was glad the shake had been brief because his hands felt clammy. Darius cocked his head to the side.

"'Lil didn't mention you were coming by," Darius said. "Isn't your appointment usually on Thursdays?"

Mo cleared his throat.

"Yeah, uh—"

Khalil popped his head through the doorframe leading to the break room, an eyebrow arched.

"Let me call you back . . . um, tomorrow," he said to the person on the other end of the corded phone in his hand as he disappeared. Mo looked back at Darius.

"I . . . had some time. I hoped Khalil could squeeze me in before you closed," he said.

"Course, Mo," Darius said. "Why don't you get comfortable in his chair?"

Mo nodded and sat down. Darius returned to brushing his own chair, and Mo took a deep breath, looking around Khalil's station, which he already knew by heart.

"Hey, bro," Khalil said, joining them. Mo caught Darius and Khalil exchanging a quick glance.

"Hey," Mo said.

"You know what, Dare?" Khalil said as he draped a cape over Mo. "Why don't you head out early. I got the shop tonight."

"You s—" Darius stopped when he made eye contact with Khalil again and nodded. "Thanks, man; I appreciate it." He returned the brush to its place on his station, hustled to grab a bag out of the back, and waved goodbye.

"Bye, Darius," Mo called out as he left.

Khalil went over to lock the door and strolled back to his station. He picked up his clippers and looked at them before returning them to their place. He leaned against the station, crossing his arms.

"Spill it," he said.

Mo frowned.

"Spill what?"

Khalil frowned back.

"One, it's Tuesday," he said. "At this time of day, you're either between your forge and your anvil, or you're home doing something with your plants. Two—"

"How do you know what I do on . . . Right. Maddie."

"Exactly," Khalil said. "And two, you never, ever change your barbering schedule. The last time I even hinted at it, you acted like I was trying to kill you."

"That sounds a little dramatic," Mo said. Khalil tilted his head to the side.

"Grouchy eldest brother can't be dramatic?" he asked.

Mo squinted at him. Khalil wasn't wrong about his resistance to change in his schedule. And he needed Khalil's help. No point in dragging his feet. He sighed.

"I kissed someone," he said.

Khalil's face broke into a smile, and his energy nearly bowled Mo over.

"Dude!" he said. "Are you serious?" He pushed off the station and knocked into Mo for a hug. Mo couldn't hug back with the cape on.

"Yeah, yeah," he said, his cheeks heating. Khalil straightened up, grabbed a stool from somewhere behind them, and sat next to Mo.

"That's awesome," he said, his grin a mile wide. "It's Jess, isn't it?"

Mo remembered the uncomfortable conversation at their parents' house. He frowned again, furrowing his eyebrows.

"Yes," he grumbled.

"Excellent! I knew it," he said, elbowing Mo. "I knew she wasn't just a friend or fellow committee member."

Mo didn't like that.

"She was . . . is just a friend. Why would you think something different?"

Khalil chuckled.

"You brought her up," he said. "And Rachid was right—if you think her advice is good enough to listen to and share, she's gotta mean something to you."

Mo chewed that over for a moment.

"You make it sound like I never take anyone's advice," he said.

"Uh . . . you don't. You're usually the giver, not the taker."

Mo wasn't sure that was fair.

"It's part of your charm," Khalil said. "You automatically know better than any of us."

Mo frowned again. Especially since he was there hoping Khalil could help him. Khalil leaned back a little, assessing him.

"Why do you look grumpy about this? Oh. Did she not kiss you back?"

"She did. But I feel guilty."

He was grateful that Khalil's expression had shifted to concern.

"Why would you feel guilty?" he asked.

"I don't know," Mo said. "It's . . . I feel . . . uncomfortable and guilty." He looked off to the side. "Not sure why," he grumbled.

"Okay. Let's look at it," Khalil said. "Did you kiss her at a bad time? Like, was she having a difficult moment, or do you think you took advantage of her having her guard down?"

Mo rolled his lips.

"I'd be surprised if she ever lets her guard down. But I haven't known her very long, maybe I'm not reading—"

Waving a hand in the air, Khalil cut him off.

"If that's your takeaway, it's the truth. My whole life, you've never been wrong about someone's character," he said.

"Oh," Mo said, not suppressing his smirk. "So you can admit that I'm always right."

"About people, jerk," Khalil said, rolling his eyes. "So she never lets her guard down, but she was cool about you kissing her. I know that didn't come out of nowhere. What was the shift? How did you go from . . . colleagues to make-out partners?"

Mo narrowed his eyes and explained. About her quickly understanding that he was too empathetic, not angry. About how she'd forbidden him from calling himself weird, and about how she'd taken up for him about "performing" and making things to sell, emphasizing that the others were asking too much of him, something they'd never noticed even though they'd known him much longer.

Khalil's eyebrows had nearly migrated to the top of his forehead.

"She really likes you," he said, grinning again and nodding.

"Why do you say that?"

"Man, I love you, but you're clueless," Khalil said.

Mo grunted.

"She's figured you out."

Mo grunted again because he wasn't sure what that meant.

"At a bare minimum, she's concerned about you. About your comfort."

"I dunno."

Khalil gave him a half-frown.

"It sounds like she gets that you're rough around the edges, but it's not some sort of ego thing, or anger at the world or something. What's she like? Personality wise?" Khalil asked.

Mo gave half a chuckle, thinking of her interaction with Doug.

"Maybe a little rough around the edges," he said.

"A match made in heaven," Khalil said.

Mo grunted again. Maybe Khalil wasn't wrong. Both he and Jess were wary with the world. For him, it was a lifestyle; for her, it might have only been a reaction to the grief she was dealing with. He kept that part to himself, though. Khalil could help him without knowing what she was going through.

"To recap," Khalil said, "this equally grouchy woman has paid close enough attention to figure you out."

"Yes."

"She stood up for you with people who should have known better because they've known you a lot longer than she has."

"Yes."

"*And* she refused to let you criticize yourself," Khalil said.

"Yes."

"I can only lead the horse to water, Mo," he said flatly.

Mo paused. He hadn't laid it out like that. He'd been too caught up in his own confusion.

"Okay," he said.

"Jess likes you, Mo," Khalil said. "Repeat that, please."

Mo rolled his eyes.

"Jess likes me," he muttered.

"Good," Khalil said. "So if she likes you and she kissed you back, what on earth do you have to feel guilty for?"

That was the problem. Mo didn't know.

"Is it Maddie?" Khalil asked.

"Maddie?"

"Well, your life has kind of revolved around Maddie since you and Diana split up. And I'm not saying that's a bad thing. But are you afraid that if you let Jess into your life, you'll have to push Maddie out somehow?"

Mo considered the possibility.

"Maybe," he said.

"I don't see that happening," Khalil said. "You're so attuned to Maddie emotionally; I'd be shocked if you did something like that. Even unintentionally. Besides, has that been an issue with Diana's new husband? Does Maddie feel like she still has her mom?"

"It hasn't been an issue at all," Mo said.

"So why would it be an issue with you?"

Maybe Khalil was right. Jess was the first person he'd really been interested in since the divorce. Staying focused on Maddie had allowed him to maintain the emotional stability he desperately needed to feel balanced.

"I mean, I guess it could be that. But it doesn't feel quite—"

"It's the girl thing, isn't it?" Khalil asked flatly.

"The girl thing?"

"You've never been the most . . . aware of female interest," Khalil said. "We almost had to hold an intervention to get you to realize that Diana was into you."

Mo chuckled in spite of himself.

"And even back then, you weren't sure it was okay to like someone, which I'll never understand," Khalil said.

"Very funny, Ladies' Man," Mo said.

"One lady man now, thank you very much," Khalil said. "I hate telling you to relax because saying it won't work, but maybe let yourself see where this goes. It might not go anywhere, maybe you'll get to know each other and realize the vibe isn't right. But it's worth trying. Especially since it seems like Jess respects your . . . uniqueness."

Mo bristled a little at the last part, but Khalil wasn't wrong. Mo could just see what happens.

"Okay," he said. "I'll try."

"You could sound a little more enthusiastic," Khalil said. "You've already kissed her."

"It's . . . a lot to process."

"It is," Khalil said. "But you can do it. You might even like it."

"Hmmph."

"Let's get started," Khalil said, standing and pushing the stool to the side. Mo shifted to the edge of the chair and stood too. He unsnapped the cape.

"What are you doing?" Khalil asked.

"Be back Thursday," Mo said over his shoulder as he walked to the door. Khalil started laughing.

"You've got to be kidding me, man. You're already here," he called out.

"No," Mo said, unlocking the door. "Stick to the schedule."

CHAPTER TEN

Jess

Wednesday afternoon, Jess dropped her whiteboard marker for the third time and cursed under her breath. She'd been shaky and distracted the entire day. Mo's dark eyes and gentle face kept bubbling up in her subconscious, spilling silly feelings like shyness and giddiness all through her insides. Taming those feelings should have been the easiest thing in the world, but she was struggling—in front of her most difficult class to manage, no less. She hadn't been able to keep them engaged for the past fifteen minutes. Her newly unruly mind was all over the place.

She shook her head hard.

Stop being unprofessional.

"As I was saying," she said, making her voice carry over the whispered conversations. "At the height of the Renaissance, women who wished to avoid being subjugated to a husband had no other real choice but to enter a religious order. While there were women who helped run their husbands' businesses, such as shopkeeping, they could not . . ." Jess trailed off. She had the attention of about four students out of thirty. Everyone else was talking or on their phones. Between her own distraction and the strange new deep aching in her legs, she just didn't have the strength to fight.

"Okay, let's wrap it up for today," she said.

Only the four began to put their things away.

"Hey!" Jess shouted. Most of the rest of the class looked up.

"Go home," she said, packing her own things. She waited for the last student to leave and returned to her office.

Once the door closed behind her, she resolved to clear out her inbox, but her thoughts would not behave. She had some privacy, and her classes were done for the day, so she settled in behind her desk and let her mind wander. As she'd been fighting off thoughts about Mo during the day, he'd shown up in her dreams instead. The way his wary expression brightened with her when they had a little privacy. The deep, gruff sexiness of his voice when he spoke to her with full sentences. The shy little kid he'd turned into at her car and then in his.

A shy smile curved her lips as she remembered his kiss that had shocked her even though she'd been wishing it would happen. Then the smile fell.

This isn't . . . a good idea.

She sighed. She'd had a plan. She was solidifying her footing in her "adult" life. She was settling into her job. Even though there was a bit of stress involved due to the threat to the Folk School, she'd picked up archery again and was being social, which could lead to real friendships. The decision to be open to new friends wasn't that far off from being open to a relationship.

Why am I struggling with it?

She was too in her own head. Even though Steph would make fun of her, and Alice would say "I told you so," Jess grabbed her phone. Thumbs over the keyboard, she hesitated, trying to find the right words for the group chat.

Fuck it.

Jess:

Emergency meeting, Ladies

The word "typing" and a dancing ellipsis appeared at the top of the screen.

Alice:

What's wrong?

Steph:

> You were with me the whole time.
> Wherever they said you were, no
> you weren't.

Jess chuckled.

Jess:

> Mo & I kissed

For a few moments, the top of the screen remained the same. No "typing" or dancing ellipsis. Then the app screen changed, and the phone started ringing in her hand.

"*Excuse* me?" Steph asked as the screen changed again. But it was dark, and Jess could barely make her out.

"Where are you?" she asked.

"Don't worry about—"

Stephanie was cut off as Alice joined in.

"You *what*?" she asked, a little breathless.

"Hi, I'm sorry, I'm sorry, I didn't mean to make you all freak out," Jess said.

Jess could see that Steph was speaking but couldn't hear anything.

"You're on mute, Steph," Alice said.

"My bad," she said, the sound coming back. Including the sound of a refilling toilet. Jess raised an eyebrow.

"You did not start a call while you were sitting on the toilet," Jess said.

"You're the one who called for an emergency meeting while I was sitting on the toilet. The least you could do is plan your emergencies for when I'm not bleeding like a stuck pig and gritting my teeth through clots," she said.

"Oh, Steph," Alice sighed. "A rough period again? I'm so sorry."

"Me too," said Jess.

Stephanie rolled her eyes and shrugged.

"Hardly the first time, and I doubt it will be the last. Until science decides to properly research the female body," she said. "Now, about this kissing."

Jess cleared her throat.

"So um, that happened, and I'm having trouble," she said.

"Trouble?" Steph asked.

"Yeah. I . . ." Jess didn't know how to say it.

"Jess. Don't try to make it pretty and correct. Just dump the box of feels. It doesn't need to be tidy for us," Alice said.

Jess cleared her throat and brought them up to speed about Mo helping with her car, the keychain, and the second meeting. And then about the moment on the doorstep that had made her happy but was messing with her head.

Neither of her friends said anything.

"Um . . . ladies?" she asked.

"Al," Steph said. "Do you see the trouble?"

Alice shook her head.

"Nope. No trouble," she said.

"But I'm all back and forth. It just does not make logical sense," Jess said. "I'm starting my career; I'm getting back into—"

"Jess, I love you, but would you kindly shut that alleged 'logic' up?" Steph asked.

Jess blinked.

"I'm sure what she means is to shut the hyperdrive analytical part up and enjoy this arguably great thing that is happening to you," Alice said.

Jess hesitated to reply.

"Avoiding a romantic relationship is not going to keep you safe. What happened to Cassie is not going to happen to you just because you let a man in," Steph said flatly.

The connection slapped her in the face. She hadn't named the concern.

"But this Mo situation doesn't have anything to do with Cassie," she said, blinking fast because the room had gotten a little blurry.

"Cassie's relationship . . . resulted in something bad," Alice said. "That doesn't mean any relationship you have would be the same. And Steph, you could be more gentle, you know."

Stephanie snorted.

"I could, but this is Jess, and she's hardheaded and stubborn. We have to be brutal to get through," she said. Then she sighed. "Okay, fine. Maybe I'm wrong. But maybe that's what's bothering you."

Truly facing that might be the root of the problem . . . Jess didn't want to go down that emotional road.

"This might not be the best question to ask," Alice said softly. "But have you really spoken with your parents?"

Anger crackled through Jess, cutting off the impending tears.

"No," she said. "My mom's left a couple of messages, but I haven't called her back. She wants me to come for a visit."

"What if you did? I think, maybe, you're kind of stuck because of the pain. If you started unraveling it, that might make things better, easier," Alice said.

Jess wasn't ready to deal with her parents. They'd known that something was off between Cassie and her husband. But her father had turned a blind eye, and her spineless mother had followed his lead.

"I don't think I can be in the same room as them yet," Jess said.

Alice sighed.

"I can understand," she said.

"Okay," Steph said. "Cheat yourself, then."

"Myself? How?" Jess asked. She certainly didn't miss the fights that blew up like clockwork between her and her father every time she set foot in her parents' house.

"With Mo," Steph said. "What if you're cheating yourself out of something great because you aren't dealing with what happened to Cassie and your parents' part in it?"

All of Jess's joints were aching. Which made no sense because she hadn't shot too much, and her legs never hurt after she'd practiced. She rolled her wrists. A stabbing pain went through the left one, and she winced.

"Jess?" Alice asked. "What was that?"

"Nothing," she said, trying to find a good spot to rest. "Just my wrist being annoying."

"It didn't sound like nothing," Alice said. "Wait, did you ever go to the doctor about your stomach?"

"Her stomach?" Steph asked.

"Um, I forgot," Jess said.

"It's been bothering her for a while," Alice said.

"And it still is?" Steph asked.

"Sometimes."

Alice narrowed her eyes.

"I really think you should see someone," she said. "And ask about your wrist."

Jess sighed.

"All right. I'll make an appointment," she said.

"Mmkay," Alice said. "But about Mo. He sounds . . . perfect for you, actually."

Jess didn't get the perfect part.

"How so?" she asked.

Stephanie let out a huge sigh and rolled her eyes.

"He's a unicorn, Jess," Steph said. "A man who puts himself in your shoes, makes you things *with his hands,* and stands up for you. Grab the unicorn, Jess. Fucking *ride* the unicorn."

Jess and Alice burst out laughing.

"You really think it's okay?" Jess asked, still chuckling.

"It is okay," Alice said. "We're telling you it is."

Later that afternoon, Jess thanked her Uber driver as he pulled up to Mo's shop. After hanging up with Alice and Stephanie, she'd seen that Mo had sent her a message that her car was ready. Glancing around for him, she returned to the reception area and waited for her turn with Beverly.

"Hi," she said. "I'm—"

"Jess," Beverly said. "I remember you, hon." She shifted through some papers in an inbox on her desk until she found the right one. "Here you are." She slid the paper onto the counter as Jess was taking out her wallet.

"No need," Beverly said. "Just your signature accepting the car back, please."

Jess didn't understand. The estimate had made her teeth hurt, so what was Beverly saying "no need" for? Jess looked at the bottom line on the paper. The total was zero dollars and zero cents. She looked up higher. The work done on the car was detailed, with the prices in a column down the right side. But the total said zero.

"I don't understand," she said, looking up at Beverly.

Beverly shrugged, focused on her computer screen but with a smile playing at her lips.

"I only follow orders," she said, clearly fighting a smirk.

Jess seriously doubted that she was the type of woman to "only follow orders."

"But I—"

Beverly looked at her sharply over her glasses.

"If the big boss says that's your bill, then that's your bill, hon," she said.

Mo wasn't making her pay for it? She leaned closer to Beverly.

"But—"

"Young lady," Beverly said, lowering her voice. "Don't look a gift horse in the mouth. You got the friends and family discount and then some. I was also surprised; that's never happened before. But if Mo says it's that, it's that. Now, I don't know exactly what that means, and it isn't any of my business. But I do find it interesting that after you left, he immediately started working on your car and stayed late on his own to finish it."

Jess slowly stood up straight. That was what she'd been concerned about, and even if he'd done only that, it would have been too much. But not charging her at all?

"Oh," she said.

"Now sign here, and grab a seat until they can bring it around front, okay?"

Jess nodded, signed, and sat down.

Why would Mo have done that?

Fixing it quickly was super helpful, but she certainly expected to pay for it. Was he one of those guys who wants women indebted to him so that they'll have to "pay him back"? No. That was in sharp contrast to the way he'd reacted when that woman brought the cookies. If there'd been a time to take advantage, the night they'd met would have been perfect.

She was still chewing things over when David walked up and told her that her car was out front.

"Is Mo out there?" she asked.

"No, he's supervising a newbie," he said.

"Oh."

"Do you want me to get him for you?" David asked.

Jess looked around. It was probably best not to attempt a discussion with so many people in the reception area. They'd want a discount, too, and having an audience would make Mo uncomfortable.

"Could you ask him to meet me at my car?"

"No prob. Here are your keys."

He handed them to her and went back out to the shop. She thanked Beverly on her way outside. Reaching her car, she realized that the whole thing had been washed. She opened the door and looked at the carpet. It had definitely been vacuumed, and the whole car smelled really, really clean. She checked the dash—not a speck of dust.

They detailed it, too?

"Hi, Jess. Everything okay?" Mo's deep rumble startled her, and she jumped, almost slamming her head on the doorjamb. She stepped back and stood up slowly.

"Mo, you didn't have to do this," she said, looking up at him.

"Just cleaned a little. Always try to."

"But it smells . . ." She leaned back over to sniff the inside again. "Did you shampoo the seats or something?"

He shrugged, his cheeks getting a little red.

She closed the door and took another step back.

"Did you figure out what was wrong with it?" she asked.

He nodded.

"No tune-up before sale, I think," he said.

Jess squinted.

"They told me they had," she said.

Mo nodded slowly, pulling his lips to one side.

"Should be good now," he said. "Faulty fuel pump. And the check engine light. It was dead."

Jess looked at the car again. At least that was why she hadn't realized that something was wrong.

"Well," she said. "Thank you."

He shrugged again and tucked his thumbs into the pockets of his coveralls.

"I appreciate it a lot," she said. "The whole thing, the inside, too. It's more than I expected."

He shrugged again, then scratched at his beard.

"You're welcome," he said.

"But you have to let me pay you," she said. "At the very least for your time."

He shook his head.

"It's nothing."

He was doing it again. Turning into a giant little boy right in front of her. His cheeks were completely pink, and he wasn't really looking at her.

"I can't fix the Ren Faire, but I can fix this." He gestured at the car.

Jess was going to melt into a puddle. In spite of reaching for it, her logic was completely outmatched by her reaction to his sweetness. Her friends said that her need to analyze got in her way. And Mo was so refreshing as a human being; Stephanie was right, he was kind of a unicorn. Jess's heart was going a little too fast, her face felt too warm, and she was clutching her purse strap again.

"You mad?" he asked, sneaking a glance at her.

"No! No, not at all," she said, as much to reassure him as to get the growing jumble of emotions out somehow. "I . . . I don't want you to feel taken advantage of."

He shook his head.

"You're not like that," he said softly in his rumbly voice.

Jess needed to get away from him. He was being far too sweet, and she was responding to it far too much. But she wanted to address the other night.

"I, um . . . about—"

She was cut off by a loud crash from the open garage doors of the shop. Her knowledge of auto body shops was nil, but she was sure that a car on one of those raised contraptions shouldn't have two wheels in the air and two on the ground.

"I better see to that," Mo said, eyebrows furrowed as he looked back at her.

"Yeah," she said, opening her driver's-side door and getting in. She adjusted her seat. "I'll find a way to repay you, or at least show my appreciation, but it won't be chocolate chip cookies."

He tilted his head, looking like a big, confused puppy.

Stop thinking like that!

"No cookies?" he asked.

"Mo!" a voice called out from the shop. He didn't turn, his attention still on her.

"You're not a fan of chocolate," she said.

He looked completely taken aback but didn't say anything.

She started the car and rolled down the window.

"See you at the School?" she said once she'd carefully backed out.

"See you," he said back, waving slowly, still looking very confused.

CHAPTER ELEVEN

Jess

The next day, after pulling into the very busy parking lot at the Folk School, Jess got out of her fresh-smelling, nicely running car and grabbed her compound crossbow and gear bag. She'd checked the schedule before leaving and saw that there was a blacksmithing class that morning, but it was being taught by Rick, the other instructor, not Mo. All the better because she was there to get out of her head a bit and wouldn't have been able to do that with him around. She couldn't help but glance through the open door of the smithy as she passed it. Her heart stopped beating and her stomach dropped.

There was just enough space between two students for her to have a clear view of Mo at the front of the room, standing beside one of the fire-things, the flames in it roaring, Mo holding the end of a thin piece of metal he was heating up. He removed it, turning to take it to an anvil. Jess took a half step, craning her neck to see what it was, but couldn't. Mo brought his hammer down, and Jess no longer cared about the metal. His forearms, corded and veined, shone as they flexed with his effort. Her breath caught. His forearms had drawn her attention when he'd picked her up, but this was an entirely different category of sexy. She caught a glimpse of his biceps straining against his dark green T-shirt and the intensity of the look on his face, the control . . . Her heart snapped into overdrive as she gasped.

Go.

She swiveled quickly—too quickly—and rushed out to the range, set up a target, and got suited up. With shaky hands, she pulled her hair into a high ponytail.

Stop it, stop it. That's exactly what you're not supposed to be thinking about right now.

She stretched her hands.

Time to get out of my head.

She needed a break after the first twenty minutes, which greatly irritated her. Even with the reduced need for effort due to the construction of the bow, her arms and shoulders were screaming. As she paced back and forth, she windmilled them and stretched her neck from side to side, pushing the Mo images out of her head. She thought about stopping but hadn't been there long enough to make the drive worth it.

At least the pain has me more in my body than in my head.

After picking up the bow again and loading it, she grimaced but decided the pain wasn't going to stop her. She had targets to kill.

Another thirty minutes later, with the pain between her shoulder blades adding to the cacophony in her arms, she decided that was enough. Emotionally, she felt eons better, and a hot shower once she got home would help physically. Passing the smithy, she glanced in, and Mo was still there, talking to a young woman with a backpack on. He glanced up, and his initial expression of surprise was replaced with a smile. He waved. Jess waved back. The young woman looked over her shoulder at Jess, then quickly back at Mo and started heading toward the exit.

Should I go talk to him?

He looked down, then back up at her with a shy smile.

The reflex to just go to her car popped up, to escape from unruly emotions that could lead to places where her logic had no footing. But she was tired of doing that, tired of clinging to logic and stifling what she felt. She wanted to simply let go, to coast, to fall into the thought that was echoing in her head.

Fucking ride the unicorn.

She smothered a chuckle at Stephanie's words and walked into the smithy.

"Hi," she said when she was close enough for him to hear her.

"Hi."

"Am I bothering you? Do you have another class?"

Mo shook his head and took a deep breath.

"All done. And you never bother me," he said quietly.

"Oh," she said as her cheeks got warm. She felt silly about getting shy like that, and she looked away for a second. He went over to a large, high table, picked up a duffel bag from underneath, and started putting his things away. She could justify staying if she was being helpful to him. She glanced around the room.

"Do you need help cleaning up?" she asked.

"Um, thanks," he said. "I always sweep after."

She noticed the broom in the corner and put her things on a low bench near the door.

"How's Madison?" she asked as she started sweeping.

He smiled.

"She's good, thanks for asking. With her uncle today."

"You have a brother?" she asked.

He tilted his head to one side and pressed his lips together like he was hiding a laugh.

"Four," he said.

Jess stopped sweeping and gawked at him.

"There's *five* of you out in the world?" she asked.

Mo chuckled.

"Not exactly," he said, giving her a full smile. "I'm the weirdo of the bunch."

She narrowed her eyes and leaned into the broom a little.

"I thought we talked about the fact that I'm not going to listen to you calling yourself weird," she said.

He blushed deep. Even the tips of his ears were tinged with red. He stopped wiping down the anvil and raised his hands in surrender.

"We did," he said gruffly. "Sorry." He shot her that shy kid smile, and her heart skipped a beat. Again, that urge to flee cropped up.

No.

She walked over to him and leaned the broom against the table. Putting her hands on her hips, she cocked her head to one side, observing him.

"You look like I'm in trouble," he said, starting to clean the anvil again.

Jess bunched her lips to the side. She thought about making a joke, maybe even the easy one about getting in trouble with the teacher. But she recognized what that urge was—another way to try to hide, to cover up her fear of leaning into her attraction to him.

You're not afraid on the range, not afraid in competitions. What the hell are you doing right now?

"I'm not attracted to weird people, Mo," she said, holding his gaze. Her heart was pounding, but she wasn't going to let whatever it decided to do stray her from her course. "So that means you're not weird," she said. "You're quiet, reserved. You help people even if it costs you sometimes. You seem . . ." She hesitated, concerned that what she wanted to say next might offend him in some way. A buzzing charge of anxiety made her throat tighten. She cleared it. "You seem like a sensitive guy. I like that about you."

He'd stopped wiping and stood straight.

"You do?" he asked, his neck and cheeks tingeing pink again.

He didn't seem angry or offended. More like astonished.

"Of course." She sighed. "I don't want to freak you out, but I get the impression that you should hear what I honestly think. You deserve to."

"Oh . . ." he said softly. "Okay."

She stepped closer to him, only the anvil between them. Resting her fingertips on it, she looked into his eyes.

"You're considerate," she said. "You're selective with your words, so when you do really speak it's like a breath of fresh air."

They were close enough that she could tell that he was breathing faster, as she was.

"And your voice." She cleared her throat. "It's . . . um . . ." She did not care for the shakiness in her hands. She rested them fully on the anvil so they would stop.

"It's?" he asked.

She took a deep breath and let it out slowly.

"Your voice is delicious. It makes me weak at the knees."

Mo searched her eyes.

"You're confident. Determined," he said suddenly. "And your hair. It's sable. I love it, especially in a ponytail."

She resisted the urge to bring the end of the ponytail over her shoulder. She opened her mouth to thank him, but he wasn't finished.

"You, um, you named it, actually. My weir—what makes me a little different." He looked down and let out a stream of air before looking at her again. "I'm an HSP, a Highly Sensitive Person. What it essentially means is that my central nervous system is turned up higher than most people's. My empathy—which you got, and you *named* . . . It flipped my world upside down that you noticed. And you don't seem to think that it's a bad thing."

She tucked that away to look into later, to learn more about what a Highly Sensitive Person was. At the moment she needed to do something else. She laid a hand on his chest. "It's not," she whispered. "Come here."

He leaned down and caught her lips with his. For a moment, Jess didn't know who she was or where she was. All that existed were Mo's lips on hers, the hand he'd curled around her own resting on his chest. She felt tingly and on fire and like her legs were going to give out any second. As he opened his mouth to hers, she became enraged at the anvil separating her from him. Without breaking the kiss, she wound around it. He let out a deep moan as she pressed herself up against him. His other hand went around her waist to bring her closer, even though that was impossible. She slid her free hand up his arm, bumping over the expansive muscles, along his shoulder and up the back of his neck. She scratched her nails on his scalp as she threaded her hand into his hair. His deep groan reverberated through her. He pulled back a little to whisper to her.

"May I pick you up?" he panted.

She nodded, breathing heavily as she slid her other hand up to weave her fingers together at the nape of his neck. He bent his knees, slid his hands under her thighs, and lifted. She wrapped her legs around his waist as he carried her over to the high table and sat her down at the edge. She caught a glimpse of his eyes, looking wild and much darker, then his lips were back on hers. It was a much better position, she was higher, so he didn't have to bend as much. She kept her legs locked around his waist and savored his groan as she scratched a hand down his chest. She wanted to pull at his shirt, get rid of it, but there was a loud bang, and they jumped, pulling their lips apart. She looked over her shoulder and saw the broom on the ground. She looked back at him, her heart racing.

"What's happening?" he asked, his breath ragged.

"I'm not totally sure," she panted.

"You don't want to," he said, like he was certain she was going to say she didn't. She frowned.

"You can't tell I want you?" she asked.

"Uh . . . I guess maybe," he said.

"You guess?"

"It's . . . uh . . . been a while?" he said. He started pulling his hands down her thighs, like he was getting ready to step away from her. She grabbed them to stop them in their tracks.

"It's been a while for me, too," she said. "But let me be clear. I want you, Mo. I'm into everything about you. I want to get to know you more. I also want to rip your clothes off right now."

His cheeks were already flushed, so she could tell that he was doing his shy thing only by the dip of his chin.

"Do you not want that?" she asked. His head snapped up.

"I do. Very much," he said.

"So we should do this?" she asked.

"Yes," he said. "But right now, we should stop."

"Why's that?"

"Because this table can't handle my weight. And I'm certainly not going to lay you down on the floor."

A searing flash went through her and her breath caught. She smiled.

"Who said I was going to let you be on top?" she asked.

He laughed. A free, open laugh she'd never seen before. It rumbled out of him, bounced off the walls, and warmed her as it passed through her body. She began laughing, too.

"You're right," he said. "I should have known better. But damn if that image doesn't turn me on even more." He leaned in close, gliding his parted lips up her neck. Her eyes rolled back in her head. "Can I call you tonight?" he whispered into her skin.

"Yes," she whispered back.

"I don't want to stop." He sighed. "But anyone could walk in on us."

He made a good point. She was a private person, and she'd already seen how mortified he'd become when someone hugged him in a room full of people. He might pass out if anyone walked in and saw her legs around him.

"You're right," she whispered beside his ear. "We should stop." She nibbled on the lobe, and he shuddered.

"Not fair," he said.

"I know," she said as he pulled back to look her in the eyes.

He chuckled and shook his head.

"I'll walk you back to your car," he said. "But you've got a good hold on me here." He gestured at her legs still around him. She didn't move. He laughed again. "Are you going to let me go?"

"No," she said. "If you give me a shot, I won't let you go, Mo."

He looked her in the eye and understood.

"Thank you, Jess," he said, leaning in for a quick peck.

CHAPTER TWELVE

Mo

*S*he said it's not a bad thing.

On a workout bench in the spare bedroom he'd turned into a weightlifting room, Mo started on a new set of reps to work his biceps. It was time to switch to a different exercise, but the need to push himself to exhaustion was stronger than the fatigue that would greet him once he'd finished. Pushing his muscles gave the buzzing anxiety from truly starting a romantic relationship with Jess somewhere to go. By this point in a workout his mind was usually quiet, but it kept returning to that moment in the smithy, to what Jess had said about him being an HSP.

She doesn't fully know what it is; she might change her mind.

Part of him hoped she changed her mind; another part would die if she did. In the past, his few relationships had been difficult—the breath-snatching overwhelm from the intensity of all the feelings, both good and bad, his painfully acute awareness of any shade of disappointment from his partner, and the screaming imperative within his every cell to prevent that disappointment from happening. For a time, though, the rewards had been well worth the risk.

Sighing, he lowered the dumbbells to the floor, pausing to rest.

He hadn't known that he was an HSP in previous relationships. Hadn't understood there wasn't something fundamentally wrong with him, that he wasn't individually weaker than the rest of the world, a failure to be a confident, never-overwhelmed adult. A fortuitous Google search, when he'd been trying to understand why Maddie's cries as a baby had made him feel like his skin was on fire and brought him to throat-closing sobs, led to the discovery of his particular neurodiversity. Once he was armed with the understanding that things like his discomfort with speaking up and his need to avoid too much attention were simply coded into his biology, he'd learned to give himself grace.

Jess understood those things, too.

The smile that had bloomed quickly faltered. She might understand him somewhat, but was he ready to deal with the physical symptoms that changing his current steady life would bring? He leaned over to pick up the dumbbells again.

"Are you okay, Daddy?"

Mo turned to face Maddie in the doorway. She'd run straight to her room when Khalil had dropped her off. She'd been focused on a coding project that Vanessa, Khalil's wife, was helping her with, so Mo hadn't stayed long when he went to check on her.

She never interrupted him while he was exercising. The fact that she'd done so, combined with her question and tone, had him on high alert.

"I am, sugar plum," he said, waving her into the room. "Why?"

She joined him.

"You feel weird," she said.

A wry smile pulled Mo's lips to the side. Maddie was watching him closely, so he did his best to let her see his appreciation for her concern and not the sadness or regret he felt when she showed symptoms of being an HSP. To non-HSPs, her statement might have been confusing. To Mo, it was crystal clear. Maddie had felt his energy, likely as a sensation in her own body, and it had affected her strongly enough for her to interrupt him in the middle of a task that she knew was important to his emotional state. He shifted a little and patted the workout bench beside him. "Good weird, or bad weird?" he asked as she sat down.

She scrunched her eyebrows, studying him. "Mostly good," she said after a few moments. "But there's some . . . fuzz?"

"Fuzz?" he asked.

"Yeah," she said. "Like when Papi is listening to his radio and changes the channels."

"Ah, when he's dialing through the *stations*," Mo said. "Static?"

Madison nodded. It tickled Mo a little that Maddie's reference for the concept of static was his father's radio habits. But he figured it made more sense for her generation than a malfunctioning television.

"Well, you're right," he said. HSP or not, it was important to him to encourage his daughter to trust the sensations in her body. "I'm mostly good. But I am a little worried, too."

"Let's talk about it, then," she said, looping her arm through his. "Maybe I can help."

Mo smiled at her. While her compassion was always appreciated, he wanted to tread lightly to avoid putting any pressure on her to feel like she needed to take care of *him*. He had to be honest with her, though; she would know if he wasn't.

"So," he said. "I'm a little worried because I'm very happy with my life right now." He paused to squeeze her arm close to his side. "But I'm also interested in maybe making some changes that could make life a little different."

Maddie scrunched her eyebrows again.

"Is it about that lady who called?" she asked. "Jess?"

Dammit. Always clever, always remembers everything.

He sighed.

"Yes, it's about Jess," he said.

Maddie's face broke into a thousand-watt smile. "Is Jess your girlfriend?" she asked.

Chuckling, Mo shook his head. "No," he said. "Jess is not my girlfriend. We just—"

"Do you like her?" Maddie asked, cutting him off.

Mo's cheeks caught fire. Khalil had named his age-old shyness about liking someone or being liked. Mo didn't think he had the strength to talk about that with Maddie. He took a deep breath, but Maddie spoke before he could.

"You do!" she squealed. "You do like her! Aww, Daddy." She wriggled around to give him a side hug.

"I mean, yeah, I guess," he said, hugging her arm.

"Does she like you?" Maddie asked.

Mo shrugged, then nodded. "That's great!" Maddie said. She pulled back and squinted at him. "Then why do you feel staticky?"

Mo sighed.

"I'm worried about doing something different," he said. "About changing anything."

Maddie stood up and put her hands on her nonexistent hips. She frowned and then cleared her throat.

"'Change can be a good thing,'" she said, her voice comically lowered the way it was when she imitated him. "'You can learn new things.'" She began strutting around the room, her chest puffed out, pontificating. "'Discover more about yourself and the world.'"

Mo wanted to be stern with her for throwing his words back at him, but he couldn't keep his laughter from tumbling out.

"Okay, okay, sugar plum," he said, still chuckling. "Point taken."

"Good." She stopped and smiled at him.

"I also want it to be okay for you," he said.

"Are you happy?" she asked.

Mo took a moment to assess. If he was honest with himself, deep down he was over the moon.

"Yes," he said.

"If Daddy's happy, I'm happy," she said. She rushed over and gave him a kiss on the cheek. "You better finish lifting. 'We see things to completion in this house,'" she grumbled, imitating him again.

"Okay, Mads," he said, picking up his dumbbells again as she went to the doorway. She stopped.

"Did you talk to her like you talk to me?" she asked.

"Um, I guess."

"See? Told you so," she said and waved at him before she walked out of sight.

———

That evening, Mo closed the sliding glass door and took the three small steps down from his back porch. He checked the patio chair that Madison had left at the foot of the stairs, but the seat had a little puddle on it from the rain the previous day. He turned it to let the water run out then tipped the back against the side of the porch so it could dry. He sat on the steps, his feet square on the grass below. Taking out his phone and holding it in both hands, he looked at the screen. Nervousness jangled and sparked his tired muscles.

Maybe there isn't enough lifting to help.

Before calling Jess, he turned his head to the side to listen. Madison hadn't followed him, and he didn't see her at the glass patio door through his peripheral vision. It seemed that she was still snug in the pillows and blankets he'd made into a nest on the couch for her to watch a movie. She'd started the day off playing basketball with Khalil. That, combined with the mental effort from her coding, had her eyes drooping over dinner. Mo doubted she'd see much of the movie. He ran a hand down his beard and opened his contacts. Letting out a deep breath to calm his nerves, he called Jess.

"Hi there," she said when she answered.

A little wriggle of nervous happiness passed through him at the sound of her voice. He smiled.

"Hi," he said. "Sorry it took so long. I had to make dinner for Maddie and get her comfortable with her tablet."

"No problem," she said. "I figured you were doing something like that. Plus, you said you'd call tonight. It's still tonight."

"Thanks for understanding."

"It's your weekend with her?" she asked.

"Yeah," he said. "But she was with Khalil, one of my brothers, this morning. I didn't want to be the third wheel; that's why I agreed to take Rick's class." He thought she might have met Rick, but he wasn't sure.

"I'm certainly glad you did," she said.

His shyness surged, his face heating both at her words and at the change in her voice. It was warmer and rich, the way it might sound if they were lying in bed together.

"Me too."

"You know," she began, "something's been bothering me since the smithy."

"What's that?"

"You said, 'I guess maybe' when I asked you if you couldn't tell I wanted you."

His shyness back twofold, his face burned. He ran a hand down it. While yes, he had understood that she was attracted to him when they'd kissed, he was accustomed to that changing the more a woman got to know him. Attraction to him always seemed temporary.

So he'd taught himself not to rely on his initial read.

"Why would you doubt that?" she asked.

"I . . ." He stood, taking a few steps to gather the courage to explain. Then he remembered what Khalil had said. A little humor would make it easier to talk about. He cleared his throat. "According to my brother, I am simply clueless when it comes to understanding that a woman is really interested in me."

"Your brother Khalil?"

"Yes." He nudged an errant pebble back into Maddie's rock garden. "I . . . uh . . . asked him for some advice about you, and he understood that there was more interest on your side than I thought."

"Well, he was right," she said. "And if it makes you feel any better, I needed advice, too. I haven't dated in forever, like I said. So I needed help from Alice and Stephanie, my two best friends."

"You talked to your friends about me?" he asked.

She laughed.

"Why do you say it like that? Do you think I wouldn't talk to someone about you?"

The thought hadn't occurred to him, and he kind of liked the fact that they both sought out advice. His curiosity kept him from fully registering one of Mrs. Sargysan's curtains moving back into place.

"What did they say?" he asked.

"Essentially that I need to get my head out of my ass," Jess said.

Mo chuckled. "That's what Khalil told me, too," he said.

They were both quiet for a moment, but Mo didn't feel like she was waiting for him to say something. That's how it felt with most people, but with Jess, he felt comfortable, not like she was expecting anything from him.

"I don't want to push you out of your comfort zone," she said eventually. "And since it's been a long time for us both, maybe we should take things slowly."

He appreciated her concern for his comfort. Most people didn't get him like she seemed to. But he didn't want her to feel like she needed to tiptoe around him.

"Thanks for thinking of me, but I don't want you to do anything that's difficult or uncomfortable for you, either. I don't want you to feel like you have to treat me with kid gloves," Mo said. "I'm a sturdy guy, I won't break."

Her breathy chuckle sent tingles down his spine.

"Oh, I know that," she said.

There was something about her voice. Mo would have been hard-pressed to explain everything it was doing to him, but the sudden weakness in his legs forced him back to the stairs to sit down.

"Uh . . . what do you mean?" His tongue felt heavy; his throat was dry.

"Um . . . have you . . ." She let out another one of those breathy chuckles. "Probably not, but have you ever seen yourself while you're working? Like maybe in a video?"

He hadn't. When she became president of the Folk School, Wendy had made a new promotional video for the website. She'd tried several times to convince Mo to participate, but he'd refused. Rick had let her film him working instead.

"Um, no," he said. "Why?" What could be interesting about watching him if it wasn't to learn something during classes?

"Mo, what's adorable," Jess said, "is your total lack of awareness of how dead sexy you are."

His scalp flashed hot as embarrassing giddiness sparked through him. Usually when that happened, he wanted to run away to process the feeling calmly. But Jess couldn't see him, there was no need to hide the emotions that would be written all over his face.

"I just . . . I have trouble believing it when anyone says anything like that," he said. "Always have." The silent anxiety he lived with whenever he wasn't in one of his safe spaces was part of him, and it damn sure wasn't sexy. So how could he be?

"Hmm," she said, her tone pensive. "Let's take just one example, then. Your arms, Mo. Your forearms should be illegal."

He looked down at the arm that wasn't holding the phone. What was she talking about? It was just an arm with a few tiny burn marks he'd gotten over the years.

"Oh," he said.

"You don't believe me, do you?" she asked.

"Well, I mean, I don't think you'd lie just to flatter me. But they're just arms," he said.

"Very sexy, very masculine arms," she said. "On a sturdy guy who I know won't break. There's a lot more I could say, but I don't want to overwhelm you. I feel overwhelmed more often than I'd like; I don't want to do it to you."

"I'd never guess that," he said. "You sometimes feeling overwhelmed."

She sighed.

"I learned pretty early that it was in my best interest to make sure no one ever knew when I was upset. My father was determined to raise tough girls. I learned to keep unacceptable emotions hidden. To seem completely unbothered in all circumstances. While, to his credit, I can say that it helped me display confidence, which has had a positive impact on my life, I think it's made me come across as cold or harsh or even like a bitch. But more often than not, I'm stuffing down feelings I don't know how to manage in the moment and trying not to run away so I can deal with them."

Mo understood exactly what she was talking about. He'd probably only picked up on her grief because he'd caught her off guard. If she usually stuffed down the larger, more erratic emotions, it would seem like she had it together at all times. He cleared his throat.

"I . . . I like that you can empathize, but it makes me sad for you. To have grown up that way," he said. "And . . ." He stopped and stroked his beard. "And I knew you weren't a bitch. I wish you hadn't had to learn to stifle your emotions at home."

Jess sighed.

"A sad story for another day," she said. "But what about . . . us? I mean, not to say that there's necessarily an 'us.'"

Her tone and subject pivot told Mo that it wasn't the time to ask about the past. She was more interested in the future.

"I understand," he said. "Why don't we start with a date?"

"A date? Okay, I like that idea."

"Dinner?" he asked.

"Yes."

But where? He'd brought it up, so he should have a suggestion. The problem was that he hadn't gone anywhere date-worthy in years. He knew lots of kid-friendly restaurants, but that probably wouldn't work. This was Jess. He could be honest.

"I have no idea where, though," he said. "Could we say seven, day after tomorrow, and I'll get back to you with where?"

"Works great for me," she said. He could tell she was smiling.

"Good," he said.

"I should probably let you get back to Madison."

Right. It wasn't that he'd forgotten that Madison was there; he'd just gotten so drawn into talking with Jess that he'd kind of lost track of his everyday life.

"You're right. I should go check on her, but I'll be surprised if she isn't asleep in her little nest," he said.

"Thanks for calling," Jess said.

"Thanks for answering."

Jess chuckled.

"Have a good evening," she said.

"You too."

CHAPTER THIRTEEN

Jess

Sitting on the examining table, Jess tugged at the sleeve of the uncomfortable paper gown. She hated going to doctors' offices, hated answering questions, hated being essentially naked with a total stranger.

Does the room have to be this cold?

Shivering, she ran a hand down her arm to warm it and ended up bending the sleeve back in the annoying way it had been before. She was grumbling to herself, trying to flatten the sleeve again, when the door opened.

"Ms. . . . Anderson," the doctor said as she stepped inside. "I understand you're here for a physical."

Jess nodded. She'd promised Alice and Stephanie to see someone about her stomach and her wrist. She might as well do a full workup while she was at it. At least then she wouldn't have to come back for a good while.

"Yes," she said after clearing her throat.

"Shall we get started?" the doctor asked, warming her hands.

As she began examining her, Jess answered the doctor's basic questions, was silent while she was listening to her heart, and breathed deeply when required. As she hated the experience so much, Jess simply went on autopilot, dying for it to be finished. When the doctor asked her to lie back on the table and warned her before palpating her stomach, Jess remembered her primary goal.

"I've been having some difficulty with pain lately," Jess said.

"Mmm?" the doctor said. She pressed under Jess's ribs, making her wince. "Ah. There?"

Jess nodded.

"My wrist, too."

"Okay, we'll get to that." The doctor was very gentle, but Jess continued wincing as the sharp pains sliced through her at each touch. She knew there was no way she'd be able to eat lunch when she got home.

"Hmm," the doctor said.

"Also my shoulder," Jess said, once she'd stopped.

"I'll check it as well," the doctor said. "Everything seems to be in order with your stomach. Have you been having trouble eating?"

Jess nodded.

"I can give you something for that. Let's take a look at your wrist and shoulder."

Thirty minutes later, Jess returned to her car with a referral for a full blood workup and a prescription for an industrial-strength antacid. She was relieved that she'd been right that nothing was wrong with her joints, but the doctor's comment about her pain was still bouncing around in her head.

"Your pain is rather . . . diffuse," she'd said. "Have you had any big life changes lately?"

For a split second, Jess had hesitated. She'd almost told her about Cassie, but losing her sister couldn't have anything to do with her body. Instead, she'd shrugged and mentioned finally starting her career and participating in a Ren Faire.

"A Ren Faire sounds like fun," the doctor said.

"Well . . ." Jess hadn't meant to lead her back to Cassie. "It can be, I'm sure. It's not really my thing. I'm just doing it to support the organization putting it on."

"Ah," the doctor had said. "That would make it more of a stressor, then. And stress *can* manifest as pain. Let's see what the blood work tells us."

Stress as pain? Tension, okay. But pain in specific places? Weird.

Standing in front of her open closet that evening, hands on her hips, Jess grumbled under her breath. She felt good about what she'd accomplished that day, from the doctor to the blood draw to the stack of papers she'd finally finished grading. The current task on her plate should have been easy. But she hadn't had a first date in years and was out of her depth on what to wear the following evening.

"Sty," she said. "Help me out."

He jumped down from the foot of her bed and ambled up beside her to face the closet. Jess pulled out a black skirt and green T-shirt. She held them up to herself and looked in the mirrored door. "What do you think?" she asked Steinem.

He raised one of his paws to clean the pads.

"Right," Jess said. "It's a dinner date. This is a little casual."

She replaced those options and chose a pair of pants and blouse that she'd worn to a conference. She'd felt confident in the outfit but caught Steinem's wide yawn in the mirror.

"Seriously?" she asked him.

He looked away.

"For someone with so many opinions on everything, you sure aren't being helpful right now," she said, stuffing the clothes back in her closet. Steinem wrapped himself around her legs and she bent to pick him up.

"Sorry, Sty Sty," she said, cradling him and scratching his upturned stomach. "Guess I'm a little anxious." He began purring, and Jess's stress stepped down a few notches. "And this isn't your area of expertise. I shouldn't ask for fashion help from someone who looks so elegant just walking around naked all day."

She booped his nose with hers before gently returning him to his original spot on her bed. She'd get better help from Alice and Stephanie during their call in an hour.

After eating dinner, Jess settled in her bed with her laptop in advance of the video call. She had an email about one of her published articles to reply to, but it took much less time than she'd expected, so she sat there, a little lost for what to do to pass the time. She was checking a news website for the latest headlines when the word "sensitive" caught her eye.

Shit. I forgot.

She typed "Highly Sensitive Person" into a browser. A preview of the first result raised her eyebrows.

Neurodivergence?

"HSPs are neurodivergent individuals whose central nervous systems are significantly more reactive than those of neurotypical people . . ." The rest of the information in the article was essentially what he'd told her about himself, but he hadn't used the term "neurodivergent." Jess didn't know much about neurodivergence beyond what she figured was common knowledge about autism or ADHD. If Mo was neurodivergent, his empathy and sensitivity weren't personality traits. His brain literally functioned differently from most people's. If they were going to date, she wanted to respect that. It must have been difficult and burdensome to exist in a world that didn't understand that difference and interpreted Mo's behavior as choices he was making, rather than logical responses to the structure of who he was.

She opened a Word file and began taking notes.

By the time her reminder alarm about the video call went off, Jess had six tabs with scholarly research reports and articles open in her browser and a page full of notes. She didn't want to stop, had always adored doing research, but she definitely needed to talk to her friends. She opened the video app. Steinem hopped up on the foot of the bed and began his lazy walk toward her.

"Well, Sty, if they're going to help me figure out what to wear, I have to tell them why."

He ambled up to her side and sat down, tilting his head up. Jess started scratching his throat as he had asked.

"They might give me a hard time, you know," she said. "Since I was resistant to the idea of dating."

Steinem started purring and turned his head a little so she could scratch the side. She chewed her lip a little. Understanding a little more about Mo also required a stronger attention to the impact her words or behaviors could have on him.

"I mean, it's not like he's a super fragile flower or something," she said to Steinem. "He's a grown man who's been managing his sensitivity his whole life."

She realized that she liked and respected the way he'd chosen to do it. He didn't completely hide from the world or hate it. He used his sensitivity to engage with it. To be compassionate with others.

Steinem turned his head the other way. Jess continued scratching.

"That actually makes him kind of special. Really spe—"

Steinem stepped away from her hand and snuggled into a ball beside her leg.

"Really?" she asked the cat.

Steinem yawned and began purring just as the screen changed as the app began ringing.

"Hey, Jess! How are you? Your students?" Stephanie asked, appearing on the screen after Jess answered.

"We're finally past the getting to know each other phase," Jess said, sidestepping the personal question. "Yours?"

Stephanie rolled her eyes.

"We've gotten to know each other. Some are endearing. But more are . . . not," she said.

"Oh, how I understand," Jess said.

"Hey, ladies, what's up?" Alice asked after joining them.

"Just commiserating about work," Stephanie said.

"That's not what we're supposed to be talking about," Alice said.

"What? Why not?" Jess asked.

"I was waiting for you to get here," Stephanie said.

"Ladies, what is—"

"Now that we're both here, it's time for our 'Mo the Unicorn' update," Stephanie said.

Alice nodded and picked up a mug from off-camera.

"We're listening," she said before taking a sip.

Jess took a breath to protest. She didn't like being a pet project or monopolizing their time together. And she wanted a little time to better digest what she'd just learned about him. But the pet project did need help deciding what to wear.

"Well," she said, "our first date is tomorrow night."

Alice put her mug down and clapped her hands, grinning broadly. Stephanie rolled her eyes then smiled.

"Fine," she said. "I owe you five bucks, Al."

"You all bet on me going out with Mo?" Jess asked, tone a bit shrill.

"I thought you were going to shut down, Al thought you weren't," Stephanie said.

"Shut down?" Jess asked. "You make it sound like I crumple if a man looks at me."

"'Shut him out' might have been a better choice of words," Stephanie said. "You know, your go-to reaction when faced with the danger of romantic entanglement."

Jess narrowed her eyes.

"It was all in good fun," Alice said. "We didn't mean to upset you."

"Hmm . . ." Jess said.

"If you're going on a date, I need to picture it. But we don't even know what he looks like," Stephanie said.

"Oh yes," Alice said, leaning forward. "Do tell."

Jess's face got a little warm. As sexy as Mo was, describing him to her friends might make her start gushing like an idiot. She was the metered but supportive friend, not the gushing friend. A picture might make things easier, but she wasn't really a picture-taking person, so she didn't have one on her phone. Even though she hadn't seen any photos of him in the blacksmithing section of the Folk School website, there might have been instructor information on it with a photo or two.

"Hold on," she said. She got the website open and found the appropriate page. Mo's profile was there so she clicked the link. There were a couple of photos of him, but he was looking off to the side or down at something he was working on. She put the link in the meeting chat.

"What. In. The. Actual. Fuck," Stephanie said after a few moments.

"*Jess*," Alice said, eyes wide. "This guy is *hot*."

Jittery giddiness passed through Jess as her cheeks warmed. She cleared her throat, stuffing that silliness away. A warm tenderness surged in its place as she realized that he seemed to be hiding a little in the photos.

I bet he's shy about having his picture taken.

"Um, yeah," she said in answer to her friends. "You can't tell from the photos, but he has really dark eyes. They're . . . kind."

"'Kind,'" Stephanie said, rolling her eyes. "Sounds like you're playing it down a little bit."

"Yeah, maybe," Jess said, rolling her eyes back.

"I am digging this beard," Alice said, her head tilted, smiling a little.

"Yeah," Jess said again. "He does the cutest thing when he's nervous or uncomfortable. He strokes it, or scratches at it. It's like a very charming tic."

"Steph," said Alice. "Jess said cute. Jess said, 'the cutest thing.'"

"Where are my smelling salts?" Stephanie asked.

"See, this is why I don't tell you anything," Jess said.

"Sorry, sorry," Stephanie said. "Alice, let's be supportive friends and listen. We can give her a hard time later."

"He *is* super-hot, but is he an ass about it?" Alice asked.

"Jess wouldn't date an ass," Stephanie said.

"No," Jess said. "He's not at all. He's completely oblivious to his sex appeal. When I told him I thought he was hot, he started hemming and hawing. I was worried I'd scared him at first."

"What's wrong with him, then?" Stephanie asked.

"Wrong?" asked Jess.

"Nice, Steph," Alice said.

Jess ran her fingertips through Steinem's fur. She knew what was "wrong" with him from the outside world's perspective. Impaired somehow. He seemed to have internalized that message if he was calling himself weird.

Impaired . . .

"Huh," she said. "He is kind of Hephaestus, Alice."

"Oh?" Alice asked, putting her mug down.

"Hephaestus . . . anybody wanna catch me up?" Stephanie asked.

"I teased her a while back about Atalanta and Hippomenes. She said Mo's more Hephaestus," Alice said.

"Okay, I think I see your vision," Stephanie said. "Muscular, blacksmith . . . but what's his limp?"

"His empathy," said Jess. "His sensitivity. They're . . . strong enough that he doesn't like a lot of attention on himself, so he's not very communicative."

She'd hesitated to outright say that they were manifestations of his neurodiversity; she didn't think he broadcasted that about himself, so it certainly wasn't her place to do so.

"Is he silent and brooding, Jess?" Stephanie asked. "Haven't we all learned from Alice's foolhardy expeditions into the land of brooding men?"

"Hey!" said Alice. "We cannot generalize from one man."

"Two men," said Stephanie. "And didn't they rhyme?"

Jess laughed.

"Eddie and Freddie," she said. "I mean, she's right, Alice. Those were—"

"Technically, Edward and Alfred," Alice said, tipping her chin. "And they were . . . learning experiences."

"More like experiments," Stephanie said. "Jess, do you—"

"Actually," Jess said. "I'm wrong. If you're paying attention, Mo does communicate. He just doesn't like to talk."

Both of her friends furrowed their brows.

"Uh . . . how does that work, exactly?" Stephanie asked.

"Hmm," Jess said. She wasn't quite sure how to explain it well. "He is very, very spartan with his words most of the time. When he speaks, it's less volunteering his opinion than responding to what someone else says. He'll grunt, or his face changes."

"Is he a Neanderthal, Jess?" Stephanie asked flatly.

"No, it's not that. When he has something to say, people listen because he doesn't say much. But he uses whole sentences when we're alone. And he's not exactly passive. When the other guy on the team said something sexist, Mo immediately called him out."

"That's a good sign," Alice said.

"Quite important," Stephanie said.

Jess felt lighter having shared. She was surprised at how much more secure she felt about going forward with Mo having talked to her friends. Even though she'd never thought of needing their approval. She did need their specific help, however.

"Ladies," she said, "I need some concrete guidance. I don't know what to wear for the date tomorrow night."

"Show us what you've got," Stephanie said.

Jess slid off the bed, carrying her laptop with her. After putting it in a good spot on the corner of her dresser, she opened the closet doors and reached for the pants she'd rejected earlier.

"Jess," Alice called out before Jess's hand closed on the hanger. "What's that on your arm?"

Jess had forgotten to remove the Band-Aid that had been placed there after her blood test.

"Oh," she said. "I went to the doctor as instructed, Mom and Mom. Had some blood work done, too."

"What did the doctor say?" Alice asked.

"I'm fine, everything looks good. She did prescribe me something for my stomach being upset all the time."

"So why the blood test?" Stephanie asked.

"I asked for a full physical, since I was making the appointment," Jess said.

"Good call," Alice said.

Jess grabbed the pants and reached for the top but remembered something else.

"One weird thing," she said. "The doctor asked about anything stressing me out, and I mentioned I'm doing the Ren Faire. Then she said stress can manifest as pain. Do you all think the Faire is making my muscles hurt?"

"Hmm," Alice said. "I guess. If it's stressing you out, that would explain why you never talk about it."

"True," Stephanie said. "Remind me why you're doing this again? You don't actually *have to.*"

Jess sighed. Rather than overthink, she co-opted Mo's explanation.

"It's for a really good cause," Jess said. She grabbed the top out of the closet and held it up with the pants for her friends to see.

"Is it a date or a research symposium?" Stephanie asked. "Next."

Jess showed them the skirt and T-shirt.

"Meh," Alice said.

Jess pulled out a long-sleeved brown dress with a high collar and flower print.

"Okay, Grandma," Stephanie said.

Jess glared at the screen.

"Maybe it will be more efficient if you pick up the laptop and pan across your closet," Alice suggested. Jess raised an eyebrow but complied.

"Wait!" Stephanie said before Jess started to pan. "What's that red thing?"

Jess followed the angle of the camera and saw what Stephanie had caught at the far end of the closet. She returned the laptop to its place and pulled out the vintage-inspired red dress that she'd retrieved among other things on her only visit to her parents' house since she returned to the States. A dress that was only in her possession because Cassie had chosen it for her so that they could attend a '50s-themed party at the end of the previous summer. The last summer her fun-loving sister had had. A dull ache began rising in Jess's limbs.

"What is *that*?" Stephanie asked. She'd leaned close to the camera, resting her chin in her hand.

"It's a dress," Jess said, pulling the hem to the side so they could see the skirt.

"No kidding," Stephanie said. "What's it doing in *your* closet?"

"It's beautiful, but isn't exactly something I'd pick out for you," Alice said.

Her friends weren't wrong. The only reason she owned such a thing was to make her sister happy. And now it lived at the back of her closet. She sighed and explained how she'd ended up with it.

"I think it's perfect for tomorrow night," Alice said.

"Me too. You're going to look stunning," Stephanie said.

"Really?" Jess held it up again, then in front of herself while looking at her reflection.

"The question isn't how it's going to look on you," Alice said. "It's how do you feel about wearing it?"

"I mean . . . okay, I think." She held the dress at arm's length again. "It should still fit."

"I swear, if I didn't know that this was just a question of old habits dying really, really hard, I would reach through the screen and strangle you," Stephanie said.

Jess looked sharply at her.

"I love you," Stephanie said. "*We* love you. With your compartmentalizing emotions and everything. The question is, are you okay with wearing this great dress even with its connection to Cassie? We tease you, but we know this is an emotional change for you, after another *much bigger* change. We just want to be sure that wearing that Cassie dress and embarking down this path isn't going to be too much."

Jess wasn't sure how to respond. Steph had brought up some good points. But before she really tried to let herself feel their weight, she wanted to get Alice's read.

"Alice?" she asked.

"What she said," Alice replied before taking a sip from her mug.

A few hours later, Jess pulled back the covers and sat on the edge of her bed to moisturize her hands and feet. The "Cassie dress" she'd hung on her closet door caught her eye.

Stephanie made some good points. Don't do flings. Just went through a big change.

She flicked off the light and slid under the cool sheets. The moon was full that night, and the light peeked through her closed blinds, illuminating the dress.

But I really like Mo. If I wear the dress, it's like taking a piece of Cassie with me. Maybe she'll like him, too.

CHAPTER FOURTEEN

Mo

Mo wasn't sure what to do with his hands. Standing outside of the Grey Ghost restaurant in Midtown, he slid them into his front pockets, but after less than a minute, he took them out to wipe his palms on the outside of his jeans. He wanted to greet Jess and walk in together, so he'd gotten there a little early.

He took a glance inside, running his hand down his beard, then he heard a familiar voice.

"Hey, Mo."

He turned around and smiled as Jess took the last two steps to reach him. He smiled back.

"Hey, Jess," he said. She looked beautiful, wearing a red dress with what Maddie would call a "swishy skirt," and her hair was in a high ponytail, the end of it resting on her shoulder. He realized he'd never seen her in a dress or a skirt.

"What's wrong?" she asked.

"Wrong?"

"Your expression changed. You looked shocked. Is everything okay?" Usually confident Jess actually looked self-conscious.

"I've never seen you in a dress before," he said.

"And you don't like it," she said, deflating a little.

He decided to be a little daring.

"You look beautiful," he said, leaning down and kissing her cheek. To his great surprise, she blushed.

"Thanks," she said softly.

"You hungry?" he asked.

She nodded. He tipped his head toward the door. Surprising him again, she slipped her hand around his arm and squeezed. Taking a deep breath for courage, he was happy to catch a whiff of vanilla. He bent his elbow, leaned toward Jess, and took another deep breath, enjoying her perfume as they walked inside.

As the hostess took them to their table, Jess looked around, admiring. She smiled at him as they sat down.

"Nice choice, Mo," she said, opening her menu.

"You think? I thought about finding something closer, but Khalil recommended it. He said they're known for their gourmet sandwiches and burgers. Figured it would be a good place to try."

"Gourmet sandwiches?" Jess asked. "I'm curious to see what that's about." She studied her menu a moment. "And you've never been here before?" she asked.

He shook his head.

"Don't come to Midtown very often," he said.

"I think I've been twice? Maybe," she said. "But I'm glad you chose a place that we could discover together." She gave him a broad smile, and he felt all tingly.

"Me too," he said. He was also quite happy that the place wasn't very busy. There were five or six people seated at the bar and maybe ten total in the large section they were in, partitioned by a half-wall.

As the waiter left with their orders, including the signature Reuben sandwich and a Wagyu truffle burger, a group of people walked in. Then another, then another. Jess looked over her shoulder then back at Mo.

"I wonder what that's about?" she asked.

"I don't know," he said, becoming increasingly uncomfortable. It almost looked like a tour bus had let out with the way they were streaming in the door. The decibel level in the room went up dramatically; the people were in high spirits and had no problem expressing it. The waiter returned with the tomato soup and beet salad they'd chosen as appetizers. Mo focused on his soup. The first few mouthfuls helped, but when he glanced up at Jess to ask about her salad, she was looking at him with a raised eyebrow.

"Are you okay?" Jess asked.

He felt bad because he'd let himself get distracted from her.

"I'm fine," he said.

"No, you're not," she said.

"What makes you say that?"

"You're stroking your beard," she said.

Mo stopped midstroke.

"Yes, I was, but is there a reason I shouldn't?" he asked, lowering his hand to rest on the table.

"Maybe I'm wrong, but I think you touch your beard when you're uncomfortable," she said. "When you're anxious or dealing with feelings you don't want to show, you reach for your beard. Stroking, scratching, smoothing. I noticed it in the first meeting. And with that woman at your shop. It's your 'tell,' I think."

Mo was dumbfounded. He was so shocked he'd stopped breathing and his body's demand for air forced him to take a breath, which pushed him back into himself.

"I . . ." He needed another breath. "I don't even know I'm doing it sometimes. You noticed that?" he asked.

Jess shrugged.

"Kind of," she said. "Unfortunately, with the Faire, there have been opportunities for you to be uncomfortable. And when you kind of apologized if you weren't talkative in your truck, I remembered that you'd done it right before you offered me a ride. It looked like you were going to pull it off your face. Which would be terribly unfortunate."

At first, Mo couldn't do anything but blink.

"What do you mean?" he finally asked.

Jess chuckled and waved him closer. He leaned toward her.

"The beard *really* works for you," she whispered.

"Oh," he said, leaning back as she had. He hadn't planned on shaving his beard anytime soon, but if Jess liked it, it sure as hell wasn't going anywhere. "I won't shave it."

"Good," she said, smiling. He wasn't sure what to do or to

say next, so he scooped another spoonful of soup. It was half-way to his mouth when a collective shout erupted from the large group of people. He jumped, the spoonful of soup sloshing back into his bowl. The group started singing, and Mo's skin felt too tight.

Jess had jumped as well, but instead of looking at the group as Mo had, she was looking at him.

"You know," she said, catching his attention. "I'm pretty good. This salad was surprisingly filling, I don't think I'll be able to eat my entrée."

Mo looked at her plate. She'd only eaten about half, and she'd said she was hungry when she arrived.

"Are you sure?" he asked.

The group started clapping along to their song, and the sound set his teeth on edge.

"Yeah, why don't we ask the waiter for doggie bags and get out of here?" Jess sat up straighter and turned in her seat, looking for the waiter.

"Jess," Mo said.

"Hmm?" she asked, still looking.

The restaurant had excellent acoustics for reflecting sharp sounds off the wall and concentrating them where most of the diners were eating, including Mo and Jess.

"Jess?"

She looked at him.

"Do you really want to go, or do you think I want to go?" he asked.

She looked him up and down, tilting her head a little.

"Both," she said.

"We can stay if you want," he said. "I don't want you to feel like you have to do something different on account of me."

"I think—" The group cheered again, cutting her off. She glared at them then turned back to Mo. "I think that's what you're used to doing. Sucking it up for the comfort or happiness of other people when sensory input is overloading you. Your body, your mind is just tuned that way. You aren't choosing that. I'm not okay with the idea of you tolerating something that harms you on account of me."

Mo's heart was going a mile a minute. She'd used some very specific language. It went beyond "You don't like being around a lot of people." Or, "You don't like loud environments." It was more targeted, almost medical.

"How do you know that?" he asked.

She resettled in her seat, squaring her shoulders. She seemed to be bracing herself.

"I hope it's okay with you that I did some research. You said that you're a Highly Sensitive Person, and I wanted to learn about it so I'd be able to respect your needs," she said. "I reviewed my notes before I came tonight."

Her face was suddenly blurry. The noise from the other patrons that had been stabbing into his ears, back, and shoulders vanished in an instant. That she would take the time to research HSPs, to take *notes* and study them . . . He felt like his throat was in a vise.

"Mo, I'm so sorry, I crossed the line," she said suddenly, reaching across the table to take his hand. "I didn't mean to upset—"

"No," he choked out. "No." He shook his head. He squeezed her hand. "It means—" He paused to clear his throat. "It means a lot that you wanted to learn more and took the time to find out."

She squeezed his hand back, smiling at him.

Outside, with the rest of their dinner in to-go boxes, Mo walked Jess to her car. The sound of cars in the street, and the few people they passed who were speaking at a normal volume, let the tension he'd been holding ease away. So much so that he began to regret the fact that leaving meant the end of the date. As they reached her car, he spoke up.

"I hate having to end early," he said.

"Me too, but maybe . . . Maybe we can do something else?" she asked.

Good idea, but what else? It was their first date, so he didn't want to suggest going back to his place. He didn't ever want her to feel like he would pressure her into anything physical. Not only was that disrespectful, but he would feel her distress in his own body.

"Wait," he said, getting an idea. He pulled out his phone to confirm that they weren't too far from Beacon Park. He didn't know if they had benches, but he did have an old army surplus blanket in the toolbox of his truck.

"Up for a picnic?" he asked her.

She laughed.

"Sure," she said.

Arriving at Beacon Park, they took a moment to find parking, but once they had, he tucked the blanket under his arm and they walked in, finding a suitable spot. The sun had set, but the sky wasn't dark yet. There was a band playing on the small stage, but they were far enough away for it to only be agreeable background noise.

"Quick thinking," she said as they settled in.

"Thanks," he said. "Maddie and I came here for one of Khalil's fundraising events a while back."

"Fundraising?" she asked, picking up her Reuben sandwich.

"Yeah, I complain about him talking too much or being too sociable, but it has its benefits. Works quite well for him in his barbershops. He also volunteers with a youth basketball team and the Boys and Girls Clubs. They do community events a lot, and he is excellent at getting business sponsors."

She raised her eyebrows as she finished her bite.

"I imagine that you're one of those sponsors," she said.

He shrugged.

"It's important." He took a bite of his hamburger. Drawing attention to any financial contributions he made always made him skin-burningly self-conscious. That had been a key source of discomfort concerning the thank-you banquet. He had started to feel a little tight in the chest thinking about it when Jess reached out and ran a finger along the edge of his beard. His heart truly started pounding.

"So, Khalil's the one who keeps you looking so sharp," she said. She winked at him.

"Uh, yeah," he said, feeling his cheeks heat.

"Did Maddie have fun at the event here?" she asked, taking another bite of her sandwich.

"Oh yeah, a blast. They had a rock-climbing wall, races, all sorts of stuff she adores. She was so tired she fell asleep on the way home."

"Sounds like she's an active girl—young lady. You said she's twelve, right?"

Mo nodded. Finishing his bite, he wished he had something to drink.

"She's still a little girl to me, but it's clear we're entering adolescence. A little too much attitude, moments where she'll cry at the drop of a hat. But apparently that's normal, that's what all the books say."

"The books?" Jess asked.

"Yeah, I've switched from the ones about childhood development to the ones about the teenage years. I don't want to get caught unawares."

"You read books about childhood development?" she asked.

"Um . . . yeah. I want to be a good parent," he said. He started to worry that he'd said something wrong.

Jess reached out and squeezed the hand he was leaning on.

"You are a good parent, Mo," she said softly. "Most parents don't do that."

"Oh," he said. He felt his cheeks getting warm again. "Thanks."

They sat in silence for a few moments, and Mo had another urge to drink something. He noticed a little concession stand near the stage.

"Do you mind if I leave you here for a second?" he asked.

"No, why?" she asked.

"I'm parched. I'm going to grab something to drink." He pointed out the stand to her. "What would you like?"

She smiled.

"A coke or some other pop. Thanks."

"Sure thing."

He stood up, then realized he was about to leave a woman alone in a park at night.

"Wait," he said. "I don't want to leave you here by yourself. Don't know who could be around."

"And you don't think that if push came to shove, I could handle it?" she asked, smirking.

"Oh, I'm sure you could. I'd feel sorry for the idiot who tried to mess with you. But I don't want 'push' to have a chance to come to 'shove.'"

"Okay, Mo, I appreciate it," she said, standing. "I'll go. What do you want?"

"Same," he said. "Any pop. Here." He pulled his wallet out of his pocket to give her some money. She waved him off.

"You got dinner, I can get drinks."

Mo didn't want to make her pay for anything, but at the same time this was Jess, and she might not like it if he pushed.

"Okay," he said. "Thanks."

He sat back down as Jess walked away. In the quiet, he realized how much he'd been talking. It had been quite a lot, but he wasn't drained like he normally was. He was out on a date with a woman he enjoyed being with, and who wanted to understand him better. She literally researched how his mind works. That thought made him a little jittery again. No one had taken the time to learn about his HSP until it became a problem for them. She'd looked into it so she could avoid problems. Jess was attractive, intelligent, confident, and thoughtful. And she was interested in him? He hoped he could rise to the challenge. Then she was back.

"Hey," she said as she got close.

"Hey," he stood up, and she handed him a paper cup.

"That one's a Cherry Coke and this one is regular. Do you like cherry?" she asked.

"I do, but you can have it if you like it," he said.

"Not necessarily. I took a guess." She smiled at him as she got comfortable on the blanket again.

He smiled back but realized he hadn't said anything about the blanket.

"Sorry about the blanket. I know it itches," he said.

She waved a hand like she was swatting a fly.

"Do not worry at all. I'm impressed that you were equipped for a surprise picnic." She picked up her sandwich and took another bite. "It sounds like you're a great dad," she said. "I hope you don't mind my asking about it, but you were married to Maddie's mom, right?"

He nodded; his mouth was full.

"It just didn't work out?" she asked.

He nodded again and swallowed quickly.

"We're better off as friends," he said. "We co-parent well, so that's the most important thing."

"It is," Jess said. "You know, I don't want to put the cart before the horse or anything, but if we do continue dating, I won't ask you to meet Maddie for at least six months."

"No?" he asked. "Why six months?"

"From what I've read, that's the recommended time frame. I think it's to make sure that you and I are compatible so that Maddie doesn't have strangers coming in and out of her life." She wiggled her straw around in her cup before having some more.

Mo wasn't sure how to respond. He hadn't thought to date, so he hadn't looked it up. But if she'd researched his HSP, it made sense that she'd research dating a parent. He smiled.

"Thank you for being concerned about her well-being," he said.

"Of course."

"It's kind of you to think about my family. I'd like to ask about yours," he said. Jess still had a pleasant expression, but it seemed like her eyes tightened for a flash. "But I . . . I feel like it might be uncomfortable for you."

She looked away momentarily, then squeezed his hand again.

"Thank you, Mo. I appreciate it. I've never had a good relationship with my parents. I was much closer to my sister. But now . . ." She sighed. "Now it's best that they live in Illinois, and I live here. I'll tell you more another day?"

He let himself run a hand down her arm.

"Sure thing," he said.

She smiled at him.

"Tell me about blacksmithing," she said. "When I read about sensory overload for HSPs, I was surprised. Blacksmithing seems like a really loud hobby. Have you been doing it long?"

He wiped his mouth and shrugged.

"Pretty much since I quit rowing. But I really wanted to do it. Took me some time to get acclimated to the noise and the smells. Now those specific noises and smells are reminders of accomplishment, so they don't get to me."

"Rowing?"

Mo held in his grimace. He hadn't meant to mention that.

"Uh, yeah," he said. "I went to college for it. UM Ann Arbor."

Jess studied him. He told himself not to blush.

"Why do you say that like it's a bad thing?" she asked.

He shrugged. Rowing was difficult to remember.

"I was injured at the wrong time," he said.

She raised an eyebrow.

"A lumbar injury will take you out for several months. I hurt myself bad right before the Olympic trials. Four years earlier I'd been an alternate; that year was my opportunity to actually row in the Games."

"I'm sorry, *what*?" Jess asked. "Are you telling me that you were an Olympic athlete?"

He shrugged again.

"I guess technically?" he said.

"Do I have to google you, Mo?" she asked.

He chuckled in spite of his nerves.

"Okay, Doug," he said.

She laughed as she fished her phone out of her purse.

"Mo Sarda rowing?" she asked.

"Mohammed," he said.

"Thank you for the precision," she said, typing on her screen. She was silent a moment, and Mo braced himself. He could tell that some results had come up but couldn't see what she tapped open. Her head snapped up and she gawked at him.

"Excuse me, Mr. 'New Hope for the Sport,'" she said. "Mr. 'UM rower favorite for the Games.' That's an amazing accomplishment. Why did you seem embarrassed about this?" she asked.

He sighed. He tried to think of a good way to explain it, but he remembered Maddie telling him to talk like he talked to her. He took a quick sip of his drink.

"Two things," he said. He couldn't bring himself to look directly at her. "One, it took me a long time to get over losing my chance. Just thinking about the sport hurt. And two, I was a complete asshole back then. Quick to anger, harsh with people. Judgmental. I didn't know that I was an HSP back then, and I was forcing myself to try to live like everybody else. I was constantly worn out by the overstimulation and didn't know how to compensate. I understand myself better today but I'm not proud of who I was back then, so I avoid thinking about it. It was better to bury the whole subject."

Jess had leaned closer to him to listen. He hadn't meant to speak quietly, but that tended to happen with things he didn't want to talk about. He glanced at her as she sat back.

"I understand," she said. She put her phone back in her purse, picked up her drink, and took a sip. He waited for the additional questions that always came when rowing came up. She put her drink back down.

"That was a very colorful necklace of Maddie's that fell out of your truck the other day. Did she make it?" she asked.

Mo wasn't sure he'd heard her correctly.

"You . . . you don't want to ask me anything else about rowing?" he asked.

"No," she said, drinking again.

He was a little off-kilter. Any time it came up, he was inundated with questions until he felt like he was going to drown. It must have shown on his face. She turned to face him completely.

"That subject will never come up between us again. You said it hurts. I'd hazard a guess that if you're willing to say that, it means the subject cuts deep enough to cause you physical pain. It seems like HSPs need to maintain wider boundaries than other people, and I want to respect yours. So unless you feel like saying something, I'll never mention it. Never refer to it," she said. "And I'm not going to talk about it with a soul."

He wasn't sure how to describe what he felt. It was big and warm, and it filled him from head to toe.

"Thank you, Jess," he said softly.

"You're welcome, Mo." She turned a little to watch the band playing in the distance.

CHAPTER FIFTEEN

Jess

Maybe this Ren Faire silliness could grow on her. Out in the expansive field behind the Folk School, Jess loudly counted out eight paces then turned sharply, raising the longbow and aiming for the target Ned had placed in the middle of the field. Brian, an archer friend of Ned's, mirrored her, raising his bow at the same time.

"Better," Ned called out from a folding chair several yards away.

They'd been practicing for the better part of an hour, learning the first of three archery shows for the guests of the Faire. While Jess had initially turned her nose up at the idea of performing, it felt kind of nice to work in unison with fellow archers to create something that was technically and aesthetically pleasing.

"We said we'd fire on 'ten,' right?" Jess called to Brian.

"Yeah," he called back. "More engaging for the patrons if they aren't sure whose arrow pierced the sack first."

Jess nodded. She stretched her neck and shoulders while shaking out her arms.

"Let's do it again," she said loudly, walking back to her original position in the routine.

"Nope," Ned said, squinting at her. He slapped his thighs and stood. "Time for a break."

Jess jogged to Ned while Brian waited for Keith, the third archer in the show, to come in from farther out in the field.

"I hope you don't want to stop on my account," she said to Ned. "I'm good."

"I'm sure you are," he said. "But no sense in overdoing it when you're on a new bow. Can't have you injuring yourself. I'd have to take your place in this brouhaha. That'll be a cold day in hell."

"Ned, you know I've shot longbow before," she said.

Ned squinted again and sucked his teeth.

"Yes, you mentioned that. When was the last time?" he asked.

Jess squinted back. Once she answered his question, she'd prove his point. She hated it when that happened.

"About ten years," she said.

Ned grunted.

"Like I said. New bow. Come on, slow pokes," he said to Brian and Keith as they approached.

The coolness of the break room made Jess shiver a little, drawing attention to the fact that she'd gotten sweatier than she'd realized outside. She decided on a water out of the vending machine while the men settled in around the table. She'd agreed to that day as their first practice session a bit reluctantly. Mo and the other Faire blacksmiths had been getting together at the School to create the items to sell for the past few weeks. But that day Mo wasn't participating—he had Maddie that weekend.

Their schedules hadn't lined up very well to get together the past few weeks, but they'd made up for it with long phone calls, texting each other throughout the day, and video call dates. The video dates had been a good way to spend time together, but they'd only made her desire to touch him, to be physically with him, grow more and more.

Didn't anticipate video calls being such an important part of my life.

"I think it's going to come together nicely," Brian said as Jess joined them. "This was a good idea, putting on a Faire to raise funds."

"Kind of you all to help out," Ned said.

Keith swatted away the praise.

"An opportunity to shoot in garb, dazzle some patrons, and slide into Ren Speak? Every Rennie's dream."

Jess blinked twice.

"I'm sorry," she said. She looked at Brian. "You said *patron* earlier, which I gathered means a person who comes to the Faire. And I've heard *garb* before." She looked at Keith. "But *Ren Speak? Rennie?* Please help me out here."

Keith smiled broadly.

"Ren Speak is the language we use at Faires. The manner of speaking. And Rennies are people who either work the Faires or go to them very, very regularly," he said.

"Oh," Jess said.

The men began discussing other things, but their voices faded away. Cassie must have been a Rennie, if that's a term that refers to regular participants. Cassie went as often as she was able. The room dimmed, Jess's throat got tight, and the muscles in her arms began screaming. She hadn't known that Cassie was a Rennie, that there was a specific word for people into Faires. She probably had friends she enjoyed chatting with in Ren Speak. Jess wondered what else she didn't know about her sister. She knew what she should have known—that she'd failed to see how abusive Cassie's relationship had become and that she'd suffered because of it. How many other ways had she failed in truly knowing her sister?

"Right, Jess?"

Ned's question shocked her back into the present.

"Uh . . . I missed that." She sat up straight. "What?"

"Said we're probably good for today. We've got a couple more sessions planned; let's wrap it up," he said.

"Yeah, sure," she said, standing as the others did.

As Brian and Keith stepped into the hall, Ned caught her elbow.

"You all right?" he asked, his brows knitted.

Jess swallowed hard. She didn't know how long she'd zoned out, and she did not like that Ned seemed to have noticed.

"Great," she said.

Ned searched her face, frowning.

"'Kay," he said. "See you next week."

The pain in her muscles had turned into a dull ache by the time she got home. But her stomach had declared rebellion. Rubbing it as she rushed to the medicine cabinet, she found the medication the doctor had prescribed and knocked back twice the dose. She leaned over the sink and took deep breaths. Steinem trilled behind her.

"Hey," she said to him with her eyes closed. "I'm okay."

He walked back and forth, rubbing his sides against her leg. She smiled.

"I am," she said. "Don't worry."

He trilled again.

"I'm gonna take a shower," she said to him. "I'm gross from today. Plus, it'll help with the aches."

After turning on the water to let it warm up, she started getting undressed. Steinem hopped on the counter and watched, squinting a little. She smiled at him.

"Thank you, Sty Sty," she said, scratching behind his ear. "I promise I'm okay."

But maybe she was lying to her cat. Her doctor's office had called on Friday afternoon, and she still hadn't checked the voicemail. Once she was out of the shower, she decided to be a grown-up about it and stop hiding. After a deep sigh, she grabbed her phone to listen to the message.

> "Hello, Ms. Anderson, this is Dr. Williams's office. Your blood work has come back, and she'd like to schedule an appointment with you to discuss the results and further tests. Please call us back at your earliest convenience."

Sitting on her bed, still wrapped in a towel with her hair dripping, Jess hung up the phone. That was not information she'd wanted to hear. She didn't want to be on an examining table again, did not want to talk about any test results, didn't want to hear anything that could be . . . scary. She gulped, willing her heart to slow down. The instinct to message Alice and Stephanie cropped up. They could help her relax, to get perspective. But she didn't want to worry them; they were so far away.

Mo is close by.

She could call him. She could even ask him to go with her to the appointment so she would feel less alone. But she didn't want to put that on him. While things were going quite well, she didn't . . . that would be a very deep form of vulnerability and Jess couldn't show that. Even though she doubted that he would see her being vulnerable with him as a weakness.

He might appreciate it.

Tossing her phone on the bed, she stood, shaking her head hard.

No. I'm an adult. I can handle this on my own.

Hair dried and fresh pajamas on, she settled at her dining table to do some work for the coming week. She was in the middle of grading a fourth paper when her focus was shattered by her phone buzzing loudly with an incoming call. She reached to pick it up but knocked over the stack of papers she'd left near the edge of the table. Cursing, she tried to pick them up and answer at the same time. She did so without looking at the caller ID.

"Hi, Jess," her mom said softly. "I . . . I was hoping we could talk."

Jess stiffened at the sound of her mom's voice but decided to stay polite. "What about?" she asked cautiously.

Her mom hesitated for a moment. "Um . . . it was wonderful seeing you when you came back. But that was months ago. We missed you so much while you were in England and were so happy that you'd be close by again," she said before clearing her throat. "We'd love for you to come home for a visit."

Jess was quiet at first. As usual, her mother was ignoring something that she didn't want to see. Her last visit to pick up some things had not been *wonderful.* Her father's habitual coldness had hardened into veiled hostility, and her mother's clinginess had been suffocating. Jess hadn't been able to breathe the whole time she was in the house. Alice had said that their behavior might have been due to grief, but Jess would not take responsibility for fixing that. They hadn't even taken responsibility for ignoring the warning signs in Cassie's relationship and for ignoring Jess's concerns about it. Just that February, Jess had called their mother, worried because she was having more and more trouble reaching Cassie. Her mom had said she'd make the drive from Rockford to Detroit to see Cassie herself, since she wasn't answering her calls, either. But she hadn't. Then April rolled around, and it had been too late. Her parents had done nothing, and her sister was gone.

But bringing any of that up at the moment would just lead to an argument, one Jess simply did not have the energy for. Alice's and Stephanie's latest encouragements to see her parents came back to her. They'd said that doing so might help her. Jess wanted to brush aside the idea that it would, but her friends were wise. Jess seriously doubted that she was ready.

She sighed. "I don't think that's a good idea," she said, trying to sound kind.

Her mom sighed, too, and tried again, pleadingly. "I know you're mad at your dad," she said. "But I can make sure he doesn't get angry when you come home."

Jess tensed up. There was no way her mother could keep him from getting angry. A dull ache blossomed in her shoulders and neck; her jaw felt locked shut. She forced herself to speak.

"He has no reason to be angry with me," Jess spat out before taking another deep breath. Alice popped into her head again. "But I'll think about it."

Jess ended the call before any more could be said. Once she placed her phone on the table, her hands began visibly shaking, her chest got tight, and a headache slammed into her temples. But she wasn't going to cry.

The thought of reaching out to Mo whispered across her mind, but she couldn't. She was too raw; she couldn't show that weakness. Her parents needed to stay in their box in her mind and feelings, Mo in his.

She pulled a file folder of student tests in front of her. Grabbing her pen, one tear tumbled onto her cheek. She swatted it away and opened the folder.

A wave of guilt was waiting for Jess when she crawled under the covers that night. She'd been fighting hard against guilt for months. Most of the time she won, but now, seeing how everything was moving on—life, the rest of the world, moving forward even though Cassie was gone—the guilt of living her life in a world without her sister was overtaking her. She was back here, in the States, in the city Cassie had moved to with her husband and that Jess had chosen so she could be with Cassie again. But her sister was no longer here, and time was forcing Jess to live each day getting further and further away from Cassie's presence. Maybe she had gone to the restaurant Jess and Mo had, but now there was no way for Jess to know that, to know if her footsteps were falling in the same places Cassie's had. Jess was going to participate in a Ren Faire. Be a Rennie. Something Cassie had apparently been but that Jess hadn't known about. It was like she was taking the place Cassie had been torn from. Jess rolled onto her side, grabbing a pillow to press against her aching stomach. And it sounded like her parents were trying to move on, too, if they wanted to have a visit and play happy family with Jess as though Cassie's sweet, conciliating temperament hadn't been the only reason that Jess and her father had ever been able to sit down at a table together.

Think of something else. Or the crying will start and never stop.

She snatched her phone off the nightstand. Unlocking it, she saw the preview of a message from Mo. The tears burned her nose. How could she even think about having a relationship when her sister no longer had the possibility of experiencing a good one? She tried to whisk the notifications away but clicked on one instead. A Google photos reminder of This Day one year ago. She felt like she was being strangled. She and Cassie, when Jess had come home for a quick visit. She swiped fast at a tear that had fallen. It didn't make sense; there had to be some mistake. A year couldn't have already passed since the last day she and Cassie sat together, in the same place. They were both smiling, making silly faces. Jess wanted to stop breathing. Stop breathing and escape from the pain. Then she remembered that Cassie had teased her about starting a relationship that day. About Jess always restricting her emotions and not having fun in life. She'd told Jess that she wanted to see her happy with someone. Cassie needed to see it. Jess swallowed. She'd completely forgotten. Steinem came walking up her leg, onto her hip. He stretched himself out on top of her. She could hear and feel him purring.

My sister, my first friend, told me she needed to see me happy with someone. Maybe . . .

Out of all the photos she could have happened upon, out of all the memories, it had to be one in the dress she'd worn on her first date with Mo. The dress she'd put on, wondering if Cassie would like Mo, too. Jess wasn't a believer in signs, but it felt like Cassie had just answered her question. Like she'd told Jess that she approved.

Steinem stretched and yawned. He looked at her with his "silly human" face.

I guess I should stop hesitating with Mo. Maybe it's worth the risk to accelerate things with him, to truly let him in.

She slid her fingertip down her sister's face on the screen.

Maybe I should listen to my sister.

CHAPTER SIXTEEN

Mo

During a lull in activity at his shop, Mo slid his phone out of his pocket and checked to see if he had any notifications. All he saw was his home screen. He'd sent Jess a text the previous evening, checking in and asking how her meeting with the archers had gone. She usually replied in less than an hour, but it was ten A.M. and he hadn't heard from her.

Probably busy. I'm sure everything's fine.

He was working with one of his apprentices, going through the checklist he had created for trainees. He had been very satisfied with her work thus far and didn't feel the need to watch her every move. What he did feel was a stronger and stronger urge to get in touch with Jess. Like other times that he'd felt the need to reach out to a family member and had found out that something was wrong, he just couldn't set the feeling aside.

"Grace," he said, tapping on the apprentice's shoulder. "Be right back."

As he walked to his office, he searched his mind, trying to name the exact feeling that was welling up inside. It wasn't quite anxiety; it wasn't fear. It was a clear need to hear Jess's voice to be sure that she was okay. He closed the door to his shop and leaned against it, pulling his phone from his pocket, then he dialed Jess's number.

"Hey," she answered after the second ring.

The uncomfortable feeling abated.

"Hi," he said. "How's it going?"

The line was silent a moment.

"Um." She sighed. "Good, I guess."

The feeling came back. Her tone was wrong, her voice too quiet.

"Am I interrupting you?" he asked.

"No, no, not at all," she said. "I came into work to get ahead on some things. Sorry, by the way. I saw your text from last night. I was going to text you back, but I kind of got lost in everything."

Something was definitely off. She sounded defeated.

"That's okay," he said. "We still on for dinner tonight?"

"Oh, yes, absolutely," she said.

He hesitated between asking if something was wrong and not prying. He hated it when other people pried with him, and he did his best to avoid doing it to someone else.

"Are you sure you want me to come over?" he asked. "I can make you dinner at my place if you want."

"No. I'm really happy to have you come over," she said. "Let's not change anything."

"Okay," he said, hoping his smile came through the phone. "Be there at seven?"

"At seven," she said.

At 6:53 that evening, Mo parked his truck at the curb in front of Jess's house. The tag at the collar of his Henley kept annoying him. He hadn't worn it in a long time and had forgotten to cut out the tag. At least unbuttoning it a bit had slackened the collar. He repositioned the bouquet of Maiden Pinks on the passenger seat. During his "hopeless romantic yet terrified of big feelings" period as a teenager, he'd learned the meanings of at least fifty flowers. The plan had been to tell a girl how he felt without having to experience the muscle-burning fear of saying the words. It had fallen flat since he'd been the only one to know the meanings. He'd chosen Maiden Pinks because they signified admiration. She probably wouldn't know that, but he liked making the gesture.

He'd considered pink roses, as they also meant admiration, but he'd been worried that their additional meaning of blossoming love might be too forward.

Why are you winding yourself up? She wouldn't jump to conclusions.

He was certainly falling for Jess, though. Even though he'd grown more confident about being open with Jess, he was still finding his feet with his own reactions. His mind interpreted his body's involuntary responses to Jess, like his heart racing or his breath catching, as mortal danger. Going slowly had given him time and space to understand that he was actually safe and that he didn't need to run away. If anything, he wanted to keep moving closer. He checked the time again. Six fifty-six. When she wasn't around, he was always thinking of her, remembering something she'd said, her determination, her laugh. That determination was lacking in her voice earlier in the day. Was it the Ren Faire situation? Now that she'd spent time with the other archers, maybe she felt resigned or sad. He checked again. Six fifty-eight. He got out of his truck, carefully taking the flowers with him. He took his time getting to her door. It opened as soon as he reached it.

"There you are," she said, smiling. "Did you need a little more time on the phone?"

"On the phone?" he asked.

"Oh, I thought that's why you were in your truck for so long. It wasn't?" She waved him inside.

"Ah," he said, realizing he may have made himself look like a stalker.

"No, not on the phone. I didn't want to ring the doorbell early. Here," he said to Jess, offering the flowers as he crossed the threshold. "These are for you."

She smiled, accepting them and closing the door.

"It would have been okay if you were a few minutes early." She shifted the flowers to one arm. "You didn't have to," she said, nodding at them. Mo's jitteriness had abated enough once she'd smiled at the flowers for him to focus on her vibe. She sounded good, but not quite like herself. As she went into the kitchen for a vase, her cat, Steinem, ambled his way over before sitting down and looking up at Mo, sniffing the air in his direction.

"Flowers are always good," Mo called to her. "Hi, Steinem," he said, smiling at the cat. "It's nice to finally meet you."

The cat meowed once.

"I've heard nothing but good things," Mo said to Steinem. Jess laughed from the kitchen. Her laughter felt right.

"Don't lie to him, Mo!" she called out. "Grab a seat on the couch."

Mo laughed and followed her instructions. Steinem joined him, walking at his side. When Mo sat down, Steinem sat beside his feet and looked at him.

"You know, you're an especially dapper tuxedo cat," Mo said to Steinem. He smiled when the cat raised his chin and meowed back. It almost seemed like the cat had smiled. Mo turned to Jess as she joined him, handing him a glass of sparkling water. He thanked her.

"Listen," he said. "I know we talked about it, and I appreciate you keeping in mind that I don't do well with a lot of people. Dinner and a movie here is great, but we can also go out for our dates. I don't want you to feel boxed in here or at my house."

Jess waved the idea away.

"Going out can be fun," she said, squeezing his hand. "But I'm basically a homebody. My friends used to have to drag me out of my apartment in England. Besides, we can watch a movie here without having to—"

Steinem jumped onto Mo's lap. He made a trilling sound, so Mo started scratching under his chin, then behind his ear.

"Where do you prefer your scritches?" Mo asked him. "Behind this ear? Maybe on the back of your neck?" He kept scratching, and Steinem began to purr. He noticed that Jess wasn't saying anything.

"I'm sorry," he said. "I was listening to you. As long as you're comfortable staying in, I'm happy with that." Steinem moved closer, bumping his head on Mo's chest. He kept scratching down Steinem's back. Jess was staring at them.

"Is everything okay?" Mo asked.

"Uh . . . It usually takes a lot more time for Steinem to warm up to somebody. When we were in England, the fastest he allowed a new person to pet him was like three days. And he certainly wouldn't approach someone right after they walked through the door. Normally, he hides."

"Oh," Mo said. "Animals usually like me. They often seek me out. And I like animals a lot, so it's nice."

He continued scratching, enjoying the low vibration of Steinem's purring. Watching them, Jess shook her head and picked up her glass with a little smile.

"I still can't believe that we both love *The Princess Bride*," she said.

Mo nodded, smiling back. That had been a lovely thing to discover when they'd been trying to decide on the movie for that evening. Steinem stood on Mo's lap suddenly, turning on himself and curling into a ball. That made him chuckle. He looked back at Jess.

"Makes for an easy movie night choice," he said.

"It does," she said. "But there's a problem."

"What's that?" he asked. Her tone had him a little concerned.

"I'm hungry," she said. "I know we said movie first, then dinner, but I don't want my stomach growling while we watch."

Mo laughed.

"Sounds like dinner first, then," he said.

Leaving her glass on the coffee table, Jess reached out and scooped up Steinem. She stood. The cat protested.

"Sorry, Sty Sty," she said. "Mo and I gotta eat."

Jess had already set the table, but Mo insisted on doing something to help, so he carefully brought the serving bowl of soup from the kitchen to the dining table.

"It smells delicious," Mo said as he sat in the seat beside hers. "Did I tell you I'm a big fan of soup?"

"No," she said. "But that tracks."

Mo didn't quite follow. She shrugged.

"Soup is warm, comforting," she said, ladling some into her bowl. "If you can call a whole type of food comforting. It's mellow. You're mellow. It fits." She winked at him and picked up her spoon. "Let's see if it came out all right."

Mo nodded and took a large spoonful. It was more flavorful than he'd expected, and he savored it, while taking the opportunity to check Jess's vibe again. It was much better than earlier that day, but something still wasn't right.

"This is amazing," he said. "But how do you get it so . . . detailed?" He chuckled. "That doesn't seem like the right word."

Jess swallowed her mouthful.

"The key is using whole herbs, except the root. Some people feel they're too strong, but you don't keep them in the pot the whole time. You cook them inside a cheesecloth, checking the intensity as you go. That's how my mom . . . does it." Her face fell when she said "mom," but she seemed to pull herself in and quickly took another spoonful.

There were two ways he could go about this. She'd never mentioned her mom before and maybe that was because it would lead to her sister. Mo could either ask some gentle questions or be direct. Jess was usually direct; he'd take a chance. He put his spoon down.

"Do you want to talk about it?" he asked.

"About what?" She took another spoonful.

He leaned back in his chair, resting his hands in his lap.

"It seems like something's wrong," he said.

"Something's wrong?" More soup.

"You aren't yourself," he said.

She stopped, about to dip her spoon in again.

"What do you mean?" she asked, not looking up.

"You don't have to tell me if you don't want to," he said. "But it feels like something's been wrong since this morning. You sounded defeated on the phone."

She rested her spoon against the bowl and sighed.

"It's hard for me," she said.

"What is?"

"Talking about my family, about what I feel." She looked up at him. He was astonished to see tears in her eyes. That wasn't Jess at all. "We don't have a good . . ." She sighed. "My sister . . . Cassie—Cassandra—would have wanted me to," she said, voice strained.

Hesitantly, he reached for her hand.

"Thank you," he said.

"For what?" she asked, letting him close his hand around hers.

"That's the first time you've told me her name."

A single tear rolled down her cheek. She rubbed it away with her free hand. He could feel her struggling, so he thought it was best to be indirect.

"Tell me more about what she liked," he said.

"What she liked?" Jess asked.

Mo nodded.

"You told me about the Ren Faires, but what else?"

Jess tilted her head to the side then squinted, the tears in her eyes shimmering.

"She *adored* doing Children's Story Hour at the public library, where she worked. She always said that reading to the children was the best part of her job. She'd even dress up, get multiple uses out of her Ren Faire garb. She also had other costumes for other sorts of stories."

Jess laughed once, the previous sadness on her face giving way to nostalgia.

"It makes sense, if you think about it. She was the 'dress up' sister. When we were kids, she'd make costumes out of anything. For her, for me. Even for our dog. Very on brand for Cassie to find ways to wear costumes as frequently as possible." Jess smiled at him, but it was a broken smile. He smiled back and began stroking the back of her hand with his thumb.

"Cassie was a librarian?"

Jess nodded, whisking away another tear.

"A children's librarian," she said, smiling. "She loved books and kids and . . . God, I feel so guilty."

Mo had wanted to ask if Jess knew the name of the branch of the library where Cassie had worked. He'd taken Maddie to Children's Story Hour, and she'd loved it. There was a small possibility that he'd crossed paths with Cassie. But Jess feeling guilty was a more important issue. He needed to tread lightly with an emotion as weighty as guilt. Especially after the shift from the positivity of happy nostalgia. He didn't see what she had to feel guilty about, and he wanted to push the feeling off of her, but he didn't want to approach it in a way that made her feel invalidated.

"Jess," he whispered, leaning closer. "Would you help me? I don't understand what you feel guilty about."

Jess slumped forward. She put her elbow on the table and supported her forehead with her hand.

"I'm . . . I'm kind of taking her place, a place that was once hers and never can be again," she said. "It's wrong; I'm wrong. I've been wrong on so many levels when it comes to her."

He began to rub her back softly.

"I didn't . . ." He needed to pause for a breath because her distress was tightening his throat. He cleared it. "I didn't have the privilege of knowing her, so I can't say what she would think. I am confused, though. Why do you feel that you were wrong?" he asked.

Jess sighed and sat up. She still had a firm grip on his hand.

"Because I didn't see the signs. Well, looking back, I can see some. But I'd just thought he was a garden variety asshole. At the time, I wasn't paying enough attention to realize what was going on. Like you did," she said.

Mo didn't follow. How could he have paid attention?

"Um . . ." he said. "What—"

"The woman with the car, with the tracker," Jess said. "You recognized what it could mean." She took a deep breath and sighed.

Again, Mo was a little lost. Then it clicked.

"Ah," Mo said. He squeezed her hand. She winced a little, so he loosened it. "Your sister was a victim of intimate partner violence?" he asked softly.

Jess nodded. Then a short, dry laugh seemed to escape her.

"Depends on who you ask," she said. "There were signs—first physical isolation, then policing her appearance, pushing her to lose weight when she really didn't need to. I was too far away to see the changes happening, but as she became more and more difficult to reach after being in near constant contact our whole lives, I began to think that something was wrong. My parents disagreed."

Jess narrowed her eyes and shifted, letting out a light cough before she continued.

"She died in a car accident. But I don't think it truly was one. It was his fault. He was driving, and he survived. Cassie didn't. The elephant in the room is that they'd been fighting in the car at the time. My mother waited until well after the funeral to mention that Cassie's husband liked to drive aggressively to scare her when they fought in the car. And somehow, he always ended up starting a fight with her in the car." Jess was completely slumped in her chair. Mo didn't know what to do or say. Tiny, spiky sparkles of ice bloomed over every inch of his skin, each fiber of his muscles. Breathing was of no interest to him. Just a yearning to say something that would help even though he understood that nothing truly could. Jess moved a bit like she was uncomfortable.

"I . . . I am so sorry, Jess," he whispered. She readjusted her hand in his and squeezed it hard. He squeezed back.

"Do you want to go sit on the couch?" he asked.

"Yeah."

He let go of her hand and followed her as she made her way over, Steinem staying at her side. When she sat, Mo got close, but not enough to crowd her.

Jess leaned into him, and he wrapped her in his arms. He took a deep breath. She wasn't crying, even though she had good reason to. She was breathing slow and deep with her head tucked into his shoulder. He stroked her beautiful sable hair. Sometimes it was good to be quiet. Just sit in sadness if necessary. So that's all he did, no more questions, no trying to get her to talk about it. He'd wait for her if she wanted to speak. After a little while, she raised her head to look at him.

"My mom called me yesterday," she said. "Wants me to come home for a visit. But it . . . it doesn't feel like home anymore. I've only been once since I got back from England." She gave him a wry smile. "Cassie sent me a message after my mom called. Or I'd like to think of it as a message from her."

Mo raised his eyebrows.

"What's that?" he asked.

She rested a hand on his cheek.

"To give you a chance. To stop holding back. It was a notification of some photos we'd taken a year ago. On the day she told me it was time for me to have a relationship. A real one. Not someone I hold at arm's length."

Mo didn't want to nod, concerned that she might take it as encouragement for her to let her hand slip from cradling his cheek. He smiled a little.

"Do you agree with her?" he asked.

"I do," she said, leaning in to kiss him, her hand sliding down to his chest.

He was thrilled to be kissed, as he always was when they did. But there was a tiny worry that she was kind of displacing emotions, and she might regret it later. He gently took her hand in his again and pulled back a little.

"Are you sure?" he whispered. "You've had a heavy day."

"I have," she whispered back. "But I trust you; I feel safe. And I've wanted a lot more for a while now."

Mo's brain stuttered for a moment. She couldn't mean . . . then she was kissing him again.

CHAPTER SEVENTEEN

Jess

Jess felt warm for the first time since the previous afternoon. The soup had helped a little, but kissing Mo made things much better. The gentle scratch of his beard on her palm, the heat from his body drawing her closer and pushing away the chill that had settled in her bones. She knew he wouldn't take the lead in deepening the kiss, so she did, nudging his lips open with her own. She shifted closer, nearly in his lap, and ran her hand into his wavy hair. He groaned, and she felt the sound moving through her, shuffling away the last traces of sadness. After a moment's hesitation, she pulled back enough to look him in the eye.

"Ready?" she asked.

"Uh . . ."

She shifted quickly, straddling his lap. The shock on his face made her laugh.

"Mo," she said. "You look a little scared."

"I . . ." His cheeks reddened as he chuckled and tipped his chin down. "I've never been the most comfortable leading, the uh . . . dance," he said. "It doesn't mean I don't want to."

"Ah," she said, taking his hands and putting them on her thighs. "Well, leading doesn't bother me one bit." She slid one hand up his arm, savoring his impressive biceps, and well-muscled shoulder. She used the fingertips of the other to caress his chest.

He was completely still, searching her eyes. She flattened her hand on his chest; his heart was pounding. She leaned closer.

"Mo," she whispered, smiling. "Why don't—"

He lurched forward, wrapping an arm around her lower back and sliding his hand into the base of her hair as he pulled her into another kiss. But it wasn't like the ones they'd shared before. This was much deeper, much more passionate. This was a different Mo and she liked it very much. She pressed herself hard against him, running both hands through his hair, dragging her nails on his scalp. He shivered and groaned but didn't let his lips leave hers. Trying to match his energy, she found herself quickly out of breath and needing much more of him. She leaned back and he loosened his grip, going along with her to continue kissing her. Pulling her lips away, she pushed him enough to make a little space.

"Wait," she breathed, grabbing the hem of her shirt and ripping it off.

His eyes went wide as his gaze fell to her chest.

"Jess," he panted.

"Mo," she breathed back, lunging at him again, greedy for his lips. Her hands back on his chest, she tugged at the collar of his Henley, unbuttoning the last button. He understood and leaned forward, pulling where it was tucked into his jeans, but he still had an arm around her, keeping her from falling off his lap. She chuckled lightly and helped him get rid of it. Suddenly, there wasn't any air in the room. She hadn't been prepared. Of course, she'd guessed, but he looked like he lived in the gym.

"Damn, Mo," she said, running two fingers down the dark, wiry hair between his muscles.

He chuckled.

"It's a 'damn' situation from my perspective, too."

She laughed.

"I am enjoying myself," she said. "But I think we could find somewhere more comfortable."

"And where would that be?" he asked.

For a second, she didn't understand. She thought what she said was pretty clear. Unless he wanted to do it on the couch or something.

"Um . . . my bedroom," she said.

"And where's that?"

"It's uh . . . down the hall." She gestured over her shoulder.

"Got it," he said, sliding his hands under her thighs and tipping her against him before he stood with her in his arms. She couldn't contain her laughter as she wrapped her legs around his waist again, linking her fingers behind his neck as she held on.

"This again?" she asked. "Do you like picking me up?"

"Do you like it when I pick you up?" he asked.

Stifling a giggle, she nodded.

"Off we go?" he asked, smiling broadly.

"Off we go," she said, still laughing.

A small part of her chided herself for turning into a giggly teenager. But she pushed that thought aside as he wound around her coffee table and started down the hall. She should enjoy all of this, even if she turned into a cliché. She leaned in to get another kiss but kept it brief so he could see where he was going.

"Straight back," she said as they got closer. Once they'd crossed the threshold, she caught the switch and turned the light on.

He walked around to the side of the bed and started to sit her down, but she began kissing him again and tightened her grip on his waist. He chuckled against her lips and laid her down on her back, resting a hand on the bed. He was close, but she wanted him closer. She tugged a little on his shoulder, but he broke the kiss.

"I don't want to crush you," he said.

"Who said I wouldn't like to be crushed?"

He raised an eyebrow, freeing his other arm so that he could stay close, but still off her.

"I'm a big guy," he said.

"That's an understatement," she said, laughing. "But I won't break."

He leaned in, resting his weight on his forearms.

"Still, I—"

She cut him off by grinding herself hard against his waist. The position wasn't right, but the message was. He groaned and shifted his weight so he could scratch his hand down her still-covered thigh. She took it as a cue to take off her jeans. As she slid her hands to her belt, he shook his head.

"I think it's time for a little slow again," he said.

Jess didn't follow until he burrowed into her neck. She let her hands go slack. He took his time, kissing and whispering along her skin from the bottom of her neck to the base of her ear.

"What does Jess like?" he whispered. He found a sensitive spot and Jess moaned. "Ah," he said. "There's a good one." He nuzzled into the same spot, kissing and nibbling. She shuddered, and he dragged his tongue across it. She moaned again, turning her head to give him better access.

"Why do you always smell so delicious?" he asked, continuing his search for sensitive spots. "Vanilla," he sighed. "Like . . . cookies."

Jess gulped. Heartache tinged the arousal that had been building.

"You like it?" she asked, voice tight. He looked up.

"I love it," he said, searching her eyes. His brow knitted together.

"Good," she said, pulling him close again. He resisted.

He kissed her chest but didn't lose eye contact. "Why wouldn't I like it, Jess?" he asked softly.

She took a deep breath and rolled her lips. Her nose stung.

"It's . . . I don't think it's really me, but . . . it was a present from . . ." She took a breath. "This way she's always—"

"Always with you?" he asked, grazing her cheek with his thumb.

She nodded. He shifted closer, tucking his cheek against hers.

"She made a good choice. I'll have to thank her," he whispered into her ear. Her eyes burned, and she swallowed hard.

"Do you need to stop?" he asked. She shook her head hard. Her emotions were all jumbled up, but she'd been wanting this to happen for too long to let him walk away. She tightened her legs around him.

"No," she said. "You stop and I'll have to threaten to shoot you again."

He chuckled, nipping at her earlobe, then moved to the other side, his beard grazing her collarbone, sending chills over her skin. She giggled. He looked up.

"What was that?" he asked, smiling.

"Your beard," she said. "I wasn't expecting it."

"Not expecting good, or not expecting bad?"

"Oh, very good," she whispered.

He grinned broadly and swept the edges of his beard across her chest. She gasped again, and he chuckled. She decided she loved feeling his deep laugh even more than hearing it.

"My turn," she said, tugging at one shoulder and pushing the other until he rolled along with her and settled on his back. He laughed.

"This seems more like you," he said, smiling.

"Does it?" she asked before kissing him briefly and nuzzling into his neck. She kissed just under his ear, then dragged her open lips down to his shoulder. He shuddered and groaned deep while tracing his fingertips down her back. She nipped him with her teeth, and he laughed again.

"You know," he said, nudging her head with his so she would raise it and look at him. "It's uh . . . I'm out of practice."

She kissed his chest and pulled back again.

"It's been a while for me, too," she said. "But I think it's like riding a bike. Well, I'll be the one doing the riding." She winked at him.

His laugh bounced off the walls, and she laughed, too. But she was impatient.

She reached behind her and undid her bra. The straps slipped down, and she held the cups in place. "Ready?"

Looking very solemn, he nodded once. She pushed a bit of nervousness aside and threw her bra across the room. Mo didn't move. She wondered if he was breathing.

"Are you all right?" she asked, throat suddenly dry.

"I'm more than all right," he said gruffly. He slid his hands up the sides of her torso, pulling her to him as he leaned up. He caught one of her nipples in his mouth and sucked. She moaned and leaned into him farther. He sucked gently, then let go to swirl his tongue around her nipple, groaning deep again. He took her breast in his hand, massaging, as he moved to the other nipple and hungrily took it into his mouth. He massaged and sucked, and Jess thought she was going to go out of her mind. As he thumbed one nipple and sucked the other, he groaned like he was starving.

"God, you're beautiful," he whispered quickly as he moved from one to the other.

Jess would have thanked him, but words were gone; she could only answer with moans.

"Your skin is perfection," he said as he shifted again. "All of it." He caressed her side.

She wanted to stop him so she could do the same to him, but she felt weak. Mustering the strength to sit up a little, she put a hand on his chest.

"Thank you," she breathed. "I think we're overdressed." She rolled off him, onto her back and went for her belt and zipper. As he did the same, she caught a glimpse of a very substantial bulge. She ripped her jeans off and started to take off her panties, but Mo grunted.

"Will you let me do the honors?" he asked.

To her complete shock, she felt bashful.

"Um . . . sure," she said, lifting her hands.

Mo shimmied out of his jeans and boxer briefs, and Jess's heart stopped. He was big all over.

"Uh . . ." she said.

He stroked himself once and looked a little embarrassed.

"Yeah," he said. "It's been a problem in the past. All the more reason for you to be on top. You'll control how deep I go."

Jess swallowed around the lump of intimidation in her throat.

"Yes," she said. "You're right."

"My turn?" he asked, sliding onto his knees on the floor. He gently pushed her legs together. She didn't get why until she remembered the picnic. He ate slowly, savored his food. He was being consistent. Placing his hands on each ankle, he slowly drew his fingertips up the outside of her legs. Chills ran all over her.

When he'd reached the sides of her panties, he hooked his fingers in them and slowly began pulling them down. She shifted so he could take them off but kept her legs together. When they were gone, he placed his hands on her knees and looked up at her. He smiled. Following his gentle lead, she let her legs fall open. He sighed.

"My orchids have nothing on you, Jess," he said, gazing between her legs. If Mo, a man who adored plants, was complimenting her in that way, it was high praise. Her skin warmed. He pressed a soft kiss into the inside of one knee. Then another a little bit higher on the opposite thigh. He turned to do the same on the first, but she leaned up to stop him with a hand on his shoulder.

"Not now," she panted. "Another time. Right now, I want you inside me."

"Your wish is my command," he said, mouthing her thigh again. She twisted herself to reach her nightstand. Thankfully, she'd bought two boxes of condoms. One the regular size, the other extra-large. She got that box open as he began kissing up her stomach, reaching one breast. He slowly licked the underside. She grabbed a condom, but her hands were shaky, and she dropped the box, spilling them all over. He chuckled.

"I do have a good bit of stamina," he said. "But not that much."

She laughed.

"Something tells me it's safer to only go one round with you." She shot a glance at his crotch. He grinned as he clambered back onto the middle of the bed. He stretched out beside her.

"Have your way with me, m'lady. And we'll see if that's true."

She laughed again.

"M'lady?" she asked. "Never been called that before."

"Since we're on this Ren Faire adventure, I'd say it fits," he said, winking at her.

"Makes sense," she said, smiling.

She knelt beside him and handed him the condom. He barely had it on before she straddled him again.

"Riding a bike," she repeated, reaching back to grab him.

"Riding a—" Mo groaned, and his eyes fluttered shut as she guided him inside.

Jess needed a second, too. She sighed as she settled onto him, before bringing his hands to her hips.

"Let's go," she breathed, not recognizing her own voice. She began to move, anchoring herself with both hands on his chest. Mo's eyes were darker, his breath keeping time with each of her strokes. After a minute or two, he let go of one hip to cup and massage her breast.

"Yeah," she breathed. He squeezed and began dragging his thumb back and forth across her nipple. Her pleasure doubled. She began riding faster and he blew a stream of air out of his pursed lips. She could feel the pressure building. Leaning back, she put a hand on his thigh to stay balanced. Her cries became more desperate when he began moving his hips to meet her thrusts.

"God yes, Mo," she panted.

"That's it, Jess," he said through gritted teeth.

Hands on her hips again, he began bucking harder, faster to meet her.

"Mo," she cried. "So close."

"Don't hold back," he growled. "I can feel you."

She leaned forward again, hands on his chest and broke, the orgasm exploding and tearing through her body. Her eyes rolled back, and her arms gave out. She fell into his chest. His arms wrapped around her, and she felt him kiss her head before he groaned long and deep and his hips stuttered a jerky rhythm.

Neither of them moved as they caught their breath. Then Mo slid a hand in her hair and ran his fingers down its length. She began drawing gentle circles on his skin. Closing her eyes, she focused on the rise and fall of his chest, the beating of his heart. She was in the perfect place, the frustration over the Ren Faires, even the almost ever-present pain in her body gone. She felt safe and free and as light as she did when she was with Cassie.

Maybe that's the feeling Cassie wanted me to have.

"Are you okay?" Mo asked softly.

She lifted her head to look at him.

"I'm great," she said.

"Me too. But are you sure it was enough?" he asked.

She didn't quite follow. He looked like a worried little kid.

"Enough?" she asked.

"Yeah," he said, his fingers still gliding through her hair. "You only came once, I think."

"Only once?" she chuckled. "Please don't tell me that you feel like you have to make a quota."

He smiled.

"I want you to be satisfied," he said.

"Oh, I am, Mo," she said, resting her head against his chest again. "Very satisfied."

CHAPTER EIGHTEEN

Mo

M o hated leaving Jess, but a client was coming in early for his car the next morning and if he didn't sleep in his own bed, he'd be useless. He tucked away his smile again as he unlocked his front door. There wasn't anything wrong with feeling a little bashful, a little happy. But he felt like his emotions would have him jittery and far too distracted if he couldn't keep a rein on things. He looked into Maddie's empty room quickly and went straight to his own for a shower. Climbing into bed, he realized that he hadn't checked on his plants, but now he was too comfortable; he wasn't getting out of bed. There was one thing that was still bugging him a little. He wasn't 100 percent sure that Jess hadn't accelerated things because she was in a bad place emotionally.

What if I did take advantage of her? Even just a little?

He rolled onto one side, then the other. He realized he hadn't texted her good night, so he grabbed his phone.

Mo:

Good night m'lady

She might have been asleep already; she'd said she was bone tired when he left. He reached over to put his phone down when it buzzed in his hand.

Jess:

> Do I have an official nickname
> now?

He smiled.

Mo:

> Sure

Jess:

> Then I wish you good night, m'lord

He chuckled but paused before replying. There was something he'd meant to bring up after the movie, but they hadn't gotten around to it.

Mo:

> M'lady. What if you dressed as
> Westley?

Jess:

> Westley?

> Well, Westley as the Dread Pirate
> Roberts. From the Princess Bride.
> For your garb. You could move
> around easily to shoot without
> worrying about how your clothes
> are moving around.

Doug had emailed garb suggestions a week earlier. All the choices for women had been oversexualized, and the blacksmith suggestions had been fire hazards. Mo and Jess had vented their frustrations to each other during a video date. They were moving closer and closer to the event, but it had been nice for Mo to keep it from his mind as much as possible. Being confronted with choosing garb had forced it to the forefront, along with the steely-cold tension of anticipatory anxiety that flared in his jaw whenever he imagined how it would go.

Right then, there had been a long pause between Mo's last message and the little ellipsis starting on his screen. Mo's throat was a little tight. He worried that he'd insulted her by suggesting she dress like a man, before her reply appeared.

Jess:

That is an *excellent* idea, Fezzik the Giant.

Fezzik?

Mo:

?

It's a basic costume. No billowing sleeves. Should be safe near fire.

She was right about the sleeves. And Mo liked basic. He smiled.

Mo:

Sounds like a plan.

She sent a smiling emoji.

The idea to say something about dressing up together and having fun together like she had with Cassie passed through his mind. But he didn't know if bringing it up would raise positive feelings or painful ones. He decided to let it rest.

Mo:

Then I wish you a good night, m'lady Roberts.

Laughing emojis appeared.

Jess:

> Good night m'lord Fezzik.

He sent a winking emoji back.

He felt better, but there was still a lingering doubt about how things had gone. Jess had already said that she was doing something she'd wanted to do for a long time. She knew her own mind, he wasn't going to ask again just because he was having difficulty processing. But he also knew that he would still be looking up at the ceiling ruminating in an hour or two if he didn't talk out his concerns with someone else.

"What's wrong?" Khalil said immediately after answering the phone.

"Why?" asked Mo.

"It is well past your bedtime. The last time you called this late, Grandpa was dying. Before that, you were at the ER with Mads for appendicitis. So who is it? I'm ready."

Mo rolled his eyes. But Khalil wasn't wrong about it being late.

"I'm sorry—"

"Oh God, it's Mom. It's Mom, isn't it? What happened? Was it an accident? She always drives too—"

"Khalil, shut up," Mo snapped. "No one is dying. I'm calling because I'm confused about something."

The line was silent for a few moments.

"You are calling this late because you're *confused*? You. Calling *me*. 'Cause you're confused?" Khalil asked.

Mo suppressed a growl of frustration.

"Fine," he said. "Confused probably isn't the right word. Unsure is better."

"What the hell?" Khalil asked. "Mister Big Brother, always

certain he's right in any circumstance is un . . . Wait a minute. It's about Jess, isn't it?"

Mo's skin flashed hot. He ran his nails through his beard.

"Yes."

"What happened?" Khalil asked.

Mo was stuck. He didn't want to say the precise words of what had happened, but he needed to share at least a general idea so Khalil could actually help.

"Let's just say," he grumbled, "that things have accelerated, but I'm concerned about the circumstances before it happened."

"Before it happened?" Khalil asked. "Oh! *It?*"

Mo sighed.

"Yes, it happened."

"I told you she was into you! This is awesome, Big Brother. Good on you."

Something about that rubbed Mo the wrong way. Like he'd attained some impossible achievement. He grunted because he didn't know what to say.

"Are you guys a thing?" Khalil asked.

Mo figured that he was right, especially since nicknames were now involved. But he hadn't asked Jess if she was okay with it being an official thing, so he certainly wasn't going down that road with Khalil.

"Let me get to the point," he said.

"Okay, shutting up," Khalil said.

That would be a miracle.

"She had a bad day yesterday. Some stuff with her family. We'd already planned dinner at her house tonight and when I got there, she was still upset. I'm worried that I took advantage of how down she was."

"Hmm," Khalil said. "Who made the first move?"

"Well, she kind of made all the moves, and I followed. I asked her if she was sure, and she said she was."

"So you're good," Khalil said. "Especially since she made the first move."

"I dunno."

"Okay. Wait and see about the next time," Khalil said.

"What do you mean?"

"Wait to see if she does the same thing. If she only turns to you when she's upset. Then you'll have your answer."

Mo considered for a moment. Maybe Khalil wasn't wrong. That was a reasonable way to know without bugging Jess. And Khalil did have a lot more experience with women than Mo did.

"Did you make sure she came first?" Khalil asked.

"Of course."

"Then she'll probably be eager for more. Wouldn't surprise me. Us Sarda men are gifted in the bedroom."

Mo's face caught fire, and he fought the urge to hide under his comforter.

"Can we please not?" he asked.

"God, you're shy. Can't even talk about it," Khalil said.

Mo cleared his throat.

"Okay," he said. "I'll consider your perspective."

"As you should," Khalil said. "But what about you?"

"Me?" Mo grunted.

"Are you good with how it went down? It sounds like you weren't expecting it to happen when it did," Khalil said.

He was right; Mo hadn't expected it at all that night, even though it was something he'd been quietly hoping for for a while. He'd been dampening his happiness about it by focusing on any bad feelings Jess might have.

"I wasn't," he said. "But I'm . . . happy it happened."

Khalil coughed.

"Happy?" he asked. "Did *you* just use the words 'I'm *happy*'?"

"Okay, I'm hanging up the phone now," Mo said.

"No, no, wait, this is a historic moment; I gotta write this down!" he laughed.

"Good night, Khalil," Mo said.

"Night, night, sleep tight," Khalil sing-songed.

Mo could hear the smile in his voice. He grunted again.

———

Late the next morning, Mo returned to the reception area of his shop and picked up the client orders that were sitting on Beverly's desk. She turned in her chair a little to face him and folded her hands in her lap.

"Mo," she said slowly. "Are you all right?"

"Um . . . yes, Bev," he said, confused. If anything, he was better than he'd been in a long time.

She tilted her head to one side and squinted at him.

"How's Maddie?" she asked.

"She's great," he said.

"Any new awards or achievements or anything? She's such a smart kid."

He did appreciate Bev asking about Maddie. She was kind and patient with her when she came into the shop. Bev always had a friendlier smile for Maddie than anyone else.

"No," he said. "Nothing new."

"Hmm . . . You've had a lot of pep in your step this morning," Bev said.

Mo wasn't sure what to do. His ears were beginning to burn, and his throat was dry.

"Have I?" he croaked.

Bev nodded slowly.

"Mmhmm . . ." she said. "It's been quite some time since I've seen you look so . . . happy."

Great. I said the word and now people can see it.

"Oh, um . . . that's good, I guess?"

"It's very good," she said. "But if it's not Maddie . . . I wonder, does it have something to do with that young lady who was in the other day when her engine wouldn't start? The one whose car you stayed late to finish?" He realized that she was fighting to keep her lips from spreading into a smile. He could cover up and say that it was something else, but Bev didn't miss a single thing that happened in his shop. She'd know that he was lying.

"Uh, yes," he said.

Bev's face lit up, and she gave him the smile she usually reserved for Maddie.

"That's excellent news, Mo. I'm very happy for you," she said.

His cheeks got warm, and he took a quick look around. There were only two people waiting on their cars. A very old man reading a newspaper and a young woman wearing headphones as she watched something on her phone. They were in the farthest seats from Bev's desk.

"Um, thanks," he said.

"Of course, Mo," she said. "Don't worry. That's all I'm going to say about that." She turned her chair back to her desk and resumed working on the forms in front of her. Mo walked back to his office, passing through the shop floor. He'd been tucking away thoughts of Jess as soon as they cropped up. It wasn't that he didn't want to think about her. He felt like his feelings were too big for him to concentrate on anything if he paid attention to them. He thought he'd done a good job of hiding what was going on inside, but evidently not.

Although Bev is always perceptive. She even notices if I'm getting sick before I realize it.

He put the client orders on his desk and felt like he should check his phone. To his very pleasant surprise there was a message from Jess.

Jess:

Good morrow, m'lord Fezzik. (did a little googling on Faire vocab, so I'm trying)

Mo:

Good morrow then, m'lady Roberts. I'm impressed with the effort.

Thanks. Just checking on you. Ready for photoshoot day?

Mo had been more than happy to be distracted from their photo-shoots scheduled for that weekend. But he couldn't continue ig-noring it if he wanted to get his hands on a Fezzik costume.

Mo:

I am not. At all.

Jess:

Is it being photographed or getting the garb?

YES

Jess replied with several laughing emojis.

Mo smiled, broad and free. Someone knocked on the not-quite-closed door.

"Hey, Mo," David said, pushing his way in. "I'm having trou-ble with the . . . Are you all right?"

Mo realized he'd looked up with the smile on his face. He quickly tucked it away.

"I'm fine," he grunted.

David blinked at him. "I don't think I've ever seen you smile before," he said, eyes wide.

Mo grunted again, narrowing his eyes.

"Right," David said. "I'll come back later." He left, closing the door behind him. A charge of embarrassment prickled Mo's scalp. He returned to his phone.

Jess:

My skin is itchy just thinking about it

Mo:

Same

Jess:

I'm sure you'll look great

Mo wanted to tell her that she always looked great no matter what, but he didn't want to be weird. But maybe that wouldn't be weird. They'd slept together. He should be able to compliment her. He started to say that, but the ellipsis started again.

Jess:

You probably don't need your official garb, since it's only advertising photos.

Mo:

You're probably right.

Class is starting in a minute, gonna go. Please don't stress too much about it today.

Okay, I won't.

She sent a winking emoji, and Mo smiled again. Then he tucked it away.

Mo:

Have a good day, m'lady.

Jess:

You too, m'lord

That evening, as he took a long shower and scrubbed the grime from under his nails, Mo finally felt like it was safe to let his feelings unfurl. Madison was at Diane's, so there wouldn't be any questions to answer. He didn't have to hide the fact that, now that he and Jess might be a thing, he didn't know what to do with himself.

He'd just sat down to trim and file his nails when he heard a crash and a muffled thud from next door. He snatched his keys off the hook and rushed over.

"Mrs. Sargysan!" he called out after letting himself in. At first there was no answer. He called out again as he started walking down the hall. He reached the kitchen and found her on the floor.

"Mrs. Sargysan are you all right?" he asked, kneeling down beside her. The kitchen light was off, the tablecloth and assorted broken dishes were on the floor. Mo pushed the upturned chair out of the way and leaned over her.

She groaned. Mo started breathing again. He took another look at her and all of her limbs were at the correct angles, so maybe she hadn't broken anything. She began to sit up.

"I don't think that's a good idea," he said. "Maybe lie still for another minute?"

"The floor is cold, Mo," she said, voice scratchy. "Are you really going to make an old woman lie on a cold floor?"

At least her spunk was intact.

"No, of course not," he said. "But what if your hip's broken?"

"Impossible," she said, grabbing his arm and pulling herself up. "That one's titanium."

Mo sat back on his heels and looked around again. The chair, the broken dishes. It was too dark to see well. He jumped up to flip the light switch, but nothing happened. He went back over and looked at the light fixture. No bulb. Then he caught sight of one in the corner on the floor and the pack of new bulbs on the counter.

"Mrs. Sargysan," he said. "Did you try to change the lightbulb?"

"So what if I did?" she said, still sitting on the floor. She reached for his hand.

"I don't want you to get up yet," he said.

"Who said you have a vote?" she asked, beginning to push herself up. He bent down to wrap his arm around her waist and lift her into the chair that was still upright.

"Are you sure you didn't break anything?" he asked, squatting in front of her. "Does anything hurt?"

"Mo, at my age, everything hurts. But nothing too out of the ordinary right now."

He couldn't tell if her color was right, but her breathing was back to normal. He frowned.

"Why didn't you call me? I was home," he said. She put a wrinkly hand on his shoulder.

"I'm not going to call you for every little thing, Mo," she said. "Besides, what if you were entertaining that young lady of yours?" She winked at him. "I hope things are progressing as they should."

His ears got hot.

Do I have a sign on my forehead?

He cleared his throat.

"Um . . ." he said. "Everything's fine. But how did you know?"

"Maddie told me you have a new friend. A woman." She shrugged.

"Oh," he said.

"She your girlfriend yet?"

His whole face lit into flames. He couldn't talk with Mrs. Sargysan about romantic *feelings*. He couldn't have a discussion that might make his shyness overwhelming and cause him to shut down. Shutting down with her would be disrespectful.

"Ha! Good," she said. "It's about time you had a little romance in your life. Good for Maddie, too."

"They haven't met yet," he said.

"That's not what I mean." She stretched her leg out and winced.

"I'm calling an ambulance," Mo said, standing quickly and sliding his phone from his pocket.

"No, sir, you are not," she said, glaring at him. "You want me to be broken and broke? Put your phone away."

Mo obeyed.

"What I was saying is that it's good for Maddie to see her dad in a happy relationship. To see you doing well with someone you like who supports you," she said, cautiously bending the arm she'd fallen on.

"Oh," Mo said.

"Have you told her yet?" Mrs. Sargysan asked.

"Jess? Yes, of course she knows about Maddie."

"No, silly," she said, looking up at him. "Have you told Maddie that Jess is your girlfriend?"

"I . . . um . . ." His voice was too shaky at first. He took a deep breath. "I don't know if she's my girlfriend. We haven't talked about that."

Mrs. Sargysan squinted at him.

"What on earth are you waiting for? Talk about it. You've been mooning around here having whispered conversations on the phone in your yard; you're out later than I've ever seen. And when you come home, you're all lit up. She's your girlfriend, and that's that."

Mo wasn't sure what to do. It wasn't a surprise that Mrs. Sargysan had noticed his behavior. He had not been acting like himself at all. But he couldn't just decide that Jess was his girlfriend. Mrs. Sargysan was eyeing him.

"She would be stupid not to say yes," she said. "And I know you're not the type to spend your time around stupid people."

"Okay," he said. "You're right, she's not stupid." Suddenly the disorder in the kitchen jumped out at him, and he realized that Mrs. Sargysan was in no state to clean it up. He grabbed a bulb off the counter and reached up to screw it into place. The room flooded with light, and Mrs. Sargysan blinked a few times.

"Yes," she said, looking around. "Definitely better."

He righted the other chair and went into her pantry for the broom and dustpan. In a few minutes, her kitchen was in order, and Mo relaxed a little. Mrs. Sargysan hadn't moved from her seat.

"I still think we should get some help," he said. "I can take you to an urgent care."

"Don't wanna," she said.

Mo stifled a chuckle. She sounded like Maddie when she was little.

"What if I call your nephew?" he asked.

Mrs. Sargysan rolled her eyes.

"Fine. I'll never hear the end of it if I don't get checked out," she said, her arms folded. "But if we're doing all that, can you help me to the couch?" She held out a hand. Mo reached out for her and held perfectly still as she pulled herself up. She began shuffling along with him to the living room but seemed winded before they'd made much progress down the hall.

"Um . . . do you want me to carry you?" he asked.

She rolled her eyes again.

"All right, fine," she said.

He scooped her up carefully and carried her to the couch. Placing her on it, he noticed that her breathing had quickened.

"Are you sure you're not in pain?" he asked.

"I'm fine. Just not used to being picked up and carried around. Got a little dizzy."

Mo's heart clenched.

"I don't like 'dizzy,'" he said. "I—"

"That makes two of us," she said, cutting him off. "Don't worry; it's stopped now. Do me a favor. There's an ice pack in the freezer. Two, actually. Bring them both, please?"

Mo hustled to do as she'd said. When he'd rearranged the pillows to better support her and put the packs where she wanted them, he stood straight.

"I'm going to go call your nephew," he said. "I'm sure he'll want to take a look at least."

Mrs. Sargysan harrumphed. "His number's on the corkboard next to the phone. Do you have a date with Jess tonight?"

"No, I'm free," he said.

"In that case, if you have to, I guess you can stay until he gets here."

Mo kept his lips straight even though a smile was fighting its way out.

"Okay," he said. "We'll have our own date night."

Mrs. Sargysan laughed as Mo returned to the kitchen to make the call.

CHAPTER NINETEEN

Jess

Jess barely restrained herself from slamming her front door when she got home. She chucked her keys in their basket and toed off her shoes.

"*More* tests?" she grumbled to herself as she walked to the kitchen, frowning.

She snatched the water pitcher out of the fridge and poured herself a glass. "I went across town for a stupid appointment just so they could tell me they didn't find anything wrong, but they want to do more tests?" she asked the empty room.

Her day had started out fine, teaching her morning classes and then getting a lovely surprise flower delivery from Mo. The bouquet of red camelias had soothed the light trepidation she'd been feeling about her doctor's appointment in the afternoon. She'd almost cracked and told Mo that she was nervous when she'd texted to thank him. But keeping things separate felt better.

Especially since he'd probably worry.

After finishing her first glass and refilling it, Jess walked down the hall to get changed when her phone started ringing in her pocket. The caller ID read "Mom." Jess's stomach tightened, the glass and a half of water she'd swallowed, churning in her stomach. Weakness surged through the hand holding the phone, pain crackling through her wrist and knuckles. She wanted to ignore the call, knowing what it would be about.

Or, I could listen to Alice and Steph and rip the Band-Aid off.

"Hi, Mom," she said, answering.

"Jess! Hi," her mom said. "So good to hear your voice."

Jess didn't want to lie and say it was good to hear hers.

"Hello," she said again, forcing an almost bright tone as she continued into her bedroom. "How's it going?"

"Good, good," her mother said. "Weather's been great, my seven-sons have come in nicely this year. It's attracted so many butterflies!"

Sitting on her bed, Jess realized her mom had just provided a nice segue. If she was going to listen to Alice and Steph—who, objectively, logically, were probably right that seeing her parents might help her—she could use seeing the flowering tree to bring up the possibility of a visit. Even though she was still very reluctant to do so, her friends had never led her astray. She'd pushed herself to make more difficult choices in her life; she could do this. She took a deep breath, preparing herself to speak, but then her mouth was suddenly dry, in spite of the water she'd just finished.

"Huh," she scratched out. "That sounds nice . . ." Her throat sealed up, cutting off her voice. She pushed, but nothing happened. She coughed, trying to force her voice back. "Maybe you could send me a picture?"

"Oh! Will do. You'll see, it's so much fuller than last year. I'll send you one from then so you can really see the difference."

"That'd be great, Mom," Jess said.

Angry with herself for failing to suggest the visit, Jess needed to get off the phone. The remaining agitation from the doctor's appointment, and her disappointment with herself, meant her temper was on a short leash. She was afraid of saying something hurtful because she was struggling with her own emotions.

"Listen, Mom," she said. "I'm expecting a work call any minute. I can't miss it. I know why you're calling, and I'm sorry, but I'm . . . I'm still not ready for a visit."

Her mother made a small, muffled whine, and Jess could just see the facial expression that went along with that sound: her mother's lips pressing together and then turning down on one side. Wincing at the pain still in her hand, Jess tugged at a loose thread on her comforter. For the first time, she noticed how strange and almost sorrowful the pattern on it looked in the meager light filtering through the blinds on her windows. Her mother's sigh drew Jess back to the call.

"Okay," her mom said. "I won't keep you. Your work is important. But the door is open whenever you feel you're ready. You know that."

"I do," Jess said. "And . . . thank you for saying that. About my work."

"Of course, honey. It's important to you, so it's important to me. Love you, Doctor," she said.

A slow, cold fog rose in Jess's bones.

"Love you, too, Mom," she said and ended the call.

Her mother hadn't called her "Doctor" because Jess had finally become one. She'd been calling her that for many, many years. At least since Jess started high school. What her mother hadn't said was the other part of the nickname, Pepper, because she couldn't say it anymore. "Doctor" for the serious sister and "Pepper" for the sweet, spunky one who had once been attached to her hip.

Jess melted into the bed, grateful for the quiet and the dark so that the cold fog morphing into a heavy ache could cement itself into her bones, and she didn't have to do anything about it. But she wasn't going to cry.

That evening, sitting on her bed with her laptop on her lap, Jess sighed as her laughter died down.

She, Alice, and Stephanie had been talking for about an hour. Jess had been having a great time. It was nice to put the heaviness from talking to her mom and her frustration about her doctor's appointment to the side. Stephanie venting about her students had made Jess laugh hard enough that her sides hurt, and she was happy to commiserate with similar stories. But the pain in her hand from the call with her mom hadn't left. The ache in her muscles had turned flu-like. Which was odd because she hadn't had pain like that in a while. She couldn't remember any at all since she'd spent the first night with Mo.

It was almost like being with Mo, being open, allowing herself to start something hopeful and new had brought in a positivity that eased her pains, at least for a little while. But now that she was digesting the call from her mom and the "need" for more tests, the pain was back, requiring a lot of energy just to stay in the conversation with her friends.

"Jess?" Alice asked, bringing her out of rubbing her arms and back into the call.

"Hmm?" she answered.

"It looks like you're trying to give yourself a deep tissue massage with your clothes on," Alice said.

"Yeah," said Stephanie. "And it looks painful. Wait—you didn't tell us what the doctor said. Any news from your tests?" Alice asked.

Jess sighed, shrugging as she stretched out her hands.

"The doctor doesn't know what she's talking about," Jess grumbled. "The tests came back fine, apparently. But rather than just leaving it at that, she wants to do even more of them."

Stephanie narrowed her eyes.

"Your doctor wants to be thorough, and that's a problem?" she asked.

Jess rolled her eyes.

"I didn't say that it was a problem. It's just . . . it's a waste of time. Clearly, I'm fine. The aches and pains will go away on their own."

Steph let out an expansive sigh.

"Do I love you, Jess?" she asked.

The exasperation in her tone tarnished the content of her question.

"Um . . . yeah . . ." Jess said, glancing between her friends on the screen. Alice looked as confused as Jess was, but Stephanie's face was hidden, her forehead supported by her palm as her elbow rested on her table. Jess couldn't read her.

"Good," Stephanie said. "Keep that in mind for the next thing I'm about to say."

Jess braced herself.

"How . . . how can a woman as intelligent and analytical and educated as you are be so fucking clueless?" she asked, raising her head and looking into the camera. A much sharper whip of pain sliced through Jess, her eyes watering a little.

"Steph," Alice said. "That's—"

"Lemme finish, Al," Stephanie said. "I love you; I adore you, Jess. You're awesome and tough and I respect you so much that I want to be you when I grow up. But we have been sitting here watching you trying to manage physical pain. Pain that you said had abated and just now flared up after talking to your mother. Al, correct me if I'm wrong, but that's been a pattern. She's talked to her mom, or she's had some reason to think about Cassie, and right afterward, pain."

"I don't . . ." Alice glanced to the side, then back at the screen. "Actually, you're right, Steph. Jess, you've almost always mentioned pain or looked like you were in pain when your family has come up."

Jess didn't know about all that. There were plenty of times when the pain just was. It was there, existing, heavy and cumbersome, requiring her to spend energy on pushing through to accomplish whatever task was in front of her. She told them so, fighting off a growing tightness in her chest.

"Huh," Stephanie said. "Kind of like grief."

In a heartbeat, Jess's bedroom became a vacuum. Air was hard to catch. Her head ached. Steinem caught Jess's eye, stretching up from the floor to place his front paws on the edge of his bed. His mouth opened, but Jess couldn't hear if he meowed because of the metallic buzzing in her ears.

". . . did you?" Stephanie said.

"I'm sorry?" Jess asked.

"You didn't tell the doctor about Cassie, did you?" she asked.

Jess couldn't say anything at first. She folded her arms across herself, squeezing tight.

"Oh, Jess." Alice sighed. "Why not? Her job is to help you. She can't do that if you keep things from her."

"What on earth could my sister—" Jess tried to catch her breath; it was too shallow and too fast. Her skin was burning, her voice louder than she'd intended. The growing, jagged confusion of frustration and anger exploding inside her kept her from reining herself in. "What could my very much *not alive* sister have to do with my very much *alive,* painful body?" she shouted.

"Everything!" Steph shouted back. "She has everything to do with it because you are refusing to grieve her." Stephanie's voice broke. The tears running down her face made Jess's heart drop, slowing her rapid breathing and deflating her frustration and anger.

"Steph?" It wasn't until she tried to speak that Jess felt the tears on her own face. "Steph?" she repeated, pushing down a sob.

"I'm sorry," Stephanie said, sniffing hard and wiping away her tears. "I'm just . . . I'm scared for you, babe. I'm so far away. We both are. We can't hug you. We can't shake you. We can't . . . we can't help." She wiped another tear.

Jess's breath stuttered. The screen was completely blurry, and she blinked fast so she could see her friends.

"You *are* helping," she croaked out. A sniff from Alice made Jess realize she was crying, too. "Al, I'm sorry. I didn't mean to upset you all. I just . . . I . . . I've already grieved for Cassie, I cried. So it's done. It can't be impacting my body now."

Stephanie glared but didn't say anything.

"Jess," Alice said softly. "She was your sister. You're never going to be done grieving."

The shaking started. A deep, violent trembling through her whole body. Adrenaline zagged through Jess as she remembered the only other time she'd experienced shaking like that—the moment her mom had called to tell her that Cassie was gone. She knew what was coming next, the fast, disorienting fall into anguish. She clung to the comforter, willing herself not to fall again as her tears flowed.

"Jess," Steph said.

"Jessica, love," Alice said. "Steph, we shouldn't have talked about this while she's by herself."

"You're right," Stephanie said. "Jess, Jess. Look at us. Open your eyes."

Jess was surprised at the need to pry them open. She didn't know she'd closed them; she'd thought the dark was the anguish gaining on her. She sniffed hard but couldn't unlock her grip on the comforter.

"Love," Alice said again softly. "Can you call Mo? Do you think he could come over and sit with you? Just so you're not on your own right now?"

"I don't . . ." She sob-hiccupped. "I don't want to bother him," she said.

"Okay," Stephanie said, wiping a hand down her face. "Then I need you to give me his number. Though based on what you've said about him, he might panic if the call comes from me."

Jess gulped. Stephanie was right. If he got a call from a stranger asking him to check up on her, Mo might think the worst and race over. What if he had an accident on the way? Her lungs seized at the thought, and she coughed.

"I'll . . . I'll call him," she stuttered.

"Now," Alice and Stephanie said in unison.

"It's ready, m'lady."

Mo's hand was heavy on her shoulder, warm and gently shaking her awake. The light hurt when she pushed her swollen eyelids open. But Mo's gentle smile from where he'd crouched in front of her stretched out on the couch made it worth the effort.

"Hey," he said when she focused on him.

"Hey," she said, smiling back. "How long have I been asleep?"

"Less than thirty minutes, I think." He tossed the dishtowel in his hands on his shoulder. "Do you want to eat here? Or should I set the table?" he asked.

Jess started to sit up but froze when she realized that Steinem had curled himself into a ball against her stomach after she'd fallen asleep. "Aww, Sty Sty. Thank you," she said, running her hand down his back. He began purring. "I'd prefer here," she said to Mo.

"Be right back," he said, heading to her kitchen.

Jess sat up slowly, pulling Steinem along with her. She tucked him more comfortably into her lap and scratched him behind the ears. The aroma of the cooking food caught her attention, making her stomach growl.

"Mo, that smells wonderful, what is it?" she called out to him.

"Algerian chorba," he said, returning to her with a soup. "The chicken soup of my family." He placed the bowl on the coffee table and left again.

A few bright green coriander leaves decorated the top of a fragrant red-orange soup. Jess thought she recognized chickpeas among pieces of carrot and stewed meat. Her mouth watered enough to force her to swallow. Mo returned with utensils, a napkin, and a glass of water, sitting down next to her and scooting close.

"Mo, this looks . . . you're not eating?" she asked.

He shook his head.

"I'm good. This is the 'I feel terrible' soup. The, 'It's not okay right now, but it will be' soup. It's all for you today," he said, wrapping an arm around her shoulders and giving her a squeeze.

"Oh," she said, hugging him back. "Thank you so much."

He shrugged.

"Thank you for reaching out," he said, smiling.

Jess smiled back and then dug in. She'd been right about the chickpeas and the stewed meat. It was delicious, but she couldn't identify what kind it was. The urge to ask was there, but the soup was so rich, so delicious, that she couldn't stop eating to speak. Hunger slammed into her, and she remembered that she'd barely eaten anything all day.

"Mo, are you sure you don't want any?" she asked quickly between mouthfuls. "This is amazing."

He chuckled.

"It better be," he said. "It's my mom's recipe. Plus..." He took a deep breath, rubbing the back of his neck. "This is an HSP thing. It's not your fault, okay?" he asked.

Mo's tone forced Jess to take a break.

"Okay," she said, raising an eyebrow.

"When someone I really care about is upset, I can't eat if I'm near them. Being able to feel what they are feeling is great because it means I can usually help. The downside is that I *feel what they are feeling.*" He laughed awkwardly. "Their feelings and my concern for them combine. Which means that digestion will not be happening. When Maddie was still very small and had very big emotions . . . let's just say that I spent a lot of time not eating."

"Oh, Mo," she said, bumping him with her shoulder. "I appreciate that you care about me a lot, but I feel bad about having that strong of an impact on you."

"Please don't," he said. "Just the way I'm wired." He shrugged. "Go on, eat."

"Mmkay," she said, taking another spoonful. "But I'm doing better now, you can feel that, right?"

He nodded.

"A little. Thanks to the chorba." He winked at her. She smiled back. "That's why I keep some in the freezer for emergency situations."

"But I didn't tell you it was an emergency," she said between spoonfuls. "I was careful not to."

He nodded and glanced away, running a hand down his beard. He shifted his shoulders a little then met her eyes again.

"You're right. You didn't *say* that," he said. "But you did say that you need additional medical tests. That your friends didn't want you to be alone. Those things certainly suggest chorba time, but your *voice* told me it was an emergency. You sounded . . . heartbroken."

She slid close, wrapping her arms around him as he hugged her back. Of course he'd read her well. Felt her emotions well. His word choice made her feel guilty because she'd intentionally not shared Stephanie's theory about grief with him, in spite of promising her friends that she would. But Mo, being Mo, had had an inkling.

She took a deep breath, squeezing him tightly, pushing herself to tell him.

"Thank you, Mo," she said.

"You're welcome, m'lady," he whispered into her crown.

She took another deep breath, steeling herself in case the tears started as she shared and . . . the words got stuck in her throat.

"I . . . I think I'm going to finish this bowl," she said instead. He loosened his hold on her as she sat up to start eating again. Her phone buzzed on the table.

Mom:

> Hi honey! Sorry, I got a bit caught up in things. Here are the photos. I thought you might like to frame the second one. Love you! Xx

Quickly, two photos popped up in Jess's messaging app. The first was labeled "today" showing the Seven Sons tree in her parents' backyard, its lush green crown thickly frosted with small white blooms. Though her mother had labeled the second photo "last year," a better name would have been "diminished." It described the way the crown was smaller, the white blossoms were fewer, and the slowing feeling that Jess felt looking at it—because she and Cassie were standing underneath the tree, their arms around each other, laughing. Jess's lungs stopped working.

Mo's hand sliding across her shoulders brought Jess back into her body.

"That's a familiar dress," he said softly.

Jess's confusion forced a breath in.

"Familiar?" She looked at the photo again. She was wearing the red dress she'd worn on their first date. Cassie was wearing her matching blue one. The photo had been taken the day of the party that Cassie had nudged her to go to.

"You looked beautiful in it then, too," Mo said as he continued rubbing her back. But he wasn't looking at the photo, he was maintaining eye contact with her, a kind smile on his face. And it felt like . . . like he was waiting, giving her space. She understood that he wasn't going to ask her anything, wasn't going to nudge her to tell him things she might not want to talk about. She smiled, her eyes tearing up.

"Thanks," she said. "So did Cassie." She stopped when her voice broke. Mo looked closely at the photo.

"Looks like she really loves her big sister," he said.

Jess nodded, looking at it again.

"I love her, too."

CHAPTER TWENTY

Mo

The cheap linen shirt still stunk. Mo held his breath as he got it over his head and pushed his arms through the sleeves. His Fezzik costume had been hanging in his laundry room for the two days since it had arrived and that still had not been enough time for the chemical smell from the packaging to fully dissipate. He'd planned to wash it the previous day but had forgotten when Jess had called him over. Now he was going to have to try to push the smell aside in addition to his discomfort about being photographed that morning and what it meant. The Faire was looming, along with his shoulder-tightening anxiety about being one of its public faces and, allegedly, "main draws." The upshot was that he would see Jess any moment. He'd be able to check in and see if visually she seemed to be doing as well as she had that morning by text.

He hung the tag-less Henley he'd been wearing on the now freed hanger hooked behind the Folk School smithy door and stepped back into his work boots, stuffing his Fezzik pants in so they billowed sufficiently. The work boots were completely wrong for the Big Day, but he was sure the photographer would want to focus on him smithing, not . . . stomping or something.

As he straightened, the door was pushed the rest of the way open, Mo stepping back just in time to avoid getting the knob to his head.

"Doth mine eyes deceive me?" Rick laughed, looking Mo up and down. "Art thou in *garb*?"

Mo scowled.

"Very funny," he said. "Where's yours?"

Rick walked over to the high table, plopping a gym bag onto it.

"Gonna get changed right now," he said.

"I'll give you privacy," Mo said, stepping around the door.

"Wait," Rick called to him. "You know, you're allowed to smile about this. Even enjoy it a little." Rick winked at him as he pulled his polo out of the waist of his jeans.

Mo would have liked to explain what was going on inside him. It would have been nice to tell someone who was more than an acquaintance that it wasn't even ten A.M. and that he was already tired from fighting to control the anxiety of being seen, feeling the weight of his responsibility to the Folk School and mentally preparing himself for the multiple times that day he'd have to live moments like this one—where he could feel the static of someone else's excitement, their confusion about his lack of excitement, and the social requirement to mitigate that dissonance in a way that didn't make the other person feel criticized or minimized.

He could either fake a level of excitement that matched Rick's own—which would require Mo to deplete some of his limited energy and be a lie; or he could simply grunt, saving a little energy for future use. But most people read that second option as a personal rejection. He sighed.

"Yeah," he said, giving a brief nod. "Maybe." He stepped through the doorway, pulling the knob behind him.

"Don't try too hard," Rick called out, laughing as he closed the door.

Mo headed for the break room. He'd planned to stay in the smithy, getting things ready for the photographer, but he could do that once Rick was changed. He could hear people shouting to one another outside, the sound of hammers and nail guns. The physical structure of the Faire was almost halfway finished. He walked into the break room and headed straight for the thermos of hot water for tea among the refreshments that had been laid out, reminding himself that everything was going to go well, and the discomfort and fatigue he was managing—and would have to manage—were going to be well worth it because the School was important to him.

You're good, you're fine. Just breathe. Can't get all jittery like you've got extra fingers.

"Do you always start conversations this way?" Jess asked from behind him, making him jump out of his skin. He turned, finding her perched on the arm of the pleather loveseat in the corner beyond the door. "Extra fingers, though . . ." she said. "Isn't Inigo the one looking for the six-fingered man? Not Fezzik?"

The charge from being surprised was washed away by warmth at seeing her, not to mention how deadly gorgeous she looked. She wasn't wearing a mask, and her clothes were brown. But other than that, she was 100 percent the Dread Pirate Roberts. Even down to the low ponytail.

"M'lady Roberts," he said, placing a hand on his heart and bowing. "I didn't know you were there." He laughed, and she joined in. "And I didn't realize that I was thinking out loud."

Smiling, she strode across the room to him and wrapped her arms around his waist. He smiled back and wrapped his arms around her. She looked up at him, her chin on his chest.

"You doin' okay?" she asked, smile lingering, but one corner of her mouth turned down. His heart warmed. She was asking precisely because she knew he wasn't. He sighed.

"Gonna be fine eventually," he said, tucking some hair that had escaped the ponytail behind her ear. "I'll just have to do a lot this evening to clear everyone else's excitement and my own stress. More important, how are you?"

Jess narrowed her eyes and shook her head a little.

"I will accept '*equally* important' . . . ," she said. "I am much better than yesterday. No doubt fortified by the chorba I had for breakfast." Her wink sparked heat in his cheeks. Her lower back tightened, followed by her arms around him. She took a breath. "And if it starts to be too much today, I'm going to imagine all the Little Cassies out there who might enjoy our Faire. Help them become as excited about it as she would have been." He squeezed her back.

"That's a great plan," he said.

"Glad you think so," she said, resting her head on his chest. "We're doing this for the best reason."

"The best," he echoed.

"Okay, m'lord." She glanced at the clock over his shoulder. "Why don't you stay here, just to breathe. I told Doug I'd meet the photographer outside a couple of minutes ago."

"Okay, m'lady," he said. He leaned to kiss her cheek, but she was already turning to leave. "See you," he called out. She waved and slipped into the hall.

Once he'd finished some tea and tossed his emptied paper cup into the trash, he headed back to the smithy. The previous construction noise was gone, a near silence wafting into the building through the open windows. Mo found it quite odd, so he passed his smithy and headed out the back door of the School.

A small crowd of School volunteers was standing in a semicircle, facing the archery field, watching Jess shoot. Even though he didn't have his sunglasses, and the light might start a headache, Mo joined them, nodding hellos. The photographer was lying on her stomach on the ground, her camera pointed up at Jess, who was down on one knee, aiming at one of the targets. Jess was listening to her instructions, and she moved a little bit this way, a little bit that, changing the way that she held the bow and arrow. Her beautiful sable hair with its warm depth glinted in the sunlight. Mo tucked in his smile at the fact that now he knew what that gorgeous curtain felt like on his skin. Then the photographer got up and the videographer came closer. Jess began shooting. The onlookers had been quiet during the photos, but the quality of the silence changed. Mo glanced at the others out of his peripheral vision. Then he let his gaze fall to the ground and go unfocused so that he could get a feel for the emotions in the group. Their quiet wasn't one of restraint; it was a quiet of surprise. Mo furtively looked around. Eyes were wide, jaws slack, watching Jess. Ned was the only one who didn't look shocked.

Arms folded and standing off to one side, he looked like a proud father. Ned glanced up, met Mo's eyes, and he smiled and nodded once. Mo returned the gesture, and then happily allowed himself to look back at Jess.

She'd gotten up from where she'd been half kneeling on the ground, and was stalking toward a bale of hay, slowly, as the videographer had asked. To a silent beat, she removed an arrow, shot. Removed an arrow, shot. Each one sailed silently through the air until it pierced the center of the bale. Mo wanted to keep watching, but he also knew he needed to get the forges going for his and Rick's photos. His stomach flopped, and his breath stuttered for a moment.

It's for the School. For the best cause.

He held on to the thought and Jess's hug to keep his nerves away as he walked back to the smithy. Just as he was about to step out of the sunshine and into the building, he looked back at the crowd, still mesmerized by Jess. He caught sight of one of her arrows piercing a disk flying through the air. The "ah" that rose up from the others brought a smile to his lips. In agreeing to step out of his comfort zone for the School, he'd gotten the chance to know her. Before he could doubt himself, he slipped out his phone to text her a little encouragement she could find when she'd finished. He began to acknowledge a tiny bit of gratitude for the Ren Faire. Without it, he probably would have kept to himself, stuck in his grumpy, as Khalil liked to say.

Maybe this is a good thing for me, too.

Twenty minutes later, the forges were roaring away. Mo had laid out the tools that he thought looked traditional and placed a few bar stocks into the fires to heat up. He was feeling at ease, approaching the relaxed state he got into while working the metal, when Rick sauntered through the door.

"Hey, man, did you see her?" he asked, hooking a thumb over his shoulder. "She's awesome."

"Uh, yeah," Mo said.

Rick shook his head as he opened his tool bag.

"Silly me. Of course you've seen your *girlfriend* shoot," he said. He peered at Mo out of the corner of his eye. Mo swallowed back the blast of nerves that had sparked at the word "girlfriend" and scowled.

"Didn't want to interrupt you guys in the break room," Rick said, winking.

Mo didn't like feeling seen, especially without his knowledge. But a small part of him realized that Rick knowing was fine with him. He just didn't want to be talked about. He didn't like people examining him and his feelings. He wanted things to continue going well with Jess, though. That would mean the people around him being aware that he liked someone. He knew on paper that was a very good thing.

It just . . . feels safer when I'm single. When I'm in my quiet little bubble and no one on the outside can see what's going on inside.

But Jess was . . . starting to feel like . . . one of his safe spaces. He'd been worried about opening up with her, and that had gone well. He could continue. Plus Rick had said *"girlfriend."* He wasn't the first person to bring it up. Maddie had, then Mrs. Sargysan. The idea made his skin tingle and throat constrict at the same time. Everyone seemed to be noticing, no matter how he felt about it. Even though it made him feel terribly shy, the idea of Jess being his girlfriend was appealing. It made his heart flutter a little. Rick was still smirking at him, holding back a laugh like Khalil would have. Mo narrowed his eyes and blasted a sigh through his nostrils.

"All right, all right, man," Rick said, chuckling a little with his palms up. "Pretend I never said anything." His hammer in hand, he grabbed the cool end of one of the heated pieces of bar stock and went to his anvil. "The photographer will be here soon, let's bang some metal."

Mo did the same, blowing out a metered breath and relaxing into smithing mode.

This is difficult, but it's for the best reason, for the best cause.

He raised his hammer, bringing it down for the first blow.

And becoming Jess's boyfriend might be the best thing for me, too.

CHAPTER TWENTY-ONE

Jess

Back at the archery supply closet, Jess smiled at the message she'd discovered from Mo.

Mo:

> Neither the Dread Pirate Roberts nor Princess Buttercup have anything on you, m'lady.

She didn't know if things had begun in the smithy yet, so she couldn't guess at his emotional state. She hoped the nervous discomfort of being photographed hadn't built too much. It had been disturbing for her, but once she could move while they were shooting video, she had been able to get into the zone, far from any anxiety or worry. Any sadness about Cassie got tucked away where Jess couldn't feel it. The applause from the other School volunteers had come as a surprise once they'd stopped filming. Jess had forgotten they were there.

Once changed, she locked up and headed down the hall to leave. Not knowing how long the photography would take for either of them, Jess had planned to head home right after and do some additional research, as she needed to update a course for the next semester, then check in with Mo in the evening. Almost to the lobby, she caught Doug's voice somewhere behind her.

"The smithy is this way," he said to the photographer following him at the end of the hall. "Make sure to get a lot of close-ups of Mo."

Jess frowned. That was exactly the sort of advice Doug would give that would make Mo crawl out of his skin. Jess couldn't let him deal with this by himself, even though Rick was in the smithy as well.

"Don't pay any attention to me, or to Sam," the photographer said to Mo and Rick while gesturing to the cameraman as Jess joined them in the smithy. "You guys just do you."

Mo gave her a curt nod. Several of the other volunteers had come in from outside, and Jess discreetly made her way to the back of the group, standing against the wall just across from Mo. She hoped to catch his eye so that he'd know that she was there for moral support, but he'd turned his attention directly to the forge just behind him after listening to the photographer. He was slowly shifting a piece of metal back and forth in the fire. Jess made a mental note to ask him about how blacksmithing worked, about some of the processes. Because looking back and forth between him and Rick, she realized she didn't know anything beyond "bang hot metal with hammer."

Mo caught her full attention as he moved the long metal rod—now glowing red—from the forge to his anvil. He picked up a hammer from somewhere to the side of it. The room faded away as he brought it down for the first strike. The shower of sparks that exploded in all directions drew Jess's attention to Mo's bare forearms. First, she had a hint of concern because they weren't protected. But that concern turned to something deeper and needier as he flexed, turning the cooling metal with one hand. The hammer came down again, and she followed its path back up, her gaze catching on the biceps flexing to move it. The room was already warm when Jess had walked in, the heat from the forges getting trapped by the walls. Mo had been in there longer than she had, and his skin glowed with a light sheen of sweat. Now that she knew what his skin tasted like, she could imagine savoring it right then, just a little bit saltier than it had been before. She let herself lean against the wall as she dragged her tongue across her now parched bottom lip to moisten it. Suddenly, the arc of Mo's hammering faltered a bit, and she looked up at his face. In the brief second their eyes met, she winked at him. If she hadn't known him better, she would have missed the red that deepened his already pink cheeks. But the way he tucked his chin, without losing his rhythm, was enough to let her know he was doing his shy thing.

So sexy yet so shy. She smiled, shaking her head a little. *Makes no sense*.

She tried to reposition to catch his eye again, but the videographer stepped in and blocked her line of sight. The photographer said something to him. All Jess caught was "blacksmithing god." She chuckled.

Sounds right to me.

She pulled out her phone to send Mo a little encouragement for later.

Jess:

Goddamn, Hephaestus.

Glancing at the top of the screen, she noticed she'd missed a call. Checking the log, she saw that her mother had called her twice in a row, just a few minutes earlier. Jess's heart leapt into her throat—her mother had only called her multiple times in a row once, to tell her that Cassie was gone. Jess inched toward the door, shooting Mo a quick glance, but he was focused on his work, clearly trying to pretend that the cameras weren't there.

Everything's fine, everything's fine.

Walking around the side of the School, she called her mother back as she reached her car.

"Jess, hello!" her mother said brightly after the third ring.

"Is everything okay?" Jess asked, tossing her bag in the backseat and locking herself in.

"Yes, of course," her mother said. "Why?"

"You called me twice in a row."

"Did I?" her mother asked. "Oh, I tried to call but it dropped.

I didn't realize I called again. I tossed the phone into my purse just after."

Jess let out an audible sigh, her shoulders unclenching as she rested her forehead on the steering wheel.

"Okay," she said. "Good. What did you want to talk to me about?"

"Um, I wanted to know what you thought about the picture?"

Something had always bothered Jess about the way her mother softened statements about her thoughts or feelings by turning them into questions sometimes. She'd learned during her master's program that it was called high rising intonation, and her mom was probably doing it from a lack of confidence in her own opinions, which saddened and angered Jess at the same time. She sighed.

"Which picture, Mom?" she asked.

"Um . . . the one with . . . the two of you," she said.

Jess swallowed down her frustration that her mom wouldn't even say Cassie's name.

"It's nice," she said.

"Oh."

Jess waited, surprised at her mother's flat tone.

"What's wrong?" she asked.

"I . . . well. You just sounded a lot like your father," her mom said.

Jess saw red.

"I'm *sorry?*" she asked, a blast of adrenaline making her heart take off.

"Well . . ." Her mom let out a whine-whimper sound that stabbed at Jess's ears. "He won't talk about Cassie; you won't talk about Cassie. You two are so similar, boxing things up inside. How can we possibly do better, feel better if you all won't *talk?*"

Jess's chest was rising and falling, head spinning. In no way, shape, or form was she anything like her misogynistic father. She *managed* her feelings, which was a perfectly logical way to deal with them. Her father simply refused to have any and tried to stamp them out of everyone around him. The tiniest flicker of a thought that there may have been a similarity between *managing* and *refusing* passed through her mind, but she ignored it. With her breathing still rapid and her heart racing with anger, she decided to end the call before she passed out.

"I have to go, Mom," she said.

"Wait!" her mom said, pitch high. "Please, come home so we can—"

Exhausted and disgusted, Jess ended the call and tossed her phone on the passenger seat.

She was pulling into her driveway, having mentally tossed her anger and frustration along the road during her drive, when her phone buzzed with two laughing emojis from Mo.

Mo:

Hephaestus?

Jess smiled. That was a much better thought to return to.

Jess:

That's your nickname from now on.

Mo:

Why?

Cuz you're a blacksmithing god.

She could just imagine how red his cheeks must have gotten. Thinking of his skin reignited the fire that had kindled in his smithy. She glanced at her front door. She did have things she should do. But there was one thing she wanted to do a lot more.

Jess:

Do you have anything going on right now?

Mo:

No, I don't.

Jess:

Feel like a little company?

Jess's hands got shaky waiting for his reply. She started to chide herself for acting impulsively, and she poised her fingers to take her suggestion back, but his reply appeared.

Mo:

I'd love that.

Jess smiled again, breathing a sigh of relief.

Jess:

Send me your address.

Thirty minutes later, Jess stood on Mo's doorstep, focusing on the potted plants nearby to get the images of Mo at his anvil out of her head. Taking a deep breath and letting it out through pursed lips, she was confident that she had her hormones under control until the door opened.

"Hey," Mo said. Jess glanced down at his forearm. It was still bare. "Glad you wanted to—"

Jess jumped on him, cutting him off, sealing her lips to his. He groaned, wrapping his free arm around her as he pulled them into his house and shut the door.

"You are so fucking hot when you're working," she said quickly before kissing him again. She felt him chuckle as he kissed her back.

"Why?" he asked into her lips.

"You are a god," she murmured back, running her hands through his hair. The combination of his smell and the smoke from the smithy was making her head spin. "You are totally Hephaestus, metalworking, big, strong, god of fire, heating me up simply by being you. I almost jumped on you, watching you work." She leaned back a little, and he slackened his grip on her. Her feet returning to the floor made her realize that he'd been holding her up. He was smiling but avoiding her gaze, his skin as flushed as hers felt.

"I'm hardly a god," he said softly before glancing up at her. "And if I were Hephaestus, you'd be Artemis."

Jess didn't scoff—while the archery part was right, she certainly wasn't in the mood to be a goddess of chastity right then, or to point out the contradiction.

"You're a sweetheart," she said. "Maddy's not here, right? It's not your weekend with her, is it?"

"No," he said. "She's at her mom's."

"Cool," Jess said. She ripped her shirt off.

Mo's eyes widened, and she caught him swallowing. Jess backed toward the couch, crooking a finger at him.

"Wait," he said. "I'm gross. I need a shower."

Jess laughed.

"Oh, I promise you are not gross." She walked back over to him and ran her hands up his chest. "You are sexy and . . ." She nuzzled close, taking a deep breath. "You smell utterly delicious. Cedarwood and smoke and . . . let's get you out of these clothes." She pulled at his shirt, and he got rid of it. She bit her lip and looked him in the eye. "And the pants?" she asked, raising an eyebrow. He laughed.

"As hot as this is, I can't," he said. "Not here." He gestured around them. "Up there." He tipped his chin over her shoulder. Jess glanced back and caught the staircase. She looked back at him.

"Beat you to it!" Jess said and took the steps two at a time while he followed, laughing.

"Which way?" she asked when she'd reached the top.

"To the right, end of the hall." She followed his hand swoop and took off in that direction.

She went through the open door to his bedroom and looked around, her hands on her hips.

"Just as I suspected," she said, her laughter dying down.

"What's that?" he asked, as his did, too.

"Very, very Mo," she said, grinning up at him. He didn't grin back. He kept looking around his room as though he were trying to see it through her eyes.

"I mean . . . it's just a bedroom," he said when he looked at her again.

She chuckled.

"Dark, masculine wood, wrought-iron touches—which I'm betting you made," she said.

He nodded.

"Immaculately clean, smelling of—" She sniffed the air. "Mmm . . . more cedarwood, leather, and . . . anise, I think." She closed the distance between them and slid her hands up his chest. "Which I adore." She snuggled into his neck and took a deep breath. He shivered.

"And of course, there's that," she said, gesturing behind her at the bed.

"That?" Mo asked softly. "The bed?"

She nodded, raising an eyebrow.

"That very sexy bed."

"How . . . how can a bed be sexy?" Mo asked, looking bewildered.

She leaned back a little to look up at him.

"Maybe because I know it's your bed," she murmured.

His Adam's apple bobbed. She stepped back, undoing her jeans and wiggling out of them. She slid up the foot of the bed, looking Mo straight in the eye and licking her bottom lip. She could tell his breathing was a little fast.

"It's big," she said softly. "And sturdy-looking. Strong." She ran a hand down one of the black walnut posts at the foot. "Looks like it can handle anything. Like its owner." Winking, she crooked a finger at him again.

CHAPTER TWENTY-TWO

Mo

Mo's heart clenched in the most exciting way. He'd begun the process of emotionally resetting after the photoshoot by focusing on the calm he always gained from cleaning up the smithy. Once he'd gotten his hands clean and checked his phone, her message had made him blush as he laughed out loud. And now that she'd come to his house, was in his *room,* and *on his bed* looking at him like that . . . he couldn't get out of his jeans fast enough. Jess laughed and slid up higher as he scrambled up to join her, laughing, too. She wrapped her legs around him as he settled between them and propped himself up with his forearms on either side of her head. Her delicious vanilla fragrance rose around him like a welcoming cloud. He started to compliment her about it, but he didn't want to invite any sadness the connection to Cassie might provoke. Instead, he returned to what she'd just said.

"I don't know if my bed can handle anything," he said, nuzzling her neck.

"Come on, Hephaestus," she whispered. "Let's find out."

He began to chuckle as he pulled back to look her in the eye, but she cut him off by catching his mouth with hers. He kissed her back, deepening the kiss, shuddering at the sparks that rained down on his skin as she dragged her nails down his shoulders. She moaned, and her kisses became more desperate as he massaged her scalp with his fingertips. She pulled her legs tight, trying to bring him closer. A flash of worry cropped up, forcing him to break the kiss.

"I don't want to crush you," he breathed. She was warm and soft and inviting underneath him, but he needed to be careful.

"Haven't we discussed this?" she panted, eyes dark, cheeks flushed. "I want you to crush me."

Watching her carefully for any discomfort, he slid an arm forward to let a little of his weight down. Her head fell to the side, and she groaned with her eyes closed. The worry slammed back into his chest until she slanted a glance at him through her eyelashes and nipped at his biceps, then licked the spot. Shock stole his breath and froze his every muscle for a moment, then he let himself fall into wanting her, plunging into the side of her neck, kissing, scratching with his beard, sucking, biting. She moaned deep, tightening her legs, grinding against him and forcing a moan out of him. He needed to taste every inch of her skin. He pulled back to work his way down her chest, to the rise of one of her breasts. He glanced up at her to check that it was okay, her open-mouthed nod freeing him to pull the cup of her bra down and graze her with his beard. She shuddered. He alternated licking around her hardened nipple with beard strokes, his heartbeat pounding in his ears. He freed the other breast and did the same, letting his eyes close as he drowned in the comforting fragrance of vanilla and her. She let out a breathy chuckle.

"You're teasing me." She sighed.

"Am I?" he breathed back, stroking again, opening his eyes to wink at her.

She looked down at him.

"Mo," she said, her voice deeper, sultry. "I want you to take my nipple into your mouth now."

He obeyed, sucking hard. He pushed his own arousal to the side so he could watch her reactions out of the corner of his eye. She groaned, her head tilting back. Lacing her fingers into his hair, her legs fell slack as he flicked her nipple back and forth inside his mouth and slid two fingers along her panties. Her hips snapped up.

"Yes, Mo," she gasped. "Please."

Getting up onto his knees in a flash, he pulled the waist of her panties along with him. He jerked them off her feet, and before she could bring her legs down, he yanked her thighs over his shoulders and bent his head to taste her.

A slight whisper of concern passed through his mind, that he was trying something ridiculous, that trying to please her in that way, in such a position—her shoulders resting on the bed, her back supported by his thighs—was maybe too ambitious. His want, his bone-rending *need* of her was too great to listen to the critical voice that often arose from his innate HSP "pause to check" response to novel situations. Right then, all he wanted to concern himself with was observing Jess's reactions so that he could drive her out of her mind.

Her eyes darted back and forth, the shock of finding herself in that position leaving her mouth agape. She pulled in a sharp breath, focusing her gaze on his for a brief second until he caressed her with his tongue, making her eyes roll back. He did it again, faster, pressing harder, binding his forearm tight around her stomach as she shuddered and squirmed. He sped up, kissing, stroking, sucking.

"Oh, God, Mo," she shuddered, her thighs tightening, bringing her closer to his lips. She grabbed onto his comforter with one hand, the other scratching down his thigh. His heart racing, he narrowed his eyes, focusing on hers as he angled his head to the side and began gently sucking her clit.

"Mo . . . ," she panted, writhing. Her face was flushed, the skin on her chest and neck turning a deep pink, as her pants morphed into high-pitched sighs. He held her tightly against him, increasing the intensity as his heart tried to race out of his chest.

"Mo!" she gasped. "I'm gonna . . ."

Come, Jess.

He winked at her.

She cried out, grinding hard against his face, her eyelids sealed shut. He rode the wave with her, continuing to lick her with softening strokes as her breathing calmed. Feeling her legs slacken, he gently guided them to rest on the bed.

"Oh, Mo." She sighed. The satisfaction in her voice was a warm glow that nestled deep in his chest as he watched her come back to herself. She rested an arm on her forehead and blinked a few times, looking up at the ceiling. He softly caressed her stomach before stretching out next to her.

"Mo," she said again, licking her lips. "That was incredible. I've never done that before . . ." She sighed. "Not like that."

Proud, but shy, he felt his cheeks heat. He cleared his throat.

"I try to do quality work," he said, running his hand along the silken sheet of her hair spread out between them.

Her laughter made him grin, but he was stuck on her hair. He adored the depth of her shade of brown, but the warmer, lighter portions mesmerized him, too. Especially how the varying colors were reflected in the shades of her eyes—an enchanting warm brown most of the time, but deep and intense when she was on the cusp of an orgasm.

"I would give you a Yelp review, five stars," she said. "But I don't want anyone to know about that particular skill. I don't plan on sharing." She smiled at him.

He chuckled.

"Let's just say you inspired me to be a bit creative," he said.

"Mmm." She sighed. "Well, I am one lucky lady to be with someone so creative."

To be with . . .

There was a difference between dating someone and *being with someone*. At least from his perspective. If she was phrasing it that way, she might see their relationship as . . . a *relationship*. He ran his fingertips through her hair again. Maybe it was time to actually put the boyfriend-girlfriend thing on the table. His heart rate picked up a little.

"What's wrong?" she asked, turning on her side to face him. "You look very serious all of a sudden."

He looked her in the eye. He could do this. He could bring it up. Why was he hesitating?

"You aren't doubting that you satisfied me, are you?" she asked.

His cheeks heated, and he chuckled.

"No, I'm not." He watched his hand, sliding along her hair again. "It's . . . I . . . Well, something Rick said. Right before our photoshoot," he said, still focused on her hair.

"Okay," Jess said, taking his hand. He looked at them woven together and pushed himself to smile, in spite of the very unpleasant hammering in his chest.

"He called you my girlfriend. I told him to knock it off, since we . . . we haven't talked about that, and I don't know if it's too soon—"

She cut him off, releasing his hand to place hers on his cheek. He made himself meet her gaze.

"You're my boyfriend, and I'm your girlfriend," she said. She leaned forward and kissed him.

He hadn't allowed himself to fully contemplate how he might feel if Jess became his girlfriend. He'd made it a point to push those anticipated sensations away, knowing that they would have been so addictive that he would have had trouble focusing on his everyday life. But right then, as the barrier against those emotions disintegrated, an intense but comforting warmth radiated out from his racing heart, flooding through him. It brought a pleasing kind of tingling across his skin. While positive, the sensations were still quite a lot and he tucked his chin, taking a few breaths to try to return to a more balanced state.

"Aw, Mo," Jess said, tipping his face back up with a cupped hand under his chin so he'd look her in the eye. "Are you okay?" She smiled at him.

He nodded.

"Just really happy you want to be my girlfriend," he said, smiling back. She kissed his nose.

"Thank you," she said, letting her eyes close as she rested her head on the bed. She squeezed his hand.

"For what?" He leaned in and kissed her forehead, letting his lips rest there.

"I had . . . a frustrating conversation with my mom after I left the smithy today. I didn't realize that I'd still been holding some stress. You made it all disappear with your acrobatic achievement just now. Becoming your girlfriend is the cherry on top," she said.

The happy warmth he'd been floating in plummeted. Worry tightened his throat. He must have seen her text and replied not long after that frustrating call. Then she'd suggested coming over. They'd ended up naked in bed about half an hour later.

She is initiating after upsetting feelings. She's running to me to escape.

"Are you okay?" she asked, snapping him out of his growing worry.

He wasn't sure what to say. It was a sensitive conversation to have. And maybe one better dealt with when they were both clothed and less likely to feel vulnerable. But waiting seemed like a bad idea.

"Um," he croaked. He cleared his throat. "You remember the first time we slept together?"

She grinned and snuggled close, tucking her head into his chest. He wrapped an arm around her, and she slid hers over his waist. He hoped she couldn't hear his heart.

"Of course," she said. "It was wonderful."

He attempted a smile, but it was tight. He was glad she couldn't see it.

"It was," he said. "I was a little worried, though. Remember? It was after a difficult call with your mom. When I went home, I talked to Khalil because I'd been worried that I took advantage of you when you were in an emotional state."

"Yeah," she said, voice a touch wary. "But I told you that you hadn't. You didn't do anything wrong."

"I remember you said that. And I know that's how you felt. I just . . . I wanted to be careful."

"Of course you did," she said. He could hear the smile in her voice, which was a good sign.

"Khalil suggested that I pay attention to the next time. To see if, when you came to me, if you . . ." He swallowed to push down the nerves pricking in his throat. "If you seemed to be turning to sex to get away from difficult feelings."

She was very, very still. He couldn't even tell if she was breathing. While being in that position had made it easier to voice his concerns, it kept him from reading her face to gauge her reaction. Which dramatically increased his worry.

"Do you feel like I've been using you?" she asked softly.

He rapidly scanned his own emotions. He'd been so concerned about hers that he hadn't checked in with himself about it. Feeling used in a sexual way hadn't crossed his radar before. Perhaps because he'd never been one for sexual encounters outside of more solid relationships. He gave himself a quick scan again, and the only thing he could come up with was that because she had shown that she *saw* him as an HSP, that she'd respected his needs and had accommodated his quirks, he didn't feel at all like she was using him. He was more concerned that she wasn't respecting her own needs by running away from them. He squeezed her in a quick hug and told her what he was thinking.

"Hmm . . ." she said, snuggling even closer to squeeze him back. "I don't think I've been running away from anything. I'm just really happy to be with you. And . . ." She sighed. "It's been a long period of *unhappy.*"

Mo could get that. In the marrow of his bones.

"It has," he said. He could have pressed, tried to move the conversation a little bit deeper, encourage her to really think about the possibility. But he knew that sometimes, for heavy subjects, the best approach was to look at in small parts, a little bit at a time, and let them digest. They could return to it later. He kissed the top of her head.

"The call today, what was it about?" he asked.

Jess sighed.

"She wants me to go visit. So we can all *talk.* I don't think she'll stop pestering me until I do go."

"Do you think you will?" he asked.

"Yeah," she whispered. "Alice and Steph have been nudging me anyway. We messaged about it a little this morning when I let them know that I'm okay after getting so upset about my doctor wanting even more tests and them both being so . . . worried." She cleared her throat. "I'll have to go home eventually. But . . ."

Mo sensed that there was more behind the "worried." He'd felt she didn't tell him everything that had been said in their conversation when she'd called him over, but it certainly wasn't the moment to pry about that, either.

"But?" he asked.

"It's strange. It didn't feel like home the last time. Honestly, I haven't felt like I'm home since I came back. Maybe I was just gone too long." She sighed again.

"Maybe," he said.

She shifted a little, draping one of her legs over one of his. Pressing her body against him, she kissed his chest. Then his collarbone. Concerned about the path she might be heading down, he pulled back a little.

"Let's just snuggle for a bit," he said, moving gently to nudge her to spoon with him.

She nodded, scooting until her back was pressed against his chest. She hugged his arm close when he wrapped it around her. Once they settled, she laughed a little.

"Funny," she said. "Feels a little more like home in Hephaestus's arms."

He chuckled, kissed her crown, and squeezed her tight.

CHAPTER TWENTY-THREE

Mo

Mo closed the almanac website and took a moment to savor the hit of ease he always received when he did. That particular site was visually "loud" for him, disturbing. It always caused an uptick in static in his mind and body when he used it. Unfortunately, it was the absolute best one he'd found to help him tend to his plants. He switched over to his plant spreadsheet and made the necessary updates. Over the past couple of days, he'd been engaging more fully with his plants, trying to flush out the higher than usual levels of static that had been buzzing in his muscles and slowing his thoughts. He hadn't been successful.

I'll probably feel more grounded with some food.

He left his computer and jogged down the stairs to the kitchen. He could heat up some of his newest batch of chorba since he was feeling unbalanced. But thinking of it made him think of Jess. If he was honest with himself, most of the out-of-sorts feeling was coming from what she was dealing with. The evening she called him over was when his static had first ticked up. The photoshoot stress had raised it, and their conversation about her turning to him to escape had put it firmly on high. In spite of his surprise about the upsetting news that she needed more medical tests, he'd refused to push her on it. She was a very levelheaded person. It seemed odd that she would be resistant to getting to the bottom of a health problem. And he'd noticed that it was a problem—he'd seen her stretching her hands or rubbing her shoulders during meetings or even their dates. It had been going on for quite some time, why not try to find a solution? However, he could certainly understand being afraid when a doctor says, "I don't know."

He opened the fridge, assessing the contents for a sandwich or a salad.

She didn't seem worried about her actual health. More like annoyed that her doctor and her friends were bothering her about it.

Then there was the impact on her from contact with her mother. When she'd sent Jess the photos, a rush of cold had passed from Jess to him, even before her body had . . . deflated? He wasn't sure that was the best word. He grabbed the ingredients for a sandwich and got to work at the kitchen counter.

He was still glad that she'd called him over. But as much as he felt honored that she'd let him be there for her in that way, he couldn't think about it too much right then. All the sensations from her upset would echo back, and his sandwich would remain intact. After laying out his placemat, napkin, and glass of sparkling water, he sliced the sandwich in half and sat at the kitchen table.

The static had made it feel like his bones were vibrating on the way to the photoshoot the following day, but he'd attributed it to being watched, photographed, seen. And when he'd had a few moments with Jess, things had calmed. He took a bite of his sandwich, chewing slowly.

That's a great sign.

But that evening, after the photoshoot . . . he swallowed his bite, his throat protesting a bit. He tried to wash down the discomfort with half of his glass of water. He'd been happy and relieved, and his muscles and skin and mind had been quiet and content—until he'd become concerned about her escaping in him. While he was glad that they'd cleared the air about the possibility of him feeling used, they had not fully addressed her potential escapism.

Her physical pain, being upset by her family, running from painful feelings . . .

It was plain as day to him that at least two of those problems were related to losing Cassie. He wondered about the pain. When Mo had imagined losing one of his brothers, it had caused him piercing, visceral pain. Allowing his thoughts to return to that moment made him push his sandwich away. If he felt that way only imagining that kind of loss, how might it feel to actually live it?

Maybe it's different for me because I'm an HSP. Any feeling is.

Needing to be sure, he downed the rest of his water, put his sandwich in the fridge, and headed back upstairs.

Half an hour later, Dr. Google had provided some answers.

"Grief may be responsible for joint pain, muscle pain, and intense stiffness . . ." read the very first result. From there, Mo had gone down several rabbit holes, trying to understand the hows and the whys.

"Efforts to avoid the reality of loss" had particularly stuck out to Mo. Not that Jess owed him a performance of grieving Cassie, but he'd only seen her specifically upset about her sister one time. And she hadn't shed a tear. She hadn't told him when exactly Cassie died, but she had said that it happened right before she returned to the States. She'd only been back a few months.

Mo sat back in his seat, slowly scratching at his beard. Google had also told him that it was possible that she was running to him to escape in physical pleasure. After some time to chew it over, he realized that her desire to feel good with him made him a bit proud—in those moments, she was secure with him and felt free. But he was very, very concerned about whether continuing to run could harm her.

He rested his elbows on the desk, scratching at both sides of his beard as he reread the last article he'd found. All of the information had been useful, if a bit sterile. He'd have liked to run it by a real person, but grief is a touchy subject. Personal.

I do know someone who might be willing to share her lifetime's worth of wisdom.

Mo took a deep breath as he raised his hand to knock on his neighbor's door.

"Mrs. Sargysan, are you in?" he called out.

"Where in the world else would I be?" she called back after a few seconds. "Come on in, use your key!"

Mo let himself in, careful to close the door behind him. Mrs. Sargysan was on the couch, watching television. She lowered the volume as Mo joined her, sitting in the loveseat. He and Maddie had been checking in on Mrs. Sargysan a little more than usual after she'd fallen. She was mobile again and had a new purple cane.

"Hi," he said. "That's a nice cane."

"It is better than that other one," she said. "If I have to have one, it sure won't be that monstrosity my nephew brought by first. Screamed nursing home."

Mo smiled but let it falter. His arms felt weak, his hands jittery, nervous about broaching the subject. He pressed his palms together between his knees. The deep breath he'd taken hitched on its way out because Mrs. Sargysan was eyeing him.

"Mo?" she asked. "What is it?"

"I need to ask you something," he said quickly. "A favor, it—"

"Yes," she said, cutting him off.

"I'm sorry?" he asked, confused.

"Yes," she repeated. "I will watch Maddie so you can take Jess away for a romantic weekend. If her mom can't watch her. We can have a slumber party, make cookies, all that jazz."

Mo chuckled.

"No," he said. "Thanks, but that's not what I wanted to ask. It does have to do with Jess, though."

"Okay," she said.

His skin felt prickly, and it was like his muscles were coated in nausea.

"Mo." She turned off the television and shifted on the couch to better face him. "You're worrying me," she said tersely.

"Sorry. I just feel bad talking about it because it's kind of Jess's private business," he said. "But I also think it's harming her, and I want to be sure I understand the situation well so I can help. And so that I don't make things worse."

Mrs. Sargysan narrowed her eyes. Mo figured he'd better spit it out.

"Jess's younger sister died," he said. "Unexpectedly. Violently. Earlier this year."

"Oh, no," she said softly, shaking her head. "No, no. May God illuminate her soul." She crossed herself, ending by pressing her open palm to her chest. "Was Jess with her?"

"No," Mo said, shaking his head and rubbing his palms together again. "She was still studying in England when it happened."

Mrs. Sargysan pulled in a breath through clenched teeth.

"How is she handling the loss?" she asked.

"That's just it," Mo said. "I don't think she really is. It wasn't long ago at all, and she never expresses grief at losing her sister. She gets very upset after she speaks with her family, seems to try to distract herself afterward. The big thing is that she's having a lot of physical problems—aches and pains—but the doctors can't find anything wrong."

Mrs. Sargysan let out an enormous sigh and slumped fully back into the couch.

"I don't . . . I don't want to bring up any difficult memories for you," he said. "I just . . . I thought you might know if grief can cause physical pain."

Mrs. Sargysan looked him in the eye. The large round lenses of her glasses magnified the tears he saw in hers, making his heart clench. She gave him a sweet half-smile.

"The only reason it doesn't cause me physical pain anymore is because I keep those difficult memories close now," she said. "I stopped running from them, trying to stuff them away. Until I did, until I looked my sorrow in the face and accepted it, the constant pain in my body was a hundred times worse than the pain from when I fell in the kitchen. A thousand times worse than what you've seen the past few weeks as I've been recovering. No one can run from grief. Either we choose to face it, or our bodies make that choice for us."

About an hour later, Mo returned to his side of the duplex. He'd had a good talk with Mrs. Sargysan while doing the washing up from her dinner, in spite of her protests. It had tickled him to realize that Mrs. S and Jess were a little alike—confident, headstrong, and caring, even though they didn't easily let on. He was surprised that he hadn't noticed before. Once he'd helped her up to her room, she'd shooed him home to call Jess. But how to begin to talk about something she didn't want to see? Was that even his place?

Well, she was happy to be my girlfriend. Girlfriends and boyfriends don't just stick to light subjects.

He pulled out his phone and dialed once he'd gotten comfortable sitting on his bed.

"Hephaestus!" she said, answering after the first ring.

He smiled, still feeling a little shy about his new nickname.

"Hi, m'lady. How's your evening been?"

He sensed the downshift in her energy before she spoke.

"It's been . . . something." She sighed.

"What's wrong?"

"That's part of the problem," she said, after a dry laugh. "Nothing. Got the results back from the second round of tests, and there is not a single thing wrong with me."

The opportunity was right there. She'd given him the perfect chance to share what he'd confirmed with Mrs. S. He took a breath to prepare himself.

"So I'm raring to go for my visit with my parents this weekend."

All the air whooshed out of Mo's body.

"You're . . . visiting your parents?" he asked, hoping his voice wasn't as shaky as it felt.

"Yeah," she said. "I decided to give in. To Alice, Steph, my mom. All of them."

"Oh," he said. Running a hand down his jean-covered thigh, he vacillated about what to ask next. The grief or the visit. He was uncomfortable about both.

"Um, I'm surprised," he rushed out. "What made you decide to go?" He swallowed thickly, hoping he hadn't sounded judgmental.

"Well," Jess said. "Alice and Stephanie wouldn't push the way they have been if they didn't think that it would truly help. They haven't let it go and probably won't until I actually do it. By the way, thank you."

"What for?" he asked, adjusting himself to sit up straighter.

"You've never nudged me about that. Never bothered me about my relationship with my parents. I realized it might be strange from your perspective, since from everything you've shared, you're pretty close to your family," she said.

Mo didn't feel he merited any sort of praise for respecting how she chose to engage with her family.

"Um, you're welcome," he said.

"You're a good boyfriend," she said, a smile in her voice.

Mo's shyness crept up.

"Uh, thanks," he said.

"About the visit," she said. "That last call with my mom really got on my nerves. I'll go and just see her so that she stops asking. But the biggest thing is what I mentioned before—that I don't feel like I'm fully home yet. It's weird. Yeah, I went to my parents' after I got back, but I didn't feel like I was back in the same way that I had been during school breaks. It was kind of right, but a little off. Slightly unsettled, like . . . maybe this is weird, but like I was hovering, I hadn't landed. Maybe if I go again and try to make the mental choice to land . . . I don't know."

"Ah," Mo said. He saw a huge, glaring difference between the times that Jess had gone home during school breaks and her most recent visit: Cassie's absence. It seemed obvious to him that a lack of one of his siblings would make him feel unsettled, but Jess seemed to be missing that possibility.

Is she missing it intentionally, or is it too painful to see? She's dealing with enough physical pain right now. Maybe that would be a realization that would bring even more. Maybe if she tries to "land" she'll feel differently.

"So," she said, breaking into his thoughts. "I told my mom I'd come this weekend since we can't do anything because you're with Maddie, right?"

"Yeah," he said. "I am."

After chatting a little longer, Mo hung up, disappointed in himself. All he'd had to say was "I'm worried about you. I think your pain might be grief. Maybe you don't feel at home because Cassie is part of home for you," and he hadn't been able to. He'd always struggled with initiating discussions that might be hurtful for other people. For people close to him, he could usually manage, even though his heart would pound and his throat would get dry. That evening he'd failed.

Some boyfriend.

He pushed off his bed, headed to the shower. There was even more sharp, painful static to wash away.

CHAPTER TWENTY-FOUR

Jess

The following Saturday, Jess started the morning early, but not bright. The drive to Rockford to finally go see her parents would take hours, plenty of time to regret going at all.

I'll try to land this time. Just like I told Mo, I'll make the mental effort to feel like I'm home. Maybe this time it will stick.

She took another long swig of coffee from her travel mug and started off, paying close attention to the GPS. A low-level grumbling started inside gnawing at the cautious optimism she was trying to maintain. She reminded herself that Alice and Steph thought a visit was a good idea. She trusted her friends' perspectives enough to try.

But realistically, there's no way for this to go well.

At least she could visit Cassie's grave. Jess hadn't been able to make it back in time for the funeral, in spite of begging her department to advance her dissertation defense by a few weeks or even do it remotely. Neither she nor her parents could have afforded for her to return to England to do it later. Once she'd returned, she hadn't been able to muster the strength to go to the cemetery. This time, she felt she could do it. Pulling onto I-96, she fiddled with the radio to find something she could stand listening to, but her heart wasn't in it. In her frustration, she reminded herself of Alice and Stephanie's arguments in favor of this visit. They always tried their best to understand, but their relationships with their parents were different. They could actually *talk* about things. The opposite was true of Jess's parents, for whom appearance mattered more than anything else. Jess sighed.

At least Mo said I can reach out anytime if I need to.

After a while, the music was irritating her more than anything else. She turned it off and listened to the sound of the tires on the pavement, the engine purring as it should. But she felt terribly alone. Most people felt happy or at least content to go back home, welcomed by their families, excited to share the things that were going on in their lives. Instead she was going someplace where no one understood her. A place where she was too opinionated, too direct, too ambitious, too athletic, too serious, too combative with her words when she stood up for herself. Where she was all-around the wrong kind of person.

Except for Cassie.

Even with her softer, meeker nature, Cassie had always made it clear that she thought Jess was just the right kind of person. From making sure their parents knew that Jess helped her to get good grades, or lauding Jess's achievements to her friends, to helping Jess come up with the arguments to get their parents to support Jess's studies abroad—Cassie always embraced who Jess was, valued Jess's feelings and opinions, and made sure she had fun and knew she was loved.

Tears welled in Jess's eyes. Blinking them away, she set her mind on something else. Mo had offered to join her on this foolhardy expedition, but she'd declined. Now she was regretting it. Mo's simple presence was comforting. Even without speaking. And when he was around, the heaviness essentially disappeared. She caught herself smiling a little. If nothing else, Mo's size might have intimidated her father enough to rein in his critical nature. But she didn't want to share that part of her life with her parents. The less they knew about her, the better.

Too many hours later, and with her stomach rumbling, Jess pulled into the driveway in front of her parents' pointlessly big house—an ostentatious two-story with a finished basement, seven bedrooms, and a double garage. Her mother had been killing herself for years to keep it clean because even though he could afford to hire a housekeeper, her father—who could not abide dust or smudges—didn't want a *stranger* touching his things. The house was a metaphor for their family: pretty on the outside but lacking love and warmth on the inside.

Appearances, appearances.

As she parked, she caught the blinds moving at the window beside the door. She wasn't all the way out of the car before the front door of the house opened and her mom stepped outside. She was smiling but wringing her hands over her floral apron.

"Jess! Jess, I'm so happy you came," she said, staying on the porch as Jess approached.

"Hi, Mom," Jess said, reaching her and giving her an awkward hug.

"Oh dear," her mom said, taking Jess's face in both hands. "Is everything all right? You look so thin." She pulled her hands away and stepped back to look Jess up and down.

"Everything's fine," Jess said.

Because that's what her mom always wanted. For everything to be "fine."

Her mom took her hand.

"If you're sure," she said.

"I am," Jess said, letting her mom guide her into the house.

Okay, time to "land." Time to be back home.

Inside, everything was precisely the same, though Jess hadn't had any other expectations. She took a deep breath. Her mom had been cooking, and while the food smelled good at first, the hunger Jess had been battling quickly twisted into an acidic feeling. She was glad she'd been careful to pack her medication. Following her mom into the kitchen, Jess transformed her grimace into a slight smile as her mom turned around.

"Everything's almost ready. I made a brisket and mashed potatoes, your favorite," she said to Jess.

The acid in Jess's stomach surged, but she didn't let it show. A meal that heavy would leave her miserable for days, and those foods hadn't been her favorites for years. She'd told her mother so at each of her last three visits. But no use hurting her feelings.

"Thanks, Mom," she said. "Kind of you to do that."

"Of course, sweetie, of course. Oh! There's also a pie. A Bob Andy," her mom said, smiling.

Oh God, I'm gonna die. A custard pie? I'll never digest that.

"You didn't have to go to so much trouble," Jess said. Her mom put her hands on both of Jess's arms and squeezed.

"How could it be any trouble if it's for you?" she asked. She squeezed again, looking at Jess's arms. "But really, honey, you are skin and bones. You haven't been taking care of yourself."

Jess shrugged.

"I'm fine, Mom; don't worry," she said. "Can I help with anything? Maybe set the table?"

"Oh, that would be helpful, thank you. I already put the plates and glasses on it, but the places need to be set."

"Gotcha," Jess said, eager to go somewhere the aroma might not be so strong. She found the dishes stacked on one corner of the table, so she placed those first. Laying down the third on autopilot, she reached back for the fourth, but nothing was there. Her breath rushed out. Her last visit, there had been other family visiting as well. The six-person table had been full. Before that, every single time she'd set this table, there had been four plates, not three. And from now on, when they ate as just immediate family, there would always be a plate missing. Jess's vision started swimming; her nose began to burn. There were also three glasses when there should have been four.

"Jess, hon, grab the utensils out of the sideboard," her mom called out from the kitchen. "I don't want to use everyday utensils on such a special occasion."

Jess took a deep breath as she turned to the sideboard. She wasn't going to break down, not here, not now. She didn't want to show her feelings in front of her parents, particularly her father. If emotions came into play, it would start a fight. Quickly grabbing three sets of everything, she straightened her spine and took another breath. As she laid the rest of the table, her vision sharpened, and her pain began to subside. She thought she was in the clear until she heard her father's voice.

"Jessica," he said, standing inside the doorway from the hall. He was holding what Jess assumed to be a glass of scotch in his hand.

A little early in the day, isn't it?

"Father," Jess said, regaining her posture after placing the last spoon. He looked at her for a moment without saying anything. His round face was distinctly redder and puffier than her last visit.

Looks like the early scotch has become a habit.

"It's been a while," he said.

Jess nodded.

"A shame," he said.

"Oh?" she asked.

"Yes. Upsets your mother," he said. "Brenda," he called out to Jess's mom. "Can we sit down?"

But it doesn't upset you, of course.

Jess shook her head internally. But she didn't ask. If she did, it would start a fight.

"Yes, yes," Jess's mom called back. "Everything's ready."

Her father's steps were a little shaky as he crossed the room and sat down at his usual seat at the head of the table. Jess wasn't sure what to make of that.

More than one glass? Before lunch?

Jess also noticed that he hadn't offered to help her mom bring the food in, like Mo did at her house. But that was who her father was, a man who expected his wife to wait on him. And she'd been doing it for years.

"Sit down, Jess," he said, motioning her to her habitual seat. Jess shook her head.

"I'm gonna help Mom with the food." She walked out of the dining room without another word. It was best if she didn't spend time with him without her mom's mediating presence. She was going to avoid a fight.

Jess did not check the time. Her father had spent the entire meal talking about himself. While she was curious to know exactly how long the monologue had been, she didn't want to show any signs of annoyance by looking at her watch. That would start a fight. She tried to push the sliver of pie she'd agreed to around on her plate so that her mom's feelings wouldn't be hurt. It did taste good, as her mom's pies always did. But Jess had eaten all that she could; her stomach already felt like it was going to explode.

"It is good that you were able to find a better supplier, dear," Jess's mom said quickly to her father, finding a break in his monologue. "Uh, Jess?" She turned to her. "You've been quiet. How is your . . . um . . . social life going?"

"My social life?" Jess asked.

"Yes. You've moved back, you're in a new city. Have you made any friends?"

Jess didn't count anyone at the Folk School as friends quite yet. And while her colleagues were pleasant, she hadn't spent enough time with them to consider them friends. Jess knew that her definition of "friend" had always been stricter than her mother's, so she was hesitant about answering. But she needed to give her mom something, or she'd start bugging Jess about it.

"Well," she said, "I'm still close with Alice and Stephanie from my PhD. We talk a lot. I've also made some friends at the place I go to practice."

"Oh, that's wonderful," her mom said. "That's good news, isn't it, Ray?"

"Yeah, yeah, sure," he said before taking a sip of his refreshed scotch.

While her father's lack of interest didn't surprise her, Jess didn't understand why her mother would think it was *wonderful* that she had friends.

"Although . . ." her mom added, "is there anyone who is . . . I mean, um, maybe more than a friend?"

Of course. Jess should have seen that coming. Her mom was being all weird and nosy because she wanted to know about Jess's love life. She kept herself from rolling her eyes.

"Well, Mom, if you have to know, yes, I am seeing someone," she said.

"Oh," her father said, chuffing a laugh. "Unexpected." He opened his mouth like he was going to say something else, then closed it. His gaze drifted to his plate, then he raised his glass to his lips again.

Unexpected?

Jess swallowed hard. She'd spent so much of her life holding her tongue under this roof. So much time biting back the comeback, the question, the demand for an explanation. So much energy stuffing feelings down, every bit of her ached. But if she responded naturally, it would start a fight. The thing she was trying hard to avoid.

"I'm so happy for you, Jess," her mother said, pulling Jess's attention to her. Her mother's eyes were a little wide as she darted a glance at Jess's father, then back to Jess again. "I'm glad you're not alone. What's his name? What does he do? Are things serious yet?" her mom asked breathlessly.

Jess kept her face neutral, but inside she was partially screaming and partially confused. Why did her mother look at her father as though she was worried? But then, her mother always looked like she was worried. Her eyes were boring into Jess for answers about Mo. Maybe she would drop the subject if she felt like she had some information to chew on. Jess sighed again.

"His name is Mo," she said. "He has his own successful automotive repair business. He's divorced and co-parenting well with his ex to raise their twelve-year-old daughter."

Her father harrumphed. Jess was not surprised.

"Jessica," he said through a burp. "A kid? Blue-collar? Get a man who doesn't have baggage and who uses his brain, not his hands."

Jess didn't say anything. She didn't trust herself to at first. She'd kept it together so far and didn't want to destroy the "nice" family time her mom had clearly worked so hard to put together. She did. Not. Want. To. Start. A. Fight.

Fuck it.

"Better that he works with his hands than uses them to beat me up," she said, keeping her face placid and taking a small bite of pie. Her father's face, on the other hand, was reddening. Her mother's eyes looked like they were going to shoot out of her head.

"Oh, um . . . Jess, it's good he owns his own business," she blurted in a rush, the pitch of her voice far too high as she glanced worriedly at her father. "And he has a good relationship with his ex."

"What's that supposed to mean?" her father asked Jess, his voice a threatening growl.

"It means exactly what it's supposed to mean," she said. "Left to their own devices, your daughters, I mean your remaining daughter, can choose a caring man who doesn't see her as his property or a punching bag."

Her father's face was bright red and contorted. Jess could see the veins at his temples bulging.

"And," Jess said, delicately taking another small bite of pie, "I'm building a support system in Detroit so that if Mo were to become violent with me, someone would step in. You two have made it clear that five and a half hours is too far a drive to check on your daughter."

"Jess!" her mom gasped.

"No one talks to me like that in my house," her father said.

"I didn't talk to you like anything," Jess said to him. "I stated a fact. The fact is, Cassie was in a dangerous situation. You knew; you did nothing."

Her father stood up fast, his chair dragging back on the hardwood floor.

"Insolent," he said. He grabbed his scotch, some splashing on his hand. "Always difficult." He looked at Jess's mom.

"I told you this was a bad idea," he said. He stomped out of the dining room, his steps wavering more, and went up the stairs.

Jess took another small bite of pie. His barb would have stung if Jess weren't inured to his bullshit after hearing the same criticism for years. She was astonished that he'd left the room without saying that academia was a waste of time, or that she should have taken her archery further—things he usually did each time they were in contact. She looked across the table at her mom, who had tears in her eyes. Jess reached across the table to take her hand.

"I'm sorry, Mom," she said. "I know you tried today."

"You couldn't try a little harder?" her mom said. She glanced at the empty doorway. She almost seemed fearful. "He's been struggling. You know it wasn't our fault," she whispered.

Jess snatched her hand back.

"I'm not struggling, too?" Jess asked. "You aren't? You *knew* what was going on. You told her to stay. And you turned a blind eye."

"I tried to tell her that it wasn't . . . that . . ."

"That it wasn't that bad. You told her that sometimes marriage is hard and the best thing to do is to stick it out," Jess said. Her mom looked astonished.

"Yeah," Jess said, nodding. "She called me, too. But she didn't tell me everything, probably didn't want me to worry, being so far away. If I'd known how bad it was, I would have pushed her harder to ignore your advice, to leave him. If I'd known that he was abusive, I would—"

"He . . . he wasn't abusive," her mother said meekly, her eyes filling with tears.

"After she died, *you* told me he used to drive erratically to scare her. And now look. She died. In a car accident while he was driving. That's some coincidence."

"It was an *accident,*" she hissed, her eyes shifting back and forth across the table, followed by a quick glance at her father's empty seat. "He didn't set out to harm her."

"Why are you making ex—"

Jess's throat sealed up, the pounding of her heart deafening her. She stared at her mother, whose eyes were wide as they seemed to plead with Jess, full of the same worry that they'd shown when she'd glanced at her father during the meal. Jess's initial impression hadn't been wrong, it *had* been stronger than her mother's general worried nature. Suddenly, her mother's excuses for Cassie's husband, her minimization of what he did, her focus on the intentions she imagined that he had, made sense. If she truly recognized that Cassie had been in an abusive marriage, she'd begin to see that to a degree, her own wasn't so different.

"You don't understand," her mother said, tears streaming down her face. "We did our best. It just wasn't enough."

Numb, Jess nodded. The realization about her mother, her parents' marriage was far too large with implications much heavier than she could begin to approach at that moment. Jess felt like lead. Weighed down. Her anger was gone. All that was left was a grainy emptiness. One she knew would never be filled in that house. It was just a building with nowhere for her to land. It would never feel like home.

Jess stood. "I love you, Mom. Okay?"

"Um, I love you, too, Jess," she said, looking confused.

Jess left the table, headed to the front door.

"Where are you going?" her mom called out.

"To see my sister," Jess said. "I won't be back."

"Jess, wait!"

Jess grabbed her bag out of the hallway and went out to her car.

The groundskeeper pointed Jess in the right direction once she'd arrived at the cemetery. Her grandparents were buried there, but it had been many years since her last visit, so she would have ended up wandering without help. She'd turned her phone off once she'd gotten there, concerned that its near constant buzzing from her mother's calls might disturb other mourners.

"Hey, Pepper," Jess said, her voice breaking, once she'd found Cassie's headstone. A thousand and one thoughts and words and colors and memories bubbled and swirled and clashed in Jess's mind. She fought hard to find one, choose something, to express a single idea to her sister, but one of them was all of them, and before she could be aware of anything else, she crumbled to her knees, her face against the grass, nails clawing into the earth. Some part of her, seemingly off in the distance, nudged the idea of decorum, of holding herself together in public, of having some degree of self-control. But it was obliterated by the great giant mass of anguish she had fought so hard against on the call with Steph and Alice. Jess let herself sob into the earth, pressing her mouth against the ground when she couldn't hold back her screams.

After a time that Jess could not measure, the wave passed. She let herself slump onto her side, her cheek still against the grass. She blinked and wiped at her face until she could read her sister's name.

"Hey, Pepper," she tried again. Looking at Cassie's name, she talked. Told her about everything that had been happening over the past few months, even though it felt a little silly because it seemed like Cassie had already been there for parts of it. She shared her frustrations, admitted that maybe Steph and even their mom was right, that Jess compartmentalized too much, and it wasn't healthy. She told her about work, about Mo, about how much she missed her.

"I don't know, Cas," she said. "I'm not ready for this, for life without you. If I really . . . I can't. I can't start some process of grieving. If I accept that you're gone, that means I'm accepting a life without you—"

Something thick and wet landed on her cheek, cutting her off. She wiped at it, her fingers coming away with a goopy white-and-brown liquid. Confusion stunned her for a moment, and she looked up into the empty blue sky. She caught two birds flying away.

A memory surged forward. She and Cassie walking back to the car after grocery shopping. Jess had been trying to convince Cassie of something, but Cassie wasn't having it. A bird had pooped on Jess's head, stopping her mid-sentence. Cassie had simply smiled.

"See?" she'd said. "I call *bird shit*." Then she'd winked at Jess.

"Cas!" Jess asked, back in the present, looking at the headstone. "Did you just get a bird to poop on me? Did you just call *bird shit*?"

Her heart in her throat, Jess's eyes teared up again as she smiled with poop on her hand and her cheek.

CHAPTER TWENTY-FIVE
Mo and Jess

The following evening, Mo parked in his driveway after dropping Maddie off and took the few steps to his porch. Inside, his keys on the hook, he toed off his shoes. His "no-Maddie" ache was there to meet him. Even though it wasn't as sharp as usual, the change was unpleasant. It felt like something heavier was weighing it down. He tidied the couch cushions and refolded the throw, putting it in its place. He would need to plan dinner soon, but thinking about food put an ashy taste in his mouth, which was very odd. He chalked it up to missing Maddie and went upstairs to take a shower.

That didn't work. Out on the bathmat, drying himself, he got what was wrong with him. It was past time for Jess to have returned from Rockford. She'd only messaged him the day before to let him know that she'd arrived safely. Beyond that, he hadn't wanted to disturb her while she was with her parents. Apart from a good night text and a good morning one, he'd given her space. Maddie had had a tough week at school, and he'd spent a good bit of energy trying to help her feel better. Now that she was with Diana, Mo became concerned about the radio silence from Jess.

"Hi there," she said with a sigh when she picked up the phone.

"Uh, hey, m'lady, are you back home?" he asked.

"Yeah."

"Are you all right?"

Jess cleared her throat.

"I'm okay," she said.

She was not okay; Mo could tell. He didn't want to press. Though he'd kicked himself the last time he hadn't.

"Are you sure about that?" he asked.

"Sure?"

"That you're okay."

"Oh, sorry." There was no "Jess energy" in her voice. "I should have called you when I got here. I just . . . I've had a lot on my mind since I got here last night," she said.

"Last night?" The words shot out of him before he thought about it.

"Yeah. I . . ." She sighed. "The visit was . . . emotionally complicated."

Mo felt slow and muddy. It seemed like her sadness was sticking to her, pulling her down as it hardened. When she'd called upset before, her energy had been more pointed, staccato. This felt more like . . . grief?

"Do you mind if I come over?" he asked.

He heard her swallow.

"Um, sure," she said. "If you want."

"Lemme take care of one or two things, and I'm on my way," he said.

"Okay," she said. "See you soon."

Thirty minutes later, Mo rushed up her steps and rang the doorbell. He'd fought to push aside the sandpaper worry chafing at him on the drive there. No reason to get too far into his head before he could look into her eyes and truly see how she was doing. She opened the door, and his skin was instantly scored by a million papercuts.

"Hi," she said, voice thick, eyes puffy and red. Her shoulders were slouched, her hair hanging limp and wet. She gave him a little smile.

"M'lady . . ." he said.

She let out a short, dry laugh.

"I know, I must look terrible," she said. "Come on in."

"Uh, no, I mean, thanks," he said as he crossed the threshold, and she closed the door behind him. "You don't look terrible. You look . . . really hurt."

Her smile in response was larger than the one before, but sadder. She tipped her head at him. "You didn't have to do that," she said.

"Do? Oh." In his shock he'd forgotten about the bouquet of flowers in his hand. "Here," he said. "It's my pleasure."

"You always bring interesting ones," she said, accepting them. "Never generic gas station flowers." She gestured for him to follow her as she went into the kitchen to put them in water. Steinem walked alongside her, completely ignoring Mo. The cat knew his mistress wasn't herself. "Do you know what kind these are?"

"Uh, yeah," he said, stepping close to her. "The ones with the white petals are cranberry flowers. The purple ones are penstemon. Beardtongue."

"They are beautiful. Great choice, Mo," she said, arranging them in their vase.

He kind of wanted to tell her their meanings. But that would start a discussion about him, and he wanted her to be the focus right then. They could be a segue, though.

"I was hoping they'd brighten your mood because you seemed sad on the phone and like you could use a boost." He ran a hand down her back. "Now that I'm here, it looks like I was right."

Close-lipped, she nodded. After placing the vase in a prominent spot on the counter, she took his hand and led him to the couch. As soon as she tucked her legs to nestle into one of the corners, Steinem leapt onto the back, stretching himself to lie against her shoulders. Jess squeezed Mo's hand and then let go so she could rub her own as he sat as well, close to the middle, but careful not to crowd her. Her rubbing stiffened Mo's resolve to tell her what Mrs. S had said, but he wanted to start closer in time first, to what had happened the day before at her parents' house.

Just as he took a breath to speak, it struck him that Jess wasn't looking him in the eye. She hadn't at all after letting him in. That fact flipped a tiny switch of worry, but he couldn't really assess it. The slow, heavy energy he'd picked up on over the phone was much stronger. Much deeper. Even the way she'd spoken when he'd arrived was *just not Jess*—too much space between words, her tone a little cold.

"What happened yesterday?" he asked.

She sighed and stopped rubbing her hands. Rather than reach for him, she curled them in her lap. He folded his together loosely in his own.

"We had a fight. During lunch," she said. "I had been biting my tongue, stuffing down my frustration pretty much from the moment I stepped out of the car. My father made one of his trademark hurtful comments, and things snowballed. I think . . ." She stopped and ran a hand down her face. There hadn't been any tears. She seemed to have tried to wipe away heavy frustration. "I think I have a better idea of why my mother was so . . . inert when it came to Cassie's situation. But it's . . . more than I can handle right now. Suffice it to say, I felt even less at home than the last time."

Mo hated seeing her so defeated. And he was disappointed that things had gone poorly.

"I'm sorry, Jess. I'm really sorry that it was so difficult." He couldn't put his arm around her shoulders with Steinem in the way, so he scooted closer, rubbing her crossed legs and forearm. She smiled a little, but her gaze was unfocused, toward the coffee table. She sighed.

"Then, I went to see Cassie, and I couldn't keep it in any longer, and Stephanie is probably right, and maybe even my mother is right, and I can't keep doing this because it's going to hurt and be bad."

Mo wasn't sure where to begin to make heads or tails of everything that had rushed out of Jess just then. That was the fastest she had spoken since he'd walked through the door and even with understanding each word, their meaning all together was lost on him. She looked him in the eye, and her eyes were redder than before and full of tears. She took another deep breath and let it out slowly.

"Stephanie had gotten really upset because she thinks that I've been having the pain and the stomach problems because I'm refusing to grieve," she said.

"That's what Mrs. S said, too," Mo said. Jess looked at him sharply, squeezing the air out of his lungs. He returned his hands to his lap.

"Mrs. S?" she asked.

Mo swallowed hard. He'd wanted to bring up his discussion a little more delicately, but if her friend already had, maybe Jess would take it well.

"I was worried," he said. "You seemed to be running away from pain. Either through seeking physical pleasure when your mom upset you, or by ignoring your physical pain and being angry that your doctors wanted to investigate further. So I did some research into grief. And I asked her because she lost her husband of forty years. She knows something about it."

Jess narrowed her eyes at him, but she didn't move. He tried to push the billiard ball down his throat again and kept talking.

"She told me that either we choose to grieve, or our bodies force us to do it."

His heart thudding and cutting off his air supply, he shut himself up to see what she would say. It was impossible for him to find the origin of the tight band around his chest—he was too stressed to take a breath, but he could tell that she wasn't really breathing, either. He might have been sensing her tightness.

"So you did feel like I used you," she said, her eyes marginally softer.

"What?" he asked.

"'Seeking physical pleasure,'" she said flatly. She was stock-still. Her hands hadn't budged from where she'd curled them, arms and legs in the exact same position. Not a single strand of her hair had shifted from where it had come to rest when she'd sat down. There was something about that utter stillness that

Mo *did not like,* but he couldn't understand what it was communicating.

"Not at all," he said. "I, um . . . I had been concerned about *you.* Where your mind and emotions were. It was just tough to bring it up because I didn't want you to think I was doubting your ability to know your own mind."

She crooked an eyebrow. Mo had wanted to move forward and hug her, but the flash over his skin held him in place.

"You're sure?" she asked.

"I'm sure," he said. "You just said that your mother was right," he added, needing to get the focus off him. "What do you mean?" He took the risk to take her hand gently.

"She said I bottle things up, stuff them away, refuse to deal with them," Jess said, returning her gaze to the coffee table. "Another way of saying I refuse to grieve." Fat tears began to roll down her cheeks. Mo dared to squeeze her hand. She didn't squeeze back.

"Cassie . . . said I should grieve, too. It's okay for me to do it. I'm not accepting a life without her just because I let myself grieve," Jess said. "So, I'm going to."

"That's great," Mo said, smiling.

She raised her head, meeting his eyes. But the distance in her gaze shot a foreboding, prickly chill all over his skin.

"Then I can't do this anymore," she said.

"Do what?" he asked, his voice scratchy. And then finally, she moved. She slipped her hand out from under his and pointed back and forth between them.

"This," she said. "Us."

Usually, Jess detested being wrong. At that moment, a deep loathing at being right wrapped itself around her, squeezing into her skin. She had felt like it would tear her soul to ribbons if she faced her grief, had walked into it. Looking at Mo, she knew she'd only scratched the surface of her pain.

"I don't understand," he said.

I don't either, she wanted to say.

She'd made her way home the day before, collapsing on her couch as the sun was setting. The little spark of hope that had stuck with her after she'd cleaned herself up and gotten behind the wheel flickered out as she pulled into her driveway. Inside, the bawling had begun. Deep, wrenching cries as powerful as the ones that had thrown her to the ground in the cemetery forced her to run to her bathroom and cling to her toilet bowl. Once the retching had stopped, she slid to the floor, her gaze catching on a cracked ceiling tile. She'd understood that the path ahead of her was going to be ugly, embarrassing, and painful to live through. It would be even more so for a Highly Sensitive Man to experience by her side.

She drew her knees up, wrapping her arms around her legs and hugging herself tightly. Mo was watching her carefully.

"Do you remember, when you came over with the chorba?" she asked.

"Of course," he said, eyes guarded.

"You told me you couldn't eat any. Because I was upset."

"That's true," he said, his eyebrows coming together.

She took a breath but couldn't maintain eye contact with him. She let her gaze fall to his hands.

"Things are going to be difficult for a while," she said. "Very ugly and difficult. I don't want to subject you to that emotional ride. I don't want you to get flooded with what I'm going through and have it impact you."

"Isn't that kind of my choice to make?" he asked.

"It could be," she said. "But I know that I won't be able to really commit to letting myself feel all the grief and the pain if I'm worried that you're going to feel it, too. I'm not going to make you starve yourself so that I can heal."

Mo didn't say anything else. He shifted hard into the couch, like he'd been holding himself tight for too long.

"And even . . ." She cleared her throat and took a deep breath. This next part would be painful to say, she wanted to get it out in one fell swoop. "Even if I try not to run to you to avoid the pain, I may do it without realizing I am. Which might ruin any progress. Plus, I don't know how to trust myself to be around you. What if I think I'm acting out of healthy motivations when I'm not? Until you said something about it, I wouldn't have thought that I was using sex to escape. It's better to remove the possibility so I'm forced to face the pain. And while I am, while I'm living it, I don't want to harm you."

Mo sighed, then looked up at her. The tears in his eyes clawed at her heart.

"But not being with you is going to harm me, too," he said softly.

A hiccup-sob shot through her. She tried to take a quick breath to shove it down, but it was followed by another and another. A fight broke out inside of her—the desire to hold herself together, to take back what she'd said, to reach out and comfort him, the imperative to stop running away from her feelings—everything became a jumbled mess fighting to get out. She couldn't breathe. She sat up a little straighter to help her lungs and caught the lightning-quick expression on Mo's face: teeth clenched, eyes narrowed. He was in pain. And she was causing it. She jumped to her feet and went to the front door, a hand clamped over her mouth to hold in her cries. He sighed, stood, and joined her. Wrapping his arms around her, he pulled her close, tucking her cheek against his chest. She let her arms wind around him and her tears soak his shirt.

"I'm a sturdy guy, m'lady," he whispered. "I won't break."

That just made more tears fall. Even though she felt like a monster, she squeezed tighter, wishing she could burrow inside him and hide from everything. He stroked her hair.

"I appreciate what you're trying to do," he said. "I understand that you want to protect me. It hurts, but I'll respect it."

She sniffed hard, gorging herself on the cedarwood, leather, and hint of anise. And him.

"I know you have to do some of this on your own. But the minute you're ready for some help, the moment you need anything, I'm here, okay?" he asked, his voice rumbling through her. She nodded. He pressed a long kiss to her crown, gently released her, and left. As she closed the door behind him, a wrenching cry tore out of her and she sprinted to the bathroom, even though there couldn't have been anything left to come up.

CHAPTER TWENTY-SIX

Mo

Mo turned onto his parents' street, a light charge of tension cementing itself between his shoulder blades. It was a perfectly lovely Saturday afternoon and he should have been in a good mood, on the way to celebrate his father's birthday with his family. But he'd been under a cloud for coming up on two weeks and he didn't know if he had the ability to "people," even with ones that he loved.

Those first few days, an hour hadn't gone by without Mo turning Jess's arguments over and over in his mind, trying to understand how she could see the pain of breaking up as less than the pain that might have come from supporting her in her grief. The conflict between appreciating her desire to protect him and the pain of being rejected made it hard for him to see straight. It also drove him to lift to the point of fatigue multiple times a week, and to double his production of the goods they were going to sell at the Faire.

At least Doug'll be happy.

The care and attentiveness Jess had shown by researching what it meant to be a Highly Sensitive Person had led her to become intentional about supporting him. Unfortunately, that concern had turned into overprotection. Mo wondered if it had been because she hadn't been able to protect Cassie.

"I'm so excited," Madison said, drawing his attention back into the truck as she bounced in her seat.

"I can tell, sugar plum," he said, parking along the street.

"You're gonna be okay, Daddy," she said, catching him off guard as he unbuckled his seatbelt. He looked up at her and smiled sadly.

"I am okay, Maddie. Don't worry about me," he said.

She unbuckled her seatbelt and leaned across the seat to hug him.

"I love you and so does everybody else here," she said. She squeezed him tight and hopped out of the car.

Mo's nose burned a little, so he sniffed to make it stop. He hadn't told Maddie that he and Jess had broken up, but words weren't necessary. She'd seen through him the moment Diana had dropped her off that Sunday evening. Maddie was demonstrating more and more HSP traits with each passing day, which saddened him. The upside, he reminded himself as he stepped out of his truck, was that Maddie didn't get as overwhelmed as he did at the same age.

He walked through the empty kitchen and into the den in time to see Maddie launch herself into Khalil's arms. He caught her and swung her in a circle, laughing as he almost knocked his wife, Vanessa, out with Maddie's foot.

"Hi, Mo," Vanessa said, laughing. She pushed herself off of the couch and came over to greet him. "It's good to see you," she said, reaching up to give him a hug, careful not to spill the Coke in her hand on his shirt.

He smiled and hugged her back.

"How's it going?" he asked.

"Pretty good," she said. "But better now that Khalil's getting his Maddie fix." She laughed, and Mo followed her gaze over to where Khalil and Maddie were in the middle of a complicated-looking special handshake. Mo smiled, feeling free for a moment.

"I think she's happy to have her fix, too," he said. "How are things at work?"

Vanessa nodded, looking back at him.

"Very good, thanks for asking. We're in the process of acquiring another tech company. It's a little stressful, but I think it should be worth it."

Mo was impressed at first, but then he realized he shouldn't have been surprised. This was Vanessa he was talking to. If anyone had the acumen to choose the right sort of company to acquire, it would be her.

"I can't wait to congratulate you on the acquisition," he said, trying to give a supportive smile.

"Thanks," she said, patting his arm. "But no chickens before they're hatched."

"I understand," he said. Vanessa squeezed his arm and returned to the couch, taking small sips of her Coke.

"Maddie!" Karim's wife, Isadora, said as she walked through the open sliding glass door that led to the deck. "I've been looking for my husband all over. Thank you for finding him for me."

"Auntie Isadora!" Maddie gasped. She ran into Isadora's arms for a hug. "I didn't know you'd be here!"

Isadora hugged her back, laughing.

"But that's Uncle Khalil," Maddie said. "Not Uncle Karim." Isadora kissed her head.

"I know, sweetie; I was joking. But I am looking for Uncle Karim, have you seen him?" Isadora asked.

"No, I haven't, but I'll help you find him." Maddie grabbed her hand and pulled her toward the living room. Isadora waved at Mo and mouthed a "hey." He waved back.

He wanted to smile. He had a lot to smile about. Brothers who cared about him and his daughter. A family that had never done anything but accept him, apart from teasing him when they felt like it. But what stung, as he watched Khalil lean down and kiss Vanessa before he went out on the deck, was his loneliness. He hadn't felt that way before meeting Jess, but now it was a bone-deep feeling that was getting harder to manage.

He wove around the back of the couch and went to look for his dad outside. As expected, he found him next to the grill, in a hushed conversation with Mo's mom as she flipped the burgers.

"Hey, Dad, happy birthday," Mo said gruffly, reaching out for a hug.

"Mo, so glad you're here," he said, squeezing tight. "Where's my poulette?"

Mo smiled.

"She's inside with Isadora. Hey, Mom," he hugged her, too, and started to step away from the heat of the grill, but his mom put her hand on his cheek.

"Mo, is everything okay?" she asked, searching his eyes. He couldn't look at her.

"Yeah, some stress at work," he said. He caught the quick glance between his parents.

"Are you sure?" she asked.

He nodded. She raised an eyebrow.

"If you say so," she said. "Is it . . . just you and Maddie with us today?" She was looking at the chicken thighs she was nudging with the tongs. Mo cleared his throat.

"Yes," he said.

"What lucky parents we are," she said to Mo's dad. "All of our boys here together."

Mo appreciated what she was doing. His dad nodded at him and clapped a hand on his shoulder.

"We are lucky," he said.

Twenty minutes later, his mom called out to the house in general, letting everyone know that the meat was ready, so they could sit down at the large table on the deck. Mo and Khalil volunteered to get the cold things out of the fridge. Reaching the kitchen, Khalil turned around quickly.

"How are things with Jess?" he asked.

Of course Khalil would be the one to say Jess's name. Mo took a deep breath and let it puff out his nose. Khalil's eyes went wide.

"Mo, hi, I didn't know you'd arrived," Rachid said to him as he joined them in the kitchen. He glanced at Khalil, who was shaking his head hard. "Oh," Rachid said. "I guess I shouldn't ask about Jess?"

Mo exhaled again and walked past Khalil to the fridge. He wasn't sure which big bowl to take out first, so he started from the top.

"I think it's better to not mention her name," Khalil said to Rachid as he accepted the bowl of Berber salad from Mo.

"Whose name?" Amir asked, walking in from the living room. Mo wanted to let the figs and burrata in his hands fall to the ground. He was not going to make it if everyone was asking questions.

"Don't worry about it," Khalil said.

Amir scratched at his disheveled hair. Mo assumed he'd been somewhere asleep as he always was when Mo came by during Amir's visits from college.

"Just wake up?" Mo asked gruffly. It wasn't that he didn't love his youngest brother. He just had trouble with people who lived their lives imitating sloths.

Amir rolled his eyes.

"Not this again," he said. "I'm a human being; I need sleep. We can't all be Mr. Industrious." He reached across the kitchen island. "Give me the mustard and stuff."

Mo obliged, and Amir shuffled out of the room, yawning. Mo was contemplating whether he should take the cans of soft drinks out, but he'd noticed a cooler outside. Knowing his dad, it was already filled to the brim. He grabbed a large bowl of tzatziki and a similar one of hummus and nudged the fridge closed with his elbow. Khalil was right behind the door.

"Hey," he said softly. "I guess something went wrong?"

Mo squinted at him.

"I um . . . I'll take the extra napkins outside," Rachid said, throwing a wary glance at Mo. He escaped the kitchen quickly as Khalil got even closer to Mo.

"What happened?" he asked.

Mo frowned.

"Don't want to talk about it," he muttered.

"Maybe I can help?" Khalil asked.

Mo frowned and kept his mouth shut. Khalil sighed.

"I'm here, okay?" he said.

"K." Mo walked around the island to get outside and away from Khalil. He focused on the cold seeping into his hands from the bowls so he could get away from the prickly feeling in his heart.

Two hours later, with all the serving dishes and platters of meat picked clean, Mo tapped his sunglasses back into position to avoid crossing his arms again. He knew he'd brought the atmosphere down a little by failing to participate in the laughing and joking, but he couldn't do it. The only thing prompting a little bit of levity for him was the powdered sugar dusting Maddie's lips and cheeks from the phalanx of gazelle horns she'd devoured. He'd had the instinct to tell her to slow down, but it was his dad's birthday; she could enjoy herself. He poked at his baghrir again. But they had vanilla in them, and he could not bring himself to force them down. Nothing had tasted good since he and Jess had broken up, but anything with vanilla was like swallowing ash. He crossed his arms again. His mom had disappeared into the kitchen, and Mo wondered if he should go help her, then she appeared with a small round cake, a lit candle in the center.

"Happy birthday to you . . ." she began singing. Everyone else joined in with energy, and Mo pushed himself to do the same. His mom carefully deposited the plate in front of his dad, who caught her hand and pulled her toward him to kiss her on the cheek. Mo looked away.

"Clafoutis! My favorite," his dad said, blowing out the candle. "But . . ." He looked at Maddie. "There's no way I can enjoy it without sharing some with my granddaughter."

"Maybe you'll enjoy it with another grandchild soon," Khalil said. The table went silent as all eyes shifted to him.

"*Soon*, soon?" their mom asked. Khalil shrugged.

"In a little less than seven months," he said, grinning.

The table erupted. Their mom shot around it to hug Vanessa as their dad shoved his chair back and did the same. Karim clapped his hand on Khalil's shoulder to pull him in for a hug. Even Amir clapped his hands and shouted his congratulations.

"Daddy?" Maddie's voice was soft but urgent as she scooted close enough to whisper to him. "Does Uncle Khalil mean . . . is Vanessa *pregnant*?"

"Yes, sugar plum," he said to her.

"I'm going to have a cousin?" she asked, her face lighting up. He nodded.

"You are," he said. She let out a small shriek and pushed her chair back to go hug Khalil and Vanessa. Mo's arms were still crossed. He couldn't undo them. Naturally, he was happy about the announcement. Small details he hadn't fully processed suddenly made sense—Vanessa staying on the couch sipping her pop, the fact that he'd seen her walk out to the gazebo deep in the backyard, giving the grill a wide berth. She'd kept her plate relatively empty when everyone else was stuffing themselves. As she was still in the first trimester, she was probably nauseated out of her mind.

When the initial rush had subsided and everyone was chattering away, he pushed his chair out and went over. He squatted down beside her.

"Congratulations," he said. "But are you okay? I'm sure everyone would understand if you needed to go inside."

She smiled at him.

"Was I that obvious?" she asked. He shook his head.

"I only put everything together just now. You don't have to push yourself, you know," he said.

She nodded.

"I'm okay, the nausea has calmed down a little. But I can tell that you aren't okay," she said.

He blinked. She put a hand on his arm and leaned closer.

"Of course, I don't know the details. Things might not be hopeless, though. Khalil told me how different you were, how clearly happy you were every time he picked up Maddie. And now . . ." Her lips dipped to one side. "I can see that you're hurting. If Jess made such an impact on you, I think she might be worth fighting for."

Mo wasn't sure what to say. His throat had gotten scratchy. He swallowed.

"I don't know," he said.

She rubbed his upper arm.

"Maybe try again. For you," she said.

CHAPTER TWENTY-SEVEN

Jess

Lunch had been a bad idea. A misguided attempt to maintain the normalcy of a schedule, but Jess had eaten too many fries, and now she was paying for it. She plopped down at her desk in her office and rolled her chair forward as she opened her laptop. It had been two weeks since she had ended things with Mo. The pain still refused to deaden.

She hadn't finished putting the most recent grades into the platform and several students had brought it up in that morning's last class. Getting behind like that was not usually permissible in Jess's mind, but her first tentative steps in facing her grief through online research had opened up so much that it was all she could do to keep putting one foot in front of the other in her everyday life. An additional challenge was that the aches and pains she'd been dealing with were still there. Sometimes worse than before.

"Ms. Anderson?"

Jess looked up to find one of her most attentive students tapping on her open door.

"Hi, Sophia," she said, waving her inside. "You're welcome to sit down."

Sophia shook her head.

"Thanks, but I just have a question."

Jess smiled.

"What's going on?" she asked.

"Um . . ." Sophia took a few steps closer, so that she could lower her voice. "Is everything okay with you? I mean, I don't want to intrude, but . . . in class . . . you haven't seemed like yourself."

Jess retained her frown. Apparently, she hadn't been covering things up as well as she'd hoped.

"It's quite nice of you to ask. Just some stuff, but I'm okay," she said.

"You're sure?" Sophia asked and pulled the test Jess had handed back that morning off the top of notebook she was holding pressed to her chest. "The grade you gave me doesn't match the number I got wrong."

Sophia handed the test to her and Jess took a look. She was right; Jess had skipped including the points from a whole section.

"I'm sorry, Sophia," she said, grabbing a red pen and making the corrections. "I'll fix it on the platform right now."

"Thanks," Sophia said. She took a step toward the door when Jess returned her test. "I . . . um . . . I hope the stuff works out soon," she said.

Jess was caught off guard by the sting in the backs of her eyes.

"Thanks, Sophia. That's kind of you," she said.

After Sophia was gone, Jess waited a couple of beats then stood to cross her office and close the door. She sighed and let her head rest against it as she turned the lock.

Unprofessional in class, unprofessional with my grading. Unacceptable.

The Faire was fast approaching. She'd been grateful for the distraction of practicing with Brian and Keith, trying to nail down the routine for the show. When she hadn't been shooting with them, she'd been shooting at an indoor range she'd found a week earlier. The need to shoot had been intense. When she was in the middle of shooting, everything else disappeared. It was a reprieve from the physical and emotional pain of grieving Cassie, and from missing Mo. She just had to go to the Folk School as little as possible to avoid running into him. Otherwise she might crumble and beg him to get back together.

Then we'd both be miserable.

She sighed, pushed off the door, and returned to her desk. The joints in her hands were wailing, but she only stretched them once and got back to inputting the grades. Her phone beeped, and her heart jumped, hoping it was a message from Mo. Instead, it was Doug with more of his rambling excitement now that the Faire was a little over a week away. As she put the phone back down, she rolled her eyes, as much at Doug as at herself.

Just keep going. You wouldn't force a lung cancer patient to chain smoke.

She wasn't sure that was the best analogy for the situation. But she was going to be toxic waste for a while. She refused to poison Mo. Her eyes burned again, and a wave of sadness started to rise. She shook her head hard.

It's fine. You're a big girl. You can do this.

She whisked a rebellious tear off her face and returned to the grades.

That evening, after a cup of tea for dinner, Jess stuffed her pillows against her headboard and settled in for her video call with Alice and Stephanie. She'd already skipped the one right after she broke up with Mo; she couldn't avoid this one, as much as she wanted to.

They'll probably be happy I went to Rockford, at least. She didn't know if she'd be able to talk about Mo.

She let out a deep sigh and clicked on the icon to start the call.

"Hola, cariño!" Alice said as soon as she appeared on the screen.

"Um . . . hi?" Jess asked. "That sounded pretty." Steinem hopped up on the bed and nudged himself into her lap, forcing Jess to make space for him. He stretched in view of the camera and Alice laughed.

"Good, I'm glad," she said. "Been practicing. The ladies have been saying it to me and it's supposed to be like, 'Hi, dear,' so I think it fits." She winked. "And hello to you, too, Steinem."

Jess smiled.

"It sounds like things are still going well," she said.

"They are. We had—" Alice glanced down, out of range of the camera. "Hold on a sec," she said. "Lemme just reply to this message." Jess nodded, stroking a hand down Steinem's back.

"Okay, sorry," Alice said. "We had a great community meeting a few weeks ago. Some local politicians came and heard what our volunteers had to say. It went really well," she said.

"That's great," Jess said. "Do you want to wait for Steph to talk about it?"

"Oh, we can talk about it now," Alice said breathlessly.

She began explaining the event, the planning, its goals. And while it interested Jess, Alice seemed off. She was speaking quickly but repeating herself every now and again. It seemed like she was having trouble catching her breath. She also kept looking to the side a lot.

"Al," Jess said, interrupting her. "Is everything okay?"

"Yeah, yeah," Alice said. "Why wouldn't it be?"

"You seem stressed. Or nervous," Jess said.

"No," Alice said. "I'm—"

Jess's doorbell rang, pulling her attention out of the call.

"What's wrong?" Alice asked, her lips flashing a quirk to one side. It was an odd little expression. The doorbell rang again. Twice. Jess frowned.

"Be right back," Jess said, sliding the laptop and Steinem onto her bed. "I'll go see what this is about."

"De nada!" Alice said. "Wait. That's not right. Go take care of it. I'll be right here."

The ringing became more incessant as Jess got down the hall and through the living room. Whoever was at the door was apparently interested in pissing her off before she opened it. She checked the peephole, and the bright purple hair she saw made her heart drop.

"Steph!" she shouted, ripping the door open.

"You know," Stephanie said, readjusting her backpack on her shoulder. "It's not very polite making people wait on your doorstep. I thought you Midwestern folks were supposed to be nicer than that."

Jess, who had shrieked with happiness maybe twice in her life, let out an enormous shout of joy and launched herself into Stephanie's arms. Stephanie hugged back, laughing, and Jess joined in. But something shifted. She needed to hug Stephanie tighter and tighter, even as her friend's arms loosened. Suddenly a sob bubbled up, and Jess pressed her face against Stephanie's shoulder to stifle it.

"Jess?" Stephanie asked, tone serious. She tightened her arms again. "Jess."

Jess couldn't answer. She was thrilled but also felt that the slightest inhale to reply would burst the dam holding back her tears. She shook her head, eyes crunched tight. "Jess," Stephanie warned. "Inside."

Jess let go enough so that they could get in. Stephanie awkwardly kicked her other bag in and shut the door. Jess clung to her again. Then the sobs exploded.

"It's okay, it's okay," whispered Stephanie. "Come on. Couch."

They made their way over, crumpling together.

"Jess, babe," Stephanie said, rubbing Jess's back as she cried into her shoulder. "I don't want to let go, but where's Alice? She's going to worry."

Steph was right. Jess got a couple of quick breaths in. "My bed," she said quickly. "Straight down the hall."

"I'm coming right back," Stephanie said. She kissed Jess on the crown of her head and rushed to get Jess's laptop.

An hour later, the storm had subsided. Jess was lying on the couch with her head in Stephanie's lap, the two of them facing Alice on Jess's laptop screen. Her empty mug of tea sat beside it, next to a pile of crumpled tissues waiting to be tidied up. The surprise visit her friends had planned behind her back was the thing she didn't know she needed the most.

"So," Stephanie said, placing her mug of tea on the other side of the laptop. "The game plan."

"Yes," Alice said, pen in hand, looking at the notes she had been taking. "First things first, Jess is going to make an appointment with two of the grief counselors on the list we made. She'll see which one she prefers and continue working with them for the foreseeable future."

"Right, Jess?" Stephanie asked.

"Well, yes," Jess said. "But I still don't see why an individual counselor *and* a grief support group is necessary."

Alice sighed.

"I've avoided bringing this up before because it seemed like you . . . weren't in a place to hear it," she said. "But a lot of the ladies my NGO works with became active in justice and gender equality after the murder of a sibling. They've been doing this work for years, and every now and then something triggers a memory, and they start sobbing. They told me that the grief doesn't leave. But they got better at accepting it and living with it specifically by *spending time with people who have experienced the same thing.* And I'm sure a group will be especially helpful since it seems things are going to have to be on pause with your parents for the foreseeable future."

"Oh," Jess said. "Okay."

"Next point," Alice said. "Jess is going to get back in touch with her doctor and do the final round of suggested tests, just to be absolutely sure."

"I think it has been established that my health problems were due to grief. As much as it pains me to admit that you were right, Steph," she said flatly. "Now that we've figured that out, I don't see why I need more tests." Stephanie pinched her upper arm.

"Ouch!" Jess cried out.

"I did not just take three planes to get here *and* have to make small talk with an idiot taxi driver for you to be stubborn. We are going to be thorough with this," Stephanie said.

"'Kay, fine." Jess sighed, already a little queasy from her distaste of doctor's offices.

"Lastly—on this game plan," Alice said. "Jess is going to get in touch with Mo. She's going to—"

Jess sat up quickly.

"Ladies, I can't. I told you. It's going to be too much. My stuff is going to be too hurtful to him."

"Yes, you did say that," Stephanie said. "But it's an excuse."

"It's also kind of arrogant," Alice said.

Shocked, Jess glared at Alice wide-eyed. She shrugged.

"Men have been telling women what they can and cannot handle for centuries," Alice said. "Any time a man has done that to you, it's gone over really well, Ms. Archery Champion."

Jess narrowed her eyes and cleared her throat.

"Okay, okay, I get it," she said. "But . . ." She pressed her lips together. She hadn't told them the full truth about Mo's sensitivity and still didn't feel like it was her place. But there wasn't any other way for them to understand.

"But . . . what?" Stephanie asked. "You raved about this guy, Jess—which, that's a miracle in and of itself. This guy, who's shown he respects you, doesn't act like some *dude,* has a good relationship with his family and his employees, whose biggest flaw according to you is that he's gruff around the edges but is really a big softie, was worried about you and did research to help, and you've decided that supporting you is going to be too much for him because . . . ?"

"He's neurodivergent!" Jess snapped, jumping to her feet. "It's beyond being sensitive. It's going to emotionally *and* physically harm him if he's around me when I'm upset, and it's not right for me to ask him to do something that's going to be too much for him."

"Hmm," Stephanie said, nonchalantly checking her nails. "Did he tell you that it would be too much for him?"

"Well, no, not exactly," Jess said.

"You just decided that on your own?" Alice asked. "Just made the decision to end the relationship in order to protect him?"

"Umm . . ." Jess didn't like where her friends seemed to be heading.

"Al, does deciding what a neurodivergent person can and cannot handle without discussing it with them sound a little ableist to you?" Stephanie asked.

The air whooshed out of Jess's lungs. She glanced at Alice.

"It does, indeed," she said, shrugging again and putting her pen down.

Embarrassment crashed over Jess, making her skin go cold. What they were saying—that she was being a hypocrite, and even ableist—hurt, but they weren't wrong. Her actions could certainly be read that way. Being called out was a gut punch. However, as her best friends, that was kind of their job. She plopped onto the couch. Stephanie reached out, pulled her close and hugged her. Alice picked up her pen.

"Sorry, Atalanta," Stephanie said into her hair. "But you can be hardheaded. Sometimes we have to thump to get our message across."

"It doesn't mean we don't love you," Alice said.

"I know," Jess said. "I love you, too."

"So," Alice said. "Jess is going to get in touch with Mo. See if he is interested in working things out. Because he clearly wanted to be there for her. To support her."

"Okay," Jess said. "I will. But I have you all, too."

"You do," Steph said. "But Mo doesn't need three planes and a taxi driver to give you a hug when you need one."

CHAPTER TWENTY-EIGHT

Jess

It was simply too hot. In the small strip of shade under the edge of the archery canopy, Jess waved the cutaway collar of her brown linen pirate shirt up and down, trying to get more air to reach her skin as she leaned against the support post. It was the opening day of the Renaissance Faire, and while her garb had been comfortable to practice in and for the photoshoot, it was a bit too much for a surprisingly hot fall day.

Most of that morning had been a bit too much: the colors, the music, the smell of meats being roasted and kettle corn being popped. It had been strange to see the stands prepared and festooned with their brightly colored banners and ribbons at the final archery practice the day before. They'd been pretty, yet frozen in time. Now they'd come alive, the aisles packed with people in flashy and audacious garb—from the School volunteers, to "Rennies" that Brian, Keith, and Theo had recruited, to smiling patrons. Everyone laughing and bowing to one another, speaking with overcomplicated words and phrases. Jess might teach classes on the period, but she had no desire to *speak* the period. Brian and Keith were kind enough to speak normally with her.

Her gaze drifted up the row, but she snapped it back. The smithy was that way, and she couldn't risk seeing Mo. In spite of the promise she'd made to Alice and Steph; in spite of repeating that promise to Steph three days ago during their tearful goodbye at the airport, she still wasn't ready. But the proximity of the smithy and the archery stand might force her to cross paths with him at any moment. The town crier walked past, making Jess's head throb with his clanging bell and announcements about the events of the day. Jess winced.

My senses are overloaded; I can't imagine what it's like for Mo.

Twenty minutes later, after helping a little girl earn her Wee Archers Guild certificate, Jess was putting the child-sized bow and arrows back in their places, smiling to herself. A man's voice called out to her.

"My fair Lady Archer! By Odin, it maketh me joyous to see thee merry!"

Confused, Jess turned toward the voice as Theo joined her at the stand. His friendly grin was a mile wide, a contrast to his dark, long-sleeved tunic belted under a deep gray cloak with a mottled silver fur mantle. The hair on the top of his head had been braided flat against his crown, but the ends were much longer and fuller, resting loose on his shoulders except for a few small sections that had been braided and adorned with detailed silver and black cuffs. Jess forced her eyebrows back down.

"Theo," she said. "Looks like"—she looked him up and down—"you're in your element."

He laughed.

"But how are you not burning up?" she asked. He leaned close to her.

"I'm dying here," he whispered. "But beauty is pain. And Viking men were serious about their beauty."

"Oh," Jess said. "I'm new to this, I didn't realize that 'Viking' garb fit under the Ren Faire umbrella."

He shrugged.

"Depends on who you ask, I guess. But I'm not going to let any naysayers stop me," he said, watching the people file by. "I've always loved putting on a fun costume and stepping into a different world."

"Always?" Jess asked. He gave her his broad smile again.

"Oh yeah. Ever since I was a kid. Even dressed up my dog. He was easier to catch than my big sister," Theo said, winking.

Jess managed a tight laugh, looking away from him so he wouldn't see the tears blurring her vision. Even though she was taking more and more tiny steps in grieving, she'd been running from thoughts of Cassie that day. Neither of the counselors she'd spoken with had been able to see her before the Faire. In spite of her hesitations about compartmentalizing, Jess was afraid that if she thought about her sister, she would break down. She couldn't let her emotional state have a detrimental effect on the Faire. She'd just keep her thoughts under control and fall apart in the car or at home each evening. The last thing she'd anticipated was someone she barely knew voicing one of her Cassie memories.

Glancing at the other end of the stand, she was relieved to see a couple watching Ned as he taught a masked noblewoman to shoot. Jess focused on the opportunity to help them so she could put Cassie out of her mind. Theo followed her gaze.

"Oops, sorry," he said. "I'm keeping you from your duties. Fare thee well." He bowed his head and stepped out from under the awning, joining the passersby.

Jess took two deep breaths, steadying herself and purposefully blanking her mind. Then she walked to the end of the stall to ask the couple if they'd like to learn how to shoot.

A short while later, Keith began pulling a rope across their stand while Brian put away the bows and arrows for guests. The couple Jess was working with caught the message and left. It was time for the team to take their places in the arena for the show. Jess was seriously regretting not wearing some sort of hat. Even if the ones she'd seen online were too fussy-looking for her taste. When she'd arrived, Lana had appeared out of nowhere and shook her head at Jess's ponytail. She'd hauled her over to a booth called "bawdy braids" and the woman running it had pounced on Jess's head. In the end, Jess admitted that the result, with intertwined braids on her crown and the rest of her hair down, was pretty and

would keep her hair out of her face when it was time to shoot.
Keith approached her, tucking in his green arrows and pulling up
his green-and-brown hood.

"You ready?" he asked.

"Just need my tack," she said. He nodded as she went to the
back of the stand and filled her quiver with her red arrows. The
crowd needed to clearly see which archer shot what. Brian was
the blue archer, Keith was green, and Jess was red. She tied a long
red sash around her waist and grabbed her longbow. She was
about to step out of the shadows when she saw Mo walking past
the archery booth. She stepped back to remain hidden. He slowed
his pace a little, glancing at the closed booth. He looked back in
the direction he was walking, but not before Jess caught a forlorn
half-smile bend his lips. Her heart skipped a beat.

Maybe Al and Steph are right. Maybe he doesn't hate me.

In her hiding place under the wooden stage, Jess listened as Doug,
playing the role of the queen's servant, addressed the crowd in the
risers on either side of the arena, revving them up for the competition between Brian and Keith. Ned had told Jess that there had
been a bit of behind-the-scenes drama when Doug learned that
Wendy was to be the Queen of the Faire, and in Elizabethan tra-
dition, she was not going to have a king. When Ned told her that
Doug suggested he play Sir Robert Dudley, Jess had had to give
the reason behind her guffaw. She didn't know if her explanation
that Doug had been trying to imply that he was Wendy's lover had
gotten back to her. All that Jess knew was that Doug had not
ended up as a noble as he'd seemed to hope. His garb was nice,
but his role was little more than the queen's crier, announcing the
events taking place in front of the stage.

Jess let herself smile as he assigned each side an archer to
cheer for. She was happy to have a moment in the shade under the
stage, a few degrees cooler than in the sunshine. The following
night, the Faire would be over, and she could put the madness
behind her. If she kept her mind focused on her tasks and com-

pletely avoided Mo, she'd be fine. Her knees began aching, and she uncrossed her legs, stretching and gingerly repositioning into a kneeling position. It wasn't pain-free, but it was better.

The show began. As Brian, Good Archer Blue, and Keith, Good Archer Green, took turns firing, the crowd cheered for their respective archers. Off in the distance, one of the Rennies, dressed in garb, examined the targets, pretending he wasn't sure who had won. Brian and Keith had intentionally shot around the bull's-eye. But the crowd didn't know that. Jess picked up her tack and aimed.

"I declare, Archer . . ." Doug cried out. That was Jess's cue. She pulled back, released, and watched her arrow land dead center in the left bull's-eye. A gasp went up from the crowd. Jess emerged.

"My good sir," she shouted. "Thou hast finished the contest too soon!"

While Brian and Keith loudly expressed their disagreement to gain the crowd's attention, Jess drew back again and fired, piercing the balloon tacked to the top of the left target. The crowd cheered. She fired again, puncturing the matching balloon at the right target. The crowd cheered even louder.

"My good men," Doug said to Brian and Keith. "Verily, if we are to crown the best archer in the land, Her Majesty requires that we take all comers." He gestured and bowed to Wendy, in garb fit for her station, seated in the middle of the stage. Jess mimed lifting skirts as she curtsied to the queen. Wendy nodded at her, barely concealing a smirk.

"A curse on your bow," Keith shouted at Jess as she stood straight. He aimed and landed his arrow in the ring outside Jess's in the left bull's-eye.

"A pox on your arrow," Brian shouted. His arrow landed on the other side of hers.

"My good masters, wherefore such malice?" Jess cried out, turning so the crowd could hear her. She drew another arrow. "Methinks you fear defeat at the hands of a woman!" She released, and the arrow landed just on the inside of Keith's. The crowd roared while she fired again, grazing along Brian's as it pierced the target. Jess took a few steps forward and bowed wth a flourish to each side of the audience. They were so loud, Jess almost broke character. She'd never heard as much cheering in all her years competing.

Once Jess had returned to the firing line, Doug raised his hands.

"My good people," he called out. "My good people, what say we test the mettle of our competitors?"

While the crowd was cheering, two Rennies dressed as squires came running onto the field carrying baskets of bean bags. Brian, Keith, and Jess lined up. This next part was technically more difficult, but it would be hard for the crowd to keep track if they got it right. The squires got into position.

"The archer who doth collect the most quarry shall be champion," Doug shouted. "Shall it be our Good Archer Green?"

Keith took a few steps forward and stretched his arms wide to his side of the arena. There were shouts of encouragement and applause. He returned to the line.

"Our Good Archer Blue?"

Brian did the same.

"Or . . . Mistress Archer Red?"

The crowd roared again, but rather than step out for her applause, Jess drew back her bow, as Brian and Keith had. The crowd's reaction was the cue for the squires. They began tossing the bags high into the air and Brian, Keith, and Jess fired again and again. What the crowd didn't know was that Brian and Keith were purposefully missing every other shot they took. Jess was trying to hit each one. As planned, the squire on the right threw the last bag high into the air. Its trajectory was different because it had a lot fewer beans. Brian and Keith shot low intentionally, but Jess pierced it as it flew into the middle of the arena. It exploded, confetti flying everywhere. The crowd was on its feet.

The squires ran onto the field, collecting the pierced bags strewn all over. They built up the anticipation, counting them slowly. Then one stood straight, pulling a red scarf out of his pocket and waving it in the air. The crowd went wild.

Brian clapped her on the shoulder as they left the arena after she'd bowed and waved to the audience on both sides.

"Excellent job," he said. "Especially for your first time. You're a natural at this. Why aren't you a Rennie already?"

"I—" Jess felt her smile fall, her throat closing up. In a small way, she had been a reluctant Rennie in the past. Encouraged along by the sweetest, kindest Rennie there had ever been. The buzz, the energy from the crowd was still running through her, wrapped around her—like an impossible hug from her sister. She realized tears were on their way, so she shook her head and shrugged.

"Jess, that was great," Keith said, jogging up to join them as they walked back to the stand.

"Thanks," she squeaked out. She needed to get a drink, something, to get herself under control. She cleared her throat. "Listen, I need a drink. Can you guys take my tack?"

"Sure, take a long break, we got the stand," Brian said, taking the things she shoved at him. "Is everything—"

"Be back," she said, walking away from them as quickly as her legs could carry her.

CHAPTER TWENTY-NINE

Mo

Thankfully, Rick had given Mo very little resistance about maintaining the role of lead blacksmith that morning. Mo had already been in a battle with his discomfort before the gates opened. The arrival of this sensory nightmare of an event was bad enough. Knowing Jess was around but that he couldn't reach out was sandpaper on his skin. When he'd arrived at the tented, temporary smithy where Rick was lighting the forges, his frustration must have been all over his face. Rick had jumped when he saw him.

"Good morning, sunshine," Rick had said.

Mo had only been able to scowl in return.

Now, hours and a steadily growing number of patrons later, Mo felt somewhat better, calmed by his hobby. The heat from the forges was tolerable due to the breeze passing through overlaps in the tent fabric and the open-frame doorways on each side. There was just enough light for the patrons to watch as he, Rick, and one of their students worked. Mo had made a good number of brooches for purchase, and having shifted to blacksmith's knives, his mind had gone blessedly quiet. But a boy had taken a spot directly in front of him on the benches that had been installed for patrons to sit and watch. The boy was staring with an unnerving intensity. And he'd been sitting there for a very long time. A woman Mo guessed to be the boy's mother had tugged on his sleeve several times, to no avail. He was about Maddie's age, but from the way he was ignoring his mother, it seemed he was a lot more stubborn. Mo was starting to get annoyed at the kid's lack of respect, between the staring and the ignoring, until he realized that the boy wasn't staring at *him,* but at his hands.

Mo turned to switch knives, returning the one whose blade he'd just flattened to the forge and using a pair of tongs to pick up the one he had been reheating. As he submerged it into a tub of oil hidden inside a period-style wooden bucket, the boy shot to his feet and leaned forward, looking inside.

"That's not water!" he gasped. "Why don't you use water?" he asked Mo.

"Adam, let the man work," his mother said with a sheepish smile, tugging on his sleeve. "I'm so sorry," she said to Mo. "He gets overexcited sometimes."

Mo looked at the boy. His eyes had been wide when he'd spoken, but now he looked self-conscious and guarded.

"You can use water or oil for quenching," he said to the boy. "I prefer oil."

"Quenching?" the boy asked.

"To harden. Strengthen. You don't want your project to break because it's brittle," Mo said.

"Oh," the boy said, beginning to sit back down again.

"No, no," his mother said. "We've been here forever, sweetie. It's almost lunchtime. Aren't you hungry?"

Mo recognized the mom's desperate urge to do something, *anything* else. She had been patient and supportive of her son's curiosity, but there's only so long a parent can be immobile before getting bored out of their skull. An experience Mo knew far too well. He rolled his lips to smother a lip quirk.

"But, Mom, this is really, really cool," the boy said. "I'd love to be able to do it."

"It might be a bit early," his mom said. "Look how strong this man is. I think you have some growing to do first."

Mo rested his hammer on his anvil. He might have thought the same before he started, but after several years of teaching, he knew it wasn't true.

"Actually, ma'am," he said to her, "you don't have to be muscular to start blacksmithing." He looked at the boy, sizing him up. "Are you . . . maybe twelve?"

The boy's eyes went wide.

"Yeah," he said with a big smile.

Mo shrugged.

"You're old enough for a couple of our classes," he said.

"Will you be my teacher?" the boy asked breathlessly.

"Hold on, Adam. Let me see if I can swing it first," his mom said. She looked at Mo. "Could I ask someone about them? I'm sure we've distracted you enough."

"There's a stand near the entrance with info about our classes," he said.

The boy shot to his feet and dashed through the doorway to the right of Mo. His mom laughed, and Mo caught himself chuckling.

"Thanks," she said to him. "Have a good day."

She stepped through the doorway, waving goodbye. Mo waved back. Then he winced at Rick's elbow in his ribs.

"Nice job," Rick said. "New students mean more money."

Rick wasn't wrong, but that wasn't why Mo had said the kid could learn. He'd been really interested, and Mo had just made a suggestion to help him follow that interest.

"That's not—"

"I know," Rick said, cutting him off. "Just giving you a hard time. Looked like the kid caught the smithing bug. Why don't we break for lunch?"

After smothering the fires and helping Rick and Emma tie off the flaps designed to block the doorways, Mo walked down the path between stands, the sun getting to him a little. He hadn't brought his sunglasses, trying to stay in character in his garb. He'd had to wash his shirt three times before the chemical smell went away. At least the knee-high brown boots he'd found were comfortable. The interaction with the boy had brightened his mood a little. He tried to use young Adam's excitement about smithing as a buoy against drowning in all the smells, sounds, and masses of energy the patrons were dumping all around him. But most significantly, against his Jess-ache.

Maddie-ache when she's gone. Now Jess-ache without her. Shouldn't be a surprise.

He just wondered how intense it would get as his garb and the Faire itself were sparking memories of her.

"Fezzik!" A masked noblewoman walking down the path called to him. "Are there rocks ahead?" She and her group smiled expectantly.

The direct reference to the *Princess Bride* hurt, making it hard for him to reply. But the guests needed to have a good time.

"If there are," he answered back, "we'll all be dead."

The woman and her friends laughed, clapping their hands as he continued on his way. The outdoor bar of the Ale's Faire ale house came into view. Suddenly a man in a colorful padded vest sort of thing stepped directly in front of Mo. He stopped.

"No more rhymes now, I mean it," the man said. Mo caught the mischievous look in his eye before he glanced at a woman and two children in garb just to his right. Mo sighed.

"Anybody want a peanut?" he asked, forcing a smile.

The man and woman exploded in laughter, while the children looked lost.

"Gramercy, my good sir," the man said, clapping Mo on the arm before stepping out of his way. Unsure about the meaning of that word, Mo nodded and continued on.

The crowd on the path was much bigger than he'd realized from inside the smithy. Thankfully, there were enough people to make it easy not to glance at the archery stand as he passed it. He wove around other families and couples fully decked out. Some of them nodded to him or waved, and he gulped and waved back. It was intensely uncomfortable for so many strangers to be looking at him, engaging with him. His chest was tightening, his heart rate picking up. He didn't understand why they were doing it; then he noticed everyone was acknowledging one another that way. As long as no one spoke directly to him, the atmosphere was actually kind of nice. He could feel everyone's good mood. When he reached the bar, it was several people deep, so he made his way to a clear spot down one side. Eventually, a bar wench he didn't recognize noticed him and asked what he'd like. He asked for a Coke, and she returned, thunking a large stainless-steel tankard in front of him.

"You're the blacksmith teacher, right?" she asked.

"One of them, yeah," he said, nodding slowly.

"No charge," she said and walked away.

Mo took a long, deep sip, grateful for the generous helping of ice she'd included. As he was lowering the drink, a "huzzah" went up from the other end of the bar. And there was Jess, surrounded by a small group of people, raising their drinks to her. Mo's heart dropped. He didn't want to see her, it hurt too much. But he'd barely made a dent in his drink, and there was no way for him to toss a big metal mug in the trash can a few feet away. Trying to drink quickly, he scooted to the very corner of the bar and hoped for the best.

But Jess looked miserable. It was obvious that she was trying to humor the people around her, raising her tankard to clink with theirs as they motioned to her. He could tell that she was putting their comfort ahead of her own. Her smile was tight, and she kept taking long gulps of her drink, probably doing the same thing as he was, trying to finish quickly. One of the young men pretended to fire a bow, and the young woman next to him quickly turned to Jess to ask something. Mo realized that they must have been talking about Jess's performance, which he surmised must have gone well for them to be so excited, but Jess wouldn't have wanted this much fuss. She answered the young woman with a smile and nod, her face flushed. Just as the young woman turned away, Jess's face dropped completely, looking stricken before she took another long drink. Mo couldn't stand by and do nothing.

Taking a deep breath, he picked up his tankard and strode over to the group. He stood to his full height and cleared his throat loudly. They went silent and looked up at him.

"Good morrow, Master . . . brewer?" one young man said, eyes wide.

"Good morrow," Mo said as deeply as possible. "Not to spoil your fun, but methinks Lady Archer needs a break."

The group looked at one another, then at Jess, and began apologizing. Jess nodded, and they took their drinks, moving farther down the bar. Mo put his tankard down and crossed his arms on the bar beside her.

"You have fans," he said, hoping his voice wasn't as tense as he felt.

"Thank you, Mo." She sighed. "Um, are you okay? There's uh . . . there's a lot of people and noise."

He appreciated her asking, her knowing. But the pitch of her voice was too high, her jaw tight. He didn't want her worrying about him just then.

"It is a lot," he said. "But I haven't had groupies."

The laugh she attempted fell flat.

"I didn't want to offend them, but . . ." She trailed off.

"Too much," he said.

"Exactly." She took another long drink, put down her tankard, and rested her palms on the bar. "And . . . and the girl. She looked—" Jess's face was pale, her eyes glistening as she looked up at him. There was a sharp blast around his heart. He swallowed hard.

"Like Cassie," he said softly, remembering the photo of her and Jess laughing together.

She nodded; her lips pressed tightly. Mo hesitated before gently putting his hand on her back.

"Do you need to leave?" he asked. She shook her head hard.

"If I do, I won't be able to come back."

Mo nodded and began slowly rubbing her back. He wanted to take her in his arms, but that probably wouldn't look right, and he didn't know if it was what she wanted. She took a long, deep breath. Letting it out slowly, she picked up her tankard for another drink. The bar wench who'd served him earlier came by and raised an eyebrow.

"You all right?" she asked Jess.

Jess nodded.

"A little too much heat," she said.

The bar wench nodded and grabbed her tankard. She added more ice and a little pop.

"Normal," she said as she returned it. "'Specially the first time."

"Thanks," said Jess, taking another drink. The bar wench winked at her and left.

"I think everyone would understand if you had to go," Mo said under the noise around them, leaning close. Jess shook her head again, the air filling with vanilla. He swallowed hard.

"I had a plan," she said. "And everything was going okay . . . ish. I was going to focus on the things to do, give the patrons a good time. Think about her when I got home. But now . . ." She took a deep breath, letting it out slowly as she straightened her shoulders. "I can do this. Cassie would want me to. She wouldn't want me to run away. She'd want me to have fun."

Jess did not look like she was having fun, but Mo certainly wasn't going to point that out. While being beside her had washed away the Jess-ache, seeing her struggle was twisting his insides.

"Okay," he said. "You got a couple minutes? Need to get back to your stand, or have another show soon?"

"No, no show. And I'm sure the guys have everything under control."

"All right." He caught the bar wench's attention. "Can we bring these back?" he asked, gesturing at the tankards.

"Sure," she said.

"Come on," he said to Jess, taking her hand and curving it in the crook of his elbow.

"Where are we going?" she asked as she let him pull her away from the ale house.

"Doing what Cassie wants. We're having some fun."

They strolled down the paths, past ax throws and strongman games. The experienced Rennies and School volunteers manning them encouraged Mo to compete, but he brushed them off for another time. Jess actually smiled when a tarot reader told her that a handsome, bearded man would beat out two competitors for her heart while glancing meaningfully at Mo. Jess suggested bringing Maddie to see the live mermaids and the petting zoo, and he agreed that it was an excellent idea. She tugged at his arm, pulling him to the far side of the path as they passed a roasted turkey leg stand. Confused, he raised an eyebrow at her. She tapped the side of her nose.

"Not too much for you?" she asked. "Lots of smells, too."

His cheeks heated, and he tucked his chin at her concern. "Thanks, but it's okay right now," he said.

As they passed the stage just after the bend in the horseshoe of the path, Jess slowed down. Mo thought it was because she was trying to find a path around the large group gathered between two booths, but she surprised him by trying to make her way to the front. A woman wearing an ivy crown and with long brown hair gilded by a ray of sunlight was singing and playing a harp. Mo thought the music sounded Celtic, but he didn't know enough to be sure. He was struck by the silence of the people listening. Shifting his attention from Jess, he caught sad half-smiles on the patrons' faces that he could see. Their positive mood warmed him, like what he'd picked up on in the rest of the Faire, but it was crinkled with a little wistfulness. He saw Jess's hand dart up to her face, even though her back was to him.

". . . it will not be long, love, till our wedding day . . ." sang the woman playing the harp. She repeated the phrase, gracefully drawing and curving the lyrics in that Celtic way as she brought the song to an end. There was a moment of complete silence before the crowd applauded. The woman bowed her head as people stepped forward to put coins in a decorated basket on a stool in front of her. Jess turned around and walked back to Mo. Her eyes were glistening. Mo offered her his arm. She tucked her hand into the crook again.

"Are you okay?" he asked as they moved through the dispersing group. She nodded.

"Cassie loved that song," she said.

"It's not too hard hearing it?"

Jess shrugged.

"A little bit. Especially as some interpretations say that the couple didn't get married because the woman died," she said. Mo squeezed her hand on his arm. "But . . . it's nice hearing it. Here. With you." She looked up at him and smiled. He smiled back.

"And thank you, for earlier," she said.

"For earlier?"

"You said, 'what Cassie wants.' You referred to her in the present tense. You've . . ." Mo caught the shimmer of tears in her eyes just before she glanced away. Taking a deep breath, she looked back up at him. "You've done it in the past, and it means a lot." She smiled, waveringly, but warmly.

Mo swallowed, trying to ignore his jackhammering heart. He squeezed her hand again.

"I . . . I hadn't noticed. You're . . . welcome," he said through a scratchy throat.

Her eyebrows rumpled. She took a breath like she was going to say something, then looked away, sniffing.

"I wanna say something," she said, voice tight. "But I can't right now, not here, with . . ." She gestured around them, at the people, the stands. "I will, though. Okay?" She looked back up at him, eyes still glistening. His throat sealed shut. He nodded and bent his arm tighter, pulling her close again.

When they'd strolled the entire Faire and almost reached the archery stand, Jess stopped and slipped her hand off Mo's arm.

"Thanks, Mo," she said, looking up at him.

"You're welcome, m'—Jess," he said, his face warming.

She gave him a half-smile.

"Maddie's at her mom's tonight, right?" she asked.

"Um . . . yeah?"

"It'll take us a bit to get everything closed here, go home, and get cleaned up. But can I stop by? Maybe around nine?" she asked.

Mo's mind had kind of stuttered off for a second, and he was trying to reboot.

"I mean, I understand if . . . you know, I'm sorry," she said. "Never mind, forget—"

"No, yes, yes, it's fine," he said quickly. "It's fine. I'd like that. Nine is good."

"You're sure?" she asked.

"I'm sure. Nine is great."

She smiled.

"Perfect." She looked at her empty tankard. "Guess we gotta take these back."

He reached for hers.

"I'll take it," he said.

"Thanks," she said, handing it to him. "See you at nine?"

"See you then."

CHAPTER THIRTY

Jess

Jess raised her head from her steering wheel, dragging the back of her hand across her cheek to wipe the tears away. She stopped, surprised at the friction, and looked at the back of her hand. The moisture left streaks through dust she hadn't realized was there.

The first day of the Faire had come to a close, and while she'd been able to change quickly into regular clothes inside the School, she hadn't been able to stay and chat with the others. The mix of pride at their work, wistfulness, grief about Cassie, and the trepidation of the conversation she was about to have with Mo had been so overwhelming that she'd nearly sprinted to the privacy of her car so she could let it all out in a crying jag. Apparently, in her haste, she hadn't been thorough in washing the dust of the day off her skin.

Okay. Get it together. You're not gonna keep Mo waiting.

Forty-five minutes later, Jess pulled back the shower curtain to find Steinem sitting on the bathroom counter. He meowed at her.

"Hey, Sty Sty," she said, grabbing a towel. "What's up?"

He let out a long yowl. Jess smiled as she dried her hair.

"Yes," she said. "You're right. I was in there for a while. But I was gross. And I can't go apologize to Mo with gross skin and hair. I'm already embarrassed and uncomfortable enough." Wrapping another towel around herself, she flicked the light off as she left the bathroom, Steinem following at her heels.

She checked her phone, relieved to see replies in the group chat. During the drive home, she'd gone over and over what she could say to Mo, but none of her words felt like enough. She'd sent an SOS to her friends, along with the idea of buying Mo a plant or some other gift.

Alice:

> I googled "Good plants to apologize." Noticed something when I was poking around. Didn't you say he gave you unique flowers?

Jess:

> Yes. Why?

Stephanie:

> Why? Flowers and plants have meanings, J.

Jess knew that they had historically, but she'd never extrapolated that fact to the modern day.

Jess:

> Yes, but. Do you think he knows that?

Alice:

> He gave you cranberry flowers after you saw your parents?

> Yes.

A screenshot appeared in the chat. Jess clicked it open.

"A cure for heartache."

Knowing that she was upset after her visit "home," Mo had handed her a gift with the specific meaning of *easing her pain,* and she'd dumped him. Her eyes flooded with tears. As she blinked them away, she noticed the time.

Jess:

> You were right, Steph. I AM clueless. And I'm gonna be late. Al, can you find a couple good plants or flowers that mean I am sorry, I'm the biggest moron on the planet? Send me their names?

Laughing emojis from both popped up.

Alice:

> I'm on it. I'll have them for you asap.

Jess:

> Thx

Stephanie:

> You got this. Go get your sensitive man!

Just before nine, Jess stepped out of her car in front of Mo's house. Her hands were shaky enough that she needed to readjust her grip on the ivy plant she'd chosen from Alice's list. While waiting at the florist, she'd also learned that all the flowers Mo had given her had communicated something specific. And she, Ms. Clueless, hadn't realized it.

She was almost to his porch when Mrs. Sargysan's front door swung open. Leaning on her cane, she shuffled to the edge of her porch, leaving the door open behind her.

"You!" Mrs. Sargysan spat. Jess gulped.

"Good evening, Mrs. Sargysan," she said. "It's good to see you again."

"Don't 'Good evening' me," she said, narrowing her eyes. "You dumped him, didn't you?" Mrs. Sargysan asked, leaning into her purple cane, squinting down at Jess.

"Well . . . um . . ." Jess's throat felt thick, her tongue gummy. She hadn't even thought about Mrs. Sargaysan, but she should have known that the older woman would not be happy with her. Her hands began to stick to the paper around the plant.

"Don't sugarcoat it. I know you did. He didn't say anything, but I can tell."

"Yes, I did." She took a few steps closer to Mrs. Sargysan's porch, not wanting to be impolite.

"And why is that?" Mrs. Sargysan snapped.

"I'd rather not get into it," Jess said.

Her inquisitor didn't say anything, but the way she raised her chin told Jess that her answer was insufficient.

Pepper. Help me.

"Hm," Mrs. S said. "If you're back to make it worse, I suggest you be on your way; you've done enough. Mo deserves better than some wishy-washy nonsense."

"You're absolutely right, Mrs. Sargysan," Jess said. "He does."

"Course I'm right." She readjusted herself on her cane.

"I just want to apologize to Mo and see what he wants from there," Jess said. "If it's over, it's truly over. That's his choice."

Mrs. Sargysan harrumphed.

"Maddie can't have some flighty woman darting in and out of her life. I know Mo won't stand for it and neither will I," she said.

"Of course not, ma'am," Jess said. "They both deserve stability."

"Hmm." Mrs. Sargysan furrowed her brow and bunched her lips to one side. Then her face softened just a little. "My deepest condolences about your sister. Truly. I know what that pain is like."

Jess swallowed hard, her heart clenching.

"But if you don't face your hurt, deal with it? It's going to make you hurt other people. And yourself," Mrs. Sargysan said, squeezing the handle of her cane. "Which would be stupid things to do, wouldn't they?"

Vision blurring, Jess nodded quickly, wanting to say more but incapable of doing so. Mrs. Sargysan gestured to Mo's door.

"You can make your case now," she said. "But I've got my eye on you. No more hurting Mo. Or my little kuzu."

"Yes, ma'am," Jess said. "Have a good evening."

"We'll see," Mrs. Sargysan said, narrowing her eyes at Jess before she slowly turned and began making her way into her house. Taking a deep breath and letting it out, Jess took the steps to Mo's door.

Thanks, Pepp—

Jess's thought was cut off by Mo swinging the door open the moment she reached it.

"H—"

He swept her into his arms, cutting her off. A tiny part of her protested, feeling like she didn't deserve his affection, but his warmth and his broad chest and strong arms and utterly irresistible Mo-smell turned off her thoughts. She almost purred when he rested his cheek on her crown and drew a slow, deep breath. Her bones became weak and rubbery, and she wanted to give in to the temptation to just melt inside him. She got a little dizzy from a lack of air and suddenly remembered his present squished between them.

"Can't breathe," she said, the word muffled by his chest.

"Hmm?" he asked.

She tried to shift a little, but he didn't budge.

"Hard to breathe."

"Oh! Sorry," he said, letting her go. He stepped back, waving her inside as he closed the door. Being able to take a full breath was great, but she was gutted to lose his warmth and smell.

"What was that?" she asked, smiling.

He smiled back.

"Eavesdropping," he said. "I didn't realize that the window was cracked until you and Mrs. Sargysan were in the middle of your conversation."

Jess's face flashed hot. She swallowed hard.

"Well," she said. "If nothing else, you know that you have an ardent protector."

He chuckled.

"That I do," he said.

For a moment, she wasn't sure what to do. She wasn't sure how to transition into what she wanted to tell him. He was looking at her, face open and sweet. He'd seen the gift; she could start with that. Or maybe the apology should come first. Or the gift? Being indecisive was strange and uncomfortable.

What would Cassie do?

The gift. She liked seeing people enjoy her gifts. Jess raised the ivy plant, ready to give it to him, then froze when she looked him in the eye. His lips were curled together, hiding in his beard.

"What's wrong?" she asked. "Are you okay?"

"Are you?" he asked, smiling. She smiled back.

"No, not really," she said.

"Let's go sit down," he said. She nodded, and he rested a hand on her back as they walked to the couch. His touch steadied the jumble inside of her.

"You know what," she said, sitting down. "Let's do it like a Band-Aid."

"Okay," he said, sitting beside her.

She placed the ivy on the coffee table and took a deep breath.

"Mo, I am intensely sorry. I was an idiot. Multiple times over," she said. "I decided what you are capable of handling and then made a decision for both of us based on that. And I did it with the full knowledge that that choice itself would cause you pain. So I hurt you to not hurt you, which makes zero sense."

"Jess, it's—"

"Wait," she said, cutting him off. "Please let me just say all this. I don't want to forget anything."

"Okay," he said, smiling and folding his hands in his lap.

"So," she said, "it would be beyond reasonable for you to decide to return to your life the way it was before, maintaining your safe spaces and spending time with people who respect you and the way that you manage your HSP, respect your agency. If that's what you want, I'll one hundred percent respect it and won't bother you in any way. At first, I was just going to do that. Keep my mouth shut and keep out of your way. But that's another form of compartmentalizing, and I've decided that I'm not going to do that anymore. And I'm taking action. I've started on a plan that Alice and Stephanie helped me put together. It's mainly for my grief, but you're part of it, too."

"I am?" he asked, eyebrows raised.

"Yes."

"What . . . about me?" he asked.

"This." Jess gestured between the two of them. "Me apologizing for being an arrogant dumbass." He frowned, then raised his arms like he was asking for a hug. She happily melted into them.

"You are not an arrogant dumbass," he said. His words were nice to hear, but better to feel reverberating from his body into hers. "You just made a mistake in trying not to hurt me because you know it can be easier to do so than with other people. I knew you were coming from an overabundance of concern, not of malice. Things were jumbled up for you because you're struggling about Cassie."

"I'm working on that," she said, resting her head on his shoulder. "I have my first appointment with a grief counselor next week, and I'm going to a support group meeting on Tuesday." He pulled back so he could make eye contact with her, his smile a mile wide.

"That's great, Jess. I'm really happy for you."

She smiled and pulled him in, snuggling close. She closed her eyes, drowning herself in Mo-smell as he began running his fingers through the ends of her hair.

"That's a nice ivy," he said after a few moments.

"I wanted to get some purple hyacinths, too. But they didn't have any," she said. He went stock-still. His fingers stopped moving, his chest no longer rising and falling. She smirked but kept her head tucked so he couldn't tell.

"Why . . . an ivy and purple hyacinths?" he asked softly.

"Why cranberry flowers? Or any of the flowers you've given me?" she asked, raising her head. She held in her giggle at the shock on his face. "I didn't realize it at the time," she said. "But I asked Alice and Steph for help for tonight. Maybe a plant as a gift. When they pointed out what you've been doing, I decided to speak your language to apologize."

He glanced down at his lap but not before she caught the shimmer in his eyes.

"I can't tell you how sorry I am, Mo." She took his hand. "You didn't deserve that. I wanted to show you I'm sorry, and I'd like another chance. Even if it might be bumpy as I work through things."

His cheeks reddened and he tucked his chin.

There's the big shy kid.

"That's why I chose the ivy," she said, smiling. "For fidelity. If you do give me another shot, I won't let you go again."

Mo sniffed and blinked quickly. He closed his other hand around hers.

"I won't let you go, either," he said. "Let's take that shot."

CHAPTER THIRTY-ONE

Mo

"Well," Mo sighed as he parked his truck in the Folk School lot on Monday afternoon. He looked at Jess in the passenger seat. "Here goes something."

"Yeah." She sighed back, reaching for the door handle. "The moment of truth. Let's go."

The Faire was over, and Mo's body hadn't begun to recover from two days of blacksmithing and sensory overload. Part of him was joyful with Jess by his side, but the deep, metallic anxiety about the School was still there. Wendy had called the team for a meeting to discuss options before she went to the board. On the phone the previous evening, she had been very light on details. And while Mo knew that there had been a lot of people at the Faire, and it seemed that everyone had had a good time, he had no way of knowing if it had been the financial success they were counting on.

While it would be a shame in general to have gone through all that effort for nothing, it would be much worse for Jess to have gone through the struggle he'd witnessed if the Faire plan didn't work out. She'd been majestic in the show he'd caught the day before, but she'd melted in his arms when he'd gotten to her house, emotionally drained. Grief was shitty that way—events and experiences that brought back good memories could also set off an avalanche of sadness over the impossibility of making new ones.

Walking through the parking lot beside her, he tried to pick up on her energy without asking. The evidence of the visitors struck him instead. The gravel crunching under his feet was significantly disturbed, the festooned path to guide patrons out to the field still in place, its green and purple flags hanging loose in the absence of a breeze. He could still hear the chatter of the crowds and feel their excitement. He stretched and rolled his shoulders a little, trying to shuffle off the energy all those people had left behind so he could focus on Jess. As they reached the building, she surprised him by sliding her hand into his. He stopped, looking from their hands to her face.

"Yeah?" he asked, shooting a glance at the door.

"Yeah," she said. "Between the photoshoot and our stroll on Saturday, I'm sure everyone's already made up their minds. Even if we haven't openly said we're together." She looked at the door and then back at him. "I know privacy is important to you, though. What makes you feel more comfortable, Hephaestus?"

Skin tingling, he smiled. She hadn't called him that in weeks.

"That everyone in the world knows that you're m'lady," he said, bringing her hand to his lips and kissing the back. Her cheeks tinged pink. She repeated the gesture with his hand and mimed a little curtsy.

"And I want everyone to know that you're m'lord."

He smiled, his heart beating fast.

"Off we go, then," he said, leading her inside.

Guided by the smell of coffee, they found Lana and Doug at the table in the break room. Lana was blowing across the top of a steaming mug held in both hands. Doug was beside her, clacking away on his laptop. Lana grinned broadly as soon as Mo and Jess walked in.

"Hello, hello!" said Lana, standing and rushing over to squeeze their arms. "So," she said, looking at their clasped hands. "Is it official? Can we all stop pretending like we don't know?"

Mo didn't do a good job of concealing his discomfort with Lana being Lana. Jess just sighed.

"All right, Lana, yes. Mo and I are together. Do you feel better now?" she asked.

"Oh, so much better," Lana said, clapping her hands. "Isn't this wonderful?" she asked, turning to Doug.

"Of course, Lana," he said without looking up from his laptop. "Come, come, you two, sit down."

"Wasn't the Faire spectacular?" Lana asked. She launched into a lot of chatter that Mo just did not have the ability to pay attention to. He was doing his very best to stay calm because walking into the building had brought home the fact that if the Faire hadn't been a success, he didn't know what else they could do. He loved the Folk School too much to see it disappear.

As he sat down with Lana and Doug, Jess poured a cup of coffee from the maker. She picked up another mug and raised it in Mo's direction to ask if he wanted one, too. He nodded and tried to smile. He realized he'd folded his arms. He took a deep breath, loosening them to rest his fingertips on the table.

"Guys, look at this," Doug said, turning his laptop so that Mo could see the screen.

"People were posting about the Faire all weekend long. There're even a couple of posts today," he said, looking smug.

"Really?" Mo asked, nodding a thanks to Jess as she sat next to him, sliding him the mug.

"Oh, yeah," Doug said. "I've been paying attention since the beginning. *Hashtag MFSchoolRenFaire* has been doing great. Everybody loved it."

"Told you," Theo said from behind Mo. He and Jess shifted in their seats to look at Theo as he walked into the break room. He'd come into the smithy once over the weekend, and Mo had been surprised that he'd gone so far as to change his hair for the event. He hadn't changed it back.

"I knew it was going to be a success," he said, joining them at the table and opening a bright blue energy drink.

"You're still wearing your hair . . . style," Jess said, raising her mug to her lips. Mo could tell that she'd tried to sound neutral, in spite of the laughter that was trying to escape.

"Yeah," Theo said, grinning slyly as he finished his sip. "Haven't been home yet. Made a friend near the end last night. She was into the hair."

"Ah," Jess said.

"The magic of a Faire," Lana said, smiling. "You two weren't the only ones who fell under its charms." Theo's face lit up as he followed Lana's gaze to Mo and Jess. Mo didn't want to get into it.

"People are *talking* about the Faire," he said quickly. "But that doesn't mean that it was a success." He looked at Doug while turning the mug between his fingertips. "What has Wendy said? She was tight-lipped with . . . me." He'd almost said "us" but didn't want the others to continue on that path.

"She wasn't very forthcoming with me, either," said Doug. Jess squeezed Moe's thigh under the table.

"I'm sure it will be—"

"Hey, everyone," Wendy said, rushing into the break room, cutting Jess off. "How are you all?" Her smile was broad, and she seemed enthusiastic.

Maybe things aren't bad.

"I have great news," she said, taking a seat. She put her phone on the table in front of her. "To get straight to it, after all the expenses, we reached fifty-five percent of our goal."

Mo's stomach dropped. *Fifty-five percent?*

"How is that great news, Wendy?" Jess asked. "That's not nearly enough."

"It's . . . perfect," Doug said, creepy smile blooming as he leaned forward. Mo felt like Doug was about to high-pressure sell him a house infested with termites. "We've had so much good press, so many new student sign-ups. So many patrons asked when the next Faire will be. We can make it a twice-yearly event. During the summer and . . . at Christmas, maybe."

"Billing it as a winter solstice event would probably sell better than Christmas," Theo said. "Pagan is big right now."

Mo wasn't sure what Theo was talking about but couldn't ask. A jittery charge had been building since Wendy announced the percentage. The idea of doing a Faire multiple times made blisters of heat bloom on his skin. Right then, he was wiped out after just one. He knew that he would be struggling at least for the coming week.

"Oh!" Lana said. "I would love for this to be a recurring event."

"And we can make it bigger!" Doug said. "We could add things like a joust with horses and fire dancers and aerial acrobats and—"

"Those things cost money, Doug," Jess said, cutting him off. "Both in paying performers and liability insurance, I'd imagine. We probably shouldn't try to do too much too soon if there's only ten percent wiggle room in the budget. Right?" She looked at Wendy.

Wendy was smiling broadly again. Mo began to worry if being out in the heat of the past two days had gotten to her.

"Well," Wendy said, "that's where the even better news comes in. We may have a new benefactor. Her name is Lindy Libet. She comes from a family well known for supporting the arts throughout the state. She and her friends visited the Faire both days; you might have seen her." Wendy picked her phone up off the table, unlocked it, and scrolled a little bit. She held it up so that the others could see. Mo immediately recognized the masked noblewoman who had initiated the *Princess Bride* quotes with him after pegging him as Fezzik.

"Wait a minute," Jess said. "I think Ned taught that woman to shoot at our stand."

"She's familiar," Doug said, squinting at Wendy's phone. He turned his laptop back, facing him, and started moving his finger around on the pad.

"I think . . ." said Lana, also squinting at Wendy's phone. "Yes. I think that woman came to my stand. She asked questions about the School. Other people did, too, but she stood out because her dress was so well made. I saw her again the following day, and she was wearing a different dress. That one was even better. I didn't recognize her until she stopped by to say hello. Even her masks were exquisite."

Mo was surprised that someone would have visited more than once. The Faire had been small enough to see everything in one afternoon. But the more he thought about it, had he seen her more than once as well? He took a deep drink of his coffee as he flipped through his memories.

"Lindy approached me at the end of the day yesterday, as we were wrapping up," Wendy said. "She wanted to know if we needed any financial help. She loves what the School is doing and what it's bringing to the community. She wants to make sure that we can keep doing it."

Mo wasn't really sure how he would pinpoint the feeling that was growing in his chest. He would have attributed the racing of his heart to anxiety, or maybe the strength of the coffee, but he also felt calmed. Safe. He looked at Jess. She looked equally as surprised. And relaxed.

Well, glad I played along with Lindy's joke rather than snapping at her.

"While I'm happy about the possibility of a new benefactor," Wendy said, "I don't want us to find ourselves in a difficult position again. So if you all agree, I'll go to the board with a suggestion of two Faires a year plus Lindy's help."

Mo rolled his lips.

At least not a year-round stress.

"You all know I'm in," Theo said, leaning back in his seat, arms crossed, looking satisfied with himself.

"Of course, I agree," Doug said, attention back on his laptop screen.

"Don't have to ask me twice," Lana said. She looked expectantly at Mo and Jess. "Come now," she said. "I know you two had fun."

Mo wouldn't have called it fun, precisely, but it had been satisfying. And beyond what he'd felt, the people who had visited had enjoyed themselves, too. The joy that had lit up the boy's face when Mo said he could learn blacksmithing was exactly how he'd felt about rowing as a teenager. Then about blacksmithing later on. But it wasn't just about Mo's feelings. He glanced at Jess, sliding her thumb up and down the handle of her mug on the table. What if she didn't want to go through that again? What if she couldn't?

"I think it's a great idea," Jess said to Wendy, surprising him.

While the others expressed their excitement, and Doug began to talk about having a more significant role, Mo shifted down a little to whisper in Jess's ear.

"Are you sure?"

She looked up at him, squeezing his thigh under the table again.

"For Cassie," she whispered, winking at him.

Walking back to the truck, hand in hand again, Mo felt lighter but tethered in the very best of ways. The School would be okay. And in spite of the stress, he was okay. Better than okay. He was with Jess.

"Even though neither of us wanted to do it, I'm glad it worked out," he said to her as they reached the passenger side of his truck. He opened the door for her.

"Yeah, me too," she said, getting in.

He joined her in the cab and started the engine.

"Maybe Fezzik was wrong," she said.

"I'm sorry?" Mo asked.

"Maybe people in masks can be trusted," she said. "Especially when they come in and save the day."

Friday evening, Mo stood at the sink in the now vacant workshop next to his own, soaping his hands. He had intended to give himself at least one week's rest before returning to his anvil, but the seed of an idea had taken root Monday night, and on Tuesday afternoon he'd left work early to get started. While he'd never tried this sort of project before, it had come together in just a few days, with only minor hiccups. Rinsing and drying his hands, he glanced up at the broken mirror and smiled.

Here goes something.

He collected the carefully wrapped package from his workshop and walked briskly to his truck. The finishing touches had taken longer than he'd anticipated, and he was due at Jess's for dinner soon.

As soon as Mo pressed Jess's doorbell, a loud, yowling meow sounded on the other side of the door. Mo chuckled, grateful to release some of the low-level nervousness that had weakened his muscles, making it difficult to hold the gift across his forearms. Steinem yowled again.

"Hi, Steinem," Mo said through the door.

He yowled again.

"I'm coming!" Mo heard Jess call out from somewhere deep in the house. Steinem kept yowling. Mo couldn't stifle his laughter.

"I'm coming, I'm coming," Jess called out, her voice getting closer. "Goodness, Sty Sty," she said as she opened the door. Steinem darted out and immediately wound himself around Mo's legs. "I wasn't moving fast enough, I guess," she said to Mo, smile bright.

"I guess not," he said, giving her a quick kiss as she waved him inside. He took a deep breath, his stomach grumbling to life. He'd forgotten about lunch that day, and whatever Jess had made smelled divine. "What's for dinner?" he asked.

"Chili," she said. "I did consider soup for Mr. Soup. But I thought that chili would be more filling. It's soup-adjacent, though. It kind of works."

"Oh, it works," he said. Steinem meowed again, standing on his hind legs, stretching to paw at Mo's leg.

"Um, you better give that to me," Jess said, nodding at the package in Mo's hands. "I think Steinem requires some Mo-love."

Smiling, Mo handed her the gift and scooped up the cat. He burrowed into Mo's chest and immediately began purring. Mo's anxiety calmed but didn't abate entirely.

"Can I open it?" Jess asked, smirking at him a little. Mo nodded and followed her to the couch. He focused on the softness of Steinem's fur against his palm, the warm, vibrating weight against his body as he held his breath.

"Mo!" Jess gasped as she unwrapped the three wrought-iron roses. "These are beautiful."

His cheeks heated and he glanced down at Steinem as his heart rate picked up in a good way.

"You made these for me?" she asked, marveling at them.

"I did," he said.

"They're incredible. The petals are so detailed. And the leaves . . . they even have thorns!" She ran her fingertips carefully over each one.

"Do you like them?" he asked.

"I adore them," she said. She leaned in close to kiss him then went back to examining the roses. Even if she hadn't said anything, the happiness flooding out of her was enough to put him on cloud nine.

"It was a little difficult to find the right thing," he said.

"The right thing?"

He shrugged.

"To say what I wanted. I thought about something linked to Artemis," he said. "You know, to go with Hephaestus." She smiled at him, and he felt all tingly and shy. "But that didn't really suit you. I thought about something else related to archery or the Renaissance."

"Wait," she said. "There's a little pink stone inside each rose."

He nodded.

"Rose quartz," he said. "It was a symbol of love in Greek mythology."

Jess froze, then looked up at him.

"Roses are also a symbol of love," she said. He nodded again. "You've never given me roses before. You've always been careful about the meaning of the flowers you've given me. This time, you *made* me flowers that mean love."

His heart thudding in his chest, he looked down at Steinem in his arms, caressing him slowly to gain a little courage. He drew a slow breath.

"That's because—"

"I love you, too," she said and launched herself into his arms.

There wasn't a single way to describe the sensations that exploded through Mo. There was happiness and sparks and joy and a soothing wave. He wanted to simply bask, but everything was cut short by a loud yowl as Steinem shot up, pressing himself against Jess, forcing her to let go of them both. Laughter erupted out of her, and Mo joined in. "Okay, bossy," she said to Steinem. "You've had your Mo cuddles. It's my turn." She scooped Steinem out of Mo's arms and slid into them herself.

"I love you, Jess," he whispered into her crown as their laughter died down.

"And I love you, Mo," she said, squeezing tight. "So, so much."

Mo closed his eyes and inhaled, filling his lungs with vanilla, as he melted into peace and calm and "safe."

EPILOGUE
Jess and Mo

Nine Months Later

Jess stood up straight from the kitchen table, letting her hand stay on the back of Maddie's chair.

"You are so much better at this than I am, my friend," she said to Maddie. "I'm sorry I'm not more helpful."

"I am useless," Maddie said plaintively. "Everyone else in class is a thousand times better than me. There's no way I'm not going to fail the test." She dropped her pencil and plopped her elbows onto the table, face falling into her hands.

Seventh-grade math was kicking Jess's butt; she was a word person, not a numbers person. The last thing she was going to do was let Maddie get down on herself, though.

"Nope," she said, gently pulling on one of Maddie's arms. "That's not what we're going to do. Come on, time for a break."

Maddie let herself be pulled out of the kitchen and out onto Mo's porch. Jess lifted the lid of the large storage box Mo had installed for Maddie's archery tack.

"Jess . . ." Maddie whined. "I suck at this, too . . ."

"Bah! Bull—crap," Jess said, correcting herself as she slid the foam target out from its place against the side of the house.

"You can say 'bullshit.' I won't tell Daddy," Maddie said.

"Shh," Jess said quietly. "It's not your dad I'm worried about." She shot a look at Mrs. Sargysan's back door. Maddie giggled.

"Okay, good point," she said.

Jess took the target down to the end of the yard and jogged

back. Maddie was adjusting her arm guard as Jess hopped up the steps.

"Okay, Mads," she said, getting in place a few steps behind her and to the left. "Make yourself proud."

Maddie turned and looked at her with a raised eyebrow.

"Don't you mean, 'Make you proud'?" she asked.

"No," Jess said. "I meant exactly what I said." She crossed her arms, leaned against the back of the house, and winked.

Mo walked through his front door, placing his smithing bag in its spot just inside. He took a deep breath, savoring the smell of Maddie's sugar cookies in the air.

"Daddy, we're in the kitchen!" she called out to him.

"On my way, sugar plum," he called back.

He hung his jacket on the coat rack and ran a hand down Jess's jacket beside it. He took a deep breath, checking that his present for Jess was snug in the pocket of his jeans, and followed the delicious aroma.

Maddie was carefully moving some cookies from a cooling rack to a large plate as Jess straightened, taking a freshly baked set out of the oven. She smiled at him.

"M'lady," he said to her, winking and nodding. He joined Maddie, giving her a side hug. "What's this about, sugar plum? Are all of these for me?" He reached for a cookie, and Maddie swatted at him.

"No, Daddy, this plate is for Mrs. Sargysan," she said. "I'm trying to get the best ones."

"Ah, makes sense," he said. He went over to Jess, who tiptoed up as he leaned down.

"Have a good day?" he asked after a quick peck.

"Not bad," she said. She darted a glance at Maddie. "My classes went well."

Mo didn't quite get the quick glance at Maddie, but he decided not to push.

"I'll be back," Maddie said, carefully picking up the plate piled high with cookies and leaving the kitchen. "I want to give them to her while they're still a little warm," she said over her shoulder.

"Good idea," Mo called out to her. He looked back down at Jess. "Everything okay?"

She sighed.

"Tough therapy session. Don't want to get into it; the water-works are going to start again," she said.

Mo nodded, rubbing her back and taking her in his arms. She'd been working hard for months. Her aches and pains had disappeared. He was proud of her, but he felt at a loss as to how to truly help. The anniversary of Cassie's death had been crippling for her, and it took weeks to get back the progress she'd made. He squeezed tight.

"You're doing so great," he said into her hair.

"Doesn't feel like it," she said against his chest.

"You are, I promise." He'd thought to wait until later that evening, but he decided not to. His nerves shot up, and he had to take a deep breath to calm the jitteriness in his muscles. "M'lady?"

"Hmm?" She pulled back a little to look at him.

"I, uh . . ."

She raised an eyebrow.

"You okay, 'phaest?"

He chuckled a little. The shortened form of Hephaestus that she'd come up with was still cute enough to tickle him.

"Pretty much," he said, slipping a hand into his pocket. "But better soon, I hope. Brought you a little present. Give me your hand."

She took a step back and did as he asked, her eyebrow still raised. He put the freshly cut key in her palm.

"What's this?" she asked.

"I hope it's the key to your new home," he said, his voice a little weak.

She took another step back, focused on it.

"I know your lease is going to be up soon," he said quickly.

"And since, well . . . you're already part of our little family . . . I was thinking you could come live here."

She didn't move. And since she hadn't raised her head, he couldn't read her face. His heart was pounding, his hands weak.

She sniffed.

"Jess?" he asked, bending a little to try to see her.

She sniffed again and looked up at him, tears streaming down her face. His heart clenched.

"Jess, m'lady, I'm sorry," he said, pulling her into his arms. "It was the wrong day to ask. You said you had a tough—"

"Yes!" she wailed into his chest.

"Yes?" he asked, pulling back to see her well.

"Yes, yes, yes," she sobbed, nodding, her eyes clenched tight. He was thrilled and heartbroken at the same time. He pulled her back close.

"Are . . . are you sure?" he asked. "You can say no; maybe it's not a good time."

"I love you!" she cried into him. She wrapped her arms around him and squeezed.

It was far from the first time she'd told him that she loved him, and it still made his heart soar. But her shouting it while sobbing jumbled his feelings and made it hard to know what to do. He started rubbing her back again.

"I love you, too," he said. "Do you want to come sit with me?" he asked. She nodded against him.

Slowly, he walked them to the couch. She dropped down but scooted tight against his side. He kept rubbing her back as her crying subsided. She took a deep breath, swatting for one of the tissues on the end table.

"I . . . I . . ." She hiccupped as she wiped her nose. "I don't feel like I have a home," she said, looking at him, her eyes red. "That's . . . that's what we talked about today. Cassie gave me the feeling of home as a child, not my parents." She hiccupped again. "I've felt . . . untethered since she's been gone."

A lump was developing in Mo's throat, his eyes filling with tears.

"So this . . ." She raised the hand holding the key. "The fact that you want to share your home with me . . ." She started breathing fast again and held the tissue up to her mouth.

"But . . ." He shook his head. "I don't want to *share* my home, Jess. I want it to *be* your home."

Her face crunched up.

"Thank you!" she wailed, falling into him.

He hugged her tightly.

"No, m'lady," he said. "Thank you."

She sniffed hard.

"For what?" she asked, muffled against his shoulder.

"For making it safe for me to love you," he said. "For recognizing and respecting my—"

"If you say 'weirdness,' I'm going to bite you," she said. He chuckled.

"I know better than to use that word with you now," he said. "I was going to say for respecting me as an HSP and not trying to change me or criticize me. You've *become* one of my safe spaces by letting me be who I truly am."

She pulled back a little to look him in the eye.

"You made it easy to love who you truly are," she said, shrugging.

His cheeks warmed, and he darted in quick for a kiss so she wouldn't see the tears in his eyes. She kissed him back then surprised him by jumping to her feet.

"Where are you going?" he asked as she walked toward the front door. She grabbed her bag off the hook.

"Gotta put the key to my new home on the key ring you made for me," she said, winking at him.

He smiled back, not hiding his tears.

ACKNOWLEDGMENTS

No matter what I write, this portion of the book is going to be too short.

My world has dramatically changed since I sat down to write my acknowledgments for *Not the Plan*. There are nowhere near enough words to express my gratitude to the people who have been involved in making my new reality a safe and affirming one.

To my agent, Léonicka Valcius, barrister and solicitor—honestly, il n'y a pas de mots. There's no way I can truly thank you for your patience, diligence, and willingness to gently get my head right when I'm having a moment or ... five. But maybe dinner with a view on the Eiffel Tower would be a start?

To the team at Dell—thank you for your diligent work. And most particularly to Mae Martinez, for your patience and understanding.

To Alice and Lindy—my deepest, deepest gratitude for giving me a safe place to land when my whole world came crashing down. You let me breathe, you gave me hope and showed me that I wasn't alone in a country that's not my own. Little did I know that I was under the protection of a secret agent.

To Toushi and Diana—what are even men? And no, our book has not been forgotten.

To Bibi—you are a rock. Thank you for being a steady source of love and affirmation in a turbulent world.

To Stephanie—my unexpected one-woman street team! Your

enthusiasm has been a source of confidence when I have had none. Thank you.

To the Coven—Janet, Jess, and Megan, who answered my frantic call for help: I cannot tell you how much it meant to me that you did.

To Wanequé—you have no idea what a balm you have been to my writer's soul! Thank you.

To Melissa—no matter what, your face is always here.

To Thibaut—thank you for all the support and laughter. Even when I resist.

To my dad—things are so much better. Fairy Mae is proud of you.

To Marc and Gabrielle—among so many other things, thank you for the Death Candy. Bye.

GIVE ME
A SHOT

A Novel

GIA DE CADENET

A BOOK CLUB GUIDE

Dear Reader,

I hope you've enjoyed getting to know Mo and Jess.

This was a tough story to write. For many reasons but most of all because neither of them wanted to open up about themselves! With time, I understood that their reluctance made sense. When you're a Highly Sensitive Person, or dealing with loss, it's hard to be vulnerable.

Dealing with grief is probably familiar, but you may be wondering what a Highly Sensitive Person is. Psychologists Elaine and Arthur Aron coined the term in the 1990s.

Throughout his life, Mo had been called many things: grouchy, introverted, gruff, even arrogant. But he'd often *felt* overwhelmed, exhausted, and confused. He found it easier and more freeing to keep to himself and engage with others only when necessary.

In *Getting His Game Back,* Khalil chides Mo's reluctance to say much, telling him that words are free. It doesn't cost anything to get your point across.

"Doesn't cost you," Mo says.

And that's Mo in a nutshell. Interactions that seem minor, that other people barely register or are even energized by, can cost him. Either in just a slight loss of energy or in a deep, abiding fatigue, requiring hours or even days to recover from.

That's because Mo's *body* is actually doing more in any situation than a non-HSP's. His central nervous system is responding more; cognitively, he's processing more information from the stimuli around him. And all that extra, invisible work is exhausting. Mo manages it by pulling away, reducing the amount of stimuli by engaging as little as possible.

It's not that Mo has a problem with the rest of the world. It's just that he understands how he can engage with it while respecting his own needs. Sometimes that's a difficult balance to strike—especially when something important to him like the Folk School is in danger.

It's actually a good thing that it took me as long as it did to write Mo and Jess's story. In that time I learned that being an HSP isn't just a personality trait—new research indicates that it's a form of neurodiversity.

Information that has been personally freeing.

Portraying Mo accurately and respectfully was crucial to me because I see him in my son. I see him in my dad. And I feel him in me.

I hope you enjoyed reading about "grouchy," sensitive Mo. If he reminds you of anyone in your life, it might be worthwhile to learn more about HSPs. Elaine Aron's website is a great place to start: hsperson.com.

All the best,
Gia

QUESTIONS AND TOPICS
FOR DISCUSSION

1. How do Mo's and Jess's personal histories influence their initial perceptions of each other? Discuss how their backgrounds shape their interactions and the development of their relationship.

2. Jess is dealing with the recent loss of her sister. How does her grief impact her actions and decisions throughout the story? How does Mo support or challenge her healing process?

3. Analyze the nature of the conflict that arises between Mo and Jess during their first encounter. How does this initial tension set the stage for their evolving relationship?

4. The Folk School plays a significant role in both Mo's and Jess's lives. What does the School represent for each of them, and how does their involvement in saving it reflect their personal journeys?

5. Both Mo and Jess are portrayed as individuals who are initially closed off to new relationships. Discuss the barriers they face in opening up to each other and how they overcome these obstacles.

6. How do Mo's blacksmithing and Jess's archery serve as metaphors for their personalities and life philosophies? In what ways do their crafts bring them closer together?

7. Mo's interactions with his family are a key aspect of his character. How do these relationships influence his approach to romance and connection with Jess?

8. The task of organizing a Renaissance Faire to save the Folk School is central to the plot. How does this shared goal help Mo and Jess build trust and intimacy? What challenges do they face in the process?

9. Both Mo and Jess have built walls around themselves—why do you think that is? How do their interactions with each other challenge these defenses? Can you identify key moments in the book where they each take a significant step toward emotional openness?

10. How does Mo's experience as a highly sensitive person (HSP) influence his interactions with others, and in what ways does it affect his relationship with Jess? How does the author portray the strengths and challenges of being an HSP through Mo's character? Did you connect more with Mo's character or with Jess's?

PHOTO: © CÉCILE HUMENNY

GIA DE CADENET is the author of *Not the Plan* and *Getting His Game Back*. A Maggie Award finalist, BCALA Literary Award nominee, and lifelong romance reader, she is also a business school professor and former translator and editor for UNESCO. A native Floridian, she currently lives in France with her children.

giadecadenet.com
X: @Gia_deCadenet
Instagram: @gia_decad

RANDOM HOUSE BOOK CLUB

Because Stories Are Better Shared

Discover
Exciting new books that spark conversation every week.

Connect
With authors on tour—or in your living room. (Request an Author Chat for your book club!)

Discuss
Stories that move you with fellow book lovers on Facebook, on Goodreads, or at in-person meet-ups.

Enhance
Your reading experience with discussion prompts, digital book club kits, and more, available on our website.

Join our online book club community!
 randomhousebookclub.com

RANDOM HOUSE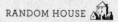